SHARPEN *your* CLAWS

TWOONY

SHARPEN YOUR CLAWS

Book Cover by M.E. Morgan

ISBN: 9798317103439 (Paperback)

Imprint: Independently published

WARNING

There will be graphic violence, suicidal thoughts, PTSD, depictions of anxiety attacks, and mentions of body dysmorphia. Please read with caution.

1

NICHOLAS

HILL CASTLE HAD MANY forms depending on the household's mood. Once the structure made an indentation into the land, sinking low as a hatchling in their nest. Then it would contort into a tower, thin as a grown man, with an interior vaster than grasslands and more treacherous than caves.

That day, Hill Castle sprouted more voraciously than unwanted weeds, shutters hanging off their latches and vines braiding over mismatched rooftops. The stonework shimmered beneath morning light, varying shades of reds and greens and blues. Birds sang from the chimneys upon their nests that would get a swat if they dared defecating on Hill Castle itself.

All knew of the castle's prickly demeanor, making offerings to its guests as snacks or flowers and growing murderously upset when one did not appreciate its efforts. Nicholas knew better than to ignore the appearance of the kitchen when he opened a door that should have led outside, but alas, Hill Castle loved keeping inhabitants on their toes.

The Darkmoon family had gotten lost in their own halls, forced through a labyrinth for making a mess or, the worst offense of all, vomiting on the floors. Years ago, he had been eaten by the wall, forced to hang from the entangling roots for a day because he dared to call Hill Castle's tastes in decorum tacky.

Baskets of fruits and vegetables lined the kitchen countertops, for perhaps Hill Castle believed he needed a snack. The castle assumed correctly because his appetite had been rather dulled for years. He thought little of rest, nothing of mingling with the hundreds of fae swarming to and from Darkmoon lands.

Many yearned to ask a million questions of him about Fearworn, the war, and his demeanor. But all Nicholas had on his mind was William. Jade eyes and golden hair softer than silk, of his voice and his laugh and his smiles. He was homesick for William's touch, so much so he hallucinated the medic in his bed. He'd wake to William's morning stubble tickling his fingertips. Then the vision vanished, and he hardly resisted the urge to burn the world to ash.

Rather than risk the house's wrath, Nicholas plucked an apple, then left the kitchen in search of an escape. Guests filled the ballroom. Their voices and laughter carried through the halls. If any caught him, they would drag him to his doom. Typically, Blair would be among them. His attention still swept the halls for the silhouette of his sister, prepared for another assault.

After Nicholas killed Fearworn, after witnessing William being torn apart, something within himself broke. Blair saw that. On the battlefield, she swept through the masses, blades drawn and pointed at his throat. He hadn't seen her, would have fallen to her if not for Arden and Amos stepping in. Upon learning of what she had tried, their father banished her, if only because Nicholas still had more use than she.

Opening another door, he clung to the doorframe to prevent himself from falling into a pit of his brother's peculiar plants. They adhered to the soiled walls, their leaves vibrant in colors, and vines snapping with snarled teeth. Solomon Darkmoon tended to them, swinging on a pair of vines that breached the earth and held him like a lover. His brown hair had never been less than a knotted mess of flowers and leaves. One could lose sight of him among the glade, his pale green skin blending in with the nursery.

"Evening, brother." Solomon snapped a dying bud. "Are you prepared for tonight's festivities?"

"I will not be attending," Nicholas replied hesitantly.

Solomon speaking to him was a rarity and always ended with one of them annoyed, injured, or both.

"Why not? Do you worry Blair may turn up and relieve you of your head?" Solomon laughed, because he would enjoy the debacle.

"If so, she would fail a second time." Nicholas slammed the door shut.

Blair had never been a sister. Solomon and Percival were not brothers. Laurent wasn't a father. And yet, remembering Blair on the battlefield, the hatred in her eyes as she ran at him, dug a hole in his chest that couldn't be filled.

Nicholas hadn't seen her since Fearworn died, but that didn't mean she wasn't waiting for him to leave. She would be given another chance to rid the world of the potential coming of the second Fearworn, or so she claimed as she tried driving a dagger into his heart. Her hatred shouldn't have surprised him, seeing as she was always more than open about said hatred, but alas, the memory left a foul taste on his tongue.

"I am in no mood to play games or attend the revel," Nicholas grumbled, with his forehead pressed against the door.

The castle groaned. Floorboards bent beneath his feet. He opened the same door. A hall greeted him. Right or wrong ways did not exist at Hill Castle. One walked with a place in mind and the castle led them there, if it was feeling generous. He suspected these games resulted from Laurent, his father, the lord of Darkmoon. Laurent had Hill Castle working overtime for the revel. A celebration supposedly for Nicholas' return after two long years of hunting the remnants of Calix Fearworn's shadowed disciples, the cursed shade bent on opening paths to new realms, even if it meant destroying theirs.

Nicholas refused to be paraded around by his father for all to fawn and gossip over. Because of Fearworn's demise at the hands of the Darkmoon family, foolish mortals lined up at their door for deals. Some would even attend tonight, unaware that that they'd drown in faerie wine, and die pirouetting on the dancefloor as they once did before the Collision Treaty.

He refused to be trapped by gawking fae, reduced to an evening entertainment. He was not an animal to be teased in a cage, not a piece of tapestry to be admired on the wall, and he wasn't to be pitied or condemned. He saw their looks, the concern, the rage, the desire, all captured in their eyes, twisted among their words.

With Fearworn's fall, Nicholas took his place upon the pedestal, to be talked about, watched, pondered by any and all. A fair few worried, perceiving him in the same way Blair had; a threat. Others, like Laurent, saw Nicholas as an opportunity, a weapon to be pointed at any he perceived as an enemy. Nicholas couldn't stand it, and few had already faced his wrath for daring to speak ill behind his back.

Finally, Hill Castle released him into the sunflower field at the back of the household. They bowed in welcome, shifting to form a path. He kicked off his shoes. The soil beneath his bare feet was soft, full of endless life that had been loud before, but now it was nearly unbearable. He saw more, in a way he couldn't explain. He sensed the weather changing, felt the earth take a breath, saw magic slipping through roots, cobwebs, from one animal to another. Even these flowers.

He pinched a petal between his fingers. Light flashed beneath in a pale grayish-blue hue. *Was this what caught Fearworn?* he wondered. The lights, the feelings, this sense of being so small in the face of an infinite wonder. Fearworn leaped forward, desperate for answers. Nicholas did not because he thought of William always.

A cavern formed in his chest, expanding by the day, consuming more and more until it wouldn't be manageable. The worries, fears, and ambitions he once had were replaced by the ravenous want of William and anything he desired. He thought of holding his hand, dancing with him, taking a stroll under the stars, the most ordinarily mundane day-to-day activities that he would have scoffed at years ago. But now he couldn't imagine anything more beautiful.

He fell to his knees and plucked the sunflowers, promising they were being remade for good reason. The lush green of their stems reminded him of William's eyes. So often his wicked forced hostility out of his heart for protection, but on nights when they forgot about the world outside their embrace, William's eyes held the first breath of spring, of promised renewal and strength like no other.

He had neither heard nor seen William in two years, but no amount of time could make him forget. He would recognize William's laughter, his scent, his voice, even at the ending of the world. Memories sustained him, but wouldn't forever. He craved to feel William's breath upon his skin, to run his lips over William's pulse, to burrow himself within William's heart, tangled among his bones, filling his veins, stealing his heart as to never to be torn apart.

I'll lock us away, my wicked, where none will dare disturb us, he thought with a sneer that flipped into a scowl. Laurent kept them apart, but deals had loopholes and Nicholas would tug the fray. He would find the loose thread, break free, and slither his way out of his father's noose. A man had Nicholas' heart, and if he could not be with William, he would tear this world apart until all that remained was them.

"Making a crown for yourself, mighty shade slayer?" Evera Bloodbane called in an angelic voice that betrayed most.

Evera and Nicholas were bound to each other as children through deals struck between their parents. They were to sire three children and let Evera's mother, Alvina Bloodbane, experiment on them to determine if children could inherit the abilities of a shade parent, or if that caused any effects on the offspring. Evera and Nicholas never got along after that, always at each other's throats since they couldn't be at their parent's.

He didn't understand his father's reasoning at first, but Laurent claimed if Alvina learned about shades, perhaps they could stop another Fearworn from being born. While Nicholas agreed a world without another Fearworn was nice, he hated the prospect of shades being treated as nothing more than experiments. He felt much like one himself, forced to bear children, to waste his time with Evera, to do Laurent's bidding out of fear, being forced down one path after the other without any say in where he wanted to go.

He continued crossing the flower stalks while imagining bringing William here. They would lie in the field together. William would read his books and drink his tea. Nicholas would worship him, his God to revere, and if any stood in his way, he would rid the world of them.

Unfortunately, it was not William who knelt beside him. Evera, with her ashen gray skin and blue tinted fingers, pinched a letter between her nails. Her long blue hair had been plaited in silver, tucked behind her sharp ears, covered in silver and jewels. Eyes of a storm, dying gray, showed no emotion, but her tone carried a devious sound.

"Why are you out here when your father works diligently to throw a revel for you? One I hear that will be so grand it will last a month," she asked.

"Because I have no interest in his revels. Let him waste his time." Nicholas twisted a stem too tight, and it snapped. "Is there a reason you are here? Last I heard, you didn't wish to see me unless absolutely necessary."

"You have made my visit necessary by being so elusive. You return home after years and hardly leave the castle."

"Does that not please you?"

"Not when you are missing an opportunity for the both of us." Evera slapped his cheek with the letter, earning herself a narrowed glare. "You haven't read this."

"Obviously. What more could the mortals want from me?" He recognized the insignia on the envelope belonging to the king of Heign. William would be at the capital, Alogan. He spoke rarely of his home, but Nicholas remembered Alogan had a library William got lost in frequently as a child. He spoke fondly during the night when the two of them whispered, as if they feared the wind would carry their secrets. Nicholas hadn't forgotten a single conversation. He cherished every moment, ensuring William's words carved themselves into his mind.

"The mortal kings and fae lords wish to throw a ball for you," Evera said.

"They have thrown plenty of those already, and I shouldn't have to tell you it is rude to read someone's mail," he countered.

"You refuse to read it, so someone has to keep an eye on things."

"This one excites you, then."

She smiled cruelly, like an executioner waiting at the block. "Read it and see for yourself."

He snatched the paper from her and scanned the letter, uncaring about the promises of drink and a good meal. Nothing truly satiated his appetite anymore, but then he caught the last few lines expressing how grateful the mortals were to him, how they owed him. The kings promised a ball to celebrate Nicholas and his accomplishments because, without him, Fearworn would have torn their worlds asunder, and so they would grant him anything he desired.

"Owed," he whispered. "Owed," he laughed.

"Do you understand the meaning of this?" Evera twirled blades of grass around her fingers. "Tell me your rattled mind isn't beyond basic comprehension."

Words were important in Faerie. One shouldn't thank a fae, it implies they are owed. They shouldn't say they owe a fae anything either. The written word was equally powerful, but to make sure, he dug a hole. His teeth pierced his palm. He bled on the page, then laid the letter to rest. The mortal kings had no power, but their words would. He deserved a gift worthy of saving two realms. Faerie would ensure the deal met because Faerie never broke an oath.

He understood what the letter meant perfectly, but his plans were not what Evera yearned for. She proved as such with her following words, "This is the best chance to end our arrangement. Laurent received word too, but according to his gossiping, the letter differed from yours. It omitted the kings wanting to bestow a gift upon you, so he is unaware. With this, you can break us free from our parents."

He broke into a smile that stretched the skin far along his cheeks and made his eyes crinkle into crescent moons. "Yes, I could."

It would free him from Laurent, and finally, he would see William again. Nicholas' phantom, his heart, his all-consuming thoughts, his world, his everything, finally within his grasp. They hadn't seen each other, hadn't spoken, hadn't exchanged so much as a letter because of Laurent.

The most he could do was watch and learn from afar. He called in a favor or two, ensuring a fae kept eyes on William to guarantee his safety and feed Nicholas in the only way he could be. He knew where William was, what he was doing, and who he spent his time with, but that wasn't enough. He wanted to be with William, to learn about the last two years through his lips, to catch his hand and never let go. If they could merge, if they could become one for all eternity, he would never ask for more.

"When the kings speak to you, remind them you are owed. We don't want to miss this opportunity," Evera said.

"Do not treat me as if I understand nothing. I know what to do," he snapped.

"Do you?" She snatched the crown from his grasp. A fierce wind ripped through the field, forcing the flowers to bend. His fingers twitched, wishing to wrap around Evera's throat and snap. Break. Crush. Pulverize her being, her very essence, into nothing because she was nothing.

"Return the crown to me. It does not belong to you," he whispered, fingers flexing unnaturally, as if the bones hadn't been set right.

"Swear to end our engagement," she demanded, but her voice didn't hold the same ferocity it once did.

The only person who spoke to him the same since Fearworn's demise was his father. Others saw him, the hue of his eyes, and they recalled all Fearworn had done, all he could potentially do now. He tasted their fear, a sweet aroma making his blood curl, and on the rare occasion, desire or jealousy.

Holding out his hand, he said, "I will do as I please, Evera."

A laugh ripped through her throat. "What makes you believe your little mortal will want you? You should see yourself when you speak of him. He will see it too, the obsession, the breakage, the threat, a monster no different from the one you fought."

Nicholas tried to argue he did not differ from before, but the words congealed in the back of his throat. He thought the words to be true. What had changed about him? He tried to recall who he was before his eyes changed, before Fearworn's sticky blood coated his fingers and William's dying breath. He couldn't remember being different, couldn't recall a moment of change, but this confusion brought Evera amusement.

She smiled with hideous delight and dropped the crown into his lap. "Make the right decision, Nicholas." Then she walked away.

"Make the right decision," he repeated once, twice, thrice, but no voice stirred. Sometimes one did. The voice came and went, calming him, but it was little more than a whisper. Then the world got too loud, too much, and he fell into humming a soothing song as he finished William's crown.

They would be together soon. Nothing would separate them ever again.

2

WILLIAM

DEATH FOLLOWED WILLIAM LIKE a newfound lover. Her claws embedded themselves beneath his skin, feral rose vines growing painful thorns. Any mistake and Death would take without remorse. He never blamed her, never saw her as anything more than the inevitable. At least Death didn't discriminate like the rest of the damned city. She came when your time was up and he knew many whose times were nearly upon them.

Sick beds packed the warehouse. Operating as a clinic for the poor of Alogan, men he served beside two years ago against Calix Fearworn filled the beds. Though they never met on the battlefield, war survivors recognized the look. A bitterness overtook them, so few defiant and most having given up after being left behind by the government that promised to care for them.

In a way, William gave up, too. Life would never be what it once was. He would never be the man he could have been without five years of war, taken from his parents at sixteen and returned as a stranger to all, including himself.

He descended the iron staircase from his office overlooking the med bay. Drapes separated the patients, although nothing deterred the stench of open wounds, rotting flesh, and the sick. One never became accustomed to the smell, always burning the nostrils and watering the eyes. Nurses scurried about donning masks and gloves, their aprons stained by excrements.

Prior to the war, the clinic hadn't been so crowded. The more time that passed, the fewer donations flowed in. High society saw no reason to donate. They paid their dues, saw nothing, knew nothing other than what the newspapers claimed. Fearworn died. The war was over. Soldiers were home. They should be grateful and move on, as if it were so easy. As if being spoken highly about for a handful of months healed their rattled minds.

High Society didn't believe in the mental torment, that the soldiers could feel anything other than triumphant. Society spun their epics, tales of adventures and honor while ignoring the consequences, the men begging for help. They learned nothing of war. They cast these men aside, took away their free hospital visits, let clinics close one by one, and denied them treatment, so the soldiers turned to the last place they could.

William wished he were nothing but charitable, but in reality, he cared for them because of selfish reasons. Patient's wants and needs kept him moving day and night. He assisted in dressing them, caring for their wounds and ailments far after the sun settled. He feared what his quiet mind would wish for otherwise.

Like the men he stitched up, he couldn't return to normalcy. Peace and comfort felt out of reach, like a friend who grew distant.

At the front of the warehouse, nurses stashed medicine into brown bags with patients' names on them. Mrs. Brigby noted visitors to ensure patients fetched their medication. He approached the table. His gloves squeaked when he flexed his fingers. His right hand locked behind his back, always further away from everyone. The cool silver at his shoulder pressed against his skin as a constant reminder of what had been lost and replaced.

Fearworn tore him apart in that last battle. He remembered little more than the pain, certainly didn't remember Laurent Darkmoon gifting him a new arm after saving his son against Fearworn, and, like everyone else, expected him to be grateful. Like Nicholas expected to be forgotten, to be nothing more than a ghost haunting the halls of his mind.

Nurse Bigby, a kindly woman with warm olive skin and plump rosy cheeks, smiled. "Good evening, Dr Vandervult. You're staying late, as usual."

"There's a lot of work to be done." He presented a hand for the nurse's clipboard. He feigned being unaware of the way her eyes clipped between his arms.

Most didn't risk touching fae objects unless absolutely necessary. Tales said gifts given by fae, even if earned righteously, would cause catastrophe. His patients, sick and dying, would sometimes ask for another doctor, even if it meant struggling through more pain because they didn't want his cursed arm touching them. He faulted no one for their beliefs because, after the years spent around fae, he knew nothing from fae ever ended well. Fools fell for their tricks, and he had been the biggest fool of them all.

Mrs. Brigby handed him the clipboard. He did his best to have daily inspections, to double check his patients' received treatment. Most became regulars, but of late, some hadn't shown.

"Mrs. Brigby, have you seen Vale lately?" He didn't see her name on the list and Vale's medicine bag sat on the furthest end of the table.

"Oh dear, no, I'm afraid I haven't." Mrs. Brigby accepted the clipboard to look through the sign-in sheet. "According to our records, she was meant to pick her medicine up two days ago. No one has marked seeing her. I'll have another nurse ask around."

"Yes, please do that."

Ever since he returned, he tended to the clinic. Robert and Matilda wanted him to rest, but nightmares haunted him, visions he couldn't forget, feelings he wanted to leave behind, and a man he didn't want to admit to being. Keeping busy and monitoring patients kept him from spiraling.

Over the years, he learned about the people of the city. They weren't as transient as the public believed. His patients grew their roots. The soup kitchen a block over advertised his clinic, so he visited frequently. That's where he met Vale, an older widow who lost her husband a decade ago. They never had much, and she was sick with weak lungs, so it didn't take long for her to lose everything and find herself on the streets. She was a kind woman, generous and sweet. She never missed her medicine pick up and brought flowers she picked from the local park for the patients. Vale's absence made the seventh person, who stopped picking up their medicine in less than two months.

"Strange," he said.

"What?" Mrs. Brigby asked.

"Nothing. Good work today, Mrs. Brigby."

He returned to the rundown storage room that he called an office. Blinds, haggard and yellowed by age, hung from the windows lining the facade. A couch too small to lie comfortably on fit against the wall, the fabric ripped and cushions thin. A desk sat at the center, enclosed by shelves on either side. Papers filled every drawer and stacked atop the desk. One page stood out; a list of names that he added Vale's to.

He kept rolls of cannabis locked in the top drawer of his desk. He struck a match to one and tapped a finger against the page, wishing to do more, to prove something was happening.

After the second missing patient, he asked around at the soup kitchen. Workers and visitors claimed they saw these people one day, then they were gone the next, having abandoned the little they had behind. On the fourth missing person, he went to the police. They said he was overreacting and there was no proof of foul play. They were transients, so they likely weren't missing at all. But in his gut, he knew there was more to this.

"William?"

He lurched for the knife secured under the desk. A silhouette crossed the threshold, long-limbed and violet-eyed, a smile wicked and cruel.

Then he blinked, and it was not a monster but Charmaine Tuckerton clutching two letters to her chest. They met during their training days when he saved her from a group of tortuous teenage boys. The two stood out among the military, considered too soft by their so-called betters. They worked together to survive and formed an everlasting friendship that no other could replicate for they had witnessed and lived through terror others wouldn't understand.

He released the blade, dread fading from his thoughts. His eyes betrayed him, as they so often did these last two years.

A beautiful gown of pale blue draped over Charmaine's brown shoulders and flowed around her legs. She loved drapery and had since taken to designing apparel for girls seeking courtship and, even more recently, social elites wishing to start the newest trend. She and her mother made names of themselves, and eagerly left behind their old lives. He never asked what happened to Charmaine's poor excuse of a father. He imagined she wasn't thinking about her father much, either.

"What are you doing here so late?" he asked, offering her the remnants of his cannabis.

Charmaine finished the cigarette, dispersing the smoke high above their heads. "An excellent question for you to answer, seeing as you should be at home with your family. Lady Vandervult gets distraught when you are out late. I imagine she will be here any moment to retrieve you."

"I am a grown man. I do not need to be home in time for supper."

"But your family would like you to be."

William knew that, but the longer he was home, the more he felt they would be better off without him.

The broken pieces of him refused to mend. Every noise made him jump. His eyes played tricks, believing friends to be enemies and shadows traps. The abrupt appearance of his niece wishing to play had him reaching for a weapon. Luckily, Alice never understood. She thought he wanted to play and tugged eagerly on his pants, filling the rooms with laughter and joy.

He tried to bask in the feeling of being home, of having a family bigger than ever, but he couldn't cease the somber thoughts of how he could lose all of them in one fell swoop, especially if they learned the truth of all he had done.

He cleared his throat. "Why the surprise visit?"

"I had to see if you received one as well." Charmaine thrust the letters toward his gloved hands. He recognized the matching insignias on the back of the envelopes, the open one addressed to her and the other to him. "An invitation from His Majesty," she whispered.

William desired no invitation from King Ellis, lest it was an invitation to his beheading.

Robert Vandervult, his father, dared to call the king out for what he truly was; greedy. King Ellis punished the Vandervult family by sending William, their youngest, to war. All of his suffering had been because of a bastard who took offense to being told about his cruelty. His family's suffering was due to the king's overly inflated ego, his desire to show the Vandervult family how easily he could destroy them.

"A ball to celebrate Nicholas Darkmoon," he said after reading over the invitation. The name tasted of poison on his tongue, acidic and sour.

He tried forgetting the destructive smile and sly words he foolishly fell for, words he dared to believe hadn't been warped to toy with him, but nothing eased the loss of Nicholas. He would never forget because one could not touch another's soul and disappear without leaving a scar.

"What foolishness is this?" He dropped the letter into Charmaine's awaiting hands. "Fearworn has been dead for two years. The king celebrated more than once already."

He would know, having been forced to attend the balls where he spent most of the evening spitting up in the toilets.

Charmaine's hands clenched at her waist where her letter wrinkled between her fingers. "He did, but the Darkmoons continued the search for Fearworn's remaining disciples after his demise. Rumors say Nicholas has been battling shadowed disciples and helping set up monitoring stations around shimmers until anyone learns how to close them permanently. Now the kings of Terra wish to throw a grand affair, probably to thank the Darkmoon family specifically, since they were such a force."

"Heard all this from the girls, did you?" he asked.

"Our customers love to gossip during fitting sessions. They act like we aren't even there." She glared down at her letter. "I received my invitation this morning. After work, I hurried to your home, but you were not there. Lord Vandervult kindly gave me the letter. I assumed it was the same, but wanted to make sure."

"This is an affair neither of us can decline?"

"Seems so," she muttered.

He shredded a piece of paper, twirling the thin sheet between his fingers. "If he wishes to thank us, he should do that by leaving us alone. This will dig up bad memories for everyone."

"I don't disagree, but we both know the kings cannot fathom our turmoil, nor do they care. We shouldn't have to stay long, at least."

That didn't matter because Nicholas would be there, and William could not avoid him.

Over the years, he imagined a reunion where he could speak his mind. Each word he threw at Nicholas became crueler than the last. But every vision ended with Nicholas laughing because William knew nothing he said would ever matter. He was another mortal upset he fell for obvious tricks. Surely, Nicholas had a long list and his name meant nothing, another forgotten conquest.

Charmaine grasped his left arm. "This could be an excellent opportunity to speak with Nicholas."

He tossed the shreds of paper into a nearby basket. "I have nothing to say to him."

"But you have much to ask."

"And if I dare to ask, he will find every path to tear me apart. Fuck him, and fuck the king." His furious gaze caught on the list of missing patients. His fury settled, little more than the usual spark at the back of his mind. "Wait... we could make this work to our advantage."

She released him. "How so?"

"I will have direct access to the king. Another patient is missing, Charmaine. That is seven now."

She grabbed the list from his desk. Her lips pressed into a grim line.

He gathered what little information he had on the missing patients. "I can take all of this with us to share with His Majesty at the ball."

"What makes you think he'll care about missing homeless people? The horrid conditions of the workhouses say exactly what he thinks of anyone outside his social circle," she countered.

"I do not believe he will, but that won't stop the guests from caring. If he is heard denying such charity, there will be gossip, even from those who don't necessarily care. He will want to save face and we need all the help we can get."

Because William did not know what they were dealing with, but his gut told him to be weary. A doctor of the mind that he spoke with called this extreme paranoia, a remnant from the war that caused him to check rooms for the quickest exit and assess situations like a battle. He worried about noises in the night that were nothing more than creaking stairs or swore he saw monsters perched along the treeline at the estate.

Simply paranoia, the doctor said, the term utterly foreign to his ears, but that time, he was certain he caught onto genuine horror.

"I fear you underestimate him, William. Gossip is the language His Majesty speaks best." Richard, William's elder brother, stood in the doorway, his heavy-lidded brown eyes settled with worry. He sauntered into the room. His normally laughing mouth descended into a grimace. "I apologize for overhearing, but to my credit, neither of you knows what a whisper is. Another patient has gone missing, correct?"

A flare of concern ignited in William's belly. "Yes."

"That makes seven, if I recall correctly," said Richard.

"You say that as if you have ever recalled anything incorrectly."

"One needs a good memory in my line of work." Richard held out his hand in a silent request to see what William had.

He hesitated. That flare of concern roared. His family shouldn't get involved. Danger lurked in the city of Alogan, after all the years he spent fighting to protect them. Monsters may have found them at their home.

"William," Richard encouraged, his voice so serene, unlike Williams' rattled mind. His brother wouldn't relent, so he gave in. Richard read through what little they had, then spoke plainly, "This wasn't enough to warrant an investigation from the authorities and it will not be enough for His Majesty."

"We have to try," said William.

"Of course we do, so long as the two of you are up for it." A self-confident smirk painted Richard's features. "This tale needs a little embellishing."

"You want us to lie?"

"Embellish," Richard corrected. "Nobles love a good story, an epic, a tragedy, a way to get their cold little hearts racing."

Rage joined William's concern, boiling at the base of his neck. "I'm not turning my patients' tragedies into a night of entertainment."

"I'm not asking you to."

Richard Vandervult could convince the Souls to reconsider their judgments. His charisma manifested through blinding smiles, suave words, and enthusiastic interest. After a minute, he could make one believe they had known him since childhood. He excelled at their charity ventures for that very reason.

William found his tactics two-faced, but the best way to survive palace life was through the game of lies. Very few played that game as well as Richard, and he was offering to play the game in William's stead.

"It feels wrong," he whispered.

"It is wrong." Richard faced the window where he watched the floor below. "These people shouldn't be clinging to life here. The king shouldn't be forcing soldiers to this damned ball. I shouldn't have to fake smiles and laughter for charity. Alas, life is not fair, but it is malleable."

He looked at Charmaine for guidance. She had as little answers as he, as much fear, too. He saw it in her eyes. If he accepted, she would stand beside him, and that eased the discomfort weighing heavy on his chest.

His shoulders deflated. "What tale will you spin?"

"I'm not sure yet." Richard tapped the papers on the desk. "I trust you will let me hold on to these?"

He nodded.

"Good. We'll speak more when I have an idea in mind. For now, it is time to head home. Mother is worried."

"I told him she would be," said Charmaine. He shot her a look.

"Come, you must sleep in your own bed tonight and, most importantly, take a bath," Richard ordered.

William curled his nose. "What are you implying?"

Richard stalked around the desk to grasp him by the hem of his coat. "You stink. Our niece shouldn't be forced to tolerate this."

Richard's knuckles brushed his right arm. He put space between them. Richard pretended the action wasn't odd.

"Alice is there?" he asked.

"She is staying the night and refuses to sleep without a story from Uncle William. I trust you won't disappoint her?"

Charmaine giggled. Richard got his way because William's niece was his greatest weakness. Alice had a light in her he hoped would never be snuffed out, that he would protect at all costs. He already did, barely six months after he returned, and she clung to him ever since.

"No, I wouldn't do that. Take my carriage home, Charmaine. I'll ride with my brother," he said.

Charmaine nodded, then giggled when Richard took her hand to give her an unexpected spin followed by a hug.

"It is always a pleasure to see you, My Lady," he said.

Donning a precious grin, Charmaine said her goodbyes, then descended the stairs.

No one asked about her, not even Henry, who had seen her with William on the battlefield. He was grateful, and hopeful his family would understand one day should he ever bring a man home, if that was possible. He lost Hugh in the war, a man he believed he could love until the end of his days. He sent Hugh's family flowers every month, anonymously. It was the least he could do. Then he lost Nicholas, the fae tricking him since day one. He wasn't doing well romantically and couldn't imagine that ever changing. Not with the way he was, with how his body had become or how broken his mind was.

"Sleeping on that couch is no good for you," Richard lectured on their way down the stairs.

"I've slept in worse conditions," he said bitterly.

"But you're home now, in better conditions. You need to take care of yourself."

He was trying, truly, but he wasn't sure how to care for himself anymore. Nothing worked, not even being home.

3

WILLIAM

MARTHA MIDDLE'S BOOK OF Riddles should have burned upon William's return. If he were in his right mind, he would have cast the book into the hearth along with anything reminding him of Nicholas. Alas, the book survived, and his niece insisted on the tales becoming bedtime stories.

Alice sat on his bed, flipping through tattered pages, notes scrawled in the corners from his younger hand. She added notes of her own, dotting the pages with stars to signify her favorite parts.

"When will you come home, Uncle?" She clutched the book to her chest, forcing the ruffles of her nightgown to bundle beneath her chin. Her brown curls were tucked under a matching bonnet. She took after her mother, Amara, more than Arthur, with doe-like eyes and a button nose.

"I am not sure. The ball may last well into the night, but I will leave as soon as I can," he replied.

He glared at the soldier in the mirror, adjusting the collar of his uniform. Under the king's orders, soldiers would don their uniforms for the party, not the tattered and stained ones covered in excrement, but the pressed ones, perfect for the king's toys.

The brush of the fabric summoned the wintry air of the Deadlands, the chittering of spions, and the cry of gunfire. The room swayed, morphing into a winter wasteland, and the dead lay at William's feet. Blood dripped from his fingers, hot and sticky. Soot coated his lungs, making every breath ragged and wheezed. He searched the perimeter for the threat.

A pair of gleaming violet eyes flickered in the trees. Fearworn's laughter slithered up his spine to coil around his neck, squeezing the life from him. His silver arm ached with phantom pains. Branches coiled together tighter than a fisherman's knot, smothering the world in darkness. All that could be seen were Fearworn's eyes, then his mouth dripping red. William reached for the revolver at his waist.

"Stay back," he warned, raising the gun high.

Fearworn's laughter had him in a stranglehold. His eyes shone in the dark, soon towering over William. A hand, blacker than ink, stretched toward him, promising a gruesome demise.

"Get away from me!" He swung out. He hit something. A quiet voice whimpered, followed by a thud.

The Deadlands liquified. He stood in his bedroom, gazing down at his mother on the floor. A delicate hand brushed her cheek. Alice had vanished, her book of riddles, too. He didn't hold a gun, but a book that had been on the dresser. His stomach lurched. He swallowed hard, trying not to vomit.

"Mother, I... I'm sorry, I didn't mean..." To raise his hand, to shout at her, to shove her and frighten her, but she smiled like nothing had transpired.

Matilda stood and dusted off the hem of her skirt as if she tripped of her own accord. Her cheek remained a dull shade of red.

"Alice fetched me saying you were having trouble breathing," she explained, like he hadn't done this before, swung at a maid, screamed at a butler, and threw his breakfast across the room. He struggled existing in his home, as a civilian, as a son. The mind played tricks, and those tricks won more often than not.

"Why don't you stay home tonight?" she suggested, somehow containing the tears brimming her eyes.

He wanted nothing more, but, "We both know I cannot. The king has summoned me."

In the late hours of the night when he woke in a cold sweat, he wondered about the list he once had, the lives he took during war times, and how desperately he wanted King Ellis to join them. If he could squeeze that vile king's neck until his face went blue, the world would be an infinitely better place, and he wouldn't regret a thing. He wondered what that made him, what kind of person and what kind of son, to want to take a life so wantonly.

"Richard will tell him you weren't feeling well. He could charm the king to forgiveness," she tried with a gentle approach that he so hated.

His family practiced a new sense of discomfort, a hesitancy where they watched his every move to ensure he wouldn't lash out, like he just had.

They happened sometimes, moments of paranoia that sent him to the past. He'd blink and find himself in the Deadlands, the place they battled Fearworn once and for all. Blood would be on his hands. He tasted copper in his mouth. He'd hear gunfire, smell smoke, taste ash, and see the faces of those he killed, then he'd awaken and realize he had been screaming in the middle of the night.

Smoking helped, so he went for one of the cannabis cigarettes locked in his bedside drawer. Matilda said nothing of it when he took a match to the cigarette, although he recalled when he was younger how she praised him for not being interested in smoking like the other men of the court. He didn't press a cigar to his lips, but alas, he felt like he was not quite the son she wanted.

Hot shame bristled behind his cheeks as he took a deep hit of smoke. "I am sorry. Does your cheek hurt?"

"There is nothing to apologize for." Matilda settled her hands around his waist. Her head fell on his back and she held him tight in an embrace only a parent could give, one so unbearably warm he wanted to turn away but also lean into it, hoping he would wither into nothing.

Their butler, Marshall, and Alice appeared at the threshold. Alice's bottom lip trembled. "Are you feeling okay?" she asked.

"I'm nervous about attending the king's ball. It's nothing to worry over, sweetheart." He put out his cigarette and hid the remnants of it in his drawer. "I will try to be home before your bedtime."

All he did was try. Try to be the person he once was, try to be a good uncle, a good doctor, a full person rather than a broken shell wandering and hopeless. Trying never felt good enough.

Matilda released him, her lips pursed. She wanted to convince William to stay home. That's all he wanted, too, but the ball was about more than the king summoning him. Tonight, they had a chance to talk to the king about the missing patients.

"Ms. Tuckerton has arrived," Marshall explained. "Everyone waits in the foyer and the carriage is ready to depart."

Alice's pout grew exponentially. William kissed his mother's cheek, then approached Alice to say, "If I am late, I will read you two stories when you next stay over."

Like fae, she wouldn't let William forget about a deal struck. She allowed him to depart without anyone having to pry her from his person.

"I hope tonight isn't unbearable," Matilda said.

"Me too." He had more to apologize for, but could never conjure the appropriate words.

He set off to meet his father, brother, and Charmaine in the foyer. Robert didn't look his way when he descended the stairs. He didn't look at William most days. Spoke to him, laughed, asked about his day. All of that was normal, but look at him? Robert proved incapable, and if he ever dared, if William entered a room when he wasn't prepared, Robert's eyes fell dark, then he hid.

William said nothing of it, nor did anyone else. He hadn't the heart to ask why.

Robert had never been a man wishing to stand out. His pressed waistcoat hugged his full figure, navy in tone and embellished with silver buttons to match the tip of his cane. His peppered mustache curled at the ends and a top hat hid his thinning hair.

Richard, on the other hand, wanted ships at sea to spot him on the horizon. He donned a peculiar canary yellow tight-waisted coat and matching trousers. The sleeves narrowed at the wrists like Robert's, but Richard adorned his with bejeweled orange cufflinks like the first dawn of summer. Noble ladies were likely to throw themselves at him. They always did, even with the wedding ring on his finger.

At least he had been home to attend Richard and Eleanor's wedding. Eleanor wouldn't be joining them. She was resting very pregnant at home, more than content to be tucked in bed rather than waddling around a party, as she so eloquently put it the other evening.

Comparatively, Charmaine stood stiff as a board, hating the uniform more than William. Ever since she and her mother opened the Gilded Lily, a clothing boutique in town, she took to wearing dresses and skirts. She kept her natural hair shaved, preferring to wear wigs her mother tended for her and learned a plethora of new makeup techniques. Charmaine worked in the back of the store to avoid potentially problematic customers, but she was happier than ever.

Alas, peace abandoned them. They were a rotting mess together, wishing for nothing more than to escape the confines of their past. Without make up, the scars along Charmaine's cheekbones stood out, a paled brown. She wore gloves, like him, to conceal the scars along her fingertips where claws once ripped the skin.

"Let us get this night over with," Robert said, sensing the tension in the air but knowing there was nothing that would truly disperse it.

Together, they crowded into the waiting carriage outside.

The city of Alogan had stories too ancient to remember. Artifacts rose from the soil, pointed as accusatory fingers, interwoven between brick buildings. The great city built by ancestors long forgotten fell and no one knew why. Historians argued over the specifics, if it was users of the Sight before the world understood this power that led to a civilization ending catastrophe or an unfortunate natural disaster. Since the Collision, historians considered a realm bumping into Terra that sent the world into a spiral. Regardless, Alogan rebuilt, but William imagined the issues had never changed over the centuries.

Concealed by the exuberant shops and steeples, lived the truth few admitted to. Down by the warehouses spitting smog, presided another city called the outer banks, the true forgotten of Alogan. They slept in tents and sucked on bones. They filled the workhouses and survived off scraps, many of whom saved Alogan from a second destruction.

Over the years, he pondered if the city deserved the first end and should have stayed that way. Fearworn could have wiped Alogan off the map, ending the Ellis family line, who sat on their thrones spewing tales of victory while those who brought that victory died. Not just on the battlefront, but cowering on the city streets they were forced to protect.

The Vandervult estate didn't sit far from the streets of Alogan. A stretch of trees led them to the brightened roadways where stores closed shop for the night. The buildings hugged one another, rarely separated by alleys and artifacts, as if the city sought warmth from the neighbors. Stone structures, once believed to be columns, erupted from the soil.

Lamplight cast the world in a low orange glow, illuminating the silhouettes of inhabitants meandering the streets.

The carriage passed his favorite book store where old tomes cluttered the windows and the sign swung in the evening breeze. At the next turn, Charmaine's favorite pastry shop, where she grabbed breakfast, stood out with its pink painted exterior. The further into the city they went, the more the landscape changed from shops and run down residences to upscale homes with their gated yards and high steeples. The castle painted the horizon in harsh white stone, looming from the heart of the city. Ladies in puffy dresses and men in top hats gathered in their carriages to join the celebration.

"We won't stay long," Robert explained. "After the royals and fae lords are announced, there may be a speech or two. We'll greet His Majesty, then take our leave."

"Don't forget, we will speak to the king concerning William's missing patients, too," Richard said.

He tapped the satchel containing all he and Charmaine had collected. He didn't have the manpower to offer more. He could hardly leave the clinic for long, considering he was the only on-call doctor. Others donated their time occasionally, but they had businesses to run so they weren't too reliable. He couldn't ask them to tend to his clinic while he searched the streets for a kidnapper, either.

Robert sighed, as if reminding himself his sons weren't teenagers he could chastise. "You're a force to be reckoned with, Richard, but we both know how the king will feel about this."

"He cannot ignore us in a room full of guests," William countered, although a sweat had taken him since the moment they departed.

"But he can insist on seeking an audience in private another day, and that day will never come," Robert countered.

"You say that, and yet, you fight against him. You've convinced him to fund our clinics."

Robert clenched the head of his cane. William didn't mean to remind his father of how he was sent to war in the first place. He worried bringing up the war or anything he went through would hurt Robert all the more, so he chose not to say anything, but the damage had been done.

Robert heaved a long breath through his nostrils. "His Majesty does what he believes will make him look best. When you inform him that the homeless are going missing, he will be pleased. Most people don't care about the less fortunate. In fact, they are often glad to be rid of them."

Robert brushed the curtains aside. They passed through the iron gates warded by roaring lions carved from granite. Rumors claimed the lions would rise and protect their king should unwelcome visitors pass, gifted to the Ellis family by fae upon the signing of the Collision Treaty. Rumors also said they would slay the royals one day so fae could take their place, but William had been around enough fae to know they didn't care about mortal royalty.

"This isn't a few people. We've counted seven in the last two months. There is darkness in this city. We must get to the bottom of it," William countered as the carriage slowed behind the procession.

"I'm not saying you shouldn't, but I am saying His Majesty isn't the route to take," Robert said.

Richard settled a hand on their father's shoulder. "There is no need to worry. We have a plan."

That would hopefully work. William itched his left arm. His right, the silver monstrosity, never itched, but it felt pain. Of course, fae would ensure that.

"I suppose there is nothing wrong with trying, but please don't take offense if his answer isn't what you hoped for," Robert said.

William didn't hope for much. If the king acknowledged their request, that may be enough. The authorities could get involved. Even if they weren't dedicated to the cause, extra eyes and ears on the streets would work wonders.

The carriage came to a halt, and the door opened. Robert stepped into the golden light followed by Richard, who earned the crowd's attention. Guests called out to him requesting his ear this evening. Richard laughed, saying his hellos and greetings while William and Charmaine shuffled along at his back.

Lanterns hung from strings tied around towering columns lining the stairwell. Visitors whispering to one another over the grandeur passed the double doors into the palace. William cursed every step, wishing the mortar would crack beneath his feet.

Inside, a floral scent overwhelmed his senses. He wished to gag and spit across the immaculate marble floor shined so well it reflected the guest's silhouettes. Butlers dressed in finely tailored black suits, faces disguised by indistinguishable white masks, guided the guests.

Guests filtered into the adjoining room, a long ballroom decorated in yellow draped silks. Chandeliers hung low, glittering in silver and gold. Fae and mortals alike filled the ballroom, though none could deny the separation. Fae flocked together along the opposite end of the room by the double staircase leading to the balcony on the second floor. The kings and fae lords would descend from there.

"Let's keep back here," he whispered.

Charmaine didn't need to hear him say it; he wanted to avoid Nicholas. The simple thought of Nicholas strangled a breath from his throat. He snatched a glass of wine from a passing butler and downed the beverage in one gulp.

Robert hummed in warning. He didn't understand. None other than the surviving soldiers understood the evening's tension.

William's mind raced with possibilities, how it'd be easy for an enemy to strike. The bright ballroom and loud music put a target on their backs. Every wall had an exit, three further into the interior of the castle and one to the gardens. With the amount of guests, an attack would incite panic.

There would be a stampede, so he kept himself close to the door. One hand lingered at his back by the blade tucked beneath his uniform.

Soldiers crowded the room. Many shared similar expressions; dead-eyed and tired. They wished to be free, to escape this torment. In his case, he hoped to escape without seeing Nicholas. That damned fae haunted him for too long. He took root in William's heart. He was a ghost appearing in the dim morning light, pretending to be capable of love.

Not long after their arrival, horns blared, and the crowd surged. The pressure between them had William gulping for air. He saw the battlefield, the last fight. Fearworn's monsters raining from the sky. Rifles in his peripheral. Soldiers crying, begging, snarling, doing whatever they could to survive. He couldn't breathe, thinking of all the blood upon his fingers, bodies broken beneath his cracked fingernails, and Fearworn's final attack ripping through his body, taking pieces of him.

A fierce hand gripped his arm. "Take a breath," Charmaine whispered, sounding as panicked as he.

He heaved through his nostrils. Shutting his eyes, he told himself where he was. The king's ballroom. Fearworn was dead. The war ended. They were far from war, safe.

When his eyes opened, he and Charmaine gazed upon the second floor landing where a man wearing a peculiar feathered hat announced the arrival of their royals.

First came King Ellis, adorned in enough gold to sink a ship. His crimson cloak billowed at his back as he descended, hands raised as if to stop the applause. Next came King Shepherd of the Krenia Kingdom, where Fearworn took his last breath. King Shepherd was equally bejeweled, albeit older in years. He walked crookedly, back bent and most of his weight held by a thick cane.

Then the fae followed. Their silhouettes swam in his blotchy vision. His heart rang in his ears, louder when Laurent appeared. Even in plain navy robes, Laurent had more presence than any in the room. It was his eyes, the way he held himself, like he believed beyond any doubt how better he was. White gems hung from his antlers, appearing like fallen snow. He was ethereal in every sense of the word, deceiving in his beauty.

And at his side was Nicholas, beautiful, breathtaking Nicholas, with his raven hair caught in a low ponytail. Unlike his father, Nicholas wore a suit in blinding gold with dark stitching. He summoned the attention of all in the room. The cursed bastard who stole William's heart then left it to rot, eyes brilliantly violet, terrifying in their hue. He nearly whimpered because for a long moment, it was not Nicholas he saw, but Fearworn. His silver hair, crooked smile, and eyes such a fierce purple they were painful to gaze upon.

William's reality shuddered. Sweat dotted his brow. His hands flexed. A woman nearby passed a curious stare, whispering to her husband. They stepped away, like they knew what he hid beneath his gloves. They may as well have.

Upon his return, King Ellis insisted the Vandervults throw a ball in their son's honor. Of course he became adored, in the only manner high society could adore anyone, because it gave mortals a person to call a hero, to parade as a fine specimen of mortal loyalty and love for country. While they all spoke ill behind his back, the half-man cursed by wild fae magic, the man with cursed limbs, a man destined to die by a fae's hand, one way or the other. He hated every moment of the event, how the king grabbed his arm to show off like a trophy.

"I need air," he muttered.

Charmaine called after him, but he skirted around the crowded room to the hall. His vision swayed. Sweat soaked through his uniform. He found an empty lounge and fell upon the carpet, convulsing.

He wheezed, clawing at his chest that refused to expand. Dark spots exploded in his vision. The walls closed in, suffocating. His head pounded, brutally painful. He laid there whimpering, waiting, hoping the fear would pass.

The panic eased little by little, from him counting backwards from a hundred because that's all he could think of doing. Then his shaking hand fell on a nearby end stand and he forced himself onto his feet.

Blood filled his mouth. He pressed a finger to his lips, then along his tender tongue. Red stained his fingertips. He bit the inside of his cheek, probably the moment he saw Nicholas with those eyes...

Nicholas fell. Losing himself as Fearworn had was his greatest fear.

William pressed the back of his hand to his mouth, silencing the sorrow he cursed himself for feeling. Nicholas abandoned him. He disappeared when William needed him. He didn't write and never showed up to ask how he fared. Nicholas played the trickery of fae well, and William had lost.

"You can't care," he whispered, leaning against the end stand. His body ached. He undid the buttons of his uniform, trying to fan himself. In his thoughts, he didn't notice the shadow within the threshold until it was too late.

"My wicked," Nicholas whispered, and his heart stopped.

4

NICHOLAS

LIKE A FAIRYTALE PRINCESS locked away in a tower, Nicholas waited for a savior. In his case, his captor was his father, desperate deals struck, an equally bored Evera, and annoying siblings.

They waited on the second floor for mortal kings, who were fashionably late. Dolled up in a gown spun from captured starlight, Evera Bloodbane did not wait to greet the courtiers before partaking in the evening festivities. She terrified a server into fetching faerie wine, which she finished in two hastened gulps. The gold caught on her pale blue lips and she sighed, sounding most content when treading along the road of intoxication.

Nicholas' brothers wandered around the overflowing dining table. Treats and delights towered atop porcelain, silverware sat polished so brightly they reflected the flickering flames atop the candelabra. Maids trailed Solomon's steps, brushing away the twigs cascading from his hair. Vines coiled themselves through his long brown hair and his green fingers caught a treat to savor, then passed one to Percival. Unlike his elder brother, Percival had his hair shaved to the scalp, skin nearly charcoal black in tone.

Percival and Solomon gossiped about slipping Faerie treats into the mortal food for a little fun. Unfortunately for them, mortals had been tasked with triple checking everything, ensuring to return any treats Percival dropped to its correct plate.

Humans couldn't consume the food of Faerie without dire consequences. If they did, all else would taste worse than ash upon their tongue. Water wouldn't quench their thirst, no matter how much they consumed. Their minds would wither, their bodies too, until they succumbed to death or the call of Faerie.

By the end of the night, Solomon and Percival would have done more than curse one to death. They'd have at least a half dozen mortals in their grasp, either for an evening's entertainment or a deal to go horribly wrong, for the mortals, of course.

Realizing he couldn't covertly poison any mortals, Percival caught a goblet in his claws. He sauntered toward Nicholas, his coal-black lips pinched into a cruel sneer. "You must be excited to see your little plaything again."

"Must you mention him?" Evera snapped. "Nicholas is bad enough as is."

"Yes, he is. Father made the right choice keeping you from him, otherwise you'd have put the man in a grave by now." Percival took a drink. He had said little about Nicholas' change, but Nicholas saw it in his demeanor. He remained on edge in his presence, although Nicholas couldn't determine if it was from a desire to rip out his throat or discover a way to use him.

"You are the one keen to slaughter anyone and anything in your path, not I," Nicholas countered.

"Not yet, but you will be. It is your destiny, as it is any cursed shade." Percival swirled the wine in his goblet, letting a drop spill over his thin fingers. "You will forget who you were, who you wanted to be, and everyone you had ever known. One day, you will be little more than the dog Father always trained you to be."

Nicholas lunged. Evera put herself between them, hands raised. "Let's play nice tonight," she insisted. "If the mortals see us going at each other's throats, we'll miss the opportunity to have a little fun with them."

Percival loved having the upper hand. He was so like their father in that regard. "You're right. That was poor of me to say."

"Fuck off," Nicholas snapped.

Laughing, Percival found another victim; a King's Guard standing at the door. Percival purposefully wore a mostly sheer outfit that left little to the imagination, its shimmering rubies covering the more lewd aspects of himself. He hung off the guard's arm and spoke sweetly, spinning a web that could capture the mortal by night's end.

"Try to behave this evening, for both our sakes. Your father may be less angry later when you make your idiotic decision," Evera warned over the rim of her drink.

"An idiotic decision by your standards," he corrected.

"By any standard," she argued. "How can you not see now isn't the time to lose yourself to your obsession? That mortal haunts your every thought. Most cannot get through a conversation with you without hearing of him. Even now, you are hardly listening to me."

His refusal to reply said enough. He could not breathe without William near. He could think of nothing other than him, of how to be with him. When others spoke, even if the topic once garnered his interest, his thoughts traveled elsewhere. To green eyes, strands of gold caught between his fingers, and the catch of William's breath when they kissed.

"If you paid attention to anything else, you would have heard Lord Darkmoon express that once this affair is over, we are expected to go through with our parent's deal. He has retrieved the Elderwood sap," she snarled.

Sap from the Elderwood, trees as ancient as Faerie itself, allowed fae to bear children, otherwise no amount of fornicating resulted in a child. He had always been grateful for that. He couldn't imagine worrying a tiny fae would pop into his life because of one engagement. How mortals put up with such concerns was beyond him. Elderwoods were rare, and they didn't stay in one place for long. Fae had to search, so if Laurent acquired the sap, he was serious, and that was worth worrying over. But as quickly as that worry arrived, it faded.

"What of your mother?" he asked. "She has been preoccupied of late, so I heard. Perhaps you should put yourself to work and ensure she doesn't veer away from whatever she's toiling with. It is she who will conduct experiments, after all. If she is busy, she may hold off my father."

Evera's expression went gravely pale. "My mother is the definition of erratic, so one never knows what she is up to. She vanishes when she pleases. We haven't spoken in nearly a month, nor have I seen her. For all we know, she could be preparing said experiments."

Alvina Bloodbane had a curiosity that could rival Fearworn's. If she had been born a shade, the world probably would have fallen long ago. She had a hand for cruelty and little care for anyone. Seeking answers to the world's questions was all she cared about, and he had always been high on her list of curiosities. Shades, in general, caught her eye.

In his youth, he had been kidnapped as a poor attempt for fae to gain power. They hoped controlling a young shade could either grant them a deal with Laurent, or Nicholas would be their weapon. However, Alvina had saved him from their clutches and he considered her the mastermind behind that kidnapping ever since. She was so curious of shades. What better way to get her hands on one than orchestrating a kidnapping where she came out the hero and thus Laurent owed her a favor? If his suspicions were correct, it didn't matter. None of the kidnappers survived to speak of it, and he heard nothing pointing to her involvement.

"I doubt she is preparing anything for us, otherwise we would have heard of it," he said. "Half of our expectations aren't paying attention. Stop worrying yourself. It's irritating."

"I will hear nothing about irritation coming from you, the most irritating bastard I've ever known."

He smirked. "I'm flattered."

"You shouldn't be."

A man dressed ridiculously in a feathered hat and bloated coat prepared to open the door leading to the ballroom below. The mortal kings expressed the guests had arrived, which meant William would be among them. He couldn't explain the temptation, the need, the want filling him.

William. William. William. William.

"Control yourself," Laurent warned. His shadow fell over his son, although his words were nothing compared to the screeching of Nicholas' mind.

William's name sang fiercer than a siren's song. His eyes strayed to the door when the announcer opened it. He pushed himself forward, intending to follow. Laurent snatched him by the chin, forcing him to meet his father's eyes. Laurent's gaze became a mirror, reflecting Nicholas' wide eyes and panting lips. The violet hue was brilliant and harsh against his pale skin, unnatural and frightening.

"You are not to see or speak to that mortal, or I may reverse the healing I gave, and you can watch him bleed out on the floor," Laurent warned.

He imagined sinking his fingers into Laurent's throat to tug out every vein like broken strings. Then he smiled. Laurent did not know it yet, but he would escape tonight. He would give anything to see William. He had already given so much, had made himself even more indebted to his father and became something... not quite him, but wonderful all the same. Chaotic. Wild. Wonderfully strange. The terrifying monster stories spoke about.

"Stay behind me." Laurent went for the door at the call of the king's names.

Evera shoved him forward to join them, with Solomon and Percival at their backs. He heard little of what was said. His eyes strayed, searching, wanting, needing Williams' attention. Evera kept him from lingering on the balcony too long or rushing down the stairs. She caught the back of his jacket or snatched his arm to guide him through the courtiers below.

"You may as well put him on a leash," Solomon chuckled at their back.

"Go bother someone else this evening," Evera chided and, with a rough tug, took herself and Nicholas to the far side of the ballroom. "Is there any Darkmoon alive who isn't an utter annoyance?" she snarled once they were clear.

"Even if there were, you would argue otherwise. You are so easily annoyed by anyone," he replied, earning a glare, then a grin.

"Well, you aren't wrong." Evera laughed and caught another drink from the servers.

He passed on refreshments. He didn't care about the people either. They flowed around him, curious of his presence but too frightened to approach. That was a relief because it allowed him to search, peering over the crowd for the one person he did care about. Nicholas felt William's presence, sensed him in the room, but if he attempted to search, Evera held tighter and yanked him back.

As much as he hated to be separated from William, Evera was right to keep him in place. Laurent would let William bleed out on the floor if Nicholas went against him. He had to be patient, wait for the kings, and take the opportunity to break their deal. Then he could see William as much as he desired.

The thought kept him still for the moments that felt so long before the kings made their approach with Laurent at their side.

"I hope you enjoy tonight's festivities, Nicholas. They are for you, after all," said King Shepherd with a clearing of his throat.

Nicholas tried to lessen his smile, if only to encourage them to stay. He couldn't frighten them off until he received what he was owed.

"There is something that already caught my eye," he replied. "And I am excited to receive my gift."

"Gift?" Laurent repeated calmly, even if internally he must be angered.

"Of course, as the savior of our realm, our kingdoms owe their lives to Nicholas. He not only defeated Fearworn but also spent these last two years scouring the world for his dreaded shadowed disciples. He is owed." Laughing heartily, King Ellis nodded at Nicholas. "Tell us what you want, boy."

Evera held fiercely to his arm. On his other side, Laurent gave nothing away. Expression placid as ever, but he felt the slight bristle in the air. Laurent wished to strike, to snatch him by the neck and prevent him from speaking, but nothing could be done now. Faerie had the king's letter and would ensure the deal was met.

"My father and I made a deal concerning a mortal medic, who sacrificed his life to save mine. Without him, we all would have fell to Fearworn," he replied, heart racing so fervently the world became muted to his ringing ears. "I would like you to absolve me from it."

The color drained from King Shepherd's face. "You wish for us to break a deal for you? Are we capable of such a task?"

"Typically, no, but considering that you admitted my actions led to saving two realms, well, Faerie will ensure our deal is struck."

"I would advise you against this," said Laurent. He maintained a calm tone, uncaring if one didn't know better. "Our deal is battling against Nicholas' deterioration."

"You think it is," he corrected, then cast his attention to the kings. "I am owed, you said so yourselves, and I made my request. Now, you must honor it."

Laurent caught his arm, forcing them closer. "This is not Faerie land. Do you truly believe they can absolve you from a deal with me?"

"Our deals have passed through worlds ever since the Collision. There is more than enough power here, even if it's against you." Nicholas snickered, then yanked his arm away and nodded at the kings. "Well?"

The mortal kings peered at one another. King Ellis whispered into King Shepherd's ear. Shuffling his weight from one foot to the other, King Shepherd asked, "Are you certain this is what you truly want?"

"Absolutely."

"Then how should we phrase our request?"

Nicholas could hardly breathe. "Order Laurent to absolve me from my deal concerning William Vandervult."

King Ellis stood taller at the name. He wasn't surprised the king of Heign knew of William, considering the position of the Vandervults. The kings did as he asked. Laurent didn't reply. The windows rattled from a fierce wind and the lights of the castle flickered in warning. Faerie heard, and Laurent sighed.

When he spoke, there was venom in his words. "You are absolved from our deal concerning William Vandervult, Nicholas."

The shade rushed through the crowd, frantic in his search for William. Many cursed at him as he passed. He spotted Charmaine attempting to hide away from the crowd by lingering against the wall. Her glass shook when she took a drink, yet to notice him. William wasn't with her, but he felt William's presence, following the feeling of him out of the ballroom and leading to a quiet sitting area used for light reading, considering it had little more than a couch, an end stand, and a wall of bookshelves.

There, leaning against the end stand, William stood, shoulders heaving.

"My wicked," he whispered like a prayer.

5

WILLIAM

NICHOLAS APPROACHED. THE SHADOWS of the dimly lit room hugged his muscular figure, though could never dim the fierce fire of his eyes. William shrank beneath the attention he once craved, that he still did in a fucked up way.

"Nicholas," he whispered, forcing his voice not to shake.

He didn't trust his eyes, so he half expected the fae to disappear. But Nicholas closed the space between them. His gaze was feral, desperate as a drowning soul. However, the eyes were not his, not the fuchsia light but a terrifying violet.

Nicholas cradled his cheeks more gently than a babe, proving he was real, that the one time he wished his eyes deceived him, they were not. Terror gripped him as desperately as desire, two conflicting emotions battling for dominance. He loved and hated Nicholas as much as he tried to deny the former.

"Two years I have worked toward this moment." Nicholas spoke hastily, making his words difficult to decipher. "I did as my father required, destroyed Fearworn, battled his shadowed disciples and beasts, and found every scar he opened. He thought he caught me, but he did not. Is this not grand, William? Nothing will keep us apart now. It is you and I until the stars go dark."

Nicholas traced his cheek. His thumb brushed William's bottom lip. He looked at William like he finally learned love. "I have yearned to gaze upon your beauty all these years," he whispered. "To have you here now, I fear I cannot control myself, my wicked."

William imagined a moment like this would be explosive, visceral anger and shouted curses. But he couldn't cease thinking about kissing the troublesome devil. He dared to want to forget the pain and loss and fall into Nicholas' embrace like nothing happened, made a fool once again by his hands.

Then the light caught in Nicholas' treacherous eyes.

"Step away," he ordered. Nicholas was not Fearworn, but the way he spoke, how he clung so ferociously to William's cheeks, made him feel like prey. Like Fearworn was about to steal more pieces of him until nothing but cold silver remained.

"I will not," said Nicholas.

"If you do not let go, I will make you."

Nicholas laughed. "You've hidden a weapon on you, haven't you? I would expect nothing less. Clever as a fox and wicked as the damned, I have missed you."

By the Souls, William missed him too, far more than he cared to admit. Being caught by Nicholas' unyielding attention and enraptured by his touch forced him to recall all he tried to forget. The many nights spent in Nicholas' arms, the unexpected sweet moments and secrets shared. Their history felt present. He struggled to escape, to steady his feet in a place of anger rather than confusion, fear, and desire.

"Do not think toying with me will work again." He gripped the knife at his back.

Nicholas smiled when the iron pressed against his neck. He continued to cradle William as if the threat meant nothing. "I remember being in a position like this with you before in that old house. Do you remember?" Nicholas asked. "You didn't slit my throat then and you won't now, although I must ask why you are doing this?"

"Why?" His words struggled to be heard through his chattering teeth. "You tricked and abandoned me. You did not visit me in the hospital. I was a game. You won. Now, leave me be."

Nicholas' hands fell limp. His expression was as if William had struck him. "You thought I abandoned you?"

"Not visiting or reaching out to me over all these years, yes, abandonment felt like the most obvious conclusion."

"I did not. I would never. Did you not hear what I said?"

The fae retreated. William lowered his blade.

"What you said made little sense," he replied.

"My father!" Nicholas screamed. The wind howled, forcing the windows to rattle and splinter. Then he grasped William's hand, the cursed one, the one without a blade, and he held tight. His eyes were erratic, swiping over William with palpable desperation. "The deal, my wicked, a deal was struck. You will listen, won't you?"

He sensed Nicholas would not give him another option. This desperation was dangerous. His gut told him to be fearful, and he learned long ago to trust his gut. There was no telling what Nicholas would do if stopped. He felt more dangerous than ever.

"I am listening," William whispered.

"Your injuries sustained from Fearworn's attacks were fatal. I did what I had to. I destroyed Fearworn when the mages closed the scar. It was luck, my wicked, for this scar led to Faerie, so I took you to Laurent. He is of power none of us can comprehend. If any could save you, it was he, and he did. He gave you this arm." Nicholas tried removing his glove. He growled and Nicholas ceased. "He spared your life. In exchange, I promised not to see or speak to you. The bastard ensured I couldn't even write. He kept us apart, but tonight has changed everything."

He cursed his lungs for daring to constrict, his mind for whimpering a cry, and his heart for faltering. So many evenings he spent damning Nicholas and any good they ever had. Now the fae returned, claiming their separation had been forced, that he hadn't abandoned and forgotten William?

He didn't know how to process the information. If it was worth processing or the past should remain in the past. He should move on because this changed nothing. Nicholas was fae, and less himself than ever, and William was little more than a crumbling shell of his former self. But the truth of it all was he had been trying to move on for two years and nothing eased his pain. He became an outsider in his own home, even in his mind. Nothing felt the way it once did. He couldn't view a future that wasn't painted in sorrow.

"Tonight, then, you escaped Laurent's deal?" he asked.

"Yes, now you understand," Nicholas replied. "The kings had this ball for me. They claimed to owe me for what I had done. When a promise is made, Faerie will ensure it through, so I asked to be repaid, to have them absolve my deal with Laurent toward you. He has no more sway over me."

"Doesn't he? You are to wed Evera, are you not?"

"We are to have children, not wed, though I do like when you sound jealous."

"I am not jealous, nor does this change anything." He snatched his hand away. The monstrosity felt Nicholas' touch as if it were normal, as if it weren't cold silver. "I appreciate what you did for me, but years have passed and I have moved on."

Nicholas smiled, but his tone was wicked. "Humans and their lies. You should be better at telling them."

He wasn't wrong about that. For a fleeting moment, William wondered what they could become, if they could be like they were, and he'd have some semblance of normalcy. He dared to imagine a future together, waking in the same bed every morning, showing each other their homes, and being whisked away by a consuming love.

Music played from the ballroom, a slow song he learned to dance at the hands of his less than chipper dancing instructor. She had been a tall, gangly woman that frightened him as a child. She scowled more than smiled and took tutoring seriously. While he performed better than his brothers, by her standards, that didn't mean she gave him compliments. In fact, that was the only compliment she ever gave him. If she saw him now, frozen in front of Nicholas' offered hand, she may have been horrified enough to spit on his shoes.

"Dance with me," said Nicholas.

The music ascended into a tempo that made one want to take part, but he retreated.

"What? No, I... I have business to attend to. I should return to the ball." He didn't go to the door because that meant getting closer to Nicholas.

The shade blocked the exit entirely by taking a step back to shut the door entirely. "We have business to attend to that I cannot wait another moment for."

"I believe our business is concluded. You gave your explanation. While I appreciate knowing the truth, it changes nothing." His heart quivered.

"Give me a dance and I will let you leave without a fuss." Nicholas took a step closer.

"You should let me leave without a fuss, anyway."

"Where's the fun in that?"

He barely contained his chuckle. Nicholas sounded like himself there, playful and annoyingly charming when William needed him not to be.

"One dance," he relented and berated himself for doing so.

Nicholas didn't hesitate to take hold. William fell against his chest, overwhelmed by the scent of lilacs and wood. His gaze fell to Nicholas' mouth, to lips he thought he remembered, but had the abrupt desire to relearn. The devilish fae smiled as if he read William's thoughts, or rather, couldn't possibly miss how tormented he became.

"I fear I do not know many songs of Terra, so you must lead, my wicked." Hearing that name from Nicholas' mouth made his heart ache in ways he wished to have forgotten.

He took a moment to settle himself, then laid a hand on Nicholas' waist. The other, his right, the cursed arm went stiff in Nicholas' grasp. His trembling ceased from Nicholas' gaze, the fae's longing so palpable it made him forget of everything save the music they danced to. They existed within a world entirely their own, pirouetting around a room too heated, too small to contain the rapacious desire burning between them.

He felt such a fool to be taken by Nicholas' mere appearance. A few words and a dance had his resolve crumbling when he willed it to grow taller. His heart and body were one, desiring Nicholas' entirely while the mind pleaded for separation. Nicholas breached every wall he dared to build without so much as a fight. He thought he would be stronger than that, but time and time again, reality proved different from fiction.

Then the songs stopped, and they stood breathless and alone. He wasn't certain how long they danced, certainly to more than one song. He got lost to the rhythm of not only the music, but Nicholas himself. He carried a tempo all his own, chaotic and unpredictable.

"I do believe that I was made for you," Nicholas whispered, with his hands descending upon William's cheeks. "Made to love you, to cherish you, to wait for you until I become forever yours."

His words were sickeningly sweet, but his tone was frightful and his eyes a vision of terror. They glistened in a violet hue that struck terror in William's heart, forcing him finally to depart. He struggled back a step and another, watching a shadow fall upon Nicholas' form until he stood as little more than a threatening silhouette.

He wasn't sure what would have happened if Charmaine didn't call his name. A knock rapped at the door. "William, are you in here?"

Charmaine opened the door.

"Good evening." Nicholas gave an exaggerated bow.

"Nicholas," she whispered, then caught sight of William. She wore his same fear, but forced an amicable smile. "It is good to see you. You look well."

Nicholas threw his head back in laughter. "More lies. Your expression is as if you've seen a ghost."

Because she had. They saw Fearworn in him. Even the way Nicholas moved, limbs not setting right and every step almost a sway, like the wind could topple him.

"Charmaine and I must take our leave." William sidestepped toward the threshold. Charmaine retreated, giving him room to run. "Goodbye, Nicholas," he muttered, uncertain if the fae would truly let him leave.

Nicholas shared a toothy grin. "For now. I will see you soon, William."

The words felt like a promise. He didn't know how he felt about that promise.

William shut the door. He met Charmaine's fearful expression, no doubt mirroring her. She opened her mouth to speak, but thought better of it. Together, they hurried toward the ballroom. His breathing stuttered for reasons he couldn't comprehend. Missing Nicholas, being terrified of him, wanting to be closer, wanting to run, every emotion surged, whipped, bit and scratched. His mind went silent in a way he didn't believe possible, but it wasn't the least bit relieving.

"His eyes," Charmaine said in the ballroom.

"I saw them," he said.

"You don't think... he wouldn't be like..."

"Nicholas will not become the next Feaworn." He wished to believe his words, but he never excelled at optimism. There were no tales that ended well for a shade.

Charmaine gazed toward the open doorway. William felt it too, as if they were being followed. Except Nicholas had not entered, nor did violet eyes watch from the crowd, but that didn't stop him from thinking they were there. Nicholas, but not. Still a ghost haunting William in another way.

"Did he say anything?" she asked.

William almost laughed. "He said he hadn't abandoned me, that he made a deal with Laurent to save my life and that's why," he glared at his right arm, sensing where the silver connected with his shoulder, "he couldn't keep in contact, but he broke that deal tonight, somehow."

Fae could not lie, but it felt like a lie. Rather, he wanted it to be because then the last two years of grief wouldn't have been for nothing. What could he do with the pent up anger? He still felt it, still wanted to kick and scream like a toddler. Still wanted to fight, argue, battle against Nicholas, as if that would remove the hollowness within. But what could possibly change? He didn't want hope. Hope always abandoned him.

Charmaine leaned forward. "What will you do now?"

"Nothing. I'm grateful for what he did, but it is done and over with. What else would we do?" He didn't believe in fairytales and happily ever after. There could be none for them.

Nicholas fell to the terrifying path of a shade. He would get worse. In what way, he wasn't certain, but he could not handle the thought of watching Nicholas' deterioration. Day by day, he witnessed horror, but he could fight it. He had the Sight. Catching broken strings and mending patients led to better outcomes, but he could not help Nicholas. They ended that day on the field. Nothing more. At least, he repeated such a thought to himself over and over, hoping for it to one day settle into an immovable foundation.

"Well, let us hope he keeps his distance." Charmaine nodded toward the crowd. "I searched for you because Richard has caught His Majesty's attention. We should hurry before he leaves."

William grappled for the satchel at his waist, double checking they had everything. "I am sorry that I ran off at all. I don't know what came over me."

"You don't need to apologize to me." Sweat trickled down her neck, darkening the collar of her uniform. He understood the nerves were from much more than their run in with Nicholas.

"You do not have to join me if you do not want to," he offered.

"No, I am going with you."

He was grateful for her company. Having Charmaine at his side made pushing through the crowd easier. Richard and Robert spoke with King Ellis on the opposite side of the ballroom near the doors to the gardens, unaware of William and Charmaine's presence until they closed in.

"Ah, there you are." Robert gestured for William to join them. "Your Majesty, you know of my youngest, William Vandervult."

"Yes, of course. It is so great to see you again, my boy. We would not be here without you, either." King Ellis had always been a tall man, towering over most. His tanned white skin wrinkled around his eyes and mouth. Gray streaked his otherwise black hair, but King Ellis wore age well. He came across kindly, if one didn't know better, but there was a darkness to his brown eyes, something deep and cold.

William bowed, grateful to do so because the king wouldn't see the anger in his eyes. "Thank you, Your Majesty. I'm honored to have been of help to the cause."

"And that cause calls for you again, for there is trouble afoot in Alogan, Your Majesty." Richard signaled for him to give the king their findings. "My dear brother may have discovered cruelties done upon the beloved soldiers of our kingdom. Those struggling in health after giving so much to protect us are taken care of by the Vandervult clinics, by my brother here, and they are going missing."

Courtiers watched Richard's flamboyant display of concern. He spoke over the music and waved a hand about dramatically. No one could miss him, and Richard knew it.

"Do you recognize that name there?" Richard tapped the page. "Harrison Wells, it is absurd I even asked because of course you would remember the name of a man who sunk the ships Fearworn tried to send across the seas. He had been attending our clinic for nearly a year, but he hasn't shown in a month now."

Richard chose not to add that Harrison Wells mentioned traveling to see family a month ago. When William mentioned this, Richard reminded him that socialites love a good story and Harrison had the best story. They wouldn't care about Vale, an elderly woman with nothing to her name, or Denison, a young boy falling on hard times. Harrison, the war hero, that would get their hearts pumping.

"There are others, you see, but my brother doesn't have the manpower to investigate. He is a proud soldier and an even prouder doctor to those like him who served in the war, who are the very reason we can have this ball at all. I know you are busy, but if Your Majesty would see to finding help for our soldiers, we would be most appreciative." Richard gave an exaggerated bow.

The growing crowd scrutinized their king, daring him to defy Richard's request. King Ellis' smile didn't reach his eyes. He didn't openly rage, but one could taste the frustration in the air, as if it poured from the king's frozen heart.

"Thank you for bringing these troubling matters to my attention. Tell me what you need and I will see what I can do," the king replied.

"There needs to be regular surveillance in the outer banks and a team to search into the disappearances. If His Majesty knows of another healer to tend to the clinic, I would appreciate it, so I could have more time to look into things myself as well," William said, hoping he hadn't pushed too far.

Richard assured him the king would be more lenient than usual, but after all he had done to so many men, William couldn't fathom the king knowing what the word lenient meant, let alone practiced it.

"So be it. I will look into dealing with these matters, but for now, please, enjoy the rest of your evening." King Ellis returned the findings and vanished into the crowd.

William didn't speak until the king was long out of earshot. "Do you believe he meant what he said?"

"Some of it," Richard replied. "He's likely to up surveillance, at least for a week or two, and find you a more permanent doctor, but I doubt he will dedicate a team to look into the disappearances."

"We'll make do with what we are given. Thank you, Richard," Charmaine said.

"Don't thank me. I wish I could do more, and perhaps I might." Richard cast a smile over his shoulder. "I'll see to getting more donations. The two of you should head home."

"I am more than happy to." William nodded at Charmaine. "I'll summon the carriage. Grab a few snacks for your mother. She'll like a late night treat."

"Thanks for reminding me. She'd have my head if I returned home without any." Charmaine pushed through the crowd in search of said treats.

Frowning, Robert kept his eyes on the ground. "I'm sorry either of you had to come."

He waited as if he genuinely believed Robert would look at him. It never happened.

"Don't apologize for what isn't your fault. I'll have the carriage sent back for you." He went for the exit, hesitating outside the doors to peer down the hall where the lounge door hung open. He felt Nicholas' presence like a lost soul lingering between light and dark, but the fae remained out of sight. He knew that wouldn't last long.

6

NICHOLAS

THE MIRROR REFLECTED A stranger, a fae wearing a cruel smile and amethyst eyes, incapable of focus. When Nicholas touched his cheek, the reflection did the same. The smile fell, replaced by a peculiar twitch beneath his skin.

He grasped the edges of the porcelain sink. His eyes flickered pink, as if something sought to breach the surface. Bright fuchsia. That should be their color, but they weren't, and he was suddenly frightened, incapable of taking a solid breath. He touched the glass. An ache formed in his temple. His thoughts muddled like a vicious swarm of wasps protecting their nest. Then he slammed his fist against the mirror. Shattered shards fell to the floor.

In their broken pieces, he glimpsed the pink light fade, overcome by violet. His nerves calmed, breathing steady and smiling wide. He couldn't remember what bothered him, why he could care about the color of his eyes, or why he would panic. Everything about him was perfect, better than ever before.

"What a mess," he said, picking shards from his bloodied knuckles.

Stepping out of the bathroom, he snatched his clothes and approached the castle window.

The rooms at King Ellis' castle were better than the tent he slept in for years. Depictions of birds decorated the walls, their silhouettes a darker shade than the maroon background. An empty bottle of faerie wine laid on the nightstand. A bed sat against the far wall, crimson sheets ruffled from his restless sleep.

All he dreamed about was William and the dance shared, especially after the party. While others drank and danced, he lingered in the shadows, avoiding conversation because no topic caught his thoughts like William.

He let William leave the other night because he looked distraught. Even Nicholas understood how troubling it had to be for William and Charmaine to attend the event. The war was rough on them, and the kings were uncaring. He had the occasional urge to break their fingers and toes, to watch the kings scramble across the dancefloor in fear like many of the soldiers had to. To seek revenge on William's behalf, show the kings what true terror was, and hopefully receive a reward. William's smile, his thanks, his laughter, even the briefest brush of his fingertips along Nicholas' cheek would be more than enough. He merely wanted William's attention.

He threw open the window, intending to seek that very attention. Mortal cities reeked of sewer and coal. Smog rose from factories along the horizon, coating the sky gray. The sight reminded him of the Deadlands. Gated yards circled the castle like the sight of old homes and busy work streets were too offensive to be so near. They lived in the castle's shadow, believing they could reap from its power in closeness alone. Far, far in the distant stood trees, isolated and abandoned, struggling to rise higher than the smothering fog of humanity. He couldn't fathom why mortals yearned to live in their brick houses, enclosed by a putrid stench, when beautiful woods were so near.

"Where are you off to now?" Laurent asked.

His entrance had been silent. His silhouette appeared too tall for the room, like he couldn't have possibly fit through the door. For all

Nicholas knew, his father simply materialized. It wouldn't surprise him if Laurent could do so.

"To see William, where else?" he replied.

A chill seeped from Laurent. After all he did, nothing kept Nicholas from William. Searching for the surviving shadowed disciples and the scars Fearworn opened preoccupied him, but that did not mean he hadn't checked on William. With the war over, more fae crossed from Faerie to Terra. There were deals to make and lands to explore. Nicholas may not have been home long, but he heard of all the trouble his kin caused. Mortals flocked to Faerie in the shadows, refusing to admit how intrigued and greedy they were. While they spat or cursed at any who brokered deals with fae, behind everyone's back, they eagerly did the same. To take a chance and ask for gold, glory, and admiration, as Laurent hoped. That meant there were more than enough fae in Terra who could check on William in his stead.

Mortals were foolish enough to believe making deals with any of Darkmoon would render them superior, safer than their peers. Once, he would be among his kin seeking havoc, but he hadn't thought of striking a deal in years. Evera was right in that regard. He thought little of anything other than William.

While separated, Nicholas ensured to remain up to date. A band of sprites owed him a favor after he prevented their lake from being contaminated by a horde of uncaring redcaps dumping their kills into the pristine waters. Sprites could fade in and out of existence, traveling at speeds even a fae couldn't contend with. They monitored William, so he knew exactly where William lived and worked. They were so close after years of separation. He wanted to be at William's side, asking about all he had missed and learning what all William hoped to do.

His back fell against the windowsill. "Are you here to stop me? If so, I fear you will have to drag me away in chains."

"I know a lost cause when I see one, but remember, if anything happens, it is your doing. All are endangered by your presence, but more so him." Laurent's hands folded over themselves carefully at his waist to make himself seem harmless.

"If you are implying I will hurt William, you are wrong."

"Am I?" Laurent slipped into a crooked smile.

Fear struck Nicholas to his core, thoughts of darkness and captivity, of Laurent's bitter voice, finding him beneath the soil.

"Soon, you will not recognize your own harm. You will see yourself as right and just. Do you believe Fearworn saw himself capable of tearing our worlds apart? That he ever considered our fate? He wished to learn, and that wish escalated. Is it not right to assume the same will happen with you?" Laurent asked, his voice always the same octave, as if no one was worthy enough to hear his raised voice.

"We are different people," he muttered.

"But shades, nonetheless, and you want that mortal so badly. It is a craving, an addiction. Eventually, you will see everything as an obstruction in the way of your so-called love. His friends, his family, mortals love their social circles, but you will not see it as such. They will be obstacles." Laurent spoke with a warning, like he cared. One of his tricks, one of his ploys to get what he wanted. But as he inched closer, breathing every word, the truth burrowed beneath Nicholas' skull. An infection he couldn't cut out.

"The more you see William, the worse you will get. Every moment spent in his presence may feel like bliss, but you are running toward an edge you cannot return from," Laurent finished, standing at Nicholas' side, casting him in shadow.

"You are trying to frighten me," he countered. "You said you aren't here to stop me, but from the sounds of it, you are trying to talk me out of seeing William."

"I am merely discussing the future you are laying out for yourself."

"You only care because of your deal with Alvina, because of what else you wish to use me for. You do not care about William and me," he countered.

"But you care about the mortal and you will hurt him. Not today, perhaps, or tomorrow, or a year from now, but one day, you will snap and he will pay the price." Laurent sighed like Nicholas put up a physical fight. He turned his back to his son. "Go to him, if you wish. I will not stop you from facing the consequences of your own actions, though I will be waiting for you once the lesson has been learned. And never forget, I am still owed. Evera will keep a close eye on you."

Evera entered at the call of her name, frustrated as ever. "You brought this on yourself," she said.

Laurent didn't smile over victories, for they were more common than air. He walked away, silent and content in the damage wrought.

Arguing further would be worthless. Laurent did not understand because he had never known love, not love for his children or their mothers. Each of his siblings served a purpose, otherwise they wouldn't be alive. Blair was the eldest, born from a fae lord who hadn't cared for her lands, so Laurent sought to steal them. Laurent believed a child with the previous caretaker would make absorbing the land easier. Solomon was the heir to his mother's lands in a southern territory. Nicholas did not know why Laurent agreed to that or why Solomon lived with them. If he asked, neither of them would have explained. Lastly was Percival, born between Laurent and another powerful fae out of pure interest to see if their blood would cause strong offspring. Percival didn't live up to their expectations, although Nicholas doubted any of them could.

As for his parentage, he knew nothing. None had ever shared a tale about how his parents met or why his mother would have wanted anything to do with Laurent. The most he knew was that she was adventurous and troublesome, so perhaps it was as simple as her wanting to cause trouble for Laurent by giving an unwanted child. Regardless, he didn't need to hear a story about her from Laurent because he couldn't possibly care about anyone other than himself. Because of that, he couldn't fathom Nicholas' caring.

"Obstacles," he whispered.

He certainly saw Laurent and Evera as obstacles, albeit Evera a little less so. That should be understandable. Laurent prevented Nicholas and William from seeing each other. They weren't even granted a proper goodbye. But William's friends and family? People like Henry and Charmaine, obstacles? He didn't... he couldn't... they made William happy. He wanted William's happiness, his love, more than anything. Right?

"I won't hurt him," he promised, but there it was again; fear. His breathing staggered and vision blurred. He took a step back, as if to leave the castle, to return to Faerie. He would put as much space between him and William if it meant his safety, but then the thought became so ludicrous that he laughed.

Nothing awful would happen. He and William would be happy together, as they always should have been. There was nothing to worry about.

"I am going to see William. Should you bother us, I'll have your head," he warned.

"I have no reason to bother either of you. I am here to observe, to make sure you don't get into trouble," Evera replied.

"The one most likely to start trouble is you."

"I can start as much trouble as I want. You're the one at the end of your leash with your father."

The world leash irritated him most. Even with this newfound power bursting within him, worry remained that he couldn't take on Laurent, that there would always be a tether between them. He wanted to be entirely unleashed, to be free, but no matter what he did, something or someone always held him back.

Shaking his head, he leapt out the window. Evera became a shadow, much like Arden had been during the war. He hadn't heard or seen much of Arden afterward, who immediately returned to Faerie. Arden's departure did not sadden or disappoint him, though he was curious what Arden owed Laurent and if their deal had ended.

Mortals wandered the streets of Alogan from home to home and shop to shop. They carried parasols to hide from the morning sun. Ladies fanned themselves outside bakeries, their sweets half eaten. Men bickered along street corners and dirtied children scampered through damp alleyways.

Smog coated his lungs, tasting of charcoal and grime. Evera's mug twisted, bothered by it too. She wiped at her eyes that no doubt burned the same as his. The air tasted foul. He couldn't fathom how mortals survived breathing it. There wasn't much greenery, save the shrubs allocated to the vibrant yards of nobles at the center of town. The further from the castle they went, the fewer trees there were until all that remained were weeds sprouting from worn sidewalks or half dead plants struggling to survive outside cracked windows.

The sprites claimed William worked at the Smelly Place. Their initial descriptions were a hassle to decipher because sprites weren't known for their exceptional communication. Many preferred physical confrontation and changing the color of their wings to express thoughts. They described the mortal world simply, in terms of color, scent, and "near the house with an ugly man who sneezed a lot" or "next to the pretty old lady and her many kindly cats."

Sprites recognized most individuals through scent. The sprites described William as clean, yet bloody. Considering his duties, Nicholas assumed he continued his medical practices outside of the military. Eventually, the sprites determined the name where William worked. Nicholas asked butlers at the castle to give him directions, which was how he stood by an ailing warehouse.

The sprites described the clinic well. Smelly was more than appropriate.

His nose curled, and he coughed, overwhelmed by the mixture of blood, body odor, and alcohol. Like patches of moss on damp rocks, rust grew in spots along the exterior. The highest windows had a thin coat of grime while the windows in reach were clean. The street itself did not have the same liveliness as those he had passed previously. Those walking the streets didn't carry parasols nor have a natural flush to their cheeks. Many had pale skin and sunken eyes, clothes dirty and ripped.

A pair of double doors led into the warehouse. One hung open, letting mortals enter and depart. They clutched brown bags and canned food. A man guarded the door, dressed in a thick jacket and with little more than an old knife tethered to his brawny waist.

Nicholas turned to Evera, intending to warn her about following, but she watched from a rooftop, letting him approach the guard alone.

"Uh, sir, you..." the guard stood an inch taller than Nicholas, and yet shrank in his presence. "This is a clinic for the needy. Fae and their accursed deals are not welcome here."

"Then it is good I am not here to conduct any deals," he replied. "Will you allow me to pass, or would you prefer to make this difficult?"

"I cannot let you in if you are to cause trouble."

"I will not cause trouble. I am here to see William Vandervult."

"Our doctor?" He glanced at the doors that had fewer visitors. Nicholas' presence thwarted others from entering. Some gathered at the edge of the building, muttering to each other.

"Yes, we served in the war together." Nicholas thought William would be upset if he harmed the guard, even if he really, really wanted to. Every moment spent speaking with him meant less time with William. It was infuriating.

"Alright." The guard sighed and shuffled inside.

Past the doors, two nurses sat at a long table filled with the brown bags and canned food. They, too, gawked at him. He waved because he saw mortals greet each other as such. The action didn't ease their pale expressions.

As they walked away, he overheard one nurse whisper, "The doctor is fae-cursed. We should have known one of the fae would show up."

The other whimpered. "Do you think he is the one Dr. Vandervult made a deal with?"

"Most likely. Why else would one be here? I should have left the moment I saw his damned arm."

"I can't imagine why he would make a cursed deal."

Nicholas cast a dark look over his shoulder. The nurses squeaked. He heaved a long breath through his nostrils, reminding himself William would be displeased if he made a mess by putting his hands on anyone. Twitching his fingers and cracking his neck, he ignored any urge to maim and kept walking.

The guard guided him past cots, patients, and nurses. Each gave a different reaction than the last, choking, spitting, or squealing. Whispers spread through the room by the time the guard and Nicholas reached stairs leading to an office.

"Dr. Vandervult's office is up there," the guard explained, trying to sound frightening. "I am right outside, so should you start trouble, I will know of it."

Nicholas didn't care. He hopped the stairs two at a time. He threw open the office door, heart swelling at the sight of William. The doctor sat at a desk overlooking mounds of paper. So many he was hardly visible behind them, save the tip of his emerald eyes more enchanting than ever.

William dropped his papers. "Nicholas?"

"Good morning, my wicked."

7

WILLIAM

NICHOLAS STOOD IN THE doorway, beaming in false cheer. His presence was too strange, familiar in an uncanny way. It had been two days since the ball, longer than he expected to go without seeing Nicholas, but he remained unprepared for the interaction.

His heart dropped, then sputtered, then stopped all together. He couldn't determine if the emotions were that of excitement or dread. He stumbled toward the windows. Work continued below, but the nurses cast his office fearful glances.

He closed every blind. "You cannot be here. This is my place of work. The very sight of you will unsettle my patients, let alone my nurses."

"Are they not frightened by you already?" Nicholas grasped his hand to kiss the silver knuckles. "They call you fae-cursed because of your arm, do they not?"

He yanked free. Every day, he had the strange urge to step into the forest with a blade and hack off the silver himself. He tried once to no avail, then felt awful for ever imagining such a thing, for not being grateful he had the use of his arm. Others were not as fortunate. They struggled on prosthetic limbs while his life hardly changed, yet; he dared to complain.

"How would you know anything about that?" His face paled and heart palpitated. "And how do you know of my workplace?"

Nicholas propped himself against the desk. "I may not have been able to communicate with you, but I made sure to know where you were."

"You had someone stalk me?"

"A couple of sprites owed me. They're useful creatures, coming and going as they please. Some say they faded through our realms long before the Collision."

His gaze shifted around the room. "And those sprites followed me?"

"I asked them to check in if they were nearby. Thanks to them, I know the mortal shops where you like to eat, your favorite library, and," Nicholas' brows furrowed, and a muscle quivered in his jaw, "The wretch you spent an evening with two months back."

"I beg your pardon?"

"I was going to kill him, but I thought you would be upset and refrained from doing so. If anything, I deserve to be praised," Nicholas spoke so earnestly he would convince most to believe him.

He struggled to form a coherent thought. He couldn't grasp Nicholas' return and that being one of their first conversations. It felt ridiculous, and yet, so unbelievably Nicholas.

"You cannot have creatures stalk me, learn of private matters, and threaten the life of a stranger I spent a night with." It rarely happened. Any who paid William any mind was normally more curious about fae, his cursed arm, and war stories. But with enough alcohol in his system, he didn't mind sharing, so long as he felt something, anything afterward.

Nicholas came for him, swift and without warning. William may have hit him if he didn't hold so firmly to William's hands. He didn't do well with quick movement. His heart leapt, and every nerve tightened like old violin strings, ready to snap. Every muscle tensed, ready to run or attack, and his mind reeled, conjuring escape or killing scenarios. Nicholas did not notice his fright. He was so focused on William's frustration, looking like a scolded child.

"Do you not understand my reasoning? I could not be with you, but I had to know you were safe. If something were to happen while we lost contact, I had to know about it. None of this was done with ill intent. I thought entirely of you. I see no reason to be upset." Though Nicholas pleaded, his voice held a fearsome edge. "Do not be upset with me. I did what I must, what I thought to be right, and thanks to that, we are together again. Is that not what you want? Did our time mean so little to you?"

He worried about what his answers might evoke. Nicholas' eyes were frightening, neither warm nor cold. Everything about him, his movements, his words, his actions, all recognizable yet slightly off, warped. All he could think of was when this change occurred, what the reasoning was, and naively wondered if he could help.

"What happened? Your eyes. When did they change?" he whispered.

"I fell when you did, when I thought your heart stopped, then there was... this feeling, a shock. The world opened, and I saw everything, things I can't explain even if I tried. It was marvelous, William, like I woke from a dream I believed to be a reality for so long only to realize there is so much more out there." Nicholas made the situation sound surreal, precious even.

"Do you think you will go the same route Fearworn did?" he muttered, terrified by the prospect in more ways than one.

He would have to go through the grief of losing Nicholas again, permanently that time. And maybe there would be another war, a worse one where they wouldn't win. Where everything would be lost, where he would have to fight against Nicholas, and lose.

"I will never be like Fearworn. I have no interest in his vile monstrosities," Nicholas growled.

"What is your interest, then?"

"You, my wicked. You are, of course."

William heaved an agonizing breath. He yearned to break free, struggling in Nicholas' fearsome grip. The fae wouldn't release him, holding tighter as if to fuse them body and soul.

"This is a poor joke," he snapped.

"You know I cannot lie. I want you desperately, now more than ever. You are my greatest love, my only one."

A sickness built in his chest, heavy and thick. When he woke in the hospital, he realized the truth; that he loved Nicholas. He imagined a different life, one where he woke to Nicholas waiting at his bedside. The fae smiled and spoke of love, but hearing that from Nicholas now made him ill. It wasn't right. It was off and strange and the man looking at him, those terrifying violet eyes, was not the same one from years ago.

"You do not mean that," he argued.

"I can't—"

"I know you can't lie!" He shoved Nicholas back. The fae let go, taken aback like a struck child. "This is not love. You're not yourself. It's an obsession. It's a sickness and I can't..."

He could not handle being the reason for Nicholas' worst fear coming true. He remembered what Nicholas said back then, when William asked if he feared his own power; *"I do not want to end up like Fearworn. When I die, I want to die as Nicholas Darkmoon, not a shell of who he used to be."*

But there he stood, his eyes startling violet and one step closer to being exactly what he feared.

Anger boiled behind Nicholas' eyes, though his voice remained soft, "This is not obsession, it is love. Why do you not believe me?"

Because William recognized the look in his eyes, the unyielding desire that led to destruction. Fearworn had such a look when he retrieved his book of monsters from Nicholas, when he gazed down at the battlefield believing he won. Nicholas looked at him like an object to obtain and keep, a trophy he may polish and care for everyday, but an object nonetheless.

He wished Nicholas meant what he said, that their love was truly shared. Deep down, past the frustration and anger, there had always been hope for Nicholas to appear and make things right. He hated admitting to that, hated thinking of how happy they could be, how he could give in when Nicholas hurt him, but now... things were different, and they weren't right.

Nicholas' worst fear happened because of him. Each day that passed, he would grow worse in ways they may not fathom. Would his presence make Nicholas' symptoms worse? If they weren't together, could Nicholas live a life in Faerie, a better one?

He hesitated to ask, "What will you do if I do not return your feelings?"

"I will have you, William Vandervult, or not one at all. My soul is forever yours," Nicholas replied.

"You didn't answer my question. What if I do not return your affections?"

He broke into a smile, sweet, save for his eyes that raged. "Why would you not? Have I done wrong?"

The room shook. Metal creaked from a wind that flung open windows and shattered glass. Lightning crashed and thunder roared when there had been sun seconds ago. Patients and nurses shouted, perplexed by the lights flickering, casting the warehouse in eerie darkness.

"Do you remain upset? I have explained myself," Nicholas snarled, and he felt a pressure on his chest, as if Nicholas' anger took physical form and laid heavy on his lungs.

"I do understand." He took a step back. The windows would be his best escape. He could jump to the floor below, risk a broken bone if it meant survival. "I merely wish to say that this is a complicated situation."

Nicholas approached. That strangling sensation strengthened. William struggled to breathe, let alone speak. His hand fell on the window, searching for the clasp. "I...I haven't seen or heard from you in years. There," he coughed, "have been a lot of misunderstandings. I need time to think over things. I will not simply fall into your arms. Besides, I have very pressing matters."

Nicholas blinked, and the storm subsided. The howling wind settled. Lights brightened, the pressure dissipated, and he snapped his fingers. "Ah yes, the missing patients?"

William took a solid breath. His fingers held the window clasp, prepared to seek freedom. Nicholas acted as if moments ago hadn't happened, like he didn't realize what he caused or might have done if William didn't say the right words at the right time.

"Yes, a handful of my patients are missing." He never removed his eyes from Nicholas or his fingers from the window. There was a knife strapped to his waist, and a gun locked in the desk. He wouldn't get the gun in time if he needed it, so the knife would have to do.

"Leave it up to you to stumble upon trouble." Nicholas snickered, then settled a hand beneath his chin. "My sprites spoke of it only recently. How lucky you are to have me on your team! I do love a good adventure."

"This is no game. These patients mean a great deal to me. I will not have you assist for the fun of it," he said hesitantly.

Nicholas gave him a slow once over, then frowned. "You claim to understand me, but you remain upset."

"My frustration has nothing to do with that." And it certainly ran much deeper. The wound Nicholas gave couldn't be sealed by his return. Rather, he dug new tunnels through William's heart, finding an entirely new way to wreck him.

Nicholas crossed his arms like a petulant child. "It seems like it does. Do you truthfully no longer have feelings for me? Do not lie. It is unfair."

"By the Souls!" He threw his hands in the air. "What does it matter how I feel? What do you expect to happen?"

"I believe the mortals call it courting."

He laughed bitterly. "What do you think courting is? Sex?"

Nicholas rounded the desk. William's back hit the window. Feeling the solid surface behind him, realizing he was trapped, made sweat trickle along his neck.

Nicholas took his waist and tugged him close. He hated how comfortable it was, how he wanted a moment like this, how he so easily settled in Nicholas' familiar embrace, even after what happened. How easily Nicholas became angered and how easily that anger disappeared without him understanding a moment of it.

"You speak as if that is all there ever was between us. Did we not have sweet moments too? I will give all that I have for you," Nicholas promised.

William couldn't forget their sweet moments, even when he tried. There was more than he could count, more than he realized after Nicholas disappeared. He dreamed of them, and most nights, they warped into nightmares. He couldn't deny wanting more, wishing for him and Nicholas to spend their days together walking the park or visiting a library, but he was not naïve enough to believe any of it to be possible.

"Need I remind you of your arrangement with Evera? I will not find myself at the center of trouble between you and your father." He did not wish to see Laurent ever again. The moment at the castle was more than enough, and he imagined Laurent didn't want to see him either.

"I broke a deal with him once. I will do so again."

"I never thought you were so naïve. Mortals and fae do not work well together. We can't—"

"Why care about that?" Nicholas' knuckles brushed William's cheek. He cursed himself for leaning into the touch. "We will have each other. What more could we want?"

Safety. A life without fighting. Without looking over their shoulders.

To Nicholas, the chance of trouble put a sparkle in his eyes. For William, he wished to yearn for the mundane, to be normal again, and happy, to not wake in cold sweats on the few nights he fell asleep and to not rely on any form of drug or alcohol to make his mind go blank on bad days. Most of all, he wanted to look in a mirror and not hate who he saw. He wanted to be different, someone else entirely.

"I will not have this conversation any longer. There are far more pressing matters." William freed himself from Nicholas' grasp. "I have seven patients who have disappeared over the last two months."

"I can help. You know I can."

But that meant giving Nicholas permission to remain. To continue showing up with no idea if it would be a detriment to Nicholas' health and all their lives.

However, saying no meant abandoning his patients. They sorely needed help. Nicholas offered that help. With him, the patients could return alive, or he could risk taking weeks or months and hope not to find corpses. And considering what Nicholas said, he would be around regardless. Much to his chagrin, Nicholas was the best option they had.

"I have spoken with the authorities and the king himself. None truly care," he said, relenting. "My patients are homeless, so there has been little to investigate. I may not even know their real names or whether they have a family to go home to. All I know is they haven't picked up their medications and all their belongings remain in the spots they called home through the city."

"No one has seen them captured?" Nicholas asked.

"No, our best guess is that the abductions happen at night or in private locations. One day they're here and the next they've vanished."

"What could someone potentially want with these people?"

"I dare not imagine. I fear they are being harmed or killed. No one will do anything until I have solid proof of deviance," he explained.

"I could acquire such proof. Little in Terra can stop me."

"Are you not returning to Faerie soon? Surely you have duties?" he asked.

"I believe I earned myself a break. Now, do you have any clothing or personal effects of these missing patients? I may be able to track them."

He grabbed a worn newspaper boy hat from the coat rack near the doorway. He found it laying in Denison's tent, the third missing patient. The lad hardly ever took off his hat. He hoped whatever Nicholas needed to track remained.

As he handed the hat to Nicholas, the door opened, and a perplexed Charmaine passed the threshold.

8

CHARMAINE

THE SIGHT OF NICHOLAS in William's office shouldn't have surprised Charmaine, but she struggled to contain her whimper. Seeing him reminded her of Fearworn, the overwhelming stench of copper, claws ripping through her flesh, and wild-eyes peering down at her body laying over a cold stone slab.

"Good morning, Charmaine," Nicholas chirped as if their meeting were as normal as friends joining for an early breakfast. He waved a hat—Denison's—and meandered toward the door. "I fear I do not have time to chat. I have missing patients to find. Let us catch up later."

He disappeared. Both gazed at the doorway, their breaths held until she finally faced him.

"What's going on?" she whispered.

"Nicholas offered his help." William's hands shook when reaching into the drawer of his desk.

She accepted the cannabis cigarette he offered. William lit one of his own and fell into his chair, deflated.

"Based on this," she took a long breath, then released a plume of smoke, "that isn't all the two of you discussed."

"No, he's obsessed, Charmaine, like Fearworn was, but his obsession is apparently me." William laughed, hollow and cold. He pressed two fingers to his temple where a vein throbbed. "He told me once that becoming like Fearworn was his greatest fear and now he's down that path because of me."

"How could you possibly blame yourself for that?"

"My wounds from Fearworn were fatal. The deal Nicholas struck with Laurent was because of me. That's how I got," he raised his right hand, glaring at his glove, then let it fall on the desk, "Nicholas fell because he thought I died, because I would have died. Now he's back and we need the help. He may actually find my missing patients, but being around me cannot be good for him."

She went over to the couch, moving a few papers to make space to sit. "Do you think he's in a position to help, given his current condition? Does he feel like a threat?"

William's hesitation answered enough.

"We may be desperate, but if he can harm others and you, then maybe he shouldn't help." She had few answers, either. She understood where William was coming from. They had every right to worry and every right to hope Nicholas could help. Fae were dangerous, and they were useful. The war proved that, and they needed someone dangerously useful at the moment.

"I don't know if I can refuse him. You should have seen him earlier. He," William took another drag, then licked his lips. "He said he loved me, but it isn't love. This is an obsession, no different from Fearworn and his monsters. I said this, and he did not take it well. The mere mention of me not returning his feelings made the entire building shake."

"Would returning his feelings possibly help his condition?"

William may have the best poker face anyone ever saw, but she knew of all the dreadful nights, the daydreams, how he crumbled at the loss of Nicholas. They shared every thought, spent many of their worst days together because no one else understood. When Charmaine had nightmares where she awoke screaming, it was William she went to the next day. It was William's home she stayed at when she knew another nightmare would come because neither of them had to explain.

On the days when William couldn't stand being home, when he thought he upset his family, he came to her shop. She and her mother lived on the floor above. Though their home paled compared to the Vandervult estate, William said he slept like a baby on the couch. If he woke up, if he couldn't sleep, they'd stay up all night drinking tea or talking about the weather, anything to keep the demons at bay.

Charmaine's mother cried through many nights, unsure of what to do or say to help her. Survivors carried scars others couldn't understand. She couldn't put these feelings into words, either, and she didn't want to. Neither could William, so they found solace in each other and ways to ease the worst symptoms.

"You still love him," she said, causing a miniscule twitch of his eye. "Do you want to be together? Do you think this is a chance worth taking?"

"I don't know, and I don't want to think about it." William slammed the cigarette into an ashtray. He hadn't denied loving Nicholas, either. "The missing patients matter more. That is what I'm focusing on and if Nicholas can help, then I'm grateful."

A knock sounded at the door. Even if William's slumped shoulders said he didn't have the energy to deal with another visitor, he called for them to enter. Josef waltzed through, one hand waving erratically. "Does anyone care to explain why a fae was here? The nurses won't shut up about it and there is at least twice as much piss on the floor."

"Good morning, Josef." William glanced at the clock on his wall. "What are you doing here? Don't you take the night shifts?"

Charmaine sat a little taller and inspected for any wrinkles in her dress. She finished making the garment about a month ago with the pale blue fabric she and her mom bought recently. The court ladies have adored the color. They almost ran out before she could make a dress for herself. She was glad to have worn it today, waiting and hopeful that Josef might say something.

Josef had gone to war, but they never ran into one another. When he returned, he couldn't hold down a job, like many others. Once thrown on the streets, he heard of William's clinic and became one of their patrol guards. Although he mostly helped nurses with heavy lifting and provided something nice to look at. No one could deny he was handsome with those dimpled cheeks, that firm jaw, and muscular arms that most of his jackets couldn't fully contain.

"Good morning," Josef said with a tip of his hat. Dark bags surrounded his deep blue eyes. Warmth blossomed behind her cheeks when Josef smiled at her. "And good morning to you, Miss Charmaine."

She offered a smile, worried that it may be too enthusiastic, but Josef made no mention of it, or her dress. She deflated a little.

Josef nodded toward the door. "So, what was a fae doing here?"

"His name is Nicholas. We fought together," William replied. "He is the one the kings threw a party for. He has offered to help with those missing patients I've mentioned."

Josef wore the same concern others had. "What did he want in exchange for his help?"

"You don't need to worry about it. If he can help, he will. Are you here to talk about anything?" William replied.

"Unfortunately, yeah, I think there are two more missing people."

Charmaine finished the last of the cigarette, already wishing for another. Her doctor had offered her the same solutions as William, though she tried not to partake too frequently. She found focusing on stitching did best for her rattled mind, the monotonous work where she had complete control, knowing exactly what to do, how to do it, and if a problem appeared, she could easily fix it. That brought her a sense of comfort, joy, and much pride, far more than serving her kingdom ever did.

"Who?" William asked, frustrated.

"Victoria and Chester. They usually come late when I'm watchin' the door, but I haven't seen them for a while. They haven't been to the soup kitchen either. When they didn't show up, I went to their tents. They weren't there and haven't shown up in three days. Their neighbors said they haven't seen them either," Josef replied.

"You went to their tents?" William hissed before she could.

She and William agreed to never go to any of the locations alone. They went together, in case of trouble, and Josef certainly shouldn't go. He didn't have the Sight and, while he was a big guy, they did not know what they were dealing with. If any of the beasts they went up against during the war were the ones wreaking havoc, then muscle wouldn't be enough.

Josef fingered the brim of his hat. "Well, yeah, I had to see if they were there. I thought maybe they weren't feelin' well."

"It could have been dangerous," said Charmaine.

Josef puffed out his chest. "I can take care of myself."

"You shouldn't go looking into anything alone. We don't know what we're up against and we don't want anyone else to get hurt," she said.

Josef frowned. "You're right. Sorry, I just wanted to check in."

"Can you tell me what you saw? Was there anything peculiar?" William asked, while making note of Victoria and Chester's name.

"Not peculiar, no. There's a nasty owner of a matchbox warehouse that sneers at those like us when we pass by, but I don't think he has the guts, or the connections, to orchestrate this." Josef yawned and his eyes watered. "This is getting worse, isn't it? People are disappearing fast."

"Yes, and I appreciate your concern, but please, leave this to us. Why don't you head home? You need your rest."

"I should head to the shop, too," she said, standing.

"Ah, I can walk you," Josef offered, making her toes curl in her heels.

"That's a great idea," William said before she could interject.

The warmth in her cheeks spread to her hairline. Any excuse she could conjure fell silent. It wasn't like she didn't want to walk with Josef. Quite the opposite, in fact. But Josef made her heart palpitate. He was charming and handsome, everything she could ever want. However, being around Josef reminded her of who she was, no matter how much she tried to be someone else.

Dating had been on her mind after the war ended. Falling in love felt so unbelievably normal that she wanted nothing more. An exceedingly average life beside a lover, but that meant meeting someone who could accept her for who she was, and she could hardly accept herself. Why would anyone else?

"Miss Charmaine?" Josef stood in the doorway.

"Right, yes, I'm coming." She gave William a stern look. "Don't overwork yourself. If Nicholas is helping, let him and take a breather."

William pursed his lips, but nodded.

She met Josef in the doorway before descending to the floor below. She didn't know what to say. Certainly Josef had more questions about Nicholas, but she didn't want to bring it up if he didn't.

Outside, she looked skyward, berating herself for considering talking about the weather. What a boring topic, so she chose silence. From time to time, Josef's shoulder knocked against hers when a carriage got too close to the sidewalk. She stifled her smiles, worried what Josef may think if he understood how much she enjoyed his presence. She wasn't sure if Josef knew she was transgender and feared what he may think if he learned the truth. She always had those fears. They were anchors tethering her to the bottom of a foreboding sea. In the end, she was always too frightened to release herself from them.

A block away, Josef worked up the nerve to ask, "Do you know that fae personally, that Nicholas Darkmoon?"

"William knows him far better than me. We worked with him against Fearworn," Charmaine replied.

"He is the one Dr. Vandervult made a deal with?"

She bit the inside of her cheek. "No, uh, he received a gift from Nicholas' father for saving his life against Fearworn. He never made an actual deal."

Josef clicked his tongue. "Is that why he dislikes his arm so much, the silver one?"

"I suppose so. I don't ask unless he brings it up, but I think he's upset that he didn't get a choice in the matter, and of course, everyone makes their assumptions."

"Yeah." Josef scratched at the back of his neck. No doubt he made those same assumptions. Charmaine understood that fear, especially after being around fae for years. Mortals were rightfully wary, but William did so much good for a community that still stiffened at the sight of him.

"This Nicholas. Is he trustworthy?" Josef asked.

"I don't know. I believe he will do whatever William asks, but I don't know if we can trust him." She hated to say that. Considering the situation, it felt most appropriate.

William became Nicholas' obsession. She saw firsthand what happened to shades after they've gone too far. She gripped her hands at her waist, knowing where the scars were beneath her gloves. She and William had that in common, hiding the past.

While Nicholas may not be Fearworn in the sense that he could start a cult to destroy the world, it didn't mean he couldn't cause extreme harm. Any who interfered in his relationship with William would face his wrath and none knew what Nicholas would consider interference.

"Well, I don't enjoy having a fae around, but I can't imagine the doc putting his patients in danger." Josef shoved his hands in his pockets.

"We're desperate, that's for certain, but he wouldn't. If Nicholas causes trouble, William will handle it." And Charmaine, should she need to step in.

She hadn't used the Sight routinely since the war ended. She didn't need it, and she didn't want to use it. Lighting candles or the stove when it wouldn't light, that was the extent of her use, even when her body ached, wishing for more. Even when she knew that, should the time arise when she needed power, it may not answer.

The Sight was like a muscle. Don't use it, and it weakened, but fire reminded her of the battlefield. Reminded her of blood and seared flesh. Sometimes she couldn't handle looking at a candle, let alone carrying flames in her palms. The sight of blood made her gag or vision go blurry, which was why she rarely assisted at the clinic. Not during any type of surgery. She would clean or help pass out medicine, but other than that, she couldn't handle it. She didn't want to go back to a time she would rather forget.

The walk wasn't far. The Gilded Lily wasn't on the main street. They couldn't afford that on the little savings her mother kept out of her father's grasp during her military days. However, they did well, more than well, and perhaps, one day, they could open a second shop.

"Please don't go out looking for anyone again, Josef. It could be dangerous," she said at the doorway to the Gilded Lily.

Their sign had been a gift from the Vandervults. William insisted most of all, saying she and Bessie worked so hard. He wanted to give more, but she felt so hopeless after coming home. She desired an achievement entirely her own, that didn't come from bloodshed. William agreed not to give her a handout, however, the least he could do was ensure they had a beautiful wooden sign that would catch one's eye.

Josef raised his hands in surrender. "I won't. I won't."

She smiled and brushed a curl behind her ear. "Thank you for walking me back."

"No problem. I have somewhere to be this way," he said while swaying on the heels of his feet.

"Really? What are your plans?"

He wore a toothy, childish smile. "I got myself a date."

Charmaine bit her tongue.

Of course he did because Josef was charming. The nurses were ecstatic when William hired him. He treated everyone nicely and helped where he could without fuss. He made everyone feel safer and would often play card or board games to keep patients focused on anything other than their suffering.

"She's smart, works at the library," he said excitedly. "I'm not that good at reading, but I had to do some paperwork for my Ma and we went to the library. She was there and helped us get through it. I asked her to lunch, couldn't believe she said yes!"

"She would have been foolish not to. I hope you have a good time," she said, tasting disappointment, then berating herself for daring to feel it.

She never planned to ask Josef for tea, even if she imagined it through the day while sewing. She would never admit to how often she pricked her fingers because she swooned at her own thoughts. At least in her daydreams, she always had a happily ever after. Reality wouldn't be so kind and she wasn't up to face such disappointment.

"Thank you." Josef tipped his head. "Have a nice day, Miss Charmaine."

"You too. Good luck on your date." She hurried inside where she took to the sewing machine, the one place where she could dream to her heart's content because that was all she believed she could do.

9

WILLIAM

"INTO BED YOU GO." William tucked the blankets around Alice. Tawny brown fingers crept over the lip of the blanket, tugging the fabric toward her chin. The purple blanket matched her bonnet and sleepwear.

"Papa is taking me into town tomorrow. If we get a new book, will you read it to me?" Alice yawned.

"Of course." He brushed her brown curls into her bonnet before kissing her temple. "Sweet dreams."

"I love you," she whispered.

He tapped her nose. "I love you more."

"Impossible."

"Very possible."

He waited in the doorway until Alice's eyes closed. She insisted on being as close to Uncle William's room as possible, so he slept across the hall. His parents could not deny their first and only grandchild anything, not that he or his brothers could say no, either.

His bedroom had changed little. His mother kept it as he left it, the same pale blue walls and his canopied bed that served no purpose. He never slept with the curtains drawn, fearful the fabric could hide someone or something. Shelves full of books, both old and new, took up half of his room. He read when he could, but didn't find as much enjoyment as he once did.

He could change the room. His parents had offered and his brothers, on the occasions they went into town, mentioned furniture stores they purchased from. He wasn't sure why he hadn't changed the room. He simply never wanted to.

Stacks of papers littered the small dining table set by his bedroom window. He dropped into the chair to overlook the thoughts he and Charmaine conjured over the days after Josef's visit. Their suspects began with locals. Josef mentioned the owner of a matchbox warehouse disliking the surrounding homeless population. There were plenty of other irritated parties, like nobles seeking to pass bills to shut down the soup kitchen and clinic. They claimed having the establishments at all encouraged citizens to be lazy, that they would gain benefits by losing work and home. The king himself made the list, seeing as he considered the outer banks an eyesore. Alas, without proof, the list was nothing more than speculation.

Soon, he could do more sleuthing. A letter sat nearby, one from the royal household thanking him profusely for bringing the issues to their attention. The king set out more patrols for the outer banks that would start in three days, although failed to state how long those patrols would last. He also found a doctor that would join full time, also not noted for how long or from where they hailed. William worried the doctor was fresh out of training and would still need a helping hand, but he wouldn't know until tomorrow when he arrived.

In short, their best bet became believing in a fae. Nicholas hadn't returned in three nights. The first thought in his mind was that Laurent forced Nicholas back to Faerie. Though he didn't want Nicholas tormented by his father, his departure could be a blessing in disguise.

Every hour, his mind changed concerning his decision, whether it was right or wrong. Nicholas was not himself. William could cause more

damage, and yet he wanted to see Nicholas again. He missed him enough
to dream of Nicholas every night since, not the ones where they fought
and struggled, but ones so sickly sweet he ached when he woke. Last
night he dreamt of their dance and how different it could have ended,
where they kissed and held one another without a worry in the world.

The thought made him laugh, a sound somewhere between disbelief
and joy. He thought he would become wiser with age, but alas, he remained as tormented as ever.

A tap sounded from the window. Nicholas balanced on the windowsill, a silhouette illuminated by silvery moonlight. He wiggled his
fingers in greeting, the violet hue of his eyes dim. William wasn't sure
if he should trust himself, but he thought he saw the faintest pink tint
around Nicholas' irises.

"By the souls, what are you doing?" He waved for Nicholas to step
back. The fae did so, clinging to the side of the manor with his bare
fingers. He swung open the window. Nicholas leapt into the room,
holding Denison's hat.

"These are you bedchambers?" Nicholas grabbed a book from the
shelf to flip through the pages. "It suits you."

"I will take that as a compliment," he replied, perturbed and overjoyed
that Nicholas had arrived. He missed him. He always missed him, even
when he was angry. Love betrayed us like that, made us want the most
painful of admiration.

Nicholas ran his fingers over a page. "You've taken to reading your
beloved romance books again."

He tried to. Some days, he couldn't stomach the words. The hope and
joy spoken of made him ill, made him laugh, then asked himself how he
could ever be so naïve to believe any of it. How could he have sat in the
library for hours on end, smiling at hundreds of wasted pages full of lies?

Then, sometimes, when his nightmares wouldn't let him sleep, those
books kept him sane. Sometimes he thought of himself and Nicholas in

their place, foolishly in love, and hated himself a little for daring to want that.

He snatched the book from Nicholas to place back on the shelf. His fingers tingled from where they had contacted Nicholas'.

"You cannot show up unannounced, especially here. Should my family learn of your presence, they will be terrified," he lectured.

"Which is why I came in through your window." Nicholas fell into the seat William previously occupied. He placed the hat on the table. "I figured you would want to know what I learned as soon as possible."

Yes, but that didn't make Nicholas' presence easier. Being so near, alone in his bedroom of all places, made his throat dry. His mind wanted one thing and his body something else entirely.

"Go on, then." He crossed his arms as if that would cease the magnetic pull toward Nicholas.

"Searching through a mortal city proved a little more difficult than I initially expected. Once I found the owner's tent, I knew something unusual had occurred. There is magic involved." Nicholas tapped a finger against the table. "A shadowed disciple, specifically."

He was meant to be done with them. The world was meant to be done with them. Fearworn died, and he desperately needed that life to have died with the bastard.

"But you tracked all of them down, didn't you?" he muttered, taken back to the Deadlands and their endless horrors.

He blinked and his room dulled gray; the curtains withered, and the floor oozed bloody snow. In the darkened corners of the room, beasts lurched, their bodies malformed and crooked. He shut his eyes and willed the visions to fade.

"I tracked down any who didn't keep their heads low," Nicholas explained. "There is no guarantee I found each of Fearworn's followers considering how many there are and how many may have popped up, even after his demise. One seems to have made it to your city and is abducting people. I sensed their magic, albeit weak, throughout the outer banks. You are right to be concerned. A shadowed disciple could easily snatch someone without any noticing."

Bile rose in William's throat. "What would Fearworn's old disciples want with them?"

"Could be anything, rituals, food for surviving monstrous pets, who knows?"

He grimaced, not only at the possibilities, but at how he thought that was too simple. That if this had to do with shadowed disciples, with Fearworn in some manner, there had to be more to the disappearances. The war hadn't ended at all; it was merely put on pause, and he found himself at the center of it again.

He settled his hands on the windowsill. The window let in a breeze that did little to calm his biting nerves. He looked to the garden below, hoping to relieve his stress, but the shadows cursed him. Vines became gnarled fingers reaching for him. Roses dripped with blood. In the trees, countless silhouettes of monsters waited to tear him and his family apart.

"Would... these disciples work for hire?" He swallowed hard, wondering if he could make it to his end stand without Nicholas noticing his peculiar nature. He tugged on the collar of his shirt, then unbuttoned it. "The social elite are not happy about the homeless population, even if many of them are the soldiers who protected them against Fearworn. Could someone have hired these shadowed disciples to abduct patients little by little?"

"It is in the realm of possibility."

Perhaps more than either of them could realize. William understood the powerful did what they wanted when they wanted. He saw it first-hand, heard it through his father's office door, listened to his parents worry over what move to make against the king when he threatened their charities or clinics. He read of it in his family's history too.

The Vandervults did not become a powerhouse through charity. His family, like most other nobles, rose through cruelty. In the case of his ancestors, they had mining operations with less than pleasant working conditions for centuries. Many lost their lives in those mountains, never to be buried and blessed by a priest of Soul. Charity didn't become part of their world until his great grandfather, who had only been the heir because his elder brother was killed during an uprising involving those mistreated miners. Whether his great grandfather became charitable out of fear or had always been, he was never certain. Their history books spoke of him like a savior, but he long since understood to be careful around history.

He moved toward the end stand, trying to recall every conversation he ever had that may point to someone with cruel intentions. The shadowed disciples appearing after Fearworn's defeat were too odd to be mere coincidence. If they were from Terra, they understood the homeless would be the best people to abduct. So few wanted to investigate the disappearances of the less fortunate. It'd have been easy. But something kept gnawing at his senses, a paranoia that hadn't left since the moment he was enlisted.

He lit one of the cannabis cigarettes, taking one puff after the other. His hand fell on the wall, keeping him upright after his knees threatened to give out. Then a hand caught his waist.

His breath stuttered when Nicholas held him close. His lips brushed the skin of William's neck when he asked, "When did you start using that?"

He released a breath; the smoke curling around Nicholas' charming features. If the scent bothered him, the fae made no sign of it.

"Little more than a year ago," he answered. "It helps."

"With stress?"

He nodded, unsure of whether he should push away. Nicholas felt like a piece of armor he sorely needed. His breathing steadied from the brush of Nicholas' hand against his waist. The fae's thumb rubbed his side, more soothing than anything had ever been. It didn't cure him of that paranoia festering in his mind, but it was comforting, and he needed that.

"Am I the cause of that stress?" Nicholas asked, eyes downcast.

"You have always been stressful, trouble." The name fell off his tongue as if it hadn't been years since he said it.

Nicholas wrapped an arm around his waist. His gaze fell on the bed where he thought of being with Nicholas countless times and did so again. Wishing for a sweet moment followed by bliss, but he feared both as much as he yearned for them.

"I like when you call me trouble," Nicholas whispered, as he had done years ago.

"Then I shall never call you trouble again."

Nicholas smiled against the back of his neck where his lips trailed, enchanting and intoxicating. His body and mind were at war. His body wanted to lean into Nicholas' touch, to be consumed by him entirely. His mind yearned to run, to not give in because it would end in more suffering. He and Nicholas were doomed from the start.

"There is no need to stress now. You have a loyal shade at your side. If you wish for me to hunt these bastards down, I will do so. All I ask is for our correspondence to be more than business talk," said Nicholas.

"What more do you want? Be specific," he asked, willing himself not to lean into Nicholas.

"You already know the answer." Nicholas kissed along his nape, devouring his pulse with wicked teeth and a soothing tongue.

Memories flashed. Desires resurfaced. Nights spent together, the heat of their bodies pressed together, and the many dreams he had afterward. He woke sweaty and breathless, overcome by memories of them together, lost to pleasure and one another. With Nicholas here, wanting and hungry, he struggled to think of reasons to stop. He craved Nicholas' touch, to relish in the brush of his hand beneath his shirt. Nicholas' fingers strayed, twisting in the curls above the waist of his pants. That woke him.

He caught Nicholas' hand, pivoting to face the smirking fae.

"I told you I need time." His feelings were turbulent, like snow tumbling down a mountainside into an avalanche.

He understood what had happened. He was relieved to learn Nicholas didn't abandon him. But the situation was far more complicated than that. His feelings were more complicated, continuously screaming to be close and far away. That Nicholas would be better off without him, and he without Nicholas.

"We are not alone here, either," he added. "My family sleeps."

Nicholas chuckled. "And we certainly wouldn't be quiet."

"May we return to the issues at hand?" he grumbled, ignoring the heat building beneath his skin.

Pouting in a far too cute manner, Nicholas muttered, "I suppose."

William finished his cigarette, then dropped it into the full ashtray.

"If a shadowed disciple is truly behind this, it is safe to assume more will go missing. Worse than that, more may be missing that we are unaware of." He paced to the center of the room, a hand caught beneath his chin. "However, if news of this broke, King Ellis would be displeased. Shadowed disciples in his own backyard? We may yet start another war."

He would not sit idly by while more children were sent to die, and more soldiers returned to a home that cared little for them.

"Is there a way to track down this specific disciple?" he asked.

"Nothing like this." Nicholas picked up the hat, then returned it to the table. "But we now know the beast's hunting grounds. I can keep watch, though if we want to discover where the bastard is hiding anyone, if they are alive, we may have to let another person be captured. That will be the most efficient way for me to follow anyone."

Letting another person get grabbed meant another potential death. If a shadowed disciple was behind the disappearances, that meant the lives of those taken were likely already lost.

He resented how his mind so easily said one more life meant saving countless more, so it had to be done. Before the war, he wouldn't have agreed. He would be naïve enough to believe he could save everyone. He wasn't sure if it was a good thing, or if good things truly existed.

"So be it. We'll start tomorrow afternoon," he said.

"Till tomorrow." Nicholas caught his left hand to bring to his mouth. The brush of his lips on William's skin nearly broke him. Then the cursed fae left the way he came.

The window shut, leaving William alone. He pressed a hand to his racing heart. It broke into a run the moment Nicholas appeared and refused to settle long after the fae left.

He tossed and turned that night, falling asleep to dream of Nicholas' touch. Then he woke and sat in bed worrying what would come next, not just about the potential threat of a shadowed disciple and his patients, but Nicholas, too.

What did he want? What did this mean? Once this was over, would they separate? Would Nicholas allow them to? He laid awake worrying, feeling himself slipping further and further into shadow.

10

NICHOLAS

EVERA GRIMACED AT THE single bedroom apartment Nicholas rented using golden nuggets. Those nuggets would morph into balls of dirt in six months' time, but that was the renter's fault for not asking the right questions.

"You are sleeping here. Willingly?" Evera knocked a heel against the bed frame that creaked in response.

The warped floorboards leaned inward. A broken chandelier swayed from the ceiling where a breeze came in through the mismatched ceiling planks. Certainly not a room like the castle's, but he had no interest in staying where the king would bother him and, potentially, his father. Laurent could find him wherever he went, but he would at least put up a challenge, if only to be mildly annoying.

"For now." He sat on the bed waiting for sun up.

William had been more receptive toward him last night than expected. He let Nicholas hold him, if only for a moment, and joked a little. It was like reuniting the moon with the ocean.

Evera snickered and spoke as if she read his thoughts. "Your mortal won't share a bed with you?"

"He said he needs time."

"That is a mortal's way of saying they don't want you."

"You don't know him," he growled.

What if I do not return your affections? William had asked. The possibility never arose in his mind. He couldn't fathom a world where William didn't share this voracious want more painful than dying. They were meant to be together, not because of fate. He didn't believe in such wanton conceptions. They were meant to be because the two of them wove their future together, stitched their story bit by bit through every interaction. They would be because they wanted to be, and nothing mattered more than that.

William would come around. He would see the truth as they spent more time together. That's what he said he needed, and last night may have proved that. They were close for a moment, and they would have more thanks to this adventure. Nicholas didn't give a damn about missing mortals. He didn't care about shadowed disciples. He cared about William, and if giving William his desires meant they could be together, then he would force the world on its axis if he had to.

Evera leaned against the windowsill where the off white paint chipped beneath her fingernails. "I know you well enough to recognize panic. Deceive yourself as much as you need, but that won't change the truth; the mortal knows you're a lost cause. The question remains whether he will escape your grasp before you choke the life out of him."

"You sound like my father," he spat.

"I hate the bastard, but he is far more intelligent than both of us combined."

He shot her a spiteful look. "With how you speak, I am wondering if you want to return to Faerie. Maybe you're waiting for me to give up hope."

Her voice rose an octave, and nails tore into the windowsill. "You missed the one opportunity we had to change this and you're too manic to realize that truth. My hope is gone and I see no reason to avoid the inevitable. The sooner this deal is over with, the sooner we can return to our lives."

"Now, who is the manic one to believe either of our parents will let us do what we want without a fight? Have they not ruled over us our whole lives?" he challenged. "Alvina may not be as ruthless as Laurent, but she has sway over you, over all her children. We're too young. We know so little compared to our parents. They will have us beneath their thumbs as long as they can. You know this, deep down in the darkest part of your heart, you know I speak true, but you are the one who refuses to see it."

Sunlight stained the window in a warm yellow glow. Evera stepped aside when he approached, her lips set into a grim line. He opened the window, letting the metallic scent of the city waft through their nostrils.

"Follow me, return to Faerie, bicker all you want, but my mind is made up. I will fight against Laurent and Alvina until the day I die, or they do, preferably by my hand. At least that may be the greatest outcome of this change within me." He held a hand over his chest where power surged. He thought this energy was loud before, but he couldn't describe the sensation now. Not an itch, not a craving, a feeling of so much more pushing against every fold of his mind, yearning for freedom.

"Perhaps I can kill them," he whispered. He didn't know his own strength, what he was or wasn't capable of, but he saw what Fearworn could do and he nearly tore their worlds apart. Why couldn't Nicholas do the same with enough understanding?

"I may have fallen, but they will fall with me and if it gives me a day, a month, a year at William's side, I will be grateful for it," he said.

"You are quite mad," she countered, but didn't sound so angry about that possibility.

He slipped outside to the streets beneath the window where the damp clung to every breath.

Laurent had a long line of victories and didn't speak of loss. At some point, Laurent had been young, impressionable, foolish even, but he never spoke on it. Why would he? That may clue Nicholas and his siblings in on a way to beat him. A story could encourage them to give defiance a chance, to stand against him and win. Nicholas never thought that possible for most of his life, but the last two years changed him. Power changed him. He knew that some way, somehow, he would get the upper hand. One may argue he already had by breaking a deal that Laurent thought would keep his son in line.

Evera didn't believe they could go against Laurent or Alvina. While she wasn't as old and powerful as Laurent, Alvina remained a force to be reckoned with. She had vast lands and knowledge that could end most. Standing against one, let alone both, would have most quivering in their boots. But if that meant he would be free to stay by William's side, he would face them. He would face anything.

At the clinic, he snuck in from the windows, using the rafters to encroach upon William's office. Last time, his presence upset the patients. No one saw him, so that should please William, and he wanted their day to start off as well as it could.

But William wasn't in his office. Believing he came too early, Nicholas waited along the rooftop for over an hour. Evera found a mortal to deceive, chatting with them in an alley. Since she was distracted, he wandered off to the Vandervult estate, the only other place he thought William could be at such an early hour.

Mortals lived in cold structures built of silent stone or wood. They had a love for architecture, though, in a way he didn't understand but could appreciate. Their yards and gardens were trimmed, unable to flourish, but had a sense of peace about them that called for a good nap.

First, he peeked into William's bedroom window. The room was empty. He shuffled along the high steepled roof, then settled in the backyard. Asiatic lilies invaded the garden. They allowed the estate to smell far better than the city. He shifted through the greenery, spotting a familiar head of blonde through a window.

Part of the Vandervult family ate breakfast together. Two had to be the heads of the household, Robert and Matilda. The other must be a brother, clearly not Henry. He hated himself for never having asked their names. He wanted to know every detail about William so he could covet it like mortals coveted gold.

William spoke with his brother, donning a smile, then he laughed, a sound so pure and light Nicholas' heart skipped, shuddered, then burned. His nails scraped the paint along the windowsill. Blood rushed in his ears. His feet carried him to a backdoor. Inside, the hall was empty. His fingers twitched and cracked, ears warmed from the sound of William's voice, the slight cheer behind his words. A cheer he didn't show to Nicholas.

Teeth gnashing, the fae crept to the dining area. The hinges were silent as he peeked in. A genuine family sat and ate like that, sharing stories, laughing, and caring. He hated this sinking feeling in his gut, how William didn't notice him, how his attention never strayed. Nicholas wanted that attention. He needed it. Deserved it after all they had been through, but the Vandervults were in the way.

They had to go.

William caught him. He didn't know how or why. But William stood, poised and gentle, in his departure. "I should head out," he said. "I have work to attend to. I'll be home for supper."

"You better be," said Matilda, with her back to the door. "Everyone will be here tonight for a proper family supper."

"I wouldn't miss it." William kissed her cheek. He nodded to his father at the head of the table, who didn't look up from the paper when he waved.

He retreated from the doorway when William caught his eye, and he waited for that door to open. William's scowl greeted him, irritating him further. Why couldn't he smile like earlier? Why couldn't Nicholas meld more easily into the family he so loved?

William took firm hold of his arm, but he wouldn't leave the hall.

"Why in the Souls are you here?" William hissed.

"You weren't at the clinic," he answered.

"You couldn't have waited?" William tugged, trying to get him away from the door. He wouldn't budge. He kept thinking of William's family in there, how they saw sides of William he never had, and maybe never would. He envied them and all they had.

"I hadn't planned to interrupt, but they were annoying me," he snarled.

William's grip tightened. "Who was annoying you?"

"Your family. You are different around them, happier. You smile so easily for them, laugh, too. They do not deserve it, not as I do."

"What are you..." William went pale. "What are you saying?"

A muscle feathered in his jaw and his voice came out strained. "You spend more time here and at that damned clinic than with me. I'm out here searching, helping you, but you won't smile at me like that. Your family brings you such joy that I should bring you instead. If they aren't here, then I may do so. I can do better, my wicked. I will make you happier once they're gone."

William caught him by the collar of his shirt; held so tight, the fae choked and stumbled. William pushed until they crossed the hall and his back hit the other side. His eyes darkened, bleak, as if he were no longer there. It was something else, but that something lasted little more than a moment. William's bottom lip trembled. His other hand caught the back of Nicholas' neck, holding so fiercely his bones ached beneath the pressure.

"Don't say that. If you harm my family, I... don't make me hurt you," William whispered with tears in his eyes.

He didn't mean to make William cry. He never wanted to put that kind of pain on William's face. He cursed himself, hated ever having thought about such things. He would do anything to make this right. His breathing became staggered and felt it again; fear, panic.

"I didn't mean to upset you. I wouldn't..." He grabbed William's hands where he couldn't tell who was trembling. He was desperate to be understood, to fix things. "Your family is important to you. I know that. I wouldn't..."

But he couldn't say he wouldn't hurt them because, deep down, he knew he could. That he would if that voice took control, if it had its way.

The more he was with William, the more he wanted. It didn't matter if they spent every moment of every day together. He craved more. And the others were right to be concerned, to fear him, for he couldn't stop thinking about ridding the world of every obstacle that prevented him from being by William's side, always.

"They will be obstacles," Laurent had warned, and he had been correct.

"Your eyes." William cradled his cheeks. "They're pink."

He released a bitter laugh and leaned against William's touch. "I am sorry. I am not myself."

"So you're aware of that?"

"Sometimes. Sometimes I think something is wrong but can't explain what it is and others I think I am someone else entirely. I'm sorry. I'm so sorry."

Fae didn't apologize. They weren't supposed to, but he would apologize to William for the rest of their lives. It was as honest as he could be, and William knew that.

"I know. You don't have to apologize." Then he trapped Nicholas in his arms, holding with an aching ferocity, as if he tried to pour every feeling into this touch alone. "It's not your fault."

He returned William's embrace. He wished they hugged for better reasons, because they missed each other, because William shared his love. Not because he couldn't control himself and they were both frightened.

The dining-room door swung open. William released him. Robert stepped into the hall, his eyes on the paper, then on them. He froze. Behind him, Matilda gasped. Nicholas raised a hand and smiled. "Good morning. I am not here to start any trouble."

Which may not have been the best opener.

11

WILLIAM

MATILDA TREMBLED BEHIND ROBERT. Acting as a shield, Arthur situated himself between their mother and the doorway. William wished he could say Arthur needn't be concerned. Unfortunately, Nicholas had shown how upset he could become merely by watching William be around his family. Nicholas didn't want to hurt anyone. What a peculiar thought about a fae. They thrived on violence, yet when Nicholas yearned to choose otherwise, he couldn't.

"Lord Darkmoon." Robert tucked the newspaper under his arm and played the part of the diplomat. He held out his hand.

"Call me Nicholas." He shook Robert's hand while sharing his usual charming smile.

"Nicholas, we weren't expecting a visit. What brings the savior of Terra to our home?"

"I came to visit William," he answered.

His face grew hot under the curious glances of his mother and brother. Robert still didn't meet his gaze. Two years and he continued to ache.

"We served in the war together," Nicholas elaborated, as if that helped. "We went through many trials and tribulations and spoke little at the ball."

"Ah, yes, we heard he assisted you a great deal in the war effort."

"More than I'm sure you've been told."

He would have pinched the bastard if he thought he could do so without getting caught.

"It is unfortunate you hadn't arrived earlier. We could have invited you for breakfast." Robert had that politician in him, capable of withholding any disdain or distrust.

He didn't believe Robert would have wanted Nicholas at their table, but he dined with those he disliked before. He could tolerate it.

"Really?" Nicholas' attention drifted between Matilda and Arthur, like he wanted them to agree. Matilda couldn't bring herself out from behind her son.

"I am not sure what fae customs are, but a breakfast among mortals might be interesting for you," Arthur said, being as friendly as their father taught them.

If he weren't worried, he would have found the awkward conversation more amusing than anything.

Then Nicholas looked at him with such hope that his heart shattered. There, among the violet, a shimmer of pink light, as if hope itself manifested. If he shared his life with Nicholas, would that help him in any way?

William didn't expect to become a doctor. It happened out of necessity, though he didn't regret the path. He always found them admirable, a job worthy of being proud of, and he took pride in his work. In a way, Nicholas became a patient, someone who needed help that he could potentially give. Deep down, the darkened voice that had taken root in him during war times said that there was no hope, that Nicholas was doomed. They could never have had more. But then there was the doctor who sought to heal in the face of overwhelming odds, saying maybe they could make life easier. He didn't know where to begin, though perhaps considering helping at all was the only way to begin.

"Another time then," Nicholas finally said.

"Aren't you heading into town?" William asked to spare all of them.

"Yes, I told Amara we would meet her on main street." Arthur presented his arm to Matilda. She often went with them rather than spend the day at home alone.

"I am about to head to the gentlemen's club," Robert said with little enthusiasm.

There had been arguments among the lords of late that irritated Robert more than usual. Alas, he still had a job to do, although Arthur had been slowly taking over. All the brothers sat down multiple times to discuss their father's retirement. Robert worried about giving too much to his boys all at once. They worried he put too much pressure on himself when he deserved rest.

"If that's the case, I will," he swallowed hard, reconsidering, but sensing Nicholas' unyielding attention, "give Nicholas a tour of the house, if that's alright. He came all this way, after all."

He understood he put his family in a position where they struggled to say no. Matilda wouldn't speak up out of fear. Robert and Arthur thought it would be disrespectful, and thus troublesome, to say no. He hoped he didn't make the wrong decision. This could be a test, a way to see if he could help Nicholas, if he could do anything to make the rest of his life as good as it could be.

"Of course." Robert nodded at Nicholas. "We couldn't possibly decline, considering all the Darkmoon family had done for Terra. Now, if you will excuse us, we should head out. William will take good care of you."

Robert offered his hand a second time. Nicholas shook his, then Arthur's hand, and offered Matilda a smile that she struggled to return. Matilda held William's hand in a way that questioned why he offered while also hoping he would be alright. He kissed her knuckles reassuringly, then the family left.

"Are you truly giving me a tour?" Nicholas asked once they were out of hearing range.

"Do you want one?" he replied.

Nicholas nodded eagerly. "I want to see everything."

"Your idea of everything would involve me tearing up the floorboards so you could count the dust bunnies between the crevices."

"Then show me everything that does not involve tearing anything apart," he said while tracing the line of William's jaw like he had never seen William's smile before.

As much as he enjoyed the attention, he stepped away. "We have attendants here, so we shouldn't do anything like that in the open."

Nicholas smirked. "Behind closed doors is acceptable, then?"

He didn't warrant that with a response. "Shall we start the tour?"

"Absolutely."

He didn't give so much of a tour as answered the endless questions Nicholas provided. When he replied, Nicholas' eyes brightened until they were painful to gaze upon.

He understood caring for patients, how to discover what ailed them and what to do. What could he do with Nicholas though, other than hope his every move didn't make a shade's condition worse? Was it right to tiptoe and see if he could do anything? By being together, by giving him what he wanted, was he leading them down a path of destruction? Perhaps the shade would be satiated for now, but would a day not come that resulted in their mutual demise, one way or the other? He couldn't be certain, and frankly, he didn't want to dwell on it.

Like he didn't want to dwell on how enjoyable Nicholas was to watch. He took his time showing Nicholas his home, from the hallways to the drapes to searching for which door hinge may creak and how many steps may shriek. Nicholas was as playful as fae were, in search of trouble, albeit nothing worth worrying over. Acting like this made it seem like the real Nicholas was still in there.

After earlier, that moment where his eyes were pink, he dared to hope Nicholas could be saved. That all he had to do was hold him and the curse of a shade would disappear. Alas, Nicholas' eyes remained violet through the rest of the day. He clung to William as if letting him go would spell disaster. Sometimes, his grip hurt. His nails pierced skin, or he'd yank William down a hall without realizing how hard he tugged. He knew the fae didn't mean it, and he hadn't the heart to say anything. Then they came upon William's favorite part of the house, which he saved for last for that very reason, the library.

Nicholas laughed. "You must spend the most time here."

"I've never counted, but that is likely correct," he said.

Nicholas moved through the towering rows that reached the hall of the second floor. A spiral staircase took them up, where Nicholas found a window perch to sit. He smiled, proud of himself long before declaring, "You sit here most."

William ran his fingers along the book spines nearby. "How are you so sure?"

"I believe you call it a gut feeling."

Humming, he sat on the perch. "Your gut is correct. It's quiet."

"And isolated." Nicholas always caught what he tried not to say. "Which I imagine isn't what you always wanted. I bet when you were a child, you sat downstairs by the fire."

"Another gut feeling of yours?"

"I know you." Nicholas locked their hands together. "All the stories you shared, it makes the most sense."

He was right again. Before he was drafted, he thrived off the attention of his family. He didn't mind them interrupting his reading, typically because they encouraged him to share his interests. Henry entered the library with a new puzzle to try. Arthur asked William for help to find whatever he needed, though he could perfectly do it on his own. Richard dragged him outside when he spent too much time with the curtains drawn. Matilda joined to read or listen to him read aloud and Robert came in for naps, where he snored like a bear, making William laugh. They hadn't done that in years.

"Yes, a lot has changed," he said.

Nicholas eyed him. "Like the relationship with your father. He won't look at you."

"Is that so?"

"You are too observant not to have noticed. Is this a recent development? You always spoke fondly of him."

He peered outside, incapable of meeting Nicholas' eyes. "I don't want to talk about this."

"Why not? Do you think I cannot understand?"

"Well, your father is abhorrent, so I imagine you would be pleased if he didn't look at you."

Nicholas chuckled. "I would, but I understand wanting someone to notice you over others." He had no issue staring at William when he added, "You pay attention to all of them, your family, and I am envious. I am envious of Charmaine too."

"What?" he balked.

Nicholas' shoulders caved inward. "The two of you have always been close."

"Yes, she's my best friend."

"You were willing to die for her."

"I did for you."

Nicholas stiffened as if he had been hit. His fingers brushed back the glove concealing William's hand to reveal a line of silver. "Do you regret it?"

"No," he replied. In a way, it felt good to admit that aloud to Nicholas most of all. "I would do it again, although that doesn't make what happened afterward easy. I don't mean to make you feel bad. I just…"

"Need time?"

He curled inwards, pressing himself back against the windowpane. "I don't know. I don't know if there's enough time in the world to heal all that is wrong with me. I'm trying."

He didn't know what else to do other than try, then be disappointed when nothing worked out.

"Heal may not be the right word. Transformation, I find that more fitting." Nicholas leaned closer, the fearsome hue of his eyes softened by the sunlight. "Losing one's past self is inevitable, is it not? All of us transform, and we are both amid that transformation."

"What if that transformation is for the worst?"

Nicholas settled a finger beneath William's chin, treasuring him in a gentle touch. "Then we shall be worse together, and I can say with confidence I would not mind that one bit."

He couldn't accept the kiss Nicholas wanted, but he embraced the brush of the fae's lips when they fell upon his temple instead.

"I should go before your family returns. They're fearful of me." Nicholas opened the window because the fae couldn't learn to use a door.

"Henry got along with you. Maybe I need to get some alcohol in them." He smiled at having made Nicholas laugh.

"That may not be a bad idea." Nicholas dropped to land elegantly in the yard. William leaned out to wave. "I shall spend the day patrolling the outer banks. If I see anything, I will let you know."

"Be careful, trouble."

"You ask for too much, my wicked." Snickering, Nicholas wandered off, leaving William wanting him right back by his side.

He told Charmaine once that hope was a disappointing mistress. He needed to learn to take his own advice.

12

NICHOLAS

THE FOLLOWING DAY, NICHOLAS used the rafters at the warehouse to reach William's office. He spent the night patrolling the outer banks as promised, although he had nothing to show for it. Nor Evera, who traced his steps and, occasionally, stuck her nose into other people's business. One had the drunken audacity to throw an empty wine bottle at her. He wasn't sure what became of the man, but he was likely a corpse at the bottom of the river.

Flinging open the office door, a chipper greeting died on his lips upon seeing William wasn't alone. Charmaine sat on a couch. Jealousy ran hot. She had been with William for the last two years, while Nicholas couldn't see him. They grew even closer while he and William were torn apart.

"Nicholas, good morning. Charmaine and I have been talking about what you shared with me the other night," William explained from where he sat behind piles of papers.

Dark bags stained the skin under his eyes and the top two buttons of his shirt were undone, revealing his tempting nape. Nicholas wanted to mark that beautiful neck.

"If a shadowed disciple is truly behind this, that explains why no one has caught them. They could have hid themselves from us, so we were thinking Charmaine could escort you to the other sites today to see if you can sense anything else," William added.

Annoyance sizzled along the edge of his mind. He wanted to see William, to spend more time together, even if that meant wandering the city streets in search of a monster. Yesterday wasn't enough. He desired more. With Charmaine there, William wouldn't give him more than a look when all he wanted was to sink into those muscular arms.

"You will not join us?" he asked, trying not to sound bitter and failing abysmally.

"William is busy and we'll return if we find anything," Charmaine countered.

"Come with us," he insisted.

William's fingers toyed with a stack of papers. Then he shoved them under his arms and stood. "I can't. A new doctor started today. He's downstairs. The king is keeping his word, for now. We have to solve this while we have the advantage."

"You're right, so this is the best opportunity for you to search with us. There is a doctor to adhere to your patient's needs. Surely he's qualified," he countered.

William huffed. "One would hope so, but this is the king's pick and, for all I know, the doctor could be a complete scam. Regardless, I should be here on his first day to help him acclimate."

"The nurses can do that in your stead."

"These people need me, Nicholas."

"Do they?" He thought their last few interactions meant something, that they were a step closer, but William kept him at arm's length. "I am beginning to think you need them, either as a distraction or as an excuse."

William's muscles tensed like he prepared for an attack. "If you are going to argue, then leave. Charmaine will handle this."

He caught William's hand, the one he so hated. He didn't understand why. Laurent's gift helped William survive, kept him here for him to wholly adore.

"What if Charmaine *and* Evera help handle things, too?" he suggested, causing William's stare to harden.

"She's here?" His eyes flicked over Nicholas' shoulder.

"Just outside, ordered to monitor me by my father. She'll be bored, no doubt, and easily convinced to go on an adventure."

Charmaine stood and shook her hands dramatically. "I'm not going anywhere with a fae I know nothing about."

"She won't cause you any harm. She knows the consequences if she does," he reassured her. "This way, we'll have two teams. William and I can go one way, Charmaine and Evera the other. Should this not be our top priority?"

Based on William's scowl, he needed more, another nudge to agree.

"King Ellis isn't a kind man, and especially not a good one. We do have the advantage, but for how long? None of this will last," said Nicholas. "You trust your nurses. Trust them to handle things here with the new doctor. They can survive the day without you."

"Will Evera truly be helpful?" asked Charmaine, her eyes downcast. "I'm not spending my day with someone who won't take this seriously."

"She has nothing better to do," he replied.

"That doesn't mean she will help," she grumbled under her breath.

William deflated. "Will you give us a moment?"

Charmaine hesitated, her gaze switching between the men. A silent conversation passed between the friends. Nicholas' envy grew. She could be close to William without worry or consequence. Then she stalked toward the threshold where the door shut upon her departure.

"I just want to see you," Nicholas pleaded, staring into the eyes he so adored.

"I know. I'm not trying to imply that I don't want you here. Do you understand that?" William had a curious look, more the doctor than the man.

"It feels you are implying you don't want to spend as much time with me as I do with you," he answered earnestly.

"I'm not. I am saying that neither of you needs me out there and that I would like to spend more time with you, but not right now."

"You misunderstand." A flush crept along William's neck when Nicholas caught his waist. He couldn't help himself. Seeing William again, finally being near, all he wanted was to run his fingers through William's hair, kiss his neck, hold him close, listen to his heartbeat. Lock themselves up where no others will find them so he could have William every second of every day until the stars twinkled out, and the world went dark.

"I need you," Nicholas repeated. "Two years and I finally have you, but I'm asked to separate from you time and time again. Do you not feel the same? Did you not miss me? Are you not wishing to spend every moment of every day together?"

"That's what I'm trying to explain. We saw each other yesterday. We can't spend every moment together and I thought you understood I need time," said William.

"How much time?"

"Certainly more than a few days. I..." He wore a pained expression. "Would you focus with me around or will you try to make this your attempt at courting?"

"Is that so wrong?" He rubbed William's waist. "Yesterday and the other night, you seemed comforted by my presence."

William licked his lips, making Nicholas want to kiss him all the more. He didn't answer, so Nicholas said, "I want to spend a day together like yesterday, but longer, exploring the city, going to your favorite book-store, whatever you want, so long as we are together."

William's mouth opened and closed before settling on saying, "That is a grave mistake. Others would see us, people who will talk."

"Why can we not be seen? You are free of the military."

William scoffed, but he didn't pull away, and that relieved Nicholas.

"The world condemns fae and mortal relations, Nicholas, and I face enough trouble already, enough ridicule," he answered with a glance toward his right arm.

"Tell me of this ridicule and I will rid you of them."

"That isn't as romantic as you likely think it is."

"I don't know. That little smile of yours tells me you like it."

William bit his lip.

"Come with me today." Nicholas swayed them from side to side. "I will work. We can talk more and I'll keep my hands to myself."

William's mouth betrayed him by slipping into a genuine smile. It lasted little more than a second, replaced by his usual scowl. He squirmed out of Nicholas' grasp. "I'll inform the new doctor of my plans."

He resisted the urge to celebrate lest William grow embarrassed and change his mind.

"However," he pointed accusingly at Nicholas. "I am agreeing because of all the years spent apart and I will be doing some studying of my own of your condition."

"How so?" asked Nicholas.

"We need to see if being together causes changes, if my agreeing to spending more time with you makes you any better or worse. I don't expect us to find answers when others haven't—"

Nicholas silenced him by cradling his cheeks. William's blush spread to his ears, and he savored the sight.

"I appreciate you trying at all," he whispered, then William playfully pushed him back.

"Wait outside. I'll be there momentarily."

He nearly walked down the steps until he remembered that wouldn't be a good idea. He hopped into the rafters and left the way he came. Charmaine waited outside the warehouse at the front doors. He fell beside her, enticing a curse.

"Where did you come from?" she barked.

He pointed up. "The window."

"Why? There are doors for a reason."

"I frightened the patients during my last visit. William was upset, so I took a path they wouldn't see me." He beamed eagerly. "Am I not unbelievably considerate?"

Charmaine gawked, then shrugged. "Sure. Now, where is Evera?"

"You called?" Evera asked, resulting in another jump and curse from Charmaine.

"Must fae pop up out of nowhere?" she huffed.

Charmaine's attention settled on Evera, making her breath catch. Nicholas disliked Evera entirely, but he wasn't foolish enough to claim others wouldn't be taken by her beauty. She had an air about her that warranted admiration until she opened her mouth.

"I was on the rooftop just there." Evera pointed across the street. "It isn't my fault if you didn't see me. Care to introduce us, Nicholas, seeing as I sense you've involved me in something without my permission?"

"Charmaine, this is Evera Bloodbane. Evera, this is Charmaine Tuckerton. We served together against Fearworn and she is a dear friend of William," he explained with a beatific smile. "You will investigate the outer banks with Charmaine today. We believe a shadowed disciple is kidnapping humans."

"So that's what you've been snooping around for." Evera crossed her arms and pointed her nose skyward. "Why should I help?"

"You're meant to keep me out of trouble, so why not get a little enjoyment out of it?"

Evera jabbed a nail into his chest. "This isn't enjoyment. You're using me."

"Isn't it better than stalking me all day?"

Her pursed lips said she agreed but refused to say so. William exited the warehouse. His attention strayed to Evera, who perked at the sight of him.

"This must be William," she said smugly. "What a pleasure to finally have a face to the name."

"Yes, I heard about you, too." William kept a distance from her. "Did Nicholas speak to you already?"

"Yes, it seems this lovely mortal and I will be searching for a shadowed disciple." Evera smirked at having made Charmaine stiffen. Nicholas bit back a laugh, if only not to earn a lecture from William. Then Evera took Charmaine by the arm and wiggled her fingers. "Have fun with your shade today. Try to keep his leash tight. He's known for wandering off."

13

CHARMAINE

CHARMAINE NEVER EXPECTED TO be alone with a strange fae, Evera Bloodbane especially. William mentioned how Evera and Nicholas were expected to have children together because of deals their parents struck. However, Evera had been nothing more than a topic of discussion. In a way, she was a novelty, a mysterious person and a figure of their imagination. There had never been a face for the name, certainly not one any could accurately imagine.

Evera shared the blessing all fae did; unnatural beauty. Her unusual gray skin made her even more alluring. She wore a plain blouse and trousers with a leather jacket, attire that would look normal on anyone else, but she had the presence of a goddess. If the Broken Soul could take a physical form, Evera could be the closest representation. It was irritating, in a way, forcing her to grapple with the fact that she could hardly take her eyes off the fae and it wasn't entirely because of distrust.

The fae prowled the streets better than natives, finding thin alleyways perfect for hiding or watching peculiar strangers from afar. If Charmaine didn't know better, she'd claim Evera took their patrol seriously. She and Evera were given the western side of the outer banks where many abandoned warehouses, factories, and homes presided. Once, the capital must have flourished because the old homes were built sturdy enough to survive prolonged years of neglect. Though their doors had caved in, porches rotted, and glass broke, the less fortunate used their interiors to escape the elements.

All reeked of wet soot, as if a perpetual smog laid over the land. The sun could be high and blazing bright, but the outer banks had a chill to it that seeped into one's soul. She thought the chill was sadness itself made true, suffering that couldn't be ignored, though she wished it would travel to the city center where King Ellis sat warm and full on his golden throne.

Evera didn't understand any of that. She had a nonchalance about her, an effortless aura, and that made Charmaine even more curious.

They walked side by side where she monitored Evera's every move in case she needed to defend herself. The other night, she sat in front of a candle and let the fire lick her fingertips. She called for the flames to dance, hardly containing the bile threatening to spill from her throat. After a minute, she let go, unable to not see the battlefield, Fearworn looming over her wrecked self, and death sprawled at her feet. Truthfully, if Evera attacked, she doubted she could fight, not the way she once had, and thus she would lose with minor struggle.

"Why did you agree to this?" she asked skeptically.

Evera kept her attention on their surroundings. "Nicholas made a point. I rather investigate the city than follow him, especially if he's with William. Those two are likely humping in an alley by now."

"Uh..." She ignored that last remark. "Is this helping? Do you sense anything?"

"Do you disagree?" Evera asked, her eyes blinking rapidly.

"On what?"

"Our companions partaking in sexual activities?"

She forced a contrived smile and wished desperately to be alone. "I am choosing not to agree or disagree because we are not here to discuss that."

"Do you struggle with multitasking?" Evera examined her like a new found specimen.

"No, but I would prefer if we speak about why we are here, the missing patients, or the shadowed disciple. Let's focus on that." She stopped at the street corner. She hadn't the opportunity to suggest a direction. Evera chose the right.

"I didn't expect you to be the shy type, but so be it." Evera walked backwards while maintaining eye contact. "I can tell you a shadowed disciple was here, but isn't nearby. There are rats everywhere. One is about to run by you."

She cursed when a rat did exactly that.

"There's a camp ahead of us. There are about a dozen people there. Two are talking about a work opportunity," Evera continued.

She and William theorized work opportunities would get people to leave their shelter and follow a stranger. It would be an effective way to get someone alone and it wouldn't be unusual to accept an odd job. Their guard wouldn't be up because they couldn't lose the opportunity.

"Your expression says you'd like to stop and chat." Evera swerved a corner without a glance. The camp she spoke of crowded itself within an abandoned building left to rot. Worn blankets hung from broken windows, fruitlessly attempting to keep the chill at bay, and a dozen barrels sat between the tents, illuminating all in an orange glow.

"There may be someone who will speak to me," Charmaine said, unsure of how to breach the topic of Evera's presence. Fae rarely traversed the back streets of Alogan unless they wanted trouble, so people would be on guard if she waltzed up.

"Them." Evera pointed at two men huddled around a barrel, warming their fingers over the fire. "Talk and I'll make myself scarce."

Evera wandered into the shadows of the warehouses, almost disappearing entirely. Charmaine rolled her shoulders, uncomfortable knowing Evera stalked nearby, but she could get more information without the fae at her back.

She approached the men, neither of whom she recognized from the clinic. Both were older, their backs hunched and hands calloused from many years of hard labor. The men were too engaged in conversation to notice her approach.

"The fellow promised three days' worth of the matchbox warehouse's wage in one," the man with a mustache said. He rubbed his hands together faster. "I'd be a fool to pass it up."

"But we don't know this fellow. I haven't heard of him till now," said the other, his peppered beard long and coiled at the tip. "He may not pay up and you'll lose a day, plus whatever the foreman takes for calling off."

"It's safer work, just moving furniture across town," the mustache man countered. "And I know the shop, Manwell's. It's right off main street, seen it when I went into town."

Manwell's was a small furniture store that many local shops purchased from. The owner was an elderly gentleman, his face so wrinkled his eyes were always closed, but she hadn't recalled noticing a sign requesting any help.

"Excuse me," she called. "Could I ask a few questions about this job?"

The men fastened their attention on her. Their scowls deepened. They saw her as someone potentially stealing their rare opportunity. Jobs that paid well were scarce in the outer banks. The only things that surpassed the importance of a decent job were fresh food and clean water.

"I'm not interested in taking it," she explained. "However, you might have heard about some disappearances of late here."

"Supposedly," said mustache before he spat on the ground. "I heard there will be more patrols comin' through. Are you the one who suggested that? They will make thieving more difficult."

"It is necessary, I assure you. A friend of mine and I are looking into these disappearances. He's the doctor at the clinic nearby." She may not have recognized the men, but they could have paid the clinic a visit, or at the very least, knew of it. "We thought a job offer might get people alone. Could you describe the man who made this offer?"

The men glanced at one another, their distaste for her lessening at the mention of the clinic. Then the bearded one slapped his friend on the arm. "I told ya it was no good," he muttered.

"She's being paranoid, and so are you," his friend argued.

"Just tell her."

Mustache scowled. "Fine. I met him last night. He said to meet him by the docks off Seventh Street at dawn the day after tomorrow, if I was interested. He said he was an apprentice at Manwell's and needed help taking furniture to a client. It's good pay."

"What did he look like?" she asked.

Mustache hesitated to share that information. His friend gave him a cursory look, then mustache grumbled, "I didn't get a good look. He wore a heavy jacket and kept his hood up."

"What about his voice? Did he sound strange?"

"Strange? I, well, it was deep and sounded like he had been smoking all his life."

She heard shadowed disciples speak once, when those monsters dragged them from camp, when they first saw Fearworn in person. Those disciples chased her and Arden, who did most of the work, otherwise she would have died out there. She never forgot that fear, their dead eyes, and their voices. They spoke little other than to threaten in gravelly tones that came straight from the forbidden depths of Elysium.

Last she checked, no one else worked at Manwell's, but the story didn't sound too far-fetched otherwise. People hired extra help all the time, although shops like Manwell's could afford to hire a company, which they normally did. Many didn't trust those in the outer banks to work well or be trustworthy. Meeting at dawn would be normal for a day's work, too. The dock off Seventh Street wasn't the busiest dock in town, but it wasn't dead, either. However, the stranger sounded to be purposefully shielding their appearance. Shadowed disciples were easy to spot and with the description of his voice, that unsettled her.

"Well?" the bearded man hummed. "Do you think it's trouble?"

"I think I will stop at Manwell's to see if he has an apprentice," she replied honestly. "I'll return and let you know. Thank you for speaking with me."

The men muttered their thanks. Charmaine set off toward Manwell's. Evera hopped down from the rooftops. She hadn't heard the fae and jumped a second time. Evera found that humorous, of course.

Rolling her shoulders, she asked, "Did you sense anything?"

"Nothing outside of the ordinary," Evera replied. "What is this Manwell's they spoke of?"

"A furniture store. The shop is near mine. I didn't hear of the owner hiring an apprentice, so we're going to investigate."

"Fun," said Evera, her lips stretched into a wild grin. "I do love a good mystery."

Charmaine chose not to say anything. She didn't want Evera treating the situation flippantly, however, her help was better than none. And she didn't know how Evera would react to anything she may perceive to be an insult or attitude. Nicholas was safer to be around, even in his unnatural state, because ultimately, he cared what William wanted. Evera was unknown.

"A shop, you said, then you own a business? From what I know of Terra, that is impressive. What is your," Evera made a peculiar face, like a toddler unsure if they needed to shit or eat. "What is it called? Experience, talent, err, trade?"

When she didn't immediately reply, Evera leaned closer, seeming to signal that she wanted an answer. In her shock, she almost missed the corner they needed to take. She stumbled toward the street. Evera caught her wrist, tugging her forward before she fell into the muddy road. Evera smelled like a rainstorm, fresh and calm, the latter of which she never expected to feel around any fae.

"Careful. If you get hurt, Nicholas will blame me and I am in no mood for him." Evera let go, but her wrist tingled from where they touched.

"How kind of you to care about your well being most of all," she mumbled while moving on toward main street.

"No one else will care for us more than ourselves." Evera stepped ahead to peer at Charmaine. "So, what is it? Your business?"

"Oh, um, I'm a seamstress. My mother and I create gowns for women of high society to wear at their social gatherings."

"Ah, we have something of that sort, clothes makers, except we call them weavers. They're typically boorish bog creatures that feed off insects. I assume you do not take insects as payment."

Charmaine chortled. "Absolutely not. In Terra, we take payment in coins. Is there truly no form of currency in Faerie?"

"Not in the same sense. Our currency is our interests, as in the weavers, they feed off insects. If you bring their favorites, they will repay you. Heal the forest after a fire and the brownies who live there will offer help when you least expect them, things of that sort."

Evera blew a kiss at a man who gawked at her. He tripped and face planted on the sidewalk. The fae cackled, proud of herself and seeming to adore the attention she received the further she went into town. She stood out with her flawless appearance and wicked smiles. Charmaine worried how many of these poor souls she'd find later to take advantage of.

"That is... what I wish we did," Charmaine admitted. Places like the outer banks wouldn't exist. As warped as Faerie was, poverty didn't exist nor did expectations of who or what a person should be. How strange that she would become so envious of a place she had always deemed terrifying.

"Mortals are peculiar in their ways. I do not envy you, that's for certain." Evera pointed ahead. "Is that it?"

Manwell's shop came into view, a two story brick building that matched most of the others. A sign hung from an iron clasp featuring the shop's name with a hammer underneath. Evera cast an annoyed glare at the clasp. She ensured Charmaine stood between her and the iron. An ornate clock tower stood in the window beside a rocking chair and an end stand. A customer left prior to Charmaine entering. The bell above the door jingled.

Upon initial inspection, there was no help wanted sign on the exterior. Inside, there weren't signs other than information on the pieces. Manwell sold the work of local carpenters, the wardrobe's sat at the back against the wall with dressers in front of them and smaller pieces such as clocks and wracks at the front. The owner sat behind his desk, little more than bones, and curled gray hair beneath his bowler hat.

"Morning ladies," he said, standing. He didn't react to Evera, although Charmaine wondered if the old man understood she was fae. His eyes had a dusty look about them. "What can I help you with today?"

"I'm looking for work, sir, and heard that you might be seeking someone to help move your furniture," she replied.

"Oh, even if I were, I couldn't possibly offer it to you girls. That's a tough job," he said.

"I see. Do you work with a company, then?"

"I do, miss, been with them for nearly two decades now. If you're looking for work, there is a florist down the street seeking an assistant."

"That's so sweet of you to mention. Thank you for your time."

The girls left the shop where Evera said, "It may be safe to conclude that we've learned how the shadowed disciple has isolated them."

"It's a good plan. Most in the outer banks wouldn't realize it's a hoax and they would be unlikely to check in person like we did. We should tell," her voice trailed off.

Down the street, Josef sat across from a girl with beautiful golden curls. They ate sweets together, smiling and laughing. It was everything Charmaine could ever want, a reminder of what she didn't have and what she couldn't imagine having. She knew Josef had gone on a date and expected the date to go well. He was a good man and that girl would be lucky to have him, but seeing them together brought upon a dark, unsettling feeling that made her feel unclean and broken.

"What is it?" asked Evera, sounding excited. "Do you see trouble?"

"No, we need to tell those men not to go to the docks." She hurried off the street to head toward the outer banks, keeping a pace that nearly had her tripping.

Evera caught up. "You have a sour face."

"Do you care if I have a sour face?"

"That depends on how sour you plan to act with me."

"Not at all. It's not your fault." It wasn't anyone's fault but her own misgivings. She told herself not to care, to shrug it off because they had far more pressing matters. Unfortunately, emotions rarely listened or gave a damn about one's desires.

"Then whose fault is it?" asked Evera.

"I do not want you to take offense to this," more so because she didn't want Evera to be angered, "but it isn't your business nor do I think it would be helpful for either of us if I told you."

"It wouldn't be unhelpful," she countered.

"I am not so certain. Don't fae love to learn of trouble?"

"Of course, but I'm not here to start trouble, save with the shadowed disciples. I need to keep an eye on Nicholas, otherwise my mother will be relentless."

"Do you fear her?" Charmaine asked, more to distract herself than anything else. Evera made conversation easier than expected and she needed to stop remembering Josef and how much she envied the woman across from him.

"No," Evera answered, surprising her. She thought all fae feared their parents, as Nicholas feared his father. "But she annoys me, and she's sneaky, even by fae standards. She would find another way to point me in the direction she so desires."

"Why do you associate with her at all?"

"I want our house when the old hag finally dies."

Charmaine burst out laughing. She didn't expect to, especially in a dour mood, then threw a hand over her mouth to silence the sound. "I—that is unexpected."

"What *did* you expect?" asked Evera.

"That you wanted her power?"

"I'm strong enough as is, but our home, Sorrows Well, is a finicky thing. It won't accept me as its master if I were to abandon it. I don't want to, either. I grew up there. It is beautiful and comforting." Evera smirked when she caught Charmaine watching her. "Did you not expect that answer, either?"

"No, I didn't think fae appreciated home in the way mortals do."

"We are mysterious creatures," she said teasingly.

Charmaine nodded and felt oddly better already. "That you are."

14

WILLIAM

SHADOWS HUGGED THE STREETS of Alogan. They swerved in and out of sight, strengthening in the alleys where animals scrounged for scraps. The chattering of claws on stone, the flickering of lanterns, and the songs drifting from open pub doorways made William's teeth grind. They had been in the open all day and into night, inspecting the outer banks for beasts meant to be dead. Years ago, Alogan's streets put life in his lungs, but now he wanted to conceal himself in a room safe from prying eyes.

Nicholas touched his hand. He crossed his arms to shield himself in more ways than one. A protection from Nicholas and his warped mind that worsened after the sun set. Nicholas hadn't witnessed one of his episodes. If it were up to him, he would ensure Nicholas never would.

As promised, Nicholas worked throughout the day. More like walked, because neither of them heard or saw anything. He guided Nicholas to the locations his patients may have gone missing, but they observed nothing or anyone suspicious. Seeming to consider the work done, Nicholas disregarded personal space as if it never existed. His eyes reflected William, a mirror dedicated to him entirely. That attention worsened his paranoia about being out in the open for so long. A fae could track disciples easier than he ever could. Nicholas was his best defense, but that defense had far too much on his mind to be reliable.

William didn't have a pistol on him. He had two knives, one tucked into his right boot and the other under his cloak at his back. They were better than nothing, but not the best defense against shadowed disciples. Arguably, pistols weren't of much use either.

"Your hair is longer," Nicholas spoke a little breathlessly, like he resented time for daring to escape them.

William tugged at a strand of his hair. "Is that a problem?"

"I like it."

He bit back a smile. "You look relatively the same."

"And is that a problem?"

"No. I like it."

"You still smell like disinfectant, though," Nicholas added, causing him to roll his eyes.

"Doctors tend to smell like that."

A man coughed from the alley. He grabbed his knife, knuckles bone white against the handle. The man's silhouette stretched, his fingers long and stained. Blood, blacker than ink, dripped from his growing fangs, ripping through his lips. He stumbled forward, feet sinking into crimson snow.

"William." A hand caught his chin. He met Nicholas' gaze, a fierce violet, but within, a dull, familiar ashen pink hue that eased the discomfort coiling in his mind.

"I lost the ring. I realized a day or so after I woke up in the hospital that it was gone."

He wasn't sure why that slipped out. The ring Nicholas gifted him during the war, that hid him from prying eyes so they could have their midnight rendezvous, had meant nothing. Rather, the ring wasn't meant to have meaning, but for weeks after waking, he touched his ring finger or searched his pockets to find disappointment. He felt foolish, childish, like he apologized to his parents for losing a new toy.

Nicholas smiled, soft and sweet. "Would you have kept the ring if you still had it?"

"Yes." He licked his dry lips. "It was useful."

Nicholas saw through the lie, but played along. "Shall I make you another, then? A more permanent one."

Warmed, William swerved around him. "You're getting ahead of yourself."

Another noise from the right had him swinging toward it. A woman stumbled through the alley, intoxicated enough to be smelled from a distance. Giggling, she waved and wandered away, singing horribly off key. He lowered his weapon, knuckles aching from the tension.

"You are paranoid," Nicholas said.

"How observant," he replied, struggling to catch his breath. He didn't like it here, feeling as unsafe as he did in the Deadlands. He never wanted those feelings to follow him home. Foolishly, he thought living as a civilian would become easier, that it would take away his nightmares. Alas, nothing stopped shadows from creeping in or familiar faces of terror. Though he slayed his monsters, they lived on through him in nightmares.

"You always wanted to come home," said Nicholas. "But you don't seem too happy to be here."

"I am happy," he corrected, even if the words weighed on his tongue.

"Oh, are you hiding that happiness, then? When do you plan to share it?"

He didn't warrant that with a response.

At the end of the street, a lantern struggled to illuminate the sharp curve. They left the warehouses and docks some time ago, moving closer to the less secluded parts of the city. That didn't lessen his nerves, but heightened them because there was more noise that could hide the more nefarious sounds. Drunkards sang from open tavern doors. Musicians played on street corners. Locals wandered home from work or to a shop for the night out. Among them, monsters could be hidden watching their every move.

"How about a drink to calm your nerves?" Nicholas nodded at a pub where a group of men battled their way through the front door, seeming to challenge who could get in first.

"We aren't out here to drink," he answered, even if his throat itched for one. Alcohol became too common in his life, necessary to take if he wanted even an hour of rest.

"That could be part of your problem. You focus on work too much, always have." Nicholas took his hand, and it felt right, like everything he wanted. "Besides, you said we would also test my limits tonight. We have done little of that yet, at least not to my knowledge."

Nicholas was right. He had been so caught up in work and paranoia that he hadn't noted Nicholas' demeanor at all.

"One drink won't spell our end," Nicholas said.

"You are..."

"Trouble." The name fell beautifully from Nicholas' lips, like a prayer, a hope that William would call him that again and again.

"Always trouble... one drink." A drink may sway his mind long enough to prevent Nicholas from seeing how broken he had become.

Together, they walked to the pub where their hands fell free in the light. Singing patrons greeted them upon entering the charming interior. While smelling of rum and sweat, that didn't detract from the comforting lantern light nor the playful bard dancing from tabletop to tabletop.

He found a corner at the back, darkened slightly where others may not notice Nicholas, though most were likely too drunk to realize he was fae in the light.

"We don't have pubs in Faerie," Nicholas explained as they sat. "But I find them rather charming."

"I'm surprised. Fae love to drink. All they did during the war was fight and party."

"Oh yes, we throw revels at our home or in the fields. No one has built an establishment for food and drink, although I imagine it may not perform as well in Faerie. There is always at least one death at a revel and much destruction."

He actually laughed, having not forgotten Nicholas' strange tales of Faerie, and thus found the story believable. "This may be too tame for you, then."

"I have no quarrels, so long as I am with you."

He watched carefully, feeling awful to treat their time like an experiment. He had to know if being together would lead to catastrophe. With an illness, one tested methods to discover what caused harm and what healed. He had to do the same for Nicholas, although he wasn't sure it would be of any help.

"Is that truly all you want, to be with me? You do not have other desires?" he asked.

Nicholas perched his elbows on the table, smiling with all his teeth.

"Why are you staring at me like that?" he muttered.

"Because you're picking me apart like a puzzle trying to get answers. Because you want me, or rather, what we had. That comforts me," Nicholas replied fondly.

A tavern girl came to the table. She didn't realize Nicholas was fae until she already spoke. He paid her no mind, focused entirely on William, who ordered for them. She ran into a patron in her rush to leave the table, resulting in a spill of ale. The commotion did nothing to deter Nicholas' attention.

"I want you to lead the best life you can," William muttered and gave the poor tavern girl a kind smile when she shakily delivered their meal.

"My best life will be one spent with you." Nicholas drank, then smacked his lips together.

"How romantic, but you didn't answer my question."

Nicholas ran a finger along the rim of his pint. "There are moments where my mind wanders, but ultimately, I think of you. I imagine us traveling, seeing both of our worlds while hand in hand, and I wonder if," he licked his lips, suddenly nervous, "if your family could accept me and I could be a part of that."

What a beautiful future that William desired more than ever. That also meant Nicholas didn't always perceive his family as obstacles. What happened the other day may not happen again. Nicholas wanted to be part of his family and if they could achieve that, maybe they could...

"Would you really like that? My family are mortals and they aren't exactly, uh..."

"Aren't like fae," Nicholas finished for him. "Which means they would be kind, as you described them, and yes, I do think I'd like that."

He warmed at the image of Nicholas seated at their dining table surrounded by family who loved and accepted them both as they were. It was the dream, the perfect happy ending that he wasn't so sure he believed in, but oh, how he wanted it.

"If my family got to know you, I believe they'd adore you," he said.

"Does that mean you are open to letting them get to know me?"

Swallowing hard, he spoke over his drink. "I'm not opposed to the idea, if you are willing to be patient."

"Fae aren't known for their patience."

"Which is precisely why I brought it up."

Nicholas laughed into his pint. They drank and ate to the bard's song and the patrons' laughter. The evening was fun, normal, so William lost track of the drinks, thus spending more time there than they should have.

By the time they left, William stumbled outside with a bottle of rum in hand. A carriage rustled down the street. The driver snapped the reins, and the horse galloped. William saw the puddle before the wheels hit, but nothing saved him from the murky water dousing him. The carriage passing left him drenched and Nicholas bone dry. The fae snickered, then snorted, then howled.

"This isn't funny," he said.

"It is terribly funny," Nicholas countered.

The chilled water made his coat heavy. He tore himself free of it, but his shirt had been dampened, too. Nicholas stared.

"Stop gawking," he said, feeling a blush form from head to toe.

He hadn't received attention like Nicholas gave since, well, Nicholas. He found a partner here or there, those curious about his affliction. They were less interested in him than the questions they could ask. To be admired so openly, he missed it, though knew not what to do with it.

"You ask too much of me." Nicholas stepped around him toward the road. "How about I make us even instead?"

Nicholas fell into the puddle, resembling a child playing in the snow. He rolled, then hopped to his feet, now equally drenched and grinning impishly.

"There, we match," he declared.

William bit back a laugh when a clattering noise nearby frightened him. He pivoted, attention darting about, searching for a threat. A black cat leapt out of an alley with a rat in its jaws.

"You remain jumpy, even full of alcohol," Nicholas said. He followed, though William knew not where they were heading. He walked with no destination.

"We're in dangerous territory now that a shadowed disciple is involved," he countered.

"That isn't it though, is it?" Nicholas challenged. "You have a knife secured beneath your desk."

He took a corner too quickly, resulting in his elbow scuffing against a building. "I have much in my office of monetary value that someone may steal."

"Yes, you do, and you refuse to let me turn a corner before you."

His teeth ached from how hard he was grinding them. "You may miss something I would notice."

"You're making a lot of excuses trying to hide what I have already guessed."

"I don't want to talk about this."

"Why?" asked Nicholas.

He took a long swig of his drink, then spat, "Because it won't change anything."

"Does that matter? I want to listen."

"I've told people before."

"Have you?" Nicholas challenged, taking a step ahead, so William saw the accusation in his eyes long before he said it aloud. "Or did you sit at Charmaine's side in silence because you knew she went through the same? Did you lie to your parents about what you went through and tell yourself it was fine? Who truly knows all you have done and all you are feeling now?"

Himself alone because—he couldn't explain why.

Matilda and Robert were his parents. He wanted them to be proud. Arthur, Richard, and Henry were his brothers. He didn't want to worry them. Charmaine was his best friend. She shouldn't have to take care of him. His doctor tried to see through him, but even he knew so little about the new sciences of the mind, picking and prodding and sometimes making William feel worse.

So he smoked, and he drank and he worked and he ignored because nothing more could be done. But there Nicholas waited, a bottomless pit to fill, and he saw William in ways others didn't. In ways, he couldn't deny or continue pretending it wasn't true.

"I'm a black mood no one can dispel, an anger that cannot be doused, a fear that cannot be quenched. My eyes and thoughts deceive me. I see Fearworn with my waking eyes and I hear him call my name. He's dead, and I'm home, but I've never felt so far away, and I don't know how to change that," William growled, for his sorrow sounded of anger always, as if that emotion alone had wound tight around his heart and mind, refusing to let go.

"I don't know what to do when I am not busy because when my mind is quiet, I think horrible thoughts. Sometimes, the castle burns with the king inside and I savor the thought of his screams. Sometimes, I take a blade to end it all and think of how simple it would be to sleep." And he couldn't breathe a word of that to his family, who waited so long for him to return. He knew the pain that would leave upon them, but they didn't understand the pain he felt every day.

"What is wrong with me?" he whispered as his footsteps echoed through the sleeping city. Windows and doors had shut, and the residents slept. Flames flickered upon lanterns lining the streets leading to Brandy Bridge ahead, where the water roared.

"You are William Vandervult, the man I love, that your family loves, a doctor, a soldier, a great many things, none of which define you entirely, so this," Nicholas laid a hand over William's heart, "these feelings do not define you, either, even when they burden you."

He knocked the hand away and walked faster, as if he could outrun Nicholas. "But all I feel is burden."

"Then perhaps you should ease that burden, as you are now. Is there anything you wish to tell someone other than me?"

"My father," he answered immediately. He recalled how his father couldn't meet his eyes, how they tiptoed around one another. "He blames himself for my enlistment. He struggles to look at me, for I am not the son he wanted to return home."

"Did he say that or do you believe it?" asked Nicholas. He rolled his eyes, but Nicholas caught up and held a finger to his lips. "He did not say so, therefore you do not know."

"But what if I'm right? I don't want to hear it. I can't."

"You aren't."

William came to a halt upon the bridge where the churning river below kept the stones eternally damp. "You are stupidly confident."

"No, I trust you," Nicholas argued and the words, so simple, warmed him. "The stories you shared of your family, I don't need to spend time with them to know what they think of you. They care for you, even this version you so despise, that you believe is so changed."

"I have changed."

"All things change," Nicholas continued. "Transformation, remember? You are kind, even if you believe you are not. You love your romance books, even if at times you find them silly. And you cannot help but garner the attention of a certain troublesome fae."

He leaned against the bridge. "I suppose that will never change."

"It will not." Nicholas hopped onto the parapet. He swayed, then steadied, walking with hands outstretched. Then he fell on his butt to let his legs sway. "Join me," he said, patting the stone beside him.

"So you can push me?" He asked.

"I already saw you wet today, my wicked. The next time I want it to be under different circumstances. Now, come here."

Warmth spread behind his cheeks from far more than the rum. Taking another drink, he swung onto the parapet where Nicholas tugged him closer so they were arm to arm. Their legs dangled above the river, the water sprinkled with feathered white lights of the stars.

"You were calmer than I expected today," William said.

"Was I?" Nicholas knocked his heel against the stones. "I suppose so. My head is clearer than it has been of late."

"Does that happen often?"

"Every few days, I think. Before, when the change began, I had episodes of delirium, you could call it. Now, I have less clarity every day."

He lost more of himself every day, but he wouldn't say that. William didn't want to hear it either. Words carried strength. To hear the truth aloud solidified it, made it less bearable, made the future feel inevitable.

"Sometimes, like right now, I think I'm able to grasp my situation. I know I'm growing more erratic, that my thoughts can drift with such ease and I'm not entirely in control." Nicholas' smiles once belonged to one who didn't know love and did their best to mimic the emotion. But that had changed too because when William looked at him, he felt full.

"I'm a danger to myself, but most of all, you," Nicholas continued. His words faltered. He faced the river. "You're all I can think about most days, all I can dream about, and that has me making less than spectacular decisions."

"You don't say," he teased.

Nicholas nudged him. "Don't mock me when we're having such a serious moment. We won't have many more in the future, I imagine."

That sobered him up quickly.

"It isn't just you, though." Nicholas held out his hands, touching fingertip to fingertip. "Before, I knew I was strong. I felt a power in me no other mimicked, but now? William, I can't explain it."

He stretched his fingers over the river and the water rippled, as if Nicholas willed the river itself to bend to his will. A wave surged to lick their heels, then settled as if the water fell asleep.

"I feel as if I'm connected to everything, that I'm absorbing the energy from the stars themselves."

Nicholas was strong before. He stood against Fearworn. He battled shadowed disciples and monsters, but this felt different. William tasted it in the air, sultry and sick.

"You're stronger than ever," William muttered, wondering what more Nicholas could do, what he may do in the future.

"Undoubtedly, but I don't know how to utilize this strength or what would happen if I tried. In a way, I'm grateful you're all I think of, otherwise I could so easily follow in Fearworn's footsteps."

"Don't say that."

"It's true. I could tear this city apart if I really wanted, if you asked it of me." Nicholas caught him by the chin, forcing their eyes to meet. "You understand that, don't you? That from here on out, you can order anything of me and I'd obey."

He liked Nicholas' touch, the brush of his fingertips and the sound of his voice and how close they were. Nicholas' warmth bled deep into his bones, where he wished it to stay forever.

"I tried ordering you to leave earlier and you wouldn't," he said.

Nicholas gave him a stern look, so unlike him. "Experiment all you like, but I fear there is nothing to be done. I will worsen until I don't have moments of clarity at all, until I forget everything about myself."

William finished his bottle, focusing on the burn in his esophagus rather than the tears in his eyes.

Nicholas laughed. "Aren't you a fine drinker? Will I meet a drunk William tonight?"

"Looks like it," he replied.

"I will take advantage of this moment entirely."

"I would expect nothing less of you."

Nicholas smiled, crooked and sweet. In his eyes, a faded hue of pink fought to show itself. This was the real Nicholas, William's troublesome bastard.

"Kiss me while you still remember yourself," he whispered, knowing full well it wasn't the rum talking, although he'd let anyone else believe otherwise.

Nicholas shouldn't be the person's whose lips felt like home, but William understood he fell in love not for the right reasons or moral ones, but because he found someone who felt as wrong as he did, who saw the darkness within and didn't try to bring it to light, but let it exist as it was without shame. He wasn't sure what peace felt like anymore, but he'd like to think it felt like Nicholas' mouth on his in the cold of night.

15

NICHOLAS

THE CITIZENS OF ALOGAN didn't sleep. Humans were as content as fae to waste their evenings however they pleased. Three muggings happened in the last hour. Men and women wandered into shadowed streets reeking of spirits and despair. Torches illuminated tavern doorways left open to welcome all. Shanty songs kept the night company.

Nicholas watched all this from the greased rooftops, pacing around the block of Seventh Street near the docks. Evera wandered around the roofs, remaining his shadow while entertaining herself in whatever ways she could.

After the previous night, he didn't want to leave William's side. He received a kiss he so desired. He felt so childish to admit that he thought his heart would burst. But afterward, William had that look; one of pain and worry, where he feared their future, same as Nicholas did. He yearned to ease William's discomfort in any way he could, which was how he monitored the docks.

Charmaine and Evera shared that someone lured people with a false job offer. They warned the men who told them about the job, but none knew how many others may have been approached. The stranger, likely the shadowed disciple, wanted to meet near this dock, so he watched for any peculiar guests.

Dawn approached on the promised meeting day. The older man hadn't come to the docks. However, a woman in a thin faded green jacket waited, searching left and right. She stood out because of how long she lingered. The dock became busy an hour prior to dawn with frequent comings and goings. Rarely did anyone stand anywhere for long. Then another peculiar figure appeared, one in a long trench coat whose scent carried over the stench of fish and despair. Nicholas would recognize that smell anywhere.

He moved, urged to take the monster's life, knowing that its existence brought William pain. Ever caught his wrist. Her voice came out stern, "If you want to help that mortal of yours, we follow the bastard, not kill them."

"William will be upset if we let someone get caught," he countered, although William implied he could do so if it meant capturing the shadowed disciple.

Regardless, he didn't want to risk causing a rift. He understood William's concern having shared it himself, but he couldn't stay away, either. His path, no matter what happened, led to William alone.

The shadowed disciple spoke with the woman. The disciple ensured no one would recognize him in the large coat with a second underneath; the collar turned up and a newspaper boy hat that shadowed his face. The disciple kept his hands in his pockets too, meaning she wouldn't notice his claws or the discoloration of his skin. All of Fearworn's followers took on an appearance that none would be foolish enough not to run from.

"William will be more upset if we miss this opportunity and never discover what has happened to any of the patients," said Evera.

He hated admitting she was right, that she had the thought process necessary to consider their options. At least she didn't rub it in when she could have. Instead, Evera scampered along the rooftops. In that way, they exchanged positions where Nicholas became her shadow.

The woman agreed to whatever the disciple requested.

"They're leaving together," Evera whispered.

"They're unlikely to head deeper into the city, especially with the extra surveillance," he explained. "But we cannot lose this one. The disappearances are speeding up. They're preparing for something."

His gut told him it had to do with Fearworn, somehow, someway. The bastard must have laid out a plan, or the disciples peered through his work and hoped to recreate it.

Together, they left the docks, and the fae followed. Evera kept them a street over, out of sight and capable of hiding, should the disciple look back. The disciple took a road that sloped toward the river, where three men huddled around a rusted barrel. Flames flickered within, warming their hands, hovering over the flame. The disciple and his unknowing captive walked past them, with no one offering them a glance.

"How is a disciple getting into the city?" Evera asked. "Don't the humans have fail-safes to prevent any unwanted visitors?"

"They should. Heign's Magical Society has formidable mages. They are the ones who learned how to close a scar for a short time, and certainly they can keep their people safe from disciples," he replied.

"If they aren't coming through the gates, then they are already here. They may not even be taking the patients out of the city."

"But that means they're holding them captive somewhere without either of us sensing them. Considering how many patients they've taken, there must be more than one, and that would be impossible to hide from us."

"I don't know about impossible." Evera gazed upon the abandoned buildings and their darkened windows. Alogan had countless places to hide. Their quarry took another corner. They hadn't left the outer banks, continuing along a pathway through the abandoned warehouses.

"If there were a group of disciples, we'd sense them, like we are now, and I've gone over this district multiple times already." And yet he missed the obvious that Evera spoke of so easily. With the cracks of his mind, he may have missed the obvious again.

"Sir, where are we going? I thought your shop was on main street," asked the girl. She stopped to examine their surroundings.

"The shop is on main street, but the furniture we are retrieving to take there is this way," the stranger replied in a hushed voice, like they struggled to enunciate their words.

The woman accepted the excuse. The disciple didn't rush, did nothing to make himself stand out. He held a conversation with her, spinning a story about a factory shutting down and having good furniture to sell. The girl did not know who she followed until the disciple stopped in the middle of an alleyway.

"Down here," he said, pointing at the street.

"There's nothing here," she replied, then he waved his hand over her eyes and she fell into his arms.

The disciple laid her beside a manhole. Once opened, he tossed her over his shoulder and descended into the sewers. Evera and Nicholas shared understanding looks. They weren't hiding in an abandoned warehouse. The disciples infiltrated beneath the city.

Nicholas stood along the manhole first, where the stench made him ill. Evera openly gagged.

"Mortals are foul," she hissed.

Sighing, he dropped into the manhole. Evera followed. The sewer ran all throughout the city, more convoluted than the streets above. They kept closer to the disciple, mirroring his movements until they came upon the answer to their many questions. The disciple approached a scar in the middle of a passage, hardly visible to the naked eye. If it were any larger, it may have caused sickness among the civilians above. The shadowed disciple walked in, carrying her limp figure over his shoulder.

Evera turned to Nicholas. They shared the same worried expression. The kidnapped patients had been taken to Faerie.

"Weren't you supposed to have slaughtered these bastards?" She hissed on their way to the exit.

"I lost count of how many I slaughtered, but some kept their heads low, and now we know why," he replied irritably.

Laurent sent him on a worthless mission. They understood Nicholas couldn't destroy all of them, considering more could rise after Fearworn's demise simply to worship the bastard. However, he hadn't expected the damn creatures to cause problems already.

"No, we have an idea why. They're up to something foul, but what do they need mortals for?" Evera corrected.

"Food?" Nicholas shrugged.

Evera caught the rings of the ladder and climbed out of the sewer. "This has to do with Fearworn. You're thinking it, too."

"I killed him. He's gone. I..." In truth, he didn't remember Fearworn's death.

That moment when William's breathing stopped, the world faded. What he recalled was anger and desperation, to finish Fearworn off once and for all so he could save William anyway he could. There was blood, Fearworn's body broken in his hands, a sudden change and the need to spare William above all else, but nothing more than that. Others spoke of the battle, how he and Fearworn became mirrored blazes of light ripping through the sky. Arden admitted to believing they would all perish as the sky caught fire and that fire rained upon them. The evergreens sparked and, before they realized it, the battlefield had been consumed, little more than fire and ash. Nicholas' first memory from that time was William laid out on a bed, his silver arm draped over his stomach and Laurent leaning over him. Laurent wore a smile, one of pure villainy, for he had Nicholas trapped.

"How could Fearworn have survived?" he muttered, angered at himself most of all for not ensuring anything remained of the bastard.

"This is the fae who tore a hole into another realm," Evera said. "Two realms went to war against him for decades. Do you truly believe him incapable of cheating death?"

He wasn't sure. He didn't want Fearworn to be. The war ended and that couldn't change.

"Let us return to William. He must know of this." He headed for the clinic.

Though it was late, William spent most of his time there, so it was the best place to check first. Evera traveled with him, her hands locked behind her head. To others, she looked relax, but he knew she watched the corners for signs of another disciple. Her presence and the help given drew about a worried curiosity. Laurent told her to monitor him. He knew she would get bored and expected she would follow around, but not take the situation as seriously as this.

"Why did you help?" he asked. "Tonight, you had no reason to stop me from making foolish decisions and don't use my father as an excuse. We both know you didn't have to intervene."

Evera shrugged. "If I'm to follow you, the least you can do is entertain me, and this is entertaining. I enjoy a good mystery."

Nicholas wouldn't admit to being grateful. Without her, he may have ruined their best chance to discover where the disciples were going.

They walked the rest of the way in silence. He ascended the warehouse with Evera snickering at his back. "Did your little pet make you promise not to frighten his patients? Poor boy, you have to sneak in."

"Don't refer to him as a pet." He opened a window to step upon the beams. "And yes, the patients are frightened by me, let alone the two of us. We shouldn't make the sick uncomfortable."

"As if that has ever stopped you before." Evera leaned over the beam. Any other would think she was about to fall, teetering on the edge. "Imagine if I dropped right now. How many do you think would croak?"

"Five." He bit his tongue. "We are not discussing this."

"I think seven, that one is hardly breathing already."

He ignored her and set his path to the office. The office blinds were open. Inside, a handsome man stood at William's back, slender fingers laid upon his shoulder. He wore lavish attire, bright and perfectly fitted. When he spoke, he wore a confident smile, eyes gleaming. William listened intently, nodding along to whatever the man said, then smiled.

Nicholas' stomach knotted. His throat tightened. His steps carried him over the rafters. The stranger leaned over William, too close. Clenching his jaw, blood filled the gaps between his teeth. He fell upon the stairs and threw open the door. The rattling of the windows brought the stranger and William's gaze to him, both paling at the sight.

"Nicholas," William hardly spoke before he lunged across the room.

Papers scattered. William fell out of his chair. Nicholas' claws wrapped around the stranger's neck. They fell to the floor together, Nicholas on top of him. The man released a strangled noise, suppressed by the tightening of Nicholas' fingers. His nails pierced the skin of his neck, staining his collar red.

16

NICHOLAS

EVERA THREW NICHOLAS OFF the man. All he saw was red. All he wanted to see was red. He lurched at Evera, the new obstacle in his path. Fire spread over his fingertips, vicious in their violet light. Evera shrieked from the flames breaking over her skin. She retreated, dousing the flames with a wave of her arm.

"What the fuck is wrong with you?" William bellowed, panicked and breathless.

That fueled his anger, that William was all over the stranger, desperate to ease him. He directed most of that anger toward Evera, who wore far too smug a smile even as her arm flared red from the burn.

"Why are you interfering?" He intended to finish the job.

Evera blocked his path. "You should be thanking me. I stopped you from making a terrible mistake."

"There is no mistake. That bastard—"

"Richard, my brother," William interrupted, his voice full of rage that made Nicholas' blood curdle. The doctor stood, eyes blistering cold and bloody, hands clenching a blade he grabbed from beneath his desk. "Put your hands on him again and I will cut yours off."

The reality of what he had nearly done sent him into a spiral. His thoughts drowned him, cursed him for putting such terror and anger on William's face.

Shaking, Richard held a hand over his heart. William fell beside him. He kept the blade in one hand and laid his other on Richard's neck. Thanks to William, the wounds upon his nape healed, but for whatever reason, he struggled to catch his breath. William pressed their foreheads together, instructing Richard to breathe in tune with him. Each of his breaths sounded painful, causing Nicholas to shrink further.

He hurt William's family, the people he loved most, and Nicholas admitted to wanting to join. How could he ever do that when he reacted in such a way? He had been a fool. Laurent was right.

Laurent was always right.

Richard stood with William's help. When he spoke, his voice came out hoarse and cracked. "I'm alright."

William watched him a moment longer, then set his angered eyes on Nicholas.

"Get out," he growled, knife raised, though he couldn't hide the tremor in his hand.

Nicholas stepped forward. "I didn't know. I thought—"

"It doesn't matter what you thought," William interrupted.

"Please, let me speak." Any good will he received over the days had vanished in the face of his mistake. William looked at him with fear, like the next monster to fight and when he next opened his mouth, Nicholas blurted out the first words he thought would silence whatever cruelty William might share. "I found a shadowed disciple today."

It was like they returned to the Deadlands, traveling the woods together with William, never giving him attention unless it pertained to information.

He knew to keep going, otherwise William would push him out the door. "Another patient has been taken. If we made ourselves known, the shadowed disciples would have realized they've been discovered."

"They'd go underground," Richard said hoarsely. "And they may go elsewhere. You could lose them entirely."

"Yes, so we followed one. There's a scar in the sewers. Whatever they are doing, they are doing it in Faerie," he said.

"Which we wouldn't have discovered if you were in charge," Evera chimed in. "You're a danger, as we've just seen. Keep him around and I may not be here to stop him the next time."

"No, I..." The words congealed on his tongue. Evera was right. He may have killed Richard, may have forced William's hand, and then what would happen? Would he have hurt William next?

"If my patients are being taken to Faerie, then I have to go." William kept a firm hold on his brother's arm. "And unfortunately, I need a guide, which I imagine you won't be unless coerced."

Evera snapped her fingers and nodded.

Richard held up his hands. "Wait, let's take a moment. You cannot go to Faerie to chase these shadowed disciples. You aren't in the military anymore, William."

"They're my patients."

"And you will care for them once they are found."

"By who? Do you believe King Ellis will look for them?" William challenged. "Or will he want to cover this up to not incite a panic? We all are suspecting the same thing, aren't we? That Fearworn is involved, somehow, and the kings won't want to admit to that. They may even send a force to ensure my patients are dead so they can't speak of what transpired."

"That doesn't mean you should go," Richard countered. "You were gone so long. To leave again, and to another realm, I... you can't. Please, don't."

"I have to." William lowered the knife reluctantly. "We have to."

"What of Mother?" Richard whispered.

"I won't tell her I'm going to Faerie. I'll tell her I'm going on a work trip."

Richard guffawed. "You want me to lie?"

"We're both good at it."

Richard gave William a hurt look, then stormed out of the office, even passing Nicholas without so much as a flinch.

"May I have a moment alone with Nicholas?" William asked.

He would be pleased if he were foolish enough to believe William had anything but ill will to share. Evera left without a fuss. The door shut, separating them from the world.

William wouldn't meet his eyes. He clenched and unclenched his fists. "Be honest, being together as often as we have these last few days has encouraged your condition, hasn't it?"

"My condition," he repeated. "What do you mean?"

"Don't play coy."

But he needed to play coy. He couldn't explain this wanting, no, this need, as if he needed to be fused to William entirely. As if he needed to crawl beneath William's skin and become part of him. Addiction did not do this feeling justice, but obsession reminded him of Fearworn.

"Is encouraging my love for you such a problem?" he whispered.

"It is if that encouragement leads to this." William gestured to the blood on the floor. "I was foolish to think we could test this out, that somehow I would be the one to put the pieces together and... cure you, for lack of a better word." William laughed, an entirely hollow sound. "Just the other night you said you wanted to be a part of my family, but you call them obstacles and you attack someone merely for being near me."

"I didn't know he was your brother."

"That doesn't make it better." William threw the knife onto the desk. "You said becoming Fearworn was your greatest fear. Now, here you are, having changed like him, even if not for the same reasons. I will not forgive myself if I am the reason you lose a little more of yourself each day. If returning to Faerie means you may have a better life, then that is what you should do."

A pain struck him that made his voice meek. "You wish me gone?"

William didn't answer. He wished to say William needn't worry. He wanted to promise they would be happy together forever, that nothing would ever go wrong. If he could spew a string of lies to ease William, he would. They would be painfully sweet and everything they ever wanted. But alas, fae were truly cursed. They could riddle their way through lies, but a man like William would catch the truth. He would see through Nicholas' foolish attempts, so it left him having to share the truth.

Nicholas spoke carefully, honestly, in a way he hadn't felt for quite a while. Maybe ever. But William deserved honesty, and maybe he genuinely wanted to tell the truth. At least there was someone he never wanted to lie to, never wanted to cheat or scam.

"I am scared, William," he said. "Scared of what I might do, what I could do, what I'm willing to do to have you, but nothing will stop my yearning for you. I will run to you wherever you go. The wretched Souls you mortals so love could not separate us."

He chanced a step forward, relieved that William didn't retreat. Then he took William's hand, rubbing his thumb against the calloused palms he remembered so well.

"I love you, my wicked. I cannot return to a time when I am not by your side. I cannot promise, though I so wish I could, that I will never harm you or anyone because of this sickness within me. But I can say that I'm sorry, that I don't mean it and I don't mean that as an excuse. I will do what I can. I promise to be here, with you, to not hide and to always help you, to the best of my ability. I would burn this world if you asked it of me. I would save this world if you asked it of me, although…"

"Although?" William repeated.

He cursed himself for saying it; "There may come a day when you will have to end me to prevent another Fearworn."

William spoke like Nicholas hurt him, like nothing worse could have been said. "Don't. I could never do that."

"We both know you could. I truly believe there is no one in this realm or another as vicious as you."

"That is not the compliment you seem to think it is."

"Is it not? I find it very appealing." He brushed away a tear before it slid down William's cheek. Twice he brought tears to his wicked's eyes. He vowed to show William such happiness he'd cry twice more from joy.

"We may not have much time left together, but should we not enjoy the time we have?" Nicholas asked.

William's words were pained. "I dislike it when you take on the mantle of being the pessimistic one."

"Realistic, for the moment. I fear I am not always capable of it, especially now. I know I frighten you, my feelings for you do."

William didn't deny it. There would be no point. His reactions were never truly hidden, not from Nicholas, who had grown to know him in ways others never would.

"We will work on this together, on breaking the unfortunate deal with Evera, as well. After all, we have to go to Faerie now. The disciples' trail leads there." Nicholas hated bringing up such a topic, but it was the truth.

"Shadowed disciples kidnapping mortals to take them to Faerie is worse than I imagined," William muttered. He didn't want to dwell on the prospect of slaying Nicholas, and Nicholas wouldn't force him to. They understood what may need to be done.

"We shouldn't focus too much on them being Fearworn's disciples. He is dead and it may not be as dark, or as deep, as we think it is."

"Or it's worse," said William.

He chuckled. "See? You are still the pessimistic one."

"I wish I wasn't. I wish they weren't starting trouble, potentially following in their master's footsteps." William's forehead creased and lips parted, then snapped shut. "Henry may know something."

"How so?"

"He has access to knowledge the public doesn't, including fae magic that has been shared during the war. Even with the Collision Treaty over, Henry spoke of fae continuing to visit magical societies. If there is something happening in Faerie, perhaps Henry unintentionally heard of it."

"Then you wish to speak to him on these matters?" asked Nicholas.

"It may better prepare us for what we might face. We should not speak of this to any others, though, to be safe." William stepped aside. Nicholas missed the sensation of his hand, but stayed in place. "I will have to conjure a believable lie to earn passage to Faerie."

"Why not take the scar we found in the sewer?"

"We do not know where in Faerie it leads. We may end up outnumbered by shadowed disciples."

"Ah, indeed." He shrugged. "We needn't worry about a reason. I know plenty of scars mortals are unaware of. We'll pass through one of them."

William cocked a brow. "And how do you know of these mysterious shimmers?"

He winked. "Fae should be allowed their secrets."

"They are secrets for fae to sneak into Terra and start trouble, aren't they?"

"Secrets, secrets." Nicholas laughed. "This is the first you will see of Faerie, isn't it?"

"It is," he replied.

"This trip will not only be for work, I hope. I wish for you to meet Hill Castle, the home I grew up in."

William clutched his right arm. "What of Laurent, and your siblings? Would it be a good idea for me to go?"

"Do not think of them. For now, I wish only to hear you say you will consider my requests from time to time in Faerie. That you will see my world, where I come from."

William gave a smile, true and breathtaking. "I would like that very much."

"Shall I see you tomorrow evening?"

"Yes, I should have talked to Henry by then." Then he heaved a long breath. "Nicholas, you cannot come to my home or office again, not when we aren't sure if this situation may repeat itself."

"Right. Of course." He hesitated in the doorway. "I am sorry, William, about Richard. I'm sorry."

William's voice trembled. "I know you are."

But that may not be enough.

17

WILLIAM

THE CLOSED SIGN HUNG on the window of the Gilded Lily. Charmaine gifted William a key when they opened. He often used it on evenings he knew he wouldn't sleep. That morning, he had another reason to enter.

He came through the back door leading to the workshop where Charmaine toiled most the days away. Just last year, they invested in a sewing machine that Charmaine slowly learned how to use. However, the chaotic counters revealed that she still relied on any other form of creation. The interior of the shop had a pedestal and a full-length mirror where Bessie took their patrons measurements, a seating area for those in line, and examples of all their offered materials along the walls to gawk over. If business kept up, they would have to expand. He had his brothers keeping their ears open for any news concerning a larger store front property on sale that would be on or closer to main street.

The scent of baked goods filled the shop. Bessie either cooked them herself or bought a batch from the bakery down the street. That rainy morning, freshly baked pancakes waited on the dining table of the second floor where Charmaine and her mother lived. Their apartment had been perfect, so Bessie claimed, with two modest bedrooms, a spacious kitchen with a breakfast nook, and a living room that looked over the street. The doors led onto a balcony big enough to stand on for a quick smoke, which he partook in more than either of them.

"William, oh, you should have let me know you would be coming." Bessie rose from the table, intending to step into the kitchen.

"Do not worry. I had breakfast already. I'm sorry to interrupt yours." He wanted to speak with Charmaine alone without bothering her during working hours.

The Gilded Lily became rather famous over the years. Many ladies wore their dresses and the more who wore them, the more society learned of the business. Charmaine didn't speak as proudly of her shop as William thought she should. However, he saw the note she kept on her dresser that declared The Gilded Lily would become a household name one day. The edges had faded over the years from the many times Charmaine picked it up to repeat the phrase, as if the chant would bring the future into fruition. He didn't doubt that future for a second.

"Don't be silly." Bessie patted the apron hugging her thick waist. When she smiled, her cheeks cushioned her eyes, slimming them into smiles of their own. "I've finished up. I am assuming you are here to discuss something?"

He nodded, then Bessie excused herself downstairs. While she prepared to open the shop, he took to cleaning the dishes. Charmaine finished her breakfast in silence, then sat her dish in the sink.

"What would you like to talk about?" she asked.

"I have a favor to ask," he said, feeling her intense attention all the while.

"Anything."

He settled the dishes into the wrack. "Will you check in at the clinic while I'm away?"

Charmaine leaned against the counter they had repainted when she first moved in. The apartment had furniture, much to her relief, although the furniture needed much love and care. He was more than happy to help. Cleaning up the place had kept both their minds too focused to think of anything else.

"Where are you going?" she asked skeptically.

He knew she wouldn't like what he had to say. He stalled by finishing up the dishes, feeling her scrutiny all the while. "Nicholas discovered the disciples were coming from Faerie. He, Evera, and I will follow their trail."

"Just you and two fae?" She barked out a harsh laugh. "You will not go without me."

He glanced at the steps. Bessie's voice came from below, chattering with a customer she let in early.

"Your mother cannot run this store on her own. Most importantly, I do not want you to come. This will be dangerous," he countered while Charmaine took to drying the dishes and setting them in the cupboards.

"Which is exactly why I will join you." She held up a hand, silencing him. "This is not up for debate, William. My mother is more than capable of handling the shop. I am always ahead and I will finish up more before we leave. Do not think for a moment that you may trick me. I will follow you, so I suggest you make this easier for yourself and accept it."

He didn't want Charmaine to get hurt, but deep down, he knew the more who helped, the better the outcome could be for his patients. For all of them. She had put a lot of work into helping until then. She would be distraught if he abandoned her to finish the job, and he understood that, but he nearly lost her once.

"If anything were to happen to you—"

"Something could happen to you, too," she interjected and flinched when she slammed a cup in the cupboard. Nothing broke, causing them both to sigh. Then she linked their arms. "We will do this together."

"It seems I have no say in any of this," he said, aggravated and only mildly relieved. "I'll gather supplies and I have a few things I must do. I will retrieve you from here in two days. Evera and Nicholas will lead the way to Faerie. They know of a shimmer we can take with no one knowing."

She shook her head. "Of course they do."

"If you'll excuse me, I have work to attend to before you coerce your way into even more trouble," he said, earning a tender smile from Charmaine.

"You certainly couldn't have expected this to go any differently," she said.

"I hoped you would understand and not have a death wish."

"One might argue you are the one with a death wish." She kissed his cheek. "I will see you in two days."

Downstairs, Bessie gave him a kiss too. He couldn't look her in the eye, knowing he was about to put Charmaine in danger. He told himself they would be alright. They battled Fearworn and survived, but all luck had to run out, eventually. It certainly felt like his ran out.

He returned home, but nothing was the same. Nicholas returned to him, but their future was bleaker than he ever imagined. Believing he lost Nicholas was tough. If he ever had to take Nicholas' life, he knew he couldn't do it as much as Nicholas believed otherwise. The utter fool.

Nothing worked out the way he wished it would. Perhaps that was his punishment from the Holy Soul.

He laughed at his own thoughts. He didn't believe in deity's, certainly didn't believe they cared about morality. If they did, the world wouldn't be so grim. Only creatures of malice would conceive of a world such as theirs and let atrocity after atrocity roll over the lands and its people, especially the ones least deserving of it.

Yet, the thought made an unpleasant sort of sense. He took the lives of monsters and monstrous men. Men, who had minds of their own, the capabilities of rationality and morality, but chose otherwise time and time again. Still, if the Souls were real, they would curse a man like him and, frankly, he felt he deserved it.

William took a carriage to Heign's Magical Society, located on the western side of the city, where businessmen scurried from their gentlemen's clubs to their banks and favorite liquor stores. The west side always reminded him of his father's office, smelling of liquor and cigars, until he came upon the magical society. That always had a pleasant aroma from the vast garden surrounding the estate. At eight stories high, the steeples threatened to scratch the stars from the skies. An unknown power kept the stones an awe-inspiring red, like the most sought after rubies.

The carriage pulled through the arched entryway carved from stone where depictions of mages stood as if to guard the society's secrets. The paved street lead into a courtyard encircled by benches where mages took to reading or shuffling around the columns with their arms full of books.

A pair of heavy doors stood open, granting access to everyone. However, he knew better; he may have the Sight and could walk the halls, but only the best of the best were truly welcome at Heign's Magical Society.

Alogan's public library housed the most basic knowledge of the Sight, but their genuine work remained hidden behind locked doors he could never imagine passing. Henry spoke of them, though never shared where they were even after Richard got wine into him. William always wondered if someone had somehow silenced the mages to prevent their secrets from spilling but, if that were true, he would never know.

The magical society wasn't as flashy as the king, though no one could deny the grandeur of the interior. Paintings depicting famous mages lined the walls and sculptures discovered from the ruins of Alogan sat beneath glass to be admired and protected.

A boy with a fuzzy mustache that wasn't quite grown right sat at a front desk. Piles of letters surrounded him as he sorted into compartments along the wall. He jumped when William called out to him. Wide brown eyes fell on him, slightly mortified, then relieved. The poor thing probably suspected a superior arrived, upset that their letter was late, or he didn't sit as properly as he should.

"Good morning, sir. How may I be of assistance?" The boy bowed his head.

"Good morning. My name is William Vandervult. My brother Henry Vandervult works here. May I speak with him?" In such a silent hall, his voice echoed.

"Ah, yes." The boy swept to an enormous book beneath the desk. He dropped the book on the table to flip through the pages. "He's on floor seven. Please, let me escort you to him."

The young mage scurried down the hall. The keys along his belt jangled, ricocheting off the walls, then the spiraling stairwell.

"You said he's on floor seven?" William peered up the steep stairwell that made him dizzy. There were no lanterns to light their path, only the windows that cut harsh shadows across the stairwell.

"Indeed." The boy smiled like walking seven flights wouldn't be a pain. He settled on the stairs, then pulled out a key. He realized William wasn't on the steps and grabbed his arm. "Please, step behind me, sir."

William did so, then gripped the railing after the boy put a key into a hole in the wall. With a turn, the stairs creaked and moved. They swung around, up and up, slowly but not as slowly as he needed. He pressed the back of his hand to his mouth, willing his breakfast to remain in his stomach. Then the stairs stopped. He'd have fallen if he weren't gripping the railing like his life depended on it.

"This way," the boy said with the nonchalance of one who had done that a thousand times.

The upstairs varied little from downstairs, save the many red oak doors. The names of mages scrawled across each one caught the chandelier light, glistening in gold. At Henry's door, the boy bowed and excused himself. That left William alone.

Henry wouldn't only have answers. There would be questions, too. Out of all his brothers, Henry was the last one he could ever possibly deceive. Arthur was the most gullible around his family because he couldn't fathom any of them having ill will. Richard could be deceived if one knew how to turn a phrase. Henry could sit in front of the best poker players in the land and call their bluffs.

William wouldn't bluff. He knocked.

"Come in."

He entered an office unlike their father's. Where Robert's office was meticulously clean, Henry's may have done better if a tornado ripped through. Papers covered the walls with crooked handwriting. Books piled high in every corner, some laid open, forgotten on the floor. A pair of large windows illuminated the office rather than the chandelier that hung unlit from a long chain. Henry sat on his desk, legs crossed, with a book in his lap and four more hovering around his head. Those four dropped with loud 'thunks' followed by Henry's surprised voice; "William? What are you doing here?"

He carefully maneuvered around Henry's chaos. He didn't know what half the items scattered about were, from crystals in the shapes of animals to items resembling jewels and ornaments teetering on the edge of shelves. Henry apparently thrived in an environment that could fall to pieces from the slightest breeze.

"I need to discuss a few things with you." He swatted at a piece of paper in the shape of a butterfly passing by his nose. "How do you work in this mess?"

Henry called upon the wind whenever he pleased after he discovered he had the Sight. Making objects float had been a favorite pastime, and an easy way to frighten his brothers in the middle of the night. Though they knew the curtains fluttering or a window open could have been Henry, in the silent dark, they often ran screaming anyway.

Henry laughed. "I work perfectly well in my mess, thank you very much. Now, what do you want to discuss? You never come to visit me at work."

Visiting was never on his agenda. Members of Heign's Magical Society spoke to him not long after he returned home. They had questions about his arm, how he survived, and what he witnessed, particularly with Nicholas and Fearworn. They hoped he had better knowledge of what happened, but he proved disappointing, and frankly, he wouldn't have shared. The questions were invasive. They saw him as an object in the same way the king did, a specimen to study and believed he would understand because it was for science. He didn't fault Henry for that, but it made him hesitant to risk a visit, considering who else he may run into.

He didn't know how to tell Henry he was leaving. He hadn't determined how to tell their parents, either.

"It seems this discussion will not be a pleasant one, either." Henry pushed himself off the desk where papers crunched beneath his boots.

"My missing patients are being taken to Faerie," William said, because being blunt was the only option he could think of.

Based on his darkened expression, Henry caught on quickly. "Meaning you will follow them, and their captors, to Faerie."

"Yes."

"Do our parents know about this?"

He wished not to tell them at all. All he could do was give a lie that would make his departure easier. Should Matilda know he might have to battle shadowed disciples again, that Fearworn could be involved, and he'd be in Faerie, land that all of Terra feared, she would be beyond distraught. Henry knew that too.

"Not yet," he muttered.

"So you have come to your dear older brother because he has more experience with Faerie."

"I hoped you would have information that may help us. Shadowed disciples took them, Henry. Something is going on and I fear what it may be."

"How did shadowed disciples make it into Alogan? My colleagues set up protection. We should know if they cross our borders," said Henry urgently.

"Nicholas said there is a shimmer in the sewer, one we never knew of."

Henry stroked his chin. "Strange. You must have Nicholas tell me where. It will have to be monitored. Now, what is it you wish to learn from me?"

"That's it?" He hardly resisted the urge to twiddle his thumbs. "You are not upset that I'm leaving? No lecture or attempts to convince me otherwise?"

"Upset that you are risking your life for your patients?" Henry replied around a laugh that rumbled in the back of his throat. "That is so very like you. I couldn't possibly be upset. Besides, there is no point telling you no. Once you set your mind to something, you will see it through, and my best bet is to help in every way I can to ensure your quick and safe return."

William appreciated that. It would be one less person to be upset with him. "You've been in contact with fae even after the end of the treaty. If you know anything concerning peculiar magic, even if they are rumors, I would appreciate it."

Henry laid his hands on the desk behind him, leaning slightly. "That is a tough question. There is much more magic in this world than most believe, particularly from Faerie. Their magic is wild and dangerous in ways they don't even fathom, more likely because they aren't so inquisitive about it. They accept everything as it is while we mortals want to pick everything apart."

"To be more specific, then, have you seen or heard anything of magic requiring people? Sacrifices perhaps?" he asked. "I can't imagine why else they would take my patients to Faerie."

Henry's frown spoke before he did. "Yes, there are many acts in Faerie requiring a life, blood rituals of sort. Most have to do with empowering oneself or their land, but if shadowed disciples are involved, this likely has to do with Fearworn." Henry stepped past him to inspect the hall. He shut the door and came to William's side. "You cannot speak of this outside of my office. Do you understand?"

He nodded tensely.

"There is an entire team dedicated to studying shimmers. We know so little about them. They can be volatile, but some believe a powerful surge of energy, like magic or souls, however we wish to describe it, could open further pathways. It could have been how Fearworn achieved it, sacrificing his disciples, beasts, or both. These disciples very well may continue their master's work, attempting to open more after his demise."

Bile rose in his throat. He forced it down with a hard gulp. "Does the king know of this?"

Henry laughed, distant and cold. "His Majesty remains updated on all we learn here. Trust that he is aware and trust that he does not want to consider the possibility of disciples continuing their master's work, especially after the war was declared over. Imagine how the public might react? There would be riots and fear. The fae lords don't want it, either. They rather remain ignorant until there is proof they cannot ignore."

"Meaning I have to go to Faerie and find that proof myself."

"Unfortunately." Henry scurried around his desk in search of something. "When are you leaving, and who is going with you?"

"Charmaine roped herself into it."

Henry snickered, sounding far too proud of her.

"Evera Bloodbane and Nicholas Darkmoon, as well. He knows of a shimmer we can pass through without being caught. We leave in two days."

"Darkmoon," Henry repeated while tearing through his desk. "The one I met and who slayed Fearworn?"

His cheeks warmed. He internally cursed them for doing so. "Yes."

"You have a valuable ally." Henry retrieved a green crystal little bigger than his thumb and threw it. William narrowly caught the gem. "Take that with you."

He examined the crystal. "Why? What is it?"

"A mage of far higher caliber than I made that with the help of a fae," Henry explained. "So long as you have that on you, I can find you, so if you're gone too long, I will drag you back."

William dropped the crystal in his pocket, swearing that Henry wouldn't make use of it. "How sweet of you."

"Aren't I always?"

A knock rapped at the door. Henry's eyes brightened, delighted.

"Oh, that must be my delivery." He skipped around his mess without causing an avalanche. William found that in itself magical.

Throwing open the door, a young woman smiled jovially on the other side. She wore a plain blue dress with a fresh coat of pale pink lipstick that matched the dusting of color beneath her cheeks. In her arms, she held a package of books, based on the shape.

"Good afternoon, Lord Vandervult." She stuck a lock of auburn hair behind her ear.

"Good afternoon, Miss Thomson." Henry took a package from her grasp. Her hand stroked his. Henry signed a paper, signaling he retrieved his package before returning the paper to her. "Thank you once again for such a speedy delivery. I hardly have to wait at all when you're in charge."

"Oh, it isn't a problem." Miss Thomson giggled, her pink cheeks darkening red.

"Good day, then." Henry smiled and Miss Thomson nearly swooned, but he shut the door and ripped into his package of books.

William tried not to grin. "Who was that?"

Henry proudly added four new books to his desk, somehow not toppling anything over. "Miss Thomson? She's a clerk employed by the society. When we need something specific, we can go to her. She's as speedy as they come."

"Yes, she seems exceptionally dedicated to getting your packages to you."

"I suppose so. It is her job."

"Henry." He gestured toward the door. "Did you not see how she looked at you?"

Henry glanced between the door and his younger brother. "She looked no different from usual."

"She was red in the face."

Henry looked at the teapot on his desk beside a half-empty cup of the beverage. "Ah, the poor girl must be in a rush. I should have offered her tea."

William mirrored his brother's expression. "Blushing, Henry, she was blushing. She likes you."

"Excuse you?" Henry checked the books individually, then took two to put on the shelves.

"Anyone could see it. She seems rather keen on you."

"Oh." The bridge of Henry's nose wrinkled. He glanced between the door and William before asking, "Whatever for? We hardly talk."

"But she must want to. You should invite her to tea outside of the tower."

"I'd rather not."

William didn't expect his brother to be so blunt. He didn't know what to say.

"Romance and the like. I have no interest in it, truthfully." Henry shrugged nonchalantly. "The future I see for myself is one of science and discovery. I suppose you and I have that in common, our futures differing from what our parents might expect."

Henry wasn't looking at him. He inspected one of his books as if he hadn't knocked the breath from William's lungs. He couldn't speak, couldn't look away from Henry, who read him as easily as the book in his grasp.

"Whatever do you mean?" William whispered, sounding like a child again, frightened and paranoid.

The corner of Henry's lips curled. "You don't need to hide the truth from me. I know if Miss Thomson was after you, you wouldn't be that interested, either. I don't mean to alarm you by bringing it up, but what I'm trying to say is, I get it. We're not exactly the same, but we want different things and that makes us stand out."

He didn't expect that and wondered if it was alright that he loved to hear it. He felt like the odd one out, but maybe he wasn't so odd anymore, and maybe it was okay to want that.

"Then you don't want marriage or children, either?" he asked.

"By the Souls, no. I adore Alice and I am excited to meet Eleanor and Richard's child, but I do not want any of my own, nor do I want to walk down the aisle. I'm not entirely closed off to the prospect of a relationship, something of mutual trust and understanding, but I can't see myself as infatuated with someone as the rest." Henry shuffled his weight from one foot to the other. "Do not tell anyone about that. You are the first person I've ever said anything about it to."

"Because I would get it?"

"I hoped you would," Henry muttered, sounding timid for once.

"I do."

"Good." Henry cleared his throat. "Sorry for holding you up. I imagine you have a lot of work to attend to."

"Not as much as I normally would. The king was ever so kind to hire another doctor for the clinic. I won't have to worry as much about leaving."

"That's relieving." Henry caught him by the shoulders to give a fierce hug. That time felt different in the best of ways. He wanted to tell his family one day about who he loved, but that had always been such a distant prospect, something that felt out of reach no matter what he did. But now Henry knew and accepted him and was a little different, too. It brought about a light in his darkened days that he never expected.

"Stay out of trouble," said Henry.

"I will do my best."

18

WILLIAM

Matilda tended to the garden, where she enjoyed plucking weeds and speaking to the flowers. She believed they would grow more beautifully when given love through words. William once tended regularly to those flowers alongside her where they spun tales, like bedtime stories made specifically for the garden. If he had such an imagination, he lost it years ago. But at least there, she would be the most comfortable, so William took the opportunity.

"Mother," he called hesitantly.

"Oh, you're out early this morning." She gestured for him to join her.

He knelt. With his gloves on, he was always prepared to pull weeds. He added a handful to the bucket behind them, wishing that was all he was there to do. He always suffered sleeping, but last night was worse than usual. Nothing eased him into comfort, so instead, he laid in the dark, considering how to break the news to his mother. No scenario ended well.

"Is there something you want to discuss? You're never out this early with me." Matilda had joy in her eyes, a hopeful gleam he hated to snuff out.

"There is." But he couldn't bring himself to say it.

He hadn't wanted to leave home since his return, even if he worried his presence caused more harm than good. Matilda worried about him traveling to town after his return. She followed him around the house, trying to make up for the years lost. He had no complaints.

But now he had to leave, and she would not take that news well. He thought of every reason he could give, the kindest way to tell her the truth. Nothing fit. The moment he mentioned leaving, even if he conjured a lie less frightening than the truth, Matilda would panic and there was no telling what could comfort her.

"Well, what is it?" she asked.

"There is potential news concerning my missing patients that requires my attention. However, it will take me to the countryside," he replied hesitantly.

Matilda's hands halted in their work.

"The king has kindly brought in another doctor to oversee the clinic while I take a short time to travel." He hated lying to her, but telling her he's going to Faerie wasn't an option. She may tie herself to him and force him to take her.

"A short time?" Her breathing turned ragged. "How short?"

"I'm not sure yet."

Her ripping of the weeds became frantic. "Then it may not be short. How long will you be gone?"

"It's for work. I'll be perfectly safe."

"You don't know that." She grabbed the weed bucket and lunged to her feet. Her heels clicked against the stone path. "What if you're gone for a year or more? What if there's trouble, if it's dangerous? You just got home!"

"I have been home for two years."

"And they took you for five!" Matilda's back went rigid, then she spun on him. Tears brimmed in her eyes. "Ask someone else to go. You have plenty of work here."

"Mama," he whispered.

"You can't go. I won't allow it. Absolutely not." She stormed toward the house, past Robert, standing in the doorway. He overheard and looked after his wife, but wouldn't look his son in the eye. His body swayed between following Matilda or approaching William. Then he sighed.

"Must you go?" Robert asked.

William thought of Nicholas, how he so easily noticed Robert refusing to look at him. An itch formed beneath his skin. He scratched, gloves creaking from the frantic movements of his fingers.

"Yes, it's important," he replied through clenched teeth.

Robert wanted to argue. William always noticed that now, the slight tension in his father's shoulders when someone said something he didn't agree with. He wished Robert would say something, if only to encourage himself to look at William and truly see him.

"Then I shall speak to her," he said, leaving William disappointed. "When are you leaving?"

"Tomorrow morning," he answered.

"Have you told your brothers and Alice? She will be distraught if you leave without saying goodbye."

"I think it's best that I don't." He worried they would talk him out of it, or see through his lies. At least this way, Alice would learn through her parents and he wouldn't break under the pressure of her tears.

Robert frowned. "Well, we should spend today together, then. It will ease your mother."

"Will it ease you?" He hadn't meant to ask that, nor do so with such bite.

"Nothing will make your leaving any easier, especially when we aren't sure how long you will be gone."

His hands clenched, irritated by the admission that he couldn't tell if it was a lie or not. How could he believe his father wouldn't be relieved by his absence when, for two years, Robert wouldn't look at him? He felt like a plague in his own home, gliding through the halls to erode whatever he touched.

"Are you certain my departure won't relieve you a little?" he asked, jaw tight enough to make his teeth ache.

"Why would you ask something like that?" Robert frowned, but that was it. William's blood boiled. He wasn't angry, only hurt.

"How could I not?" He approached, so Robert no doubt saw him from the corner of his eye. The man remained perfectly still, facing away from a son who craved his attention enough that he felt mad. "Look at me!" he screamed, voice breaking.

Robert finally did, but his expression broke instantly. His eyes darkened, swelling with tears that didn't shed. His hand shook atop his cane and William's heart broke and screamed and cried, wondering why his father couldn't stand the sight of him.

"Have I done wrong? Ever since I returned, you cannot bear to look at me. Have I disappointed you?" he whimpered.

A tear fell to drip off Robert's chin. "No, William, no."

"I am not the son you remember. I returned broken and you cannot stand the sight of me."

Robert reached out a hand. "That isn't it at all."

He retreated. "Isn't it? You needn't lie to me. I cannot stand the sight of me, either. I hate who I have become and so desperately wish I could return to the boy you and Mother and my brothers so loved. I am trying, Father, as hard as I can."

Robert grasped his shoulders, then his shaking hands fell upon his cheeks. He clutched his father's wrists, feeling every shake and unsure of who they belonged to.

"You misunderstand," Robert said, tears shaping his cheeks. "And it is my fault. I have done wrong by you, more than I could ever make up for."

"You have never done wrong by me."

"I have," he insisted.

William had never seen him look so lost. Robert had been their family's greatest foundation for most of their lives. When his grandparents died, Robert made sure his grieving wife and family had everything they could ever need. When Robert lost his parents, he didn't hide his sorrow because he wanted his family to know it was okay to mourn. If the king made a call he didn't agree with, Robert stood his ground, and if the boys ever bickered, their father was there to set things right.

"I am the reason you were taken and forced to live through all that you did, and it is my greatest shame," Robert whispered.

"That was the king," he argued.

Robert's tone carried regret. "I stood up to the king knowing he could hurt us, but I should have expected he would have gone after you. I shouldn't have said anything."

He knew Robert carried guilt, but not to such an extent, and he wished he wouldn't. "If you hadn't, no one would. I do not want you to regret speaking sense to him. You have done well by all of us, by people who will never know you because you care, and that makes me proud."

"I am glad for that, but it doesn't absolve me of this," he slammed a hand against his chest, hard enough to bruise. "This guilt I feel every time I see you flinch or wake in the night screaming or how you hesitate to walk into every room until you know all your exits."

William sucked in a breath.

"I have picked up the little things you do day by day," Robert explained. "And I dare not ask why you do it. I doubt I would understand even if you explained because I will never fathom what you went through, and that pains me all the more. As your father, I am meant to protect you, to give you the best life. Instead, I have given you pain like no other."

"I wish you wouldn't blame yourself for that," he said.

"And I wish you would know how grateful we all are to have you home, that we love you."

He couldn't breathe for a moment, then his words came out a whimper, "If you knew all I had done, you would think differently."

"I wouldn't," Robert interjected, stern and true. "You survived and survival is often cruel. I don't care what you did, so long as it led you back to us." Robert pulled him in before his first tear fell. He held with a fierce grip that William returned. "I am sorry. I never thought you would think like that."

His jaw trembled as he buried his head in the crook of his father's neck. He felt like that boy again, running to his dad after a nightmare, safe and secure in a pair of arms he believed could take on the world.

"I will get your mother." Robert followed his wife, leaving William in the garden.

He knelt by the flowerbed to continue Matilda's work. The staff would have done so, but he needed to keep his mind off the conversation Robert would have with Matilda. He need not be there to know her tears, her desperate pleas to keep him home, and the shakes. They were awful and were no longer only for him.

It's as if his appearance opened the floodgates. Matilda had this need for all her children to be home. Perhaps to have her family together as it once was. When the boys left, even if it was to reside in their own homes, Matilda's hands shook terribly. She'd wake in the middle of the night, worried that she wouldn't see her sons soon or ever again.

The war hurt many in ways none could fathom.

He stayed in the garden for a long while before Robert retrieved him. Breakfast was ready and they would eat together. William dreaded seeing Matilda after, no doubt, a tough conversation. He tried to ignore her sniffles throughout breakfast, trying not to focus on how red her eyes had become from tears. They did as Robert suggested and spent the day together, acting like nothing was changing.

William and Matilda worked on a knitting project in the library for a while. Little was said, and he wasn't sure if that was a good or bad sign. He merely did his best to comfort his mother throughout the day. She hadn't mentioned him staying. By the evening, she kissed him goodnight when saying, "Be careful."

"I'll be home as soon as I can. I promise," he swore.

That did little good. Matilda whimpered and hurried to her room for a night of unrest. William wouldn't have slept even if he tried. He spent the night ensuring he had enough supplies packed, including food, water, herbs, and rolls of cannabis. He hoped he wouldn't have to use them, but considering what they were doing and where they were going, that hope meant nothing. The supplies sat in the foyer while he went to his room, where he tossed and turned during the remaining twilight.

Then the sun rose, and he went downstairs. He double checked his belongings, including the worn satchel he hadn't planned to use again. That satchel saved many lives throughout the war. Days after he woke in the hospital, he had the energy to look through his belongings. The satchel laid there, bloodied among his worn clothes. He never had the heart to toss it because, as many poor memories that it carried, there were good ones, too. Times when he made it in time to spare a life, saw them walking around camp a week later as if nothing happened.

The satchel became one of the few things from the war that he didn't mind carrying. However, deep down, he didn't believe the bag would be of any help. Shadowed disciples took his patients, and certainly not for good reason. They would probably bring home corpses, but he swung the bag over his shoulder, anyway.

He gave the stairs one last look, relieved that no one was there. If Matilda saw him leaving, she may try to stop him, so he left quietly.

Outside, Marshall had the horse and carriage ready. He also told William to be careful before heading inside. At the end of the road, two figures appeared. Nicholas and Evera didn't have packs with them. He should have expected as such but still snorted. They'd be nagging him for snacks and drinks later.

As he loaded the few supplies they could carry, Nicholas came up behind him to kiss his neck. "I missed you."

"Is that truly the first thing you have to say to me today?" he asked.

"It is because it is true. I dislike spending even a minute away from you." Nicholas hopped onto the driver's bench. Evera sat on the roof, letting her legs hang over the side. Nicholas offered his hand, smiling. "Let our adventure begin."

"This is hardly an adventure," he replied, but took Nicholas' hand.

The fae tugged him onto the bench, where William grabbed the reins. The carriage traveled through the waking streets of Alogan, where people waddled to their workshops and bakeries. Charmaine waited outside The Gilded Lily in a pair of pants and traveling boots, neither of which he had seen on her for the last two years. Yawning, she offered a half hearted good morning prior to crawling into the carriage. Shockingly, Evera followed.

Nicholas knocked William's hands aside to take the reins. "I'll take it from here."

"Where are we headed exactly?" he asked.

"Outside the city. We should reach the scar before the sun sets."

"What will it be like going through the shimmer?" he asked.

"Like swimming through water," Nicholas replied. "You must be careful not to go downstream."

"What does that mean?"

"You can get lost. Even if you feel a tug, do not follow it. Actually," Nicholas glanced behind them toward the carriage. "It would be best if we go through hand in hand, so no one gets lost."

He didn't like the sound of that. He never heard of anyone getting lost. Then again, he didn't know many who passed through shimmers.

Nicholas' driving skills were questionable. The horse sped up and slowed at random intervals, typically due to him being distracted by their surroundings. He hadn't left Alogan since his arrival, so being outside the city intrigued him. He kept asking what languages the trees spoke, then got disappointed upon realizing they couldn't talk.

They traversed back roads so rocky the carriage swayed. If William had eaten more than a roll for breakfast, he would have gotten ill. Instead, he clung painfully to the bench and willed his brain not to spill out his ears.

Nicholas jerked the reins. Someone in the carriage shrieked. He would have fallen off if Nicholas weren't beside him. A wild laugh escaped the fae when they went off the road, flying between trees and brush. Charmaine threatened to get sick from Nicholas' careless driving. That encouraged the fae to make it worse, ripping through the trees to make the carriage wheels shriek with every turn. The carriage didn't slow until almost noon. They came to an abrupt halt that nearly sent William off the bench.

"Here we are!" Nicholas jumped down and pushed aside a bush to reveal the shimmer, little more than a thin line of blue light between the trees. One would struggle to find it if they didn't know its exact location.

"Finally." Charmaine dropped out of the carriage to kiss the ground. "He is never driving again."

Pouting, Nicholas argued, "I got us here unharmed."

"My stomach is harmed."

Nicholas glanced at William to save him, which he would not do. "You are a reckless driver," he said.

Nicholas clicked his tongue. "I'm underappreciated."

"Aren't we all?" Henry asked, causing William and Charmaine to curse. Evera and Nicholas didn't look surprised.

He thought he hallucinated his brother riding up behind them. He waited for the inevitable change, the melting of reality, colors fading to black and Fearworn clawing out of the shadows. But nothing happened save Henry closing in. A bag hung over his horse's rump.

Henry descended, clutching a stuffed satchel against his side. He wore a dark gray cloak, hood up, and a pair of slightly worn boots. William reached out, that time hoping his mind to be playing tricks, that his hand would pass through Henry's mirage. Instead, his fingers landed upon Henry's arm, firm and real.

His expression hardened to stone. "Why are you here?"

"Because I'm coming with you." Henry retrieved the supplies from his horse to swing the pack over his shoulder.

"Absolutely not." He laughed coldly. "You are heading home. Now." Henry made no move to obey. Snarling, William ran a hand through his hair. "How did you follow us?"

Henry retrieved a crystal from his pocket, the one he told William to carry. "I said I could find you anywhere with this."

"In the case of an emergency. Not to join us!" He turned his attention to Nicholas. "Did you know he was following?"

Nicholas nodded.

"Why didn't you tell me?"

"I thought he was coming with us," he answered earnestly.

"I never said he was, and he isn't joining us. You are staying here." He grabbed the pack, but Henry held firm.

"William." Henry settled his hands on his brother's shoulders. He winced. Henry had his hand on silver. Even with clothes separating them, he couldn't stand anyone touching that.

"You went to war on your own. I'm not letting you go through this without me," said Henry.

"And I am not letting you go with me. I won't risk your life. You can't..." He caught his tongue between his teeth, tasting copper.

Henry couldn't see the side of him created by war, which he would no doubt have to show while in search of the disciples. Ever since his return, he struggled to maintain a careful performance, one as close to the son and brother they lost as possible. Not the monster he became. He didn't want any of them to know what he truly went through, what he was not only willing but also more than capable of doing.

"I am going with you," Henry said sternly. "You can either let me join you here or I'll find you on my own. Your choice."

Nicholas came from behind to speak against William's ear. "Let him join us."

He wanted to argue, but he caught Charmaine's apologetic smile in his peripheral vision. She wanted Henry along, or at least understood that they were stronger as a group. He knew that, too. Another mage would be of great use, especially Henry, who had earned the attention of a magical society. But they asked William to put his brother in danger after he fought so long to keep his family safe.

Henry's hands fell, one to tighten around the strap of his pack and the other to lie upon his satchel. "If it makes you feel better, I won't leave your sight."

That did not ease him in any form. He and Charmaine now shared an affliction; sickness to the gut. Bile rose in his throat. A childish urge said to chuck the crystal into the wilds. But Henry said he would follow them, one way or the other. William would rather his brother be at his side than wandering the wilds of Faerie alone.

"I will let you join on conditions," he said. "If I say to run, you run, and if I tell you to return home without us, you will return home."

Henry had an argumentative air about him, but he gave in with a sigh. "I accept your terms."

"Alright." He yanked the supplies from the carriage to pass off, then nodded at Nicholas. "Let's go."

Nicholas approached the shimmer. His presence caused the faded blue light to brighten, sensing a presence.

"Be warned, the first passing will feel strange, as if you've fallen into a river. Let it carry you. Don't fight the flow. If you hear or see anything, ignore it. Keep your eyes ahead and move," the shade explained.

Nicholas took William's hand, interlocking their fingers. Henry had to take William's hand, making his teeth grind. He didn't want anyone touching his right hand, but there was nothing to be done. Henry also grabbed Charmaine, and she latched onto a grinning Evera.

Nicholas stepped forward, hand outstretched. The shimmer expanded at the brush of his finger. Like a snake feeding, the shimmer stretched, opening as it needed for the bodies passing through. Nicholas disappeared within the now blinding light. William was next to be consumed. He held his breath and tensed when he felt it; the submersion.

The strange sensation passed over him, warmth and water except he was bone dry. The light dimmed and, in front of him, was Nicholas' silhouette, nothing more. There was no beginning or end, no up or down, left or right. The group walked forward, or tried to, within an ocean of glistening blue, like a mirror's reflection. Emptiness below his feet made his steps sway. Nicholas' grip tightened, as did Henry's. His brother's voice became warped, too high pitched, *"Look...Will...panic."*

He couldn't understand what they said. He focused on their connection, Henry and Nicholas' hands. They didn't feel right, too soft, too cold. He swore they were slipping away, fading through his fingers.

"William." That voice was clear; Hugh. He stood among the blue, cheeks colored pink, eyes bright, his smile wide to show off his slightly crooked teeth that William always found charming. Hugh was unbelievably alive. He held out a calloused hand and smiled. "William."

He's not real, he told himself over and over. He focused on Nicholas' hand, tried to think of how it truly felt, heated and smooth, like he didn't know a day's hard work. All the while, Hugh called over and over, a siren seeking prey.

Please end. Please end. Please end, he pleaded, finding the vastness of the space somehow constrictive, as if he were drowning.

Another figure formed, this one shorter, smaller, familiar long before William peered into his own eyes. The young boy, not ruined by war, stood there brighter than a star. He laughed. The sound tugged at William's heartstrings because it sounded real, like him, like who he was meant to be. His younger self held out his hand, didn't even say a word, but William felt it; *come here and you will become who you were meant to be.*

That's all he wanted, and the want moved him. He released Henry and reached. His younger self took his wrist before William could think better. The form held tight, then his sweet smile morphed into a sneer, and they fell into darkness.

19

NICHOLAS

NICHOLAS HELD WILLIAM'S HAND, then his feet fell out from under him. Light and noise overwhelmed his senses. Worlds beyond worlds passed before his eyes, sights of green seas, orange skies, and fields of ash. Then, through it all, the tug of home, of Faerie.

They hadn't strayed far from the path. He imagined himself in the sunflower field with William by his side. They bathed in sunlight, slept atop the petals between the stalks, bathing in the other's warmth. Then he couldn't see, blinded by a bright light, and he crashed against a hard surface. His limbs ached, but he clutched William's hand, warm, twitching, alive. A thin coat of sweat coated his body. He tasted the saltiness of it on his lips.

"William," he rasped. "Are you injured?"

No one answered.

Coughing, he rolled onto his knees. His vision returned in splotches; the world interrupted by brief intervals of black. Between that black were spots of gold, William's hair, then his flushed cheeks. He ran his knuckles along William's temples. Those spring eyes fluttered open. William leaned against him, chest rising and falling sporadically, then slowly.

"What happened?" William whispered while licking his lips.

"The scar took us on an unexpected adventure." And he hadn't discovered where that adventure led them yet.

They laid bunched up like dirty laundry in the corner. Branches hung low, their leaves a pale blue and bark an off gray. They stained the ground so beautifully, perfectly still that time itself felt unfurled around them. The woods made no sound, no birds sang, or breeze whispered through the branches. It was as if the forest had died eons ago and what stood had frozen on its last dying breath. Worry settled, followed by fear upon realizing where they had landed, the only place they could be.

"The Lost Woods," he whispered, and the woods echoed them. He kept a hand on William, fearful the ground may swallow them if only to preserve its silence. Then he pushed aside grass and leaves to find no stones. Fear coiled in his gut. "We're not on the path."

"Your tone says that doesn't bode well for us," said William, still catching his breath.

"It does not. Once you lose your way, The Lost Woods take you forever, if you are lucky."

"And if you're unlucky?"

He whispered so the woods may not hear the words. "You feed The One Who Waits."

The forest trembled as if it were a living being, its heart racing at the name of its master.

"What's that?" William asked, sounding as fearful as he should be.

"A sleepless entity. One that rules these woods, always has. Even my father doesn't dare tread off the path, rarely dares to take it, in fact."

Nicholas certainly never had and never planned to. Mortals feared monsters in the closet or under the bed. Fae feared the entities so ancient they lost their true names, forgotten even to themselves. Laurent saw the first mountains formed, but these creations were before them, had become them, became the land itself and did what they wanted according to rules none knew save them.

The Lost Woods weaved itself through Faerie. Only one path had ever been laid. Dozens of tales explained why or who had done so. Some tales claimed The One Who Waits laid the path itself to lure fae through the woods, letting them believe they could escape. Then it would trick them off the path for an easy meal. Others believed the first fae battled The One Who Waits and locked it away in the woods, leaving a path to find their way and defend against the entity, should it ever try to escape.

He didn't care about either. He cared about getting them out of there alive, no matter the cost. None had ever done so. He knew of a few fools who dared the forest in stupid attempts to prove themselves. They never returned, and some used the forest as a burial ground. If a fae got on the wrong side of another, it wasn't entirely unusual for them to be thrown into the forest, where they would disappear forever.

However, between the terror, he sensed something else. Faerie felt wrong. He couldn't explain why other than calling the thought a gut feeling. A scent carried in the air of decay, brought in by a silent breeze.

"Then I suggest we get a move on. I imagine the longer we're here, the more likely we are to run into this creature." William rose, thus releasing his hand. William inspected their surroundings that were nothing more than tall trees and a ground covered in leaves.

"Yes, we should do that." He chose not to mention the stories. They had to attempt an escape. He would rip the trees from their roots and battle The One Who Waits if it meant sparing William.

He reached for William's hand again, the silver one. William stuck his hand in his pocket.

"We must stick together. The forest will not treat us kindly," he explained. He didn't trust the gnawing feeling at the bottom of his gut, either. The Lost Woods had an eerie atmosphere, but there was something else there that he couldn't decipher.

William shambled to his opposite side and held his hand. He kept any comments to himself. William so hated that silver arm and he wasn't sure how to change that, or if he ever could.

"We should keep speaking to a minimum as well. It likely knows we're here, but just in case," he added, and William nodded.

Hand in hand, they set off in search of the path or an escape, whichever would reveal itself first. Leaves crunched beneath William's boots. He flinched at every noise. The crunching echoed, swirling around them, hissing through the trees. William tiptoed, doing little to help.

"Get on my back," Nicholas offered and kneeled. "No arguing. We must be quiet."

William didn't argue, but he glared and Nicholas swore he heard every argument William could ever give. He didn't want to be carried out of the forest. He worried Nicholas would grow tired. He never wanted to be a burden, but Nicholas didn't see him as one. He deserved protection and care, which Nicholas could give and wanted to.

William's chest fell against Nicholas' back, his warmth foreign and familiar. Nicholas wanted nothing more than to bask in the sensation of William being so close, feeling William's breath on his nape and his thighs caught beneath Nicholas' fingers. It was wondrous, like a dream that he played over a thousand times since their separation.

He bit the inside of his cheek and kept moving, searching this way and that. The trees spanned for an eternity, perfectly situated in diagonal lines, and yet led nowhere. At least nothing had been led to them. There were no birds upon the branches, rabbits in the bushes, or insects crawling through the rotting leaves. They were entirely alone.

As he walked, William's breathing grew heavier. His grip tightened, then twitched. Nicholas cast a worried glance. William peered into the forest, between the trees, recognizing something Nicholas did not see.

"William," he whispered, but his voice did nothing to steady William's frantic breaths. They became erratic, his sweat so heavy that his hair turned dark. He pressed a hand against Nicholas' back and squirmed. Something was very wrong, and it affected William rather than him.

"William, take a breath." He kept a firm hold on the man, but William kept squirming, then kicking, and finally slipped free.

Nicholas caught his silver hand and knew William was too lost to realize where they were because he didn't so much as flinch. The medic swayed like he was drunk, pointing, then shaking, then stepping away.

"You're dead. You're all dead." William's eyes swerved from left to right, as if they were surrounded.

"You're hallucinating," he said.

The forest's magic toyed with William far more than him. An aroma sweeter than honey filled his nostrils, and he imagined it rattled William's head.

"You deserved it. You were monsters! I'm not the monster! I'm not... I can't be..." William's voice echoed through the trees, unbelievably loud in the forest's reticence. He tore free from Nicholas to run his fingers through his hair, then tear at it. "No, no, not me. Not me. I was scared. It was wrong. I know. I'm sorry!"

He caught William by the elbow, wanting to relax him, but did the opposite. William caught sight of him, of his eyes, and a fear like no other overtook him. Expression blanched, William shoved him off and ran into the forest.

"Wait, fuck, William!" He lurched after William, the poor man losing himself completely to the forest.

William's panted breath sounded like the trees themselves grasping out for them. His figure grew smaller and smaller, making Nicholas feel like he stood still. The Lost Woods wanted to steal William, to keep him forever. He wouldn't let that happen.

He fell to his knees, fingers shoved in the dirt. Roots breached the soil. They fought against his demands, too stubborn to bend to another. The power within surged, scratching through his center. He forced his will into the earth itself until it melded to his desires. A dozen roots wrapped around William's ankles. He dropped, then was dragged, as much as Nicholas hated to do so. William slid to a stop, his nails clawing helplessly at the soil.

"Get away. You're dead. You're dead!" William broke out in a cold sweat when Nicholas laid a hand on his arm. William didn't see him. He saw Fearworn, clawing at him fruitlessly, trying to protect his arm. "It's mine. You can't have it."

"I'm not trying to take anything. It's me, my wicked," Nicholas said, unsure of what to do. He caught William by the waist to bring them into a sitting position. He buried his face in the crook of William's neck, hiding his damned eyes.

"You can't take my other arm," William wheezed, clutching the arm already taken.

"I won't," he whispered. "I'm not here to take anything."

William struggled a moment more, his breathing so labored Nicholas feared his heart would give out. He didn't know what to do when William broke into a sweat. He shook so horribly that his eyes rolled into the back of his head. Nicholas had witnessed nothing like it, fearful that he'd lose William to his own mind.

"Look at me," he said desperately, reminded of that day on the field where William bled out. "Look at me. What do I do?"

He didn't answer. He couldn't, trembling in Nicholas' desperate hold, breathing so labored his lips nearly went blue. Then he sank against Nicholas, where his heart rate slowly steadied. William laid his cheek against Nicholas' and leaned into him entirely.

"We need to get out of here. There has to be a way out. We have to escape." William gnawed at his bloody lip.

"First, you must calm down," he warned.

"There is no calming down. Everything is a mess." William bellowed, speaking as if possessed, "I survived, but I don't feel like I did. Some days,

I wish I didn't, and then I see those who died, people I killed, people I lost, like Hugh, who would have lived far happier than me and I wish we exchanged places."

His hold on William tightened, wishing he had never heard his wicked say such things.

"Shadowed disciples have my patients. Fearworn is involved. That rat bastard must ruin us even now. My patients are likely being used, tortured, or already dead and nobody fucking cares. Then there's you." William sat up taller, retreating from Nicholas enough to gaze down at him. He hesitated to meet William's eyes, such a fierce sorrow he tasted the pain like decay.

"You show up and you're different and it's my fault. You make me question everything. For two years, I was hurt and felt more alone than ever. I never wanted to see you again, then I would have given anything to see you again. I wanted to scream at you, then I wanted to hold you. I don't know what I want. I don't know what to do. I hate that I cannot help you, that I'm the cause of..." William's eyes flooded with tears he refused to shed.

"This has always been my fate, with or without you," he said with a gentle caress against William's cheek. "I am relieved my fate is tied to you. At least I will always have this part of my life, the love for you I had before and now."

"Before? Nicholas, you're..."

"Unwell, yes, but I would not have become like this if I did not love you before. It was that love that pushed me to the edge and I wish you would not blame yourself for it. You cannot fix what is broken in a day. The shadowed disciples, your patients, they will be dealt with. I will deal with them, if it will make you happy. We know what to do and we have a journey ahead of us, both of us. But right now," he caught William by the chin and brushed his thumb against William's bottom lip. "Let us get lost in one another."

William released a sad laugh, but his hands fell upon Nicholas' neck. "Is there ever anything else on your mind?"

"Not much."

"You're ridiculous."

"I am ridiculously yours. Forever." He had never spoken truer words. Being with William was indescribably known to him, as if he understood every aspect of the world, his world. "We belong together, and that is not my curse speaking. It is the truth. I know it."

He hoped William did, too. William's body became an extension of himself, undeniably right. Like this, he felt more alive than ever, more himself, even as the desire burned brighter than the dawn. He knew, even without this damned curse, he would react the same in William's arms.

"Shall we head out then, if you are feeling up to it?" Nicholas asked.

"Not yet."

They sat silent for a long moment, then William kissed him. It was sad and desperate and wanting all in one, and still perfect, all of them and nothing else. He could stay like this forever, savoring William's feverish touch. They kissed like it was their first time, like they were back in the cold wastes of the Deadlands, so overcome by the other they couldn't resist temptation. He tasted the same too; pure revelry.

"I don't want to make you worse," William panted against his mouth.

"I never feel more like myself than when I am with you," he replied earnestly.

"I wish I could make everything better for you. I want to save you."

"Do not put such pressure on yourself," he interrupted. "This is an unfortunate path I was laid on at birth. I much rather want you than anything else. In that way, you are saving me, my wicked."

William held him, kissed him, ran his fingers through his hair and all felt right. He dreamed of those moments, the weight of William, his touch, his taste, how he'd drive Nicholas to the brink of madness. But when he caught the first button of William's shirt, he flinched. Nicholas brushed their foreheads together. Their lips touched, gentle and sweet. He undid the first button. William clung to his shoulders.

"Why are you shaking?" Nicholas undid another button, relishing the sight of William's pale shoulder.

"You know why."

Silver glistened beneath William's shirt, revealed more by his questing fingers descending to circle a pink nipple he yearned to devour. If he could rip apart William's flesh and burrow himself into his veins, then Nicholas wouldn't hesitate to do so. There, within William's heart, he would nest for all eternity.

"Mortals may see this as a curse, perhaps you as well, but I do not. I will never. I shall worship every part of you." Another button undone and another while his lips descended upon William's chest. "I love you, my wicked. I shall adore you even when you do not."

William's shirt fell. Nicholas lavished him with attention, kissing along his chest to his nape. William's response was perfect, a pleasured moan caressing his ears like a spell. Nicholas caught his lips, more addicted to the taste of William than ever. He took hold of William's wrists, departing to catch the leathered glove between his teeth.

William did nothing to stop the removal of his gloves. Nicholas kissed each silver knuckle and did the same for the other, never breaking eye contact. "Tell me to stop. Tell me if you don't want this."

William said nothing as he dragged his lips over William's palm to his wrist. There, William's heart raced on his lips. He kissed and took the skin between his teeth, then further up to his bicep, then his shoulder. Finally, he reached that delectable nape. William lifted his head, letting Nicholas mark him more and more. He tasted William's sweat, salty and addictive and promising so much more.

"I want this, Nicholas," William finally moaned, the sound reverberating against his tongue. "Touch me more."

He yearned to map out William's body to ensure nothing changed, and he could still make William a withered mess. He wished they had more time, more patience to enjoy each other, but their feverish want had them rushing to touch and kiss and grind.

William's mouth fell on his neck to mark his skin when he tugged on a useless belt. William moaned against the skin between his teeth when Nicholas curled a hand around his arousal. He felt incredible, hot and ready. He wanted to see William, to watch him. Tugging at his pants, the fabric fell enough to free him. Nicholas licked his lips at the sight of William's cock.

"I wish to have rid you of your clothes so much sooner," he said, grinning from the thrusts of William's hips.

William kissed him over and over, his words spoken between every breath. "It was foolish of us not to, wasn't it?"

"We'll have to make up for all the lost opportunities. There is so much I want to do to you."

William caught him by the hair, bringing them face to face. He licked the palm of his opposing hand before returning the favor, slipping beneath his trousers to bring him to ecstasy. His cock throbbed in William's grasp, hips rolling against a hand that could ruin him completely. Nicholas thought of this moment a thousand times, but nothing compared to the lust in William's eyes or the bliss overtaking him.

"What do you want to do to me, trouble?" William whispered, retreating whenever Nicholas tried kissing him. His hand dared to stop, and Nicholas thrust fruitlessly.

"I want to fuck you," he growled, then took William's bottom lip between his teeth while his hand slowed.

William's thumb brushed his tip, teasing him. "Tell me more."

"I want you to fuck me. I want to make you scream my name and beg for more. I want to be owned by you entirely. I want to be your last of everything."

He kissed Nicholas hard, reaping the air from his body and soul. Their hands picked up a pace that left them panting. He yanked at Nicholas' shirt and the fae rid himself of it. Their naked skin pressed together, the heat of their joining making Nicholas shudder.

William slipped out of Nicholas' lap to get on his knees. "I want to taste you," he purred, tempting as the devil.

He would give William anything he wanted if that wasn't obvious enough already. He stood, trousers falling to his ankles. William's eyes drank him in, a teasing tongue darting out to wet his perfect lips. He curled his fingers in William's hair, groaning when that delectable mouth reminded him of all it could do.

With a hand around his arousal, William pleasured himself while Nicholas' cock hit the back of his throat. He fit perfectly, like they never separated, never forgot the feel of each other. He tested the boundary, rolling his hips faster and faster.

Their moans became one, a cacophony of pleasure echoing in the forest. William's hand worked faster, his head dripping. He stopped to give the poor man a breath, William's tongue darting out to drink from his tip before he returned to the ecstasy of his throat.

"Fuck, your mouth is incredible," he groaned, relishing in the lust reflecting in William's eyes. He admired his own work, knowing he drove Nicholas wild, that a few more moments of bliss would end it all.

Then William moaned, his hips jerking as his orgasm spilled over his fingers. Nicholas shuddered, feeling William's moans against his cock. He didn't stop, driving Nicholas further toward an orgasm that nearly sent him to his knees. William swallowed every drop, departing afterward with a lewd pop. He wiped the saliva from William's lips, savoring the view of him on his knees.

"I don't know how you expect me to get us out of here when you keep looking at me like you want me to take you," he said, shivering when William pressed a kiss to his hip.

"Think of it this way, we aren't fucking on the forest floor, so get us out of here and you can have me however you like," William replied, smiling far too sweetly after such a carnal act.

He tugged on William's hair, urging the man to stand before he caught his lips, tasting himself on William's tongue. "You know the best ways to motivate me."

William chuckled, sounding more like himself.

They didn't separate, taking a longer moment to bask in one another. William traced his jawline. Then he settled his hands on Nicholas' cheeks to look into his eyes, really look. Nicholas' heart soared because there was no fear or concern, only pure admiration.

"In this light, your eyes are beautiful," William said. Nicholas kissed him and would have continued to do so if he didn't settle a finger on Nicholas' mouth. "We should get out of here first."

He knew that, but William distracted him so easily. When they separated, he admired William dressing, missing the sight of his flushed skin. But he enjoyed how William did the same, appreciating his body as he dressed. Then William held out his hand, and he took hold, intertwining their fingers.

"If you feel lightheaded or panicked, tell me," he said.

"I will."

They walked together through the shrouded forest. He brought William's hand to his lips, kissing each knuckle because he wanted to. William said nothing, but he smiled even after the third time Nicholas repeated the action. He could have done that forever, merely walking hand in hand, enjoying being utterly alone.

Then the woods shrieked like a dying animal. The scream sent them into each other's arms. Wind whipped so fiercely the trees bent. Leaves circled them, creating a vortex of darkness. The One Who Waits found them.

20

CHARMAINE

CHARMAINE HEARD NOTHING, THEN everything, a concussive cacophony that couldn't be deciphered or ignored. When she thought herself dead, she took a breath and saw the sky, a deep, endless blue and twinkling starlight. Grass caught between her fingers, damp as her pallid skin. She wheezed, her lungs recalling their natural function. Then her muscles obeyed her desire to move. She rolled onto her hands and knees, vision first blurred, then coming into focus.

Evera finally looked like she belonged, an otherworldly beauty among glorious creation. She stood in an open field searching around a peculiar horizon. Charmaine couldn't grasp what she saw. There were spires taller than trees, curled at the end, but they weren't made of stone. Flowers blossomed along their stalks, their shades iridescent, catching the sunlight so it shimmered silver. Thorns pierced the tender flesh, sharp as claws and longer than her forearm. The strange plants surrounded them, although they were spaced out almost perfectly.

"Is everyone alright?" Henry sounded far away, then his hand fell on her shoulder. He squinted, struggling to adjust the same as her.

"I'm alive," she answered.

"That was the most unpleasant passing I've ever done and a less than spectacular landing." Henry forced a laugh. "Will you be alright?"

"Yeah. I'm woozy, that's all."

Henry glanced about, brows furrowed. "Where are William and Nicholas? Did they make it through the shimmer?"

He fumbled for the crystal he had used to follow them in his bag. She stumbled onto her feet. She swayed, feeling as if she had too much to drink, upset stomach and all. Nicholas and William weren't with them. She checked in every direction, including up, because who knew, the flowers could have a mind of their own. Nicholas spoke of Faerie like tales from a storybook where nothing made sense.

"I sense them nearby." Evera took a deep breath through her nostrils, then nodded to her left. "That way."

Henry pointed the crystal in that direction. The light within flashed in quick succession. Henry slipped the crystal into his pocket.

"Why aren't they with us?" Charmaine wasn't entirely sure how she felt about Evera leading them. She hadn't proved herself a threat, but if William was there, he'd remind her to remain on her toes. Fae could change at any moment. Or maybe he would lighten up, considering Nicholas returned and William couldn't hide his feelings, even if he tried.

"William was tempted," Evera replied. "Scars do that sometimes. Try to lead you astray for whatever reason. If you go too far from the path, then you're gone for good. Luckily for your friend, Nicholas had a hold of him and is likely the reason they got through."

"Oh!" Henry held tight to his satchel, like he tried to contain his excitement. "There have been theories by my colleagues that these pathways between our worlds are more than mere pathways." He waited, as if to build suspense, then declared, "They could be a rip in spacetime."

Henry stared at her with such childish delight that she felt awful for not reacting as excitedly as he hoped. She gave the best she could, a wide smile followed by, "Meaning?"

"While we pass from one world to the other, the tunnel itself is actually between all worlds, somewhere outside of time and reality itself, so these illusions could be our past selves, our futures selves, ourselves from an alternate reality. Because we are moving in unnatural ways, our minds coalesce with these alternates creating these so-called temptations when, really, it's more likely a confusion from our addled minds too small to comprehend what we're seeing." Henry pressed a hand to his chest. "I'm keen on the concept of alternate realities, but a colleague of mine finds it nonsensical. He is a follower of the Souls and believes we cannot be broken up into alternate identities, that it'd go against the reincarnation ideology."

"Do you always talk this much?" Evera continued her path through the peculiar plants that could move. The head of the plants pointed toward them, watching. Charmaine kept her hands raised in case they needed to fight. One didn't know if the plants were perhaps carnivores and interested in the new meat.

"Don't be rude," Charmaine chided.

"I take no offense," said Henry. "Most fae are not curious of the inner workings of anything, really. They believe the world is as it is and they should leave it be, save a rare few like Fearworn, which one could argue was why he made it as far as he did. If fae were curious as we were, with their abilities? I imagine we'd have collided with a dozen worlds by now." Henry went suddenly still, then snapped his fingers and took a notepad from his bag. "Perhaps their lack of curiosity is a natural safety feature, a sort of apprehension toward the unknown that prevents them from wielding their great powers in self-destructive means?"

Henry scribbled his notes, mouthing silent words to himself. She hadn't seen this side of him, but Henry wasn't around as frequently as his brothers. He worked late most nights and took residence in Alogan, a mere block from his office. He attended dinners regularly, but they rarely discussed his work. He often said it was too dry for dinner. She suspected he didn't believe they would understand or be as interested in what he studied. She wouldn't deny she couldn't follow his line of thoughts, but he probably couldn't create a dress that would cause the ton to usher to his front door. Everyone had their unique abilities, including Evera and her internal sensor for their lost friends.

Sweat coated Charmaine's neck. She wiped it away, scowling at the feeling of her buzzed hair. She kept it shaved. It was easier to deal with, easier to wear the many wigs her mother fixed for her. They weren't going anywhere she could bring them, and it would be a little ridiculous to worry over fixing her hair while chasing down potential murderers. But that didn't stop her from feeling out of place, naked in a way, as if she wasn't herself simply because she felt a breeze on her head.

"Keep close," Evera said. "We are near The Lost Woods."

"Which I imagine is a place we can get lost?" Henry asked.

"Killed, more accurately. No one comes out once they go in."

Henry clicked his tongue. "Pleasant."

She watched his back and Evera's. They moved further ahead. She willed her legs to move, to catch up to them, but they wouldn't come closer. Sweat dripped down her cheek. She tasted it. Her muscles ached, as they had upon their arrival, but more, worse. Then her knees buckled.

"Charmaine!" Henry caught her beneath the arms. A cough ripped through her throat, then she stood tall, as if nothing happened. "What's wrong?"

"I don't know," she admitted, smacking her dry lips. She grabbed her water pouch to chug, easing the symptoms for a moment.

Henry held out a hand toward Evera. "Evera, wait a moment."

Evera huffed, visibly annoyed. "What now?"

"May I?" Henry held out a hand, gesturing toward Charmaine's forehead. She nodded, and he pressed the back of his hand to her temple. He was abnormally cold, or rather, "You're running a horrible fever."

She sweat so profusely that her clothes clung to her form. She hated it, the feeling of them, the pants, reminding her of the military uniform. A dress wouldn't be practical here where they didn't know what they would run into. But safety didn't ease her desires, wanting to wear a skirt to at least feel a little more like herself. She berated herself for thinking of that now when they had more pressing matters.

Evera approached. "She's sick from passing the scar."

"Shimmer sickness. We must get away from..." Henry pivoted, surveying their surroundings. "I don't see the shimmer nearby."

Evera pointed skyward. A thin light, little more than a golden hue, scratched the sky. Certain angles made it disappear entirely, and even from here, Charmaine would have mistaken it for a catch of the light or early stars in the sky. She never expected one to be in the middle of the sky. It had her wondering how many times they may have passed a shimmer during the war, or even day to day, and she never realized it.

"She will slow us down. Stay here. I'll search for the others." Evera made as if to head out.

"Absolutely not," Henry argued. She might have, too, if she had the energy. Her mind became more muddled, harder to think, to focus. She didn't want to stand, so she fell to the ground. Henry cursed, surprised, but deemed her sitting acceptable.

"We must get her away from the shimmer, I know that much," said Henry. "And if anything unpleasant happens to us, it would be helpful to have a fae around."

Henry presented his hand. She wasn't sure what he wanted. Then he took her arm and eased her onto her feet. Her body became sluggish, as if her limbs weren't her own.

"I can hold my own, but we must keep Charmaine safe until she can handle herself, too. Help me carry her," Henry said.

Evera gave them a slow once over. Her attention lingered on Charmaine, the intensity of which warmed her chest. She blamed the fever.

"I suppose it would be safer if we stayed together." Evera knelt at Charmaine's side, brushing her long hair over her shoulder. "Put her on my back. I can carry her easily enough."

"You won't drop me?" She didn't want to rely on Evera, or anyone. In Faerie, they needed to be prepared. Evera couldn't be her best with deadweight on her back and being that close... unsettled her.

"I am far stronger than either of you."

"I meant on purpose."

Evera grinned, mischievous as ever, cute in a way. "I would never. My tricks will be far more mature than that."

Evera grabbed Charmaine's legs. Heat pulled beneath her cheeks. Henry eased Charmaine forward, so she fell on Evera's back. She smelled of early morning dew and lilies. Her hair was soft, tickling Charmaine's cheeks and she couldn't determine if she wanted hair like Evera's or she simply liked it. If she could run her fingers through Evera's hair, she would, or maybe not. Evera probably wouldn't like that. She was truly feeling delirious.

Evera stood easily, her hands caught on Charmaine's thighs. She suddenly became grateful for the pants, the fabric between them, though she wished she wasn't so sweaty. It must feel gross, must smell gross.

"Hold tight," Evera said. "We wouldn't want you to fall and bruise that pretty face of yours."

She didn't know how to respond, so she didn't.

"Someone is shy," Evera said under her breath. "I won't bite."

"You would if you didn't believe Nicholas may snap your neck in response." Because it would upset William, not her.

Evera walked on, acting as if she didn't carry more than a child's pack. Charmaine felt odd. Being taller, broader shouldered, and long-limbed, she practically cradled Evera. And yet Evera could toss her across the field single handedly without breaking a sweat. It was oddly attractive, though she chose not to dwell on it.

"Believe it or not, I'm not always interested in murdering mortals. In fact, I quite enjoy your particular company. You are more than pleasant to look at and give wonderful reactions," Evera claimed.

She choked on her breath. That put a larger grin on Evera's face. She couldn't fathom how a fae like Evera could find her *pleasant to look at.* Fae were known for their ethereal beauty, a weapon in its own right that deceived their prey. Charmaine, on the other hand, never felt like she was ever above barely average.

Her heart beat furiously against her ribcage. She worried Evera would feel it and poke more fun, but instead, the fae added, "Not to mention, I am enjoying this little adventure of ours."

"I have to agree," said Henry, earning a surprised glance from Charmaine. He smiled haphazardly. "The trip may have started out poorly, but come now, we're in Faerie. I could never venture far into Faerie during my visits. I certainly haven't seen plants like these and now I've had a chance to take note of them. This can be exciting for all of us."

"You're both mad," she said, although she may have felt differently if she weren't sick.

Her discomfort made the idea of enjoying anything seem distant, out of reach. Her dizziness and blurred vision had her struggling to make out the world around them. They passed beneath the wild high thorns, their tips stretching toward them, but never came within reach. Then they descended a hill leading to a river, the waters a pale blue. Pearlescent rocks lined the sides, glistening brighter than gems, calling to be picked.

"The bridge is the quickest." Evera nodded at a long bridge of stone arched over the water at a seemingly impossible angle.

Evera and Henry marched on to the bridge. Charmaine peered over the edge. A shadow passed below. The water rippled, then a pair of pale white jewels floated to the surface. She admired them, how her image reflected on their surface. Then a row of sharp teeth appeared beneath them, discolored as the peculiar long tongue that darted out between them.

Charmaine's throat ached and her words came out as nothing more than a hum. Below, a creature breached the water, revealing a thin torso where her bones nearly pierced flesh. Algae spotted her sides and cheeks, her smile peeling back thin skin to show three rows of fangs. A dozen more came to the surface, their expressions gleeful and hungry.

"Mm, down," she forced out, panicked but too exhausted to give more.

"Down?" Henry repeated, then the sirens sang. She never heard a more beautiful sound, a beckoning call. There were no words, merely a tune, high pitched and ethereal. Her ears rang. Her thoughts fell away, replaced by a memory, or an illusion.

Below, the sirens disappeared. A woman stood there, brown eyes warm, her form thin and small, delicate and beautiful, everything Charmaine wished to be. If she could fashion herself a new skin, it would mirror the woman, an otherworldly beauty with curls of autumn hair and full, heart-shaped lips. The woman held out her hand, fingers long and tipped in golden jewelry.

She yearned to take her hand, to be taken by her promise, whatever it was. How could someone so beautiful be dangerous? Why would Charmaine turn her away?

She shoved off Evera's back, adhering to the summons. She couldn't move as she wanted, body too weak to lift herself over the ledge of the bridge. Tears brimmed her eyes at the thought of losing the woman below, of missing the opportunity to see her, to speak with her, feeling her hand slip between Charmaine's fingers. Then she leaned over the edge and the stranger's hand gripped hers. All she ever wanted was literally in her grasp.

The stranger smiled. Someone grabbed Charmaine's shoulder, but the stranger pulled and she fell into icy darkness. The sensation startled her. In her vision, she thought she perceived jagged rocks and crooked teeth. But those bejeweled fingers fell upon her cheeks and brought her warmth, true serenity as she peered into welcoming brown eyes. The stranger smiled, her teeth pearly white and straight as needles.

A burning pain ripped through her leg. She gasped and what she brought in was not air but freezing waters. Choking, she sputtered and flailed. The stranger blurred, then warped entirely. A siren smiled, wicked, then angered. Her once beautiful voice ebbed into horror, a string of foul sounds. Blood seeped into the churning waters, darkening after the siren dived with her claws embedded into the back of Charmaine's neck. The siren had dredged through Charmaine's darkest thoughts, the furthest recesses of her mind to reveal an exaggerated, intoxicating beauty that Charmaine believed she had to be.

Even without the sight of blood, she was too sick to conjure any strength. Fire wouldn't bloom upon her fingers. She was cold and listless, dragged further into the depths, but something tugged on her ankle where pain throbbed. Through the murk, a silhouette appeared, then silver light flickered, revealing Evera's cruel snarl. Her nails pierced Charmaine's ankle, having used the pain to wake her. In Evera's other hand, the silver light coalesced into an orb like wildfire that the water couldn't snuff out. When Evera opened her hand, that light lashed out with dozens of tiny strings that cut clean through the siren's wrist.

Her ears popped when Evera yanked her and swam above to where the sunlight breached the water. She hacked and spit, her lungs struggling to take in air. Evera kicked toward the river's edge where she hastily threw Charmaine onto the muck. Evera fell over her, heaving, clothes soaked through and clinging to her skin. Her breath caught, her eyes lingering too long on Evera's chest. The fae caught her chin to bring them eye to eye. A wild smile spread across her cheeks.

"While I appreciate the admiration, we have more pressing matters than breasts," Evera said. Charmaine tried arguing, but Evera cut her off, "Are you of sound mind or do I need to cut you again?"

The sirens continued to sing, making her brain fuzzy, but all she focused on were Evera's midnight eyes, such a deep blue they bordered on black.

"I don't think so," she replied, not for the same reason, anyway.

She wished Evera could hit her a few times to get that image out of her mind, of the perfect woman society had painted. She understood that wasn't the case, that beauty came in many forms, but how could she feel otherwise when the world seemingly always found a way to demean her? Charmaine so desperately wanted to love every aspect of herself, but that was hard, and she wasn't sure if it made her a bad person or not to crave change.

"Good, because your friend is about to drown." Evera leapt off her, leaving Charmaine to realize that she didn't see Henry anywhere.

"Shit." She dragged herself further from the water, trying to call upon flames that wouldn't obey her. The shimmer sickness had zapped her of strength, leaving her as nothing more than a worthless husk on the river side. If anything happened to Henry, William would be beyond distraught.

The river rippled outward, causing waves to lap against the sides. She dragged herself forward, otherwise the strength of the waves would take her under. Then from the center, Henry burst out nearly twenty feet above the water, arms and legs flailing. Evera popped out of the water too, half laughing. Wind caught beneath Henry's open palms, sending him away from the water to roll across the grass near Charmaine.

"You mortal mages have some interesting tricks up your sleeves," said Evera while she swam. Behind her, the sirens peeked through the water, glaring.

"Be careful," Charmaine croaked.

Evera walked onto the grass to ring out her hair. "Oh, they won't bother us after wasting all that energy, although we should hurry. Those are young ones, spiteful and weak, and probably why I didn't sense them. Their parents, however, won't let us escape so easily."

"They're quite feisty for being that young, though I suppose that is why they messed up," Henry coughed up water, then he held out his satchel. He pointed his palm out to summon the wind to dry it off.

Evera knelt by Charmaine, signaling for her to get on her back. She flushed, thinking of their wet clothes, how she'd feel Evera's body pressed against hers, and vice versa. It made her stomach twist into a painful knot. The image flashed of that woman. She marked their differences, then shook her head. The siren toyed with her, tried to make a copy of what the world wanted, not who Charmaine actually wanted to be. She'd find her own way to happiness and acceptance, some day.

"Did they show you something that wasn't of interest?" asked Evera.

"They were off to a good start by putting me into a library, but then a naked woman showed up." Henry laughed and came over to dry them off with his wind. Charmaine was thankful, and a tad confused about why a naked woman would have been what broke the siren's spell. "Well, I'm grateful, although it seemed like you were also on your way to save me. I appreciate that, Evera."

She waved him off, then pointed at Charmaine. "Help me with her."

Henry caught her under the arms to ease her onto Evera's back. At least they were dry, and she was too exhausted to do more than lean against Evera.

"Let's find our lost companions, shall we?" Henry asked, then wandered toward the bridge, but not before giving the sirens a harsh glare that sent them diving into the river.

21

WILLIAM

BRANCHES CREAKED AND CRACKED. Darkness fell, an inky black to absorb all life. William and Nicholas held one other, their pulses mirrored. Their death would be in darkness, mercifully unseen, albeit heard as the forest breathed around them. The trees laughed, an eerie sound to chill the soul. Then all went silent.

He dared not to breathe. His lungs ached, wishing to expand, choosing to risk death rather than the eldritch beast's malice. Pale blue light passed through forest leaves, but those leaves did not hang from the branches. They warped beneath the call of a darker and ancient entity, fluttering above their head where a great eye formed, then another, and another, and another, until hundreds of beady eyes coated in grime and worms gazed upon them. From the soil, little white hands no larger than a child's sprouted and wiggled. Their thin fingers slithered through the dirt to wrap around his ankles. Their chill seeped through his clothes, a cold like death.

Normally, he would fight against them, tear those hands from the person and the soil. However, even he understood they were part of a beast unlike any other. He need not learn more about The One Who

Waits to comprehend that it was beyond anything, that perhaps even Fearworn would have trembled under its many watchful eyes.

"Trespassers," the eyes spoke all at once. Their voices were many carried as one, causing the forest to shake.

He didn't comprehend what he looked upon, if any of it was real or a fabrication, an illusion from the forest itself. His thoughts lurched, grappling for answers that weren't there. Every moment he drifted further into madness.

"We do not trespass of our own volition. None would dare go against The One Who Waits," Nicholas said impassively, then gave the slightest tilt of his lips, taunting in a way. "And yet, someone has."

He put a painful squeeze on Nicholas' chest, not much different from the ghostly hands. Their nails, coated in dirt, pinched the skin, threatening to draw blood.

The last path they should take was to piss off what had caught them. Nicholas held firm to the one eye above them, the biggest one blinding to gaze upon.

"Nicholas, son of Laurent Darkmoon, Fearworn's successor," The One Who Waits laughed, if an eldritch beast could laugh. The ground shook and branches creaked. Soil and bugs rained upon them, then all went still once more. "Are you arrogant enough to try to trick me?"

"No, but I am arrogant enough to ask you to set us free," Nicholas replied, keeping passive.

Nicholas' eyes took on a faint fuchsia hue as they had once been. The calmness dared to spur another sense of hope that this meant Nicholas could be spared from following Fearworn's destructive path. Like a wound on the battlefield, if William could cauterize it, snip out the infection before it took hold, then Nicholas may have a better life. He would have laughed at his own thoughts that consistently toiled with this possibility, but he hadn't the energy to do more than stand there and pray to whatever may be listening to spare them.

"None have left my woods. None will," said the beast.

The pale hands descended. William sank. The soil went soft, dragging them lower, lower. Mud pooled into his boots, weighing heavier than stone. He struggled to no avail. The hands held tighter and tighter, ripping fabric and drawing blood. Nicholas' grip on him tightened. He didn't meet William's eyes, but he wasn't panicking. He spoke without speaking, telling William to remain as calm as he could, so he took breaths, slow and deep.

"I hunger. So long it has been since one such as yourself crossed my woods," The One Who Waits growled. "Why should I deny myself fresh meat?"

"Because you would have killed us already if that is truly what you wanted." Nicholas had a confidence about him, unwavering even as the forest consumed them up to their knees.

Bugs slithered beneath their clothes. William shut his mouth when a spider crawled across his cheek. He dared not shake it off, worried The One Who Waits would react to the movement.

"Something is wrong in Faerie, isn't it?" Nicholas asked. "You, out of all of us, must know this. You sense it as I do, and if it is enough to worry you, it should worry all of us."

He couldn't sense what Nicholas and The One Who Waits did. He hadn't seen outside The Lost Woods, which was worse than he could have imagined, but he wouldn't expect anything to be wrong with Faerie. It was twisted, as he had been told Faerie would be, but not what he perceived to be wrong. However, Nicholas said something to convince the forest because the hands stopped tugging. Those pale fingers paused at their waists, still as the dead.

"We've come to Faerie with a purpose," Nicholas explained. "We're searching for shadowed disciples once belonging to Fearworn's ranks. We believe they are at fault. When we find them, we will put an end to their schemes, whatever they may be."

"If you find them," The One Who Waits countered. "If you can end what they have begun."

"Do you know what they are doing?"

The One Who Waits blinked its many eyes, casting them in momentary darkness. "They are corruption. They are rotten. They are wrong and they will break all we have ever known."

"We can stand against them," Nicholas said sternly. "You need not leave your forest or fear your forest abandoning you. Free us and we will do the work for you."

The One Who Waits breathed, its leaves shuddering beneath a corrosive breath that tasted of metallic waste. "And if you fail?" asked the beast.

Nicholas hesitated, his confidence wavered. He looked at William, who couldn't imagine another way out. They were at the whims of the beast unless Nicholas lost control. In that case, it may end even worse.

The One Who Waits yearned to strike a deal. William didn't need to ask what it wanted should they fail, but Nicholas wanted his permission. With no other options, he nodded.

"Should we fail, you will have your feast upon what is left of us," said Nicholas.

"And your allies," said the beast.

He jerked without meaning to. The hands clawed up to his abdomen. The forest groaned in warning. Nicholas shivered in his arms. William held tighter, hoping to ease him. They were buried up to their chests and Nicholas couldn't bring himself to look down, realizing they were being slowly buried.

"Our allies?" Nicholas repeated at last.

"The ones who search outside my borders. Three of them, a fae and two mortals. I want them, too. After all, if you fail, Faerie may fall. I should like a good meal before then." The One Who Waits laughed, that same guttural sound of utter horror.

William's lungs constricted. Henry, The One Who Waits would take Henry, too. He knew he should have forced Henry to stay, no matter what that meant. He should have told Nicholas to enchant him, send him back to the estate and kept him there.

"It is unfair to make a deal when the entire party isn't here to agree," Nicholas countered.

"How unfortunate for them. Make your choice."

The One Who Waits wasn't as patient as its name implied. The hands yanked. Their nails scraped against William's cheeks. His blood stained their fingertips, causing them to shake, like they hadn't been fed in ages. Goose feathers broke out across Nicholas' arms. Though higher, the fae panicked from the earth, threatening to devour them. The promise of a burial he so feared urged him to shout, "Fine! Should we fail, you will have all of us. Now, release us."

The ground spat them out like spoiled fruit. Branches snapped loose to curl toward them, tightening around their limbs. Then The One Who Waits vanished as they were yanked through the forest. Leaves cut into William's cheeks. The air whistled in his ears. His world became a blur of colors interrupted only by The One Who Waits' laughter, ominous and promising.

He fell onto smooth grass, peering up at a cloudless blue sky. The air tasted of wildflowers and sun. His empty hand shifted through the grass, fingers shaking the longer he went without finding Nicholas until their fingers caught.

They survived, but at what cost...

"How did you know that would work?" His body ached, but he wanted to get away, far from The Lost Woods and The One Who Waits. He thought he had been prepared for Faerie. He was entirely wrong.

Sitting up, he faced the edge of the forest where the trees spread far apart, wide enough for any to foolishly step through, unaware of what fate awaited them. Even he, who had seen the monsters within, dared to think how beautiful it was, how it would be so nice to take a walk beneath its shade. The forest had an air about it that made one's senses slacken.

"I didn't." Nicholas cracked his neck. "I hoped it would work and we are lucky it did. We've made history, in fact."

"I don't care about that. I care about never setting foot in there again." And making sure Henry would never end in there. He tugged Nicholas onto his feet so they could run or rather jog.

Neither had caught up to the present, their bodies sluggish. The more distance he put between himself and The Lost Woods, the better he felt.

"Are you upset?" asked Nicholas. "About the deal I struck."

"No. We wouldn't have made it out alive and, if we fail, we'll all be dead, anyway. You did great, Nicholas." Although he wasn't certain which death would be worse.

Nicholas kissed his cheek. His face warmed. He slowed to a stop, feeling somehow childish and excited to say, "You missed."

"Did I?" Nicholas had a beautiful laugh that he wanted to hear for the rest of their lives. "Let me fix my mistake." Nicholas kissed him slowly, leaving them both breathless. "Was that better, my wicked?"

"Much better, trouble."

"There they are," Evera called. She was little more than a spot in his vision coming over the hillside. Henry shuffled along beside her and Charmaine laid spent on her back.

"You're alright!" Henry hurried forward. Nicholas let go to let William meet his brother. Henry caught him in a hug, where a salt scent affronted him. Henry laughed at his curled nose. "That smell must be from the river. We had an unpleasant run in with a group of sirens, but we're alright, as you seem to be."

"As good as we can be," he replied hesitantly, then inspected Charmaine. She hung listlessly on Evera's back, but her eyes were open and present. "What happened?"

"Shimmer sickness," she groaned. "I can walk—"

"She can't," Evera cut in. "Unless we want to crawl our way to wherever we're going." She glanced over William's shoulder toward The Lost Woods. Her eyes narrowed. "Where did you two come from, exactly?"

Nicholas laughed. "You won't believe it." Then he deflated. "And you may be a tad upset."

22

WILLIAM

WILLIAM WASN'T EXCITED TO hear what the group had to say concerning their interaction with The One Who Waits. Nicholas explained, including the less than pleasant agreement struck. Charmaine and Henry shared expressions of terror and concern, while Evera remained as nonchalant as ever.

"This was always an adventure that would end in death if we failed anyway," Evera said. "Nothing has changed."

Henry settled a hand under his chin. "She isn't wrong. We knew the risks when starting this and there is no point worrying when we can't turn back."

More reasons he didn't want Henry to tag along. The thought must have been written on his face, because Henry offered a lopsided smile.

William clenched and unclenched his hands. "Now that we agreed to help an eldritch entity, how are we meant to go about this?"

Nicholas and Evera shared knowing looks. Evera sat Charmaine down when he approached. He needed to check on her. They traveled away from the shimmer, so hopefully she would recover soon.

"The One Who Waits said Faerie has changed. Is there a way for us to determine in what ways? The patients are likely to be where this source of change is," said Henry.

William tested Charmaine's temperature. She was burning up, but not the worst he had felt. He had medicine in his pack. The least he could do was ease her fever, if that was all it was. He called upon the Sight, inspecting the strings coalescing within her. None were torn or frayed, merely burning brighter from her fever. He began the preparations while the group continued their discussion.

Evera grimaced. "If anyone potentially has answers, it's *them*."

Nicholas waved his hands in the air. "No, we are not going to them. They're revolting and vicious little gremlins."

"But well traveled gremlins."

"Do you care to share with the rest of the group? What are these vicious little gremlins?" Charmaine asked. Her words weren't slurred, and she took the offered medicine easily enough. She gagged, but when he gave her water, she drank that too.

"Red caps," Evera answered.

"Revolting and vicious, indeed." Henry shook his head. "Aren't they the creatures that kill anything in their path and bathe in their blood?"

"Bathe?" Charmaine coughed.

He expected nothing less of Faerie. They had been there for a few hours and faced multiple attacks on their life. Red caps would be another addition to the pile, but at least they'd be easier to handle.

"They don't kill everything," Evera countered, then pursed her lips. "They kill most things, but they can be bargained with. Red caps don't call any land home for long, so if anyone knows of strange happenings, it's them. They're easily trackable with the bloody mess they leave."

Nicholas pouted. "The mess is the problem. The last time I saw them, I was cleaning blood off me from crevices I didn't know I had."

Evera stuck out her tongue. "That was an image I could have gone through the rest of my life without."

"Is there any chance we can rest for the day before searching for them?" William suggested, earning wide-eyed looks from the group. "Charmaine shouldn't be traveling. She's sick and needs rest."

"We don't have time to rest. Should our parents," Evera gestured between herself and Nicholas, "learn we're here, with humans, they will stick their nose in our business and that won't end well for any of us. We must reach the bottom of this. Fast."

"Charmaine shouldn't be traveling all day. Is there a place I can stay with her?" He hated suggesting it, being left behind when this was his mission, but Charmaine could get worse if they didn't give her what she needed. He refused to lose her here, of all places. They survived Fearworn. They would survive Faerie, no matter what.

"Absolutely not. We shouldn't separate," Nicholas replied, his eyes having become more violet, and yet, he spoke calmly, or William convinced himself that the fae was. "Evera and I will take turns carrying her."

Evera agreed easier than expected. William didn't know if this was their best plan of action, but he certainly didn't know of any better option. Once again in a foreign land, he was left to the devices and decisions of others. He may as well have put on his military uniform and marched along.

Nicholas offered to carry Charmaine first. William and Henry eased her onto Nicholas' back, where she went limp, but he carried her as if she weighed nothing. Evera led the group, claiming that following the red cap's scent would be easy enough, whatever smelled bloodiest. He was grateful he didn't have the sense to pick up on that.

They traversed the wilds of Faerie, hills of lush greenery, floating rivers, trees too thick for the entire group to wrap around. Foreign flowers blossomed, their petals larger than a grown man's torso and fangs hidden within leaking nectar. Creatures frolicked through the branches, their silhouettes an arrangement of shapes and sizes. They bickered and laughed or dared to sit out trinkets, glass orbs, golden spoons, torn books, and sparkling wind chimes as if they thought the mortals would fall for the trap.

Evera warned them from time to time to avoid a mushroom ring, one so large that the mushrooms were as big as a coach, or treading over roots that would have smothered them from a touch. Henry muttered to himself while taking pages upon pages of notes. Regularly, William grabbed his brother to prevent him from lagging after getting lost in a notebook. If Faerie weren't deadly, he would find the dazzling lights flickering through the forest beautiful.

"Pixies," Nicholas explained. "They enjoy gouging out one's eyes."

He snorted. "How pleasant."

Henry wrote about what he saw, drawing a thing here or there, too. William didn't know his brother could draw. None of it was too detailed, but enough of a sketch to get an idea of what he had seen.

"You're quite good," he said.

"My teachers insisted I learn so we could catalogue anything we saw in the field," Henry explained. "I hated it at first, but now I find drawing rather soothing."

Evera led them to a river where Nicholas set Charmaine down. He and Henry stayed with her while the fae picked rocks along the riverside.

"What are you doing now?" Henry asked.

"Finding us a ride," Evera replied.

"Is that a good idea considering what happened at the last river?"

"Sirens aren't the only ones in the water." Evera had a dozen smooth rocks in her palm.

Nicholas found the same. They skipped the pebbles across the water so perfectly the rocks landed on the other side. Then the river went black. The tide strengthened, pushing against the edge, and finally a steed broke forth. Black as the rapids, the stallion with seaweed as a mane and obsidian scales along its hide sputtered at Evera and Nicholas. They replied with peculiar spitting noises that had William and Henry staring at one another.

Another steed lurched from the depths, and the two settled near the edge. Evera mounted one and Nicholas shouted, "Come. They will take us to the red caps."

"In exchange for?" William asked skeptically.

"Evera and I agreed to return in a month to clean their teeth. It's hard to clean your teeth without thumbs."

"Fascinating," Henry muttered, scribbled more, then clutched Charmaine. "She will ride with me and Evera."

"I should stay with her," William argued.

"Nonsense. We can manage." Henry moved toward Evera, where they carefully situated Charmaine behind her. Henry kept his arms on either side of Charmaine while clutching Evera's waist. He nodded behind him. "You sit with Nicholas."

There was enough room for another with them. The steeds were larger than any he had seen, but Nicholas waited. He wanted to ride with Nicholas, but he felt odd to do so with Henry around. He already knew where William's interests lied, however, Nicholas was an entirely other matter.

"Go on," said Henry, waving behind him.

Nicholas smiled when he slid behind him and took his waist.

"Hold on," said Nicholas. "They won't move too quickly, but the ride can get rough."

Evera shouted, and the horses sped off. Nicholas laughed as the wind whipped through their hair. William clung to him, feeling he could slip at any moment. The horse was wet, and the water rushed against the tip of his boots, but they didn't tumble into the rapids below.

The world around them bled together in brilliant colors, making him wonder how fast they were going. As Nicholas described, the ride was rough with a lot of bumping and the horses bucking their heads, nearly hitting Nicholas in the face, but the fae found it enjoyable based on his wide smile. He admired the expression, how the little fuchsia in Nicholas' eyes flared. He looked more like himself, felt like himself.

The horses came to an abrupt stop. They survived the ride. The horses meandered to the edge of the water, where they departed. Nicholas and Evera made the weird spitting sounds before the horses vanished beneath the black water that swirled into a brilliant blue.

"That was incredible!" Henry shouted.

Evera had Charmaine on her back. She looked better, her eyes open and taking things in, but she kept silent and eventually rested her chin on Evera's shoulder.

"The red caps are near. Maybe an hour's walk," said Evera.

"Let's get this over with." Nicholas took the lead.

They arrived in another forest, though one of a slightly perturbed nature, with trees a deep red and their leaves orange as flames. In fact, from a distance, the tree tops resembled a fire swaying in the afternoon breeze. The soil had an orange tint to it, the grass more yellow like wheat fields, and the limbs caught among one another, creating an interconnected web above their heads.

In the trees, voices carried a chattering noise, then louder. Nicholas held up a hand, signaling the group to keep behind him. Through the trees, the red caps danced together, singing or cursing. He couldn't determine if they sounded angry or joyous, or perhaps the two intermingled for them. But there were many, over a hundred of creatures with off green leathered skin and eyes a variety of shades of gold and bronze. They wore long red hats crusted around their scalps and over their long ears. Fingers sharper than blades clutched spears, shields, and maces, as they danced around a fire where a familiar face hung on a spit.

Arden hummed and knocked his feet together from the spit where the red caps looped chains around him from ankle to neck. He was nonchalant about the ordeal, passing by the flames daring to lick his abdomen. If he felt pain, he didn't show it, continuing to spin and nod along to the red caps songs.

William would never understand fae.

Nicholas faced the group and said in a low whisper, "Charmaine will stand between William and Henry, in case Evera and I need to get our hands dirty. Do not comment on their attire, especially their hats, or the smell. We know they smell awful, so do they, but they hate it if it's brought up. Don't touch them. Don't touch anything. Let Evera and I do the talking."

Without further explanation, Nicholas waltzed toward the camp. Evera let Charmaine stumble off her back to be held up between Henry and William. A series of shouts erupted from the red caps, followed by their undivided attention. They nearly all turned in unison, gazing upon the group appearing from the tree line.

He gripped Charmaine's arm harder. The poor girl winced, and he apologized under his breath. He wasn't comfortable walking up to the creatures. There were too many of them, more than he originally thought, hiding among the bushes or sitting in tree branches. Those once hidden meandered to the group, so they stood as one, a crowd of blood stained teeth and wild eyes.

"Good afternoon," Nicholas declared with a curt bow of his head. "We do not mean to interrupt your supper, but have an inquiry that only you may help us with."

He wasn't sure how admitting only the red caps could help them was a good idea, but Nicholas said not to speak, so he kept his mouth shut. The last thing he wanted was to anger the hundreds of volatile, bloody creatures wielding weapons.

The red caps muttered amongst one another, swerving inward to chatter, clicking teeth and tongue. They wandered around the fire toward the group, leaving Arden alone. The fae's fingers slipped between the chains and wiggled. Below, roots slithered from the soil to cover the fire, successfully smothering it without the red caps ever being the wiser.

"Why should we help one such as you? The lot of you look down on us, think you're better," one of the red caps said from the group. The creatures dispersed, creating a path for one to saunter out. This red cap had more scars than the others, an eye white as milk with a long gash ripping across his face and peeling some skin from his lip. He missed a claw on his right hand but wore the longest hat in the deepest crimson. Their leader.

"Because you know the lands of Faerie, you travel them frequently, and this particular question needs an answer from those with the correct knowledge," Nicholas replied. "Let me introduce myself. I am Nicholas, and you are?"

"Rorbek," said the red cap. He clicked his teeth, fangs pointed as dagger tips threatening to slice his own gums. "You need our help?"

The roots below Arden rose to catch along the chains. One wiggled toward the lock and snuck into the keyhole. The other roots caught the chains, preventing them from dropping. Silently, Arden slid free without the red caps noticing, all too busy staring at the group requesting assistance rather than the meal they believed to have captured.

Nicholas smiled, showing all his teeth. "If you are incapable of answering our inquiry, we may go elsewhere."

"We are capable," growled Rorbek.

He realized Nicholas was goading the creatures, making it seem like he would look down on them if they didn't answer

"But if you want answers, you play by our rules." Rorbek said, causing the red caps to cackle. They wouldn't be laughing if they saw Arden skipping into the woods, leaving them without supper.

"What are your rules?" asked Evera rather loudly when one of the red caps nearly glanced back at the fire pit. The creature gave her its full attention, allowing Arden to be swallowed by the dark forest entirely.

"Battle." Rorbek smiled with all his crooked teeth and the red caps cheered behind him. "A fair one. Not against either of you." Rorbek pointed at Nicholas, then Evera. "One of the mortals."

"That is hardly fair. Mortals are the weakest of all of us," Evera argued.

Henry and William shared offended glances.

"The mortal may choose a weapon of their preference. We fight in our battle circle. Whoever is cast out, or dies, will be the winner. If the mortal wins, they get answers and you leave without a fuss. If we win," Rorbek chuckled and his gums bled, leaking over his chapped lips. "The mortal who failed shall be our feast."

"I accept," Henry declared.

William paled. "What? Absolutely not."

"The challenge has already been accepted." Rorbek snickered. "Pick your weapon. We have many."

Cheering and bickering, the red caps formed a circle around them. They were too focused on the battle to realize Arden escaped. A handful of them offered Henry their weapon, explaining the construction of their blades in great detail and how many lives their blades took.

"Nicholas," William said desperately. "Do something. Henry can't—"

"I can handle myself," Henry interjected, earning a sharp glare.

He couldn't believe the fool would offer himself, and felt even worse when Nicholas said, "Henry can do this."

"Have the both of you gone mad?" he hissed and pointed at Rorbek, hefting a scythe three times his size. Rorbek swung the weapon as if it weighed less than a twig. With a wicked grin, the beast sliced through the soil, leaving a gash as if to say Henry would be next.

He couldn't breathe. His mind played their tricks, showing him Henry's bloodied corpse beneath Rorbek's scythe. He wanted to scream, to snatch Henry's hand and run. The sky overhead darkened, clouds of a storm rolling in.

In his shock, he nearly dropped Charmaine. Evera took her from under the arms, easing her into a standing position. The medicine had made her tired, her eyes drooping. She did not know what was going on when he needed her. She would side with him. There would be someone to understand his panic and save his brother from a stupid decision.

Henry settled his hands on William's shoulders. "You don't need to protect everyone all the time."

"I need to protect you," he argued, struggling to breathe. The forest caved in around them. Sweat coated his back. He felt like he was drowning. All this time, he did everything to keep his family from violence, but Henry so willfully walked towards it.

"You don't," Henry whispered, soothing and gentle. "Let me handle this."

He shook his head, but Rorbek shouted, "Have you chosen a weapon?"

"I have." Henry smiled with a confidence William found foolish. The confident died first, believing themselves capable in the face of a world too unforgiving to care.

"Off the field!" Rorbek yelled, swinging a clawed hand.

"Henry, wait." He reached for his brother. Nicholas grabbed his arm. He yanked out of the hold, too pissed off to look at him.

"The agreement has been made. If you interfere, we're all in trouble," Nicholas explained.

"You should have been on my side," he growled.

"I am."

"You let my brother throw himself into a battle he will not win."

"I wouldn't let him do anything I don't believe he can do." Nicholas nudged him toward the sidelines where the red caps watched, waiting for an opportunity to strike.

Evera kept Charmaine close. With an annoyed huff, he stormed out of the makeshift arena. Thunder roared overhead and lightning streaked across the sky. A few droplets of rain fell, hitting his cheek. Henry stood in front of Rorbek, thirsty for blood. The look reminded him of Fearworn's creatures, their hunger for destruction that Henry was never meant to meet.

"As I said, the first to die or be pushed from the circle loses. We start on opposite sides. When the gong rings, we attack," Rorbek explained. Behind him, a red cap held up a gong riddled with dents and hanging from frayed strings. It had certainly seen better days. She stood on the sidelines, jittery with excitement.

"There are no other rules?" asked Henry, while removing his pack and satchel.

"None."

"So be it." Henry walked to his side where he offered his belongings to William. He didn't want to look at his brother, too angered by his stupidity, but Henry knocked his hand and he swiped the pack to clutch against his chest.

Rorbek stood on the opposite end, smiling viciously. The red caps chanted, their voices growing louder and louder. Sweat trickled down William's neck. His legs threatened to give out. He wanted a smoke. Needed one, more like it, or a drink, the strongest they had available. He reached for his pack, itching for a smoke, feeling utterly useless and an utter fool.

Nicholas laid a hand on the small of his back. He hated that it was of any comfort. Then the gong rang, and he froze, watching in terror. Rorbek launched across the circle. He raised his scythe high. The blade aimed at Henry's neck. William stepped forward. Nicholas clutched his shirt.

"Don't break the rules," Evera warned, just as a flash of lightning erupted from the sky.

The world blazed white, blinding. Rorbek shrieked. The lightning crashed against his scythe. He released the weapon, scrambling back from the jolts rocking through him. Above, the clouds had gone black, and the rain fell harder. Henry held out his hands, the tips electrified, bristling with blue energy.

"Magic!" Rorbek hissed. "Cheating!"

"You didn't specify no magic," Henry said, his calm expression illuminated by blue light.

Rorbek shrieked louder, spitting through his teeth. He leapt for his scythe. Lightning struck Henry this time. His veins glowed blue beneath his skin. The blast redirected down his arm to the tip of his fingers. The lightning hit Rorbek square in the chest and sent him hurtling over the crowd, out of the circle. William gawked at Henry, who took a slow breath. The lightning around his fingers dissipated. The rain slowed to a light drizzle, and the storm went quiet.

"How come you didn't do that against the sirens?" Evera snapped.

"First off, I was hypnotized by their song, and second, it takes a moment to power up, so to speak," Henry replied, then settled his attention on Rorbek, snarling as he pushed through the crowd. "I believe I have won."

"You have." Rorbek spat blood on the ground. His top had been singed, revealing his charred flesh beneath. "Mortal with magic. You shouldn't have that."

Henry shrugged. "I am blessed to have it. Now, answer our questions."

Rorbek was a sore loser based on his grumbling, but obeyed. "Go on, then. Ask."

"We are in search of troublemakers," said Evera. "Strange happenings in these lands, something wrong."

"Wrong," Rorbek repeated. At his back, the red caps chattered. The one holding the gong leaned in to whisper in his ears. "Wrong, like bad soil?"

"Anything, perhaps even a place you now avoid."

"Avoid, yes, Bloodbane, your home, the soil weeps." Rorbek stuck out his tongue in disgust. "It's foul with decay, rancid in smell and taste. We will not go near it."

"We should have figured as much." Nicholas threw his arms skyward in an angry gesture. "If anyone were to start trouble, it would be your mother. What is she hiding?"

Evera met Nicholas' anger with her own. "Do you know everything your father is up to?"

Rorbek sucked on his teeth. "Are we done? We have fae to cook."

"Oh yes, we are finished." Nicholas would have snickered if Evera didn't elbow him, so he grunted instead. "Enjoy your meal."

Nicholas gathered Charmaine on his back and walked away. William followed, refusing to look back at Henry even when Henry retrieved his belongings. The brothers walked in silence, Henry snorting when the red caps shrieked. They learned Arden escaped, cursing him and scuttling about in search of their prize. It wasn't until some time later that Arden waltzed up to their group as if earlier hadn't transpired. He tucked his wild hair behind his ears and sauntered beside Nicholas. Already in a foul mood, William mentally cursed the bastard. They didn't need to be that close.

"What is this talk of trouble, then?" Arden asked.

"That is no concern of yours," Evera replied. "Our group is large enough."

"The more the merrier I say, and if it's true that a fae lord may be involved, I imagine we need all the help we can get," Henry chimed in.

He resisted the urge to look at him. He felt childish, considering he hated how their father had done the same.

Evera reached in front of Nicholas to shove Arden aside. "This one got himself caught by red caps. He is no help."

Arden pressed an offended hand to his chest. "Caught? Don't be ridiculous! I was bored and let them have their fun, but this trouble of yours sounds far more entertaining."

"Have you heard of anything strange from Bloodbane? You've been in Faerie since Fearworn's demise, haven't you?" asked Nicholas.

Arden nodded. "I have and the red caps are right. I visited Bloodbane some time ago and it was discomforting, to say the least. Alvina hasn't been seen at a revel in months."

By William's records, the disappearances began two months ago. The pieces were fitting together little by little, and he hated the outcome more than expected.

Nicholas turned his attention to Evera. "You truly know nothing of this?"

"If I had, I would have told you already," she replied. "Knowing my mother, this is nothing good, and I'd want it over with it as swiftly as you." Evera stepped ahead of the group. "We can't afford any more stops. This ends before my mother causes harm. I'll take us to Sorrows Well."

Evera led the way to Bloodbane. William lagged at the back, his gaze sweeping over his brother. Henry ran his thumb over his fingers, pressing deep one after the other. He didn't know Henry could do that earlier. His affinity had been for the wind, having summoned gales that threatened to pull trees from their roots. Lightning, however, had never occurred, certainly not a storm of that magnitude.

Then again, he had been gone for five years while his brother trained under the best magical minds of the kingdom. Since he returned, he had asked little about Henry's work, either. Regardless, Henry made a foolish move, agreeing to battle the redcaps. If something happened, he wouldn't have forgiven himself. Their parents would have been distraught and all the work he had done to ensure his family would never witness what he had would be for nothing.

"Are you going to ignore me during the entirety of our journey?" Henry asked.

William didn't notice his brother slow down to walk by his side and he refused to answer.

Sighing, Henry settled his hands behind his back. "You are upset."

"You never should have come," he snarled between clenched teeth. He watched ahead of them, ensuring the fae meandered along, although they no doubt were listening in.

"You should have asked me to come along."

He barked out a laugh. "Why would I do that? It's dangerous—"

"And you need all the help you can get." Henry stepped ahead of him, stopping William in his tracks. His brother wore a stern expression, hurt even, and it shut him up before he could begin. "I am a powerful mage, William, and that is not me being cocky."

He knew that now better than anyone. Henry called forth a storm, changed the weather in less than a minute, and commanded power as threatening as lightning. He always thought Henry had an affinity for air magic. When they realized he had the Sight, it was because he could call forth the wind through the house to flutter papers or push their shoes down the hall in a race. William had always been impressed and especially envious in his youth. He liked his abilities well enough. They proved exceedingly useful, but Henry had a freedom about him that any would envy.

"I know my limits, and I have been to Faerie before. If I were not your brother, you would have asked for my help in an instance," Henry added.

"But you are my brother and it is why you must understand why I do not want you here. If anything were to happen to you—"

"And what about you?" he challenged. "If anything happened to you, none of us would forgive ourselves, either. My life is not worth more than yours."

"It is! You, Dad, Mom, everyone, none of you have any idea what I did, what I had to do to survive, and you may say it doesn't matter, but it does. If you knew, you would know that I'm not the brother you want or deserve, that I'm not me anymore. I haven't been for a long time." He swerved around Henry to rejoin the group.

"William," Henry called, but he didn't want to listen. He didn't want to risk saying more, either. He didn't understand why he said anything, but it slipped out, and now Henry would pick at every word to piece together the meaning.

"Wait," Henry tried with his hand on William's wrist, but then Nicholas held up a hand. Everyone stopped, perturbed by the wide-eyed expression he wore.

"Nicholas." William looked him up and down. "Is something wrong?"

"Do you hear anything?" Nicholas muttered while searching their surroundings.

"Nothing," he muttered.

The forest fell silent when predators were near and one had found them, his silhouette dark beneath the trees.

"Father," Nicholas whispered.

23

NICHOLAS

LEAVES CAUGHT IN LAURENT'S antlers and tangled in his hair. He looked like a ghost of the moors, pale skinned and dead-eyed. His nimble fingers caught at his waist and lips quirked. "You've brought guests, Nicholas."

"They will not be here long," he replied skeptically.

"I could leave now, if you would like," said Arden, though he dared not step back because he wasn't that foolish. Evera had Charmaine on her back, the latter of which twitched, as if she dared to consider attacking. Laurent no doubt noticed, too. He would kill her before she lit a spark.

For a moment, he rejoiced at the thought of her being gone, at knowing how distraught William would be, so much so that he would cling to Nicholas for support. Then his teeth tore into his cheek. He tasted blood and guilt to have ever imagined such a thing. He envied their relationship, yes, that they were so close that William risked everything for her and considered her in all things. However, he reminded himself what William had done for him too, that he gave up his life to save Nicholas and walked around with a reminder of that attached to his person.

Laurent's attention strayed to William. Nicholas took a protective step in front of him.

"Why are they here?" Laurent's relaxed body language would fool most into believing they were safe. "The Heign Magical Society did not ask for permission to work on Faerie land," Laurent added with a glance at Henry.

"I am not here on society business, Lord Darkmoon," Henry replied. His calm demeanor was impressive, though nothing truly hid the worry from his eyes.

"And we are not on Darkmoon soil," Nicholas added.

"Answer the question," Laurent demanded.

They may not have been on Laurent's grounds, but that didn't mean they were safe from retaliation. Laurent would attack if he wished. Power surged within Nicholas, that potent energy that had been inside him since birth, amplified to a burning sensation. There was a charge, almost a need to fight scratching along the corners of his mind. He was stronger than Laurent in the physical sense. He understood that, however, a childish fear remained. Like a struck dog, he cowered before a master that understood the world in ways he couldn't. He didn't want to fight, to risk everything against one who was always ten steps ahead.

"There have been disappearances from Terra. They're being taken to Faerie," Nicholas explained carefully.

"Is that a problem? The Collision Treaty ended with the war. Fae are welcome to make their deals," Laurent said.

"These are not deals."

Laurent waited for further explanation that never came. None dared utter a word about shadowed disciples. Laurent would be displeased to hear of them, and a displeased Laurent spelled disaster. Although arguably they were upon the precipice of disaster, dangling off a ledge leading into darkness, with nowhere to go but down.

"So be it." Laurent chortled, then waved a hand. "Come along. Hill Castle has been waiting for you, Nicholas."

All looked at Nicholas expecting an explanation, but he, too, was confused. Laurent rarely invited mortals to Hill Castle now that the treaty ended, unless they were a toy to be discarded.

"We have places to be," he countered poorly.

The look of contempt Laurent gave could freeze the sea. "You will join me at Hill Castle."

That was not a request and he needn't imagine what the consequences would be if they attempted to leave.

William brushed their hands in encouragement, a reminder that they would do this together. The group followed Laurent in deafening silence, save the one comment from Arden: "I joined at the wrong time."

Ahead of them, the world bowed in Laurent's presence. Limbs parted for him and fields shuddered in his presence. A green walkway unfurled before them, a path leading directly to Darkmoon. Laurent needn't lift a finger. Even outside his lands the soil revered him and he honored it. Flicking his wrist or muttering under his breath, trees grew taller, flowers bloomed, and rot withered. If Nicholas could say a positive phrase about his father, it would be that Laurent loved the earth as much as he loved himself. Unfortunately, that was as far as his love went. The rest of fae and mortals alike were treated like fleas atop the back of titans. He'd squash them all if he could.

William leaned against his arm. "Why is he here? What does he want?"

"I do not know, but we must stick together. If we're separated, try to keep into groups of two, understand?" he replied.

"How did he know we were here?" Charmaine muttered. She had a wakefulness in her eyes that hadn't been there previously.

"Unfortunately, my father knows when I return. It's a sense of his," he replied. Just like he had a sense of when something was wrong.

That interaction spoke of wrong. Laurent rarely sought him out. He waited for his son to wander home because he always did. When Laurent showed up, he didn't attack. Nicholas didn't need to hear his father admit to hating William for having Nicholas wrapped around his finger because that meant he was harder to control. Something was off.

Every move Laurent took felt calculated, like a predator around prey who hadn't realized what they traveled with. They walked for hours where the sun never moved, causing William to question it. Nicholas replied, *"It is a long day today."*

Faerie was unlike Terra in more than he could ever explain. Day and night bled together because the sun rose when it wished, sometimes battling for dominance with the moon, and at times night would last so long that the Faerie became but ice and snow. The unpredictability of Faerie made the fae's love for it stronger. He couldn't imagine a world where the season came and went periodically, never offering so much as a hint of mystery.

They passed rivers where the water bubbled into shapes of animals and people to chase one another across the frothing rapids before plunging into the depths. Along the shore where the mud was thick, tiny hands poked free, followed by the faces of children, their eyes too big and noses hooked. One smiled at Nicholas with two rows of jagged teeth before sinking below the mud.

Trees towered high, their limbs hung low and stretched wide. Their leaves brushed against Nicholas' cheeks, where they whispered of pain for daring to cross their roots. Those roots slithered below the earth as if they yearned to drag them all under, but none ever did. From time to time, their shadows moved, but the trees would never be caught moving until they had their prey, which the group would have been if Laurent hadn't led the pack. None dared lift a finger against him, especially in Darkmoon.

When the forest parted, Hill Castle sat as ragged thorns and thick vines twisting together to form the warped shape of a castle. The four towers leaned too far to the right, but the windows all leaned left. High grass circled the keep and dared to travel up the vines, coating the foundation in brilliant green.

He clicked his tongue. "Hill Castle is in a foul mood."

The bridge of Charmaine's nose wrinkled. "Hill Castle has moods?"

"Of course."

"Nicholas, I've said it before and I must say it again. You need to learn to explain things," William muttered, and never received a better explanation.

Facing them, Laurent held out a graceful hand. "Welcome to Hill Castle."

"We appreciate that you guided us here yourself, Lord Darkmoon," Henry said. "Charmaine will surely recover much quicker under the protection of Hill Castle."

Laurent gave a short-lived and contrived smile, then descended the rolling hills. Nicholas held William's hand tighter, worried about what awaited them. Hill Castle had love for its inhabitants, even his annoying siblings, as it remembered all of them as infants. On days when his nursemaids were disinterested in him, Hill Castle rocked his cradle or offered the sweet aroma of flowers to drift him into blissful sleep. The castle wouldn't want to cause harm, but if Laurent ordered it to, it would obey.

Hill Castle didn't have a door until Laurent approached. The vines separated to form a doorway that swung open, leading into a warm foyer lit by crooked chandeliers constructed of the same thorns as the exterior. Their pointed tips burned bright, causing the air to have a slightly burnt smell. A set of double stairs curved upward and two halls ran next to them. Another set of doors appeared beneath the stairs, firmly shut. The floors were bare dirt. Various tapestries and paintings covered the facade, though they sat lopsided against the thorns. It was certainly nothing like the king's castle, and yet, held its own elegant beauty that put an especially enormous smile on Nicholas' face.

"There are rooms to your left." Laurent gestured to the hall that turned sharply in a dozen steps. "Make yourselves comfortable. A servant will find you for supper."

With that, Laurent disappeared into the doors beneath the stairs. Upon his departure, the group released a deep breath in near perfect unison. Evera sat Charmaine on her feet where she leaned against Evera's arm, eyes droopy but aware and watchful.

"We should rest in case Laurent has anything unpleasant planned for us," said Evera.

"For the lot of you," Arden corrected. "I could take my leave."

Nicholas smiled sickly sweet. "He already views you as a part of our group, so risk it, if you would so like."

Arden clicked his tongue. "Curses."

Laurent had nothing good planned. He assured himself he would fight against Laurent if he must, but then he thought of sinking beneath the floor. All the dark crevices far below reeking of rot and decay where Laurent would push and push until Nicholas' panic made him nothing more than a whimpering mess. He would claw and tear and kick in his cocoon of roots and bones, pleading to be given fresh air while his lungs collapsed.

Lips fell on his cheek. Nicholas woke from his trance with a start. The group had taken the hall, but William lagged. He stood with Nicholas, his lips still brushing against his cheek.

"I fear I am nothing against Laurent, but should he try to harm you, I will put up an annoying fight," said William with a sweet smile.

Nicholas chuckled, his worries having lightened. He pressed their foreheads together, taking in William's scent. He still smelled so strongly of disinfectant, but somehow that brought Nicholas joy.

"I wouldn't want you to put yourself in harm's way, but I appreciate the sentiment," he said before a kiss. They lingered there, enraptured by the other's presence. "Stay close to me. I fear what he has planned."

"Whatever it may be, we will face it together." William went after the others, who took the corner of the hall.

The two of them caught up, overhearing Charmaine say groggily, "I don't know if rest will do us any good. We're in his castle in his territory. How can we be expected to sleep?"

"It sounds like you will have no issue sleeping," said Evera, having become Charmaine's walking stick. Nicholas expected Evera to play her pranks, to release Charmaine so she'd stumble, but the fae kept a firm hold on her. He found it odd.

"If I sleep, it will be a restless one from illness and fear." Charmaine stumbled when Evera came to a stop. The fae settled a hand on Charmaine's back to steady her.

A door greeted them, thus telling them which room was to be used. Henry opened the first hesitantly, peeking in like a rabbit searching for a fox. Then he waltzed inside the autumn room, where two wide beds settled against the far wall. Windows rose high on either side, crooked and without glass. One bed made for two while the other two were smaller. Hill Castle even summoned a dining set of four chairs.

"It seems four of you are expected to rest here," said Nicholas proudly. He knew the castle would be on his side. "Evera, Charmaine, Arden, and Henry, enjoy your room."

"But there are only three beds," said Henry incredulously. "Well, I can take the floor."

Hill Castle groaned. Vines breached the soil to swat at his ankles. Henry yelped and stumbled until he fell onto the smaller bed. The vines waited, daring him to leave, but he kicked off his shoes and brought his feet onto the mattress.

"I will sleep here, it seems," he half said, half asked.

The vines turned their attention to Arden, who took the second small bed without issue. He fell onto the mattress and shut his eyes.

"Then Charmaine and Evera can have the large bed," Nicholas said, or rather, Hill Castle did, and he went along with its whims.

"Can't the magical castle conjure another bed?" Charmaine glanced at William like he could help.

"Hill Castle will conjure a bed if it wishes. Right now, it does not, so take your rest. Remember, stay together." He nudged William toward the door.

"I won't bite," Evera teased while Charmaine dropped on the bed. The mortal had a peculiar nervousness about her that revealed itself through the twiddling of her thumbs, which grew worse when Evera sat beside her.

"I should stay with Charmaine," William argued.

His eyes fell on Henry. The mage had his eyes shut, but even Nicholas learned better. Henry was an observer and he no doubt took everything in. His notebook would be filled before the end of the trip. William probably worried about leaving with Nicholas and what that might imply to his brother.

"You must come with me. Hill Castle will be angered otherwise. It clearly wishes to meet you," he whispered.

"Why?"

Rather than answer, he held a hand toward the door. William looked once more at his brother.

"We'll check in later," William muttered.

Henry waved a hand. "Don't get into trouble."

"Be careful," Charmaine said.

He took William's hand to yank him out of the room. His bedroom door materialized. William stumbled after him through the threshold. The room caught William's attention. He swerved back and forth, inspecting the vines tangled in the root rafters. A dozen rugs laid atop one another over the floor, each in varying styles because Nicholas frequently changed his mind on the style he liked best.

Hill Castle shifted beneath their feet, creating more of a high-pitched laugh than a groan. Flowers bloomed along the vines and through the window. Shelves lined the walls at odd angles, donning trinkets he wore once to the revels. A large bed constructed of vines and moss grew within a hollowed out tree. Beside that, an extensive wardrobe stood by a walk-in closet, bringing a chuckle from William.

"What?" he asked.

"Leave it to you to have a nearly endless supply of clothes," William replied.

His arm settled around William's waist. "You are welcome to them, if you'd like. I would enjoy seeing you in my clothes and feel less terribly about ripping them off."

Pink dusted William's cheeks. His attention continued to take in the room Nicholas grew up in. He imagined this happening hundreds of times. Now that William was there in his arms, he could hardly believe it.

"I like that you're here, even if it isn't under the circumstances I hoped for," he admitted.

"Me too." William settled his hand over Nicholas'. They stood like that for a moment, silent, basking in each other's presence. Nicholas kissed his nape. A shiver passed through him, then he cleared his throat. "Faerie is more interesting than you described."

"And you haven't seen the half of it. There is so much I want you to see."

"After we find my missing patients."

Nicholas pouted, but sighed. "Yes, after we find them."

"We should rest while we have the chance."

"So long as you stay here with me."

"You did say we should stick together and I think it's safe to assume Hill Castle wants me here with you," William answered.

They fell on the bed in a heap. William held him close where his head laid on William's chest, listening to the racing of his heart. There they laid in an embrace of warmth, cuddling and kissing until William's breathing evened out. William fell asleep while he did not. He couldn't possibly, considering how close Laurent was, but that didn't mean he wasn't enjoying himself. He quite liked being in William's arms without those accursed gloves. They laid somewhere on the floor after Nicholas tore them off, wishing to feel the skin of William's fingers rubbing his arm. He thought being like this every day until the world ended would be perfect.

Unfortunately, his dreamland was merely that, a dream, and reality found them in the form of steps pacing outside the door. Nicholas heard them even if the trespasser did their best to be quiet. He couldn't fathom who it was. If Solomon or Percival wanted to cause trouble, they would have broken the door down. If Laurent sought them, he would have sent someone to retrieve them. There had been no signs of Laurent holding a revel, so there shouldn't be more than a few unlucky attendants at Hill Castle.

After the twelfth pass, Nicholas removed himself from his sanctuary. William didn't stir thanks to his exhaustion and, no doubt, Hill Castle's help. He hadn't missed the flowers blooming along the walls, the same ones that put him to sleep as an infant. They weren't as potent at his age, though seemingly strong enough to knock out an anxious medic. He approached the door where the pacing continued, then threw it open, shocked to find Henry standing in the hall. Alone.

"Did I not say to go nowhere alone?" Nicholas hissed.

"I hardly went anywhere alone," Henry countered, flushed from having been caught. "Charmaine rests and Evera has been tearing through my things for the last hour, claiming there was nothing else to placate her boredom."

"And so you came out to pace?"

Henry shifted his weight from one foot to the other. "Not exactly." He glanced over Nicholas' shoulder, relieved that William slept. "I was hoping I could speak with you alone."

"I dislike leaving William unattended."

"We may speak here in the hall. Keep the door open slightly if you'd like, but let me know if he wakes. He will be upset if he overhears us."

He couldn't fathom what Henry wanted to discuss, but Nicholas would listen. He was William's brother, a piece of the family Nicholas genuinely wanted to become a part of. To think a day would come when he yearned to impress a group of mortals. He would be a laughingstock of all of Faerie if others learned how smitten he had become, not that he would care for even a moment. Once, he might have, and he didn't miss that part of him even a little.

Stepping into the hall, he left the door open enough to glimpse William sleeping on the bed. He faced Henry, who stood stiffly, like he hadn't any confidence in the world.

"What is it that you want to discuss?"

"Surely you overheard our conversation earlier? Our tiff before your father appeared," said Henry.

"I did," he replied. Mortals had horrendous hearing.

"I would like to hear your thoughts on the matter."

He was rarely rendered speechless, but Henry had succeeded.

"More specifically, I would appreciate it if you gave me advice on how to proceed," Henry said after the prolonged silence.

"Proceed with what?" He checked on William. He understood now why Henry wanted to talk in private. If William woke to hear them discussing him, he would be out there in an instant.

"He seems to believe we think differently of him, but clearly telling him otherwise doesn't work. You were with him during the war, and I am not asking for you to share any secrets. However, if you have advice, I would appreciate it."

No one came to him for advice. He would be the last person to give any, too, and yet, he was unbearably excited to receive Henry's request. So overjoyed, he hardly resisted the urge to jump and kick his feet. William's brother saw him as someone to confide in. A part of him always wanted that with his family and now he had it, a little moment of it, but better than none.

Although that mirth was short-lived as he was the one lacking confidence in this area. Henry was right that William struggled with how his family perceived him as well as himself.

"I wasn't at William's side long," he admitted, thinking of how his life changed from their first encounter.

He laughed, remembering how William shot him in front of everyone and how he so easily challenged Nicholas over everything. He had been drawn to William since day one, though for entirely different reasons.

"William thinks so highly of his family, so much so that I envy all of you," he said. "I wish he felt such happiness with me as he does with all of you, but that also means you can bring about his greatest sorrow. He believes he has done horrible things and that you'd hate him should you learn the truth, but if I am being honest with you, I think telling you the truth is exactly what he needs."

"Would he?" Henry whispered.

"Not without much toil."

"As if we would expect anything less."

Nicholas smiled. "Yes, he would not be William without a fight."

"Broaching such a topic will not come easily to me, either."

"Just ask," he said. "Do not sugarcoat your words. Sit him down and tell him what you want to hear, so long as you truly believe you can accept whatever the answer is."

"I can." Henry had a sternness about him that Nicholas respected. He hadn't known the man long, but Henry showed courage and strength in the face of adversity. He was no doubt William's brother, even if they showed their merit in different ways.

"I will," Henry repeated. "I have met many survivors of the war and I have heard their tales of horror. William has his. Our family knows it, has heard him whimpering in the dark and seen the hollowness of his eyes. There is sorrow in us too upon realizing that there is so little we can do, but we end up running in a circle exactly because of that. We don't take a step forward and neither does he so we're always ten paces away from each other and that must change."

Henry settled a hand on Nicholas' shoulder, firm and true. "I appreciate you talking to me, and should you need advice when being," he smirked impishly, "properly introduced to the rest of our family, I will help and intervene in case of a catastrophe."

He suspected Henry knew more than he let on, certainly more than William believed. His reaction proved as such and eased Nicholas knowing that one of William's brothers accepted their relationship, so much so that he would stand beside them.

"That is kind of you, but I am quite charming, so I am unlikely to need your assistance," he replied teasingly.

"William is the baby of the household, so unfortunately for you, that means you have more than parents to win over." Henry placed his hands in front of his waist, pointing his nose skyward in poised arrogance. "I am much more understanding than our brothers and more intelligent, of course."

"Of course," he mocked. Then the two shared a smile and a laugh that had William sitting up in bed.

Rubbing his tired eyes, he wandered to the door to ask, "What are you two laughing about?"

"Nothing at all." Henry pivoted on his heel to head for his room. "I should make sure Evera hasn't broken any of my things. She's nosy as a cat, that friend of yours."

"Friend." Nicholas snorted, but couldn't deny the accusation after what had transpired. Then, at the end of the hall, a mortal girl rounded the corner. Henry and William shared confused looks. Nicholas bit back a scowl.

The girl came closer, revealing her clouded eyes, nearly milk white. She walked stiffly, her hands behind her back and hair falling in knotted waves. She walked without shoes, showing bloody and bruised feet. When she smiled, it was painful, though her voice held mirth. "Lord Darkmoon demands your presence in the dining hall. I am to escort you to him."

William looked at Nicholas with an unspoken question.

"Glamoured, all the attendants here are," he explained. "Get the others, Henry. We shouldn't keep my father waiting."

24

NICHOLAS

HILL CASTLE CONSTRUCTED A dining room rather than a revel hall, which was typically the norm. A long table sprouted from the floor out of roots, flattened to hold an arrangement of food and beverage. Laurent sat at the head; his hardened stare illuminated by the candles burning from warped chandeliers. Percival and Solomon scurried to a pair of seats at the opposite end of the table. They dug into the food, though never removed their eyes from the entering guests.

Charmaine had a restful sleep because she walked steadily on her own, though Evera kept close to her side. Henry kept a calm facade, save for the hands clasped tightly behind his back. Nicholas and William sat together. Yawning, Arden dropping into the chair by William. Henry took the chair on Laurent's left. He praised the human for being brave enough to do so. William, however, scowled.

Solomon and Percival made a mess, gnawing on fruits and meats, spitting pits across the room and dripping blood on the floor. Both preferred their meat on the raw side, encouraging bugs to flutter around their heads. They shouldn't be there. He had them sitting at the dining table acting as if this were normal.

"The food and drink are safe. I acquired a stash from Terra when we had human guests more often," Laurent said.

He moved with a grace that mortal kings envied, sitting elegantly, speaking gracefully, and summoning the attendants with a flick of his eyes. The mortal girl who led them hurried to pour his drink, faerie wine that resembled silver paint and tasted of the greatest delights. If a mortal partook, they would die thirsty while drowning in water.

The mortal attendants, with their clouded eyes, ensured all had their meals. Fresh fruit lined their plates beside freshly cut meat from the steaming hog at the center of the table. It smelled strongly of paprika and thyme, so savorful that their stomachs growled. Laurent wore a proud grin. He disliked mortals at his gatherings unless they were under his control, but he remained ever the perfect host. He enjoyed when others couldn't deny his hospitality.

Though Laurent stated the safety of their meals, he tasted the food on William's plate. To his surprise, Evera sampled Henry's and Charmaine's. Arden shoved food in his mouth without care.

With their reluctant nods, the humans of their group partook in their meal. In a strange way, he took pride in William eating, rather voraciously, because it meant he had William's trust. They had a long journey and ate little of their supplies, seeing as Laurent didn't stop in their travels, so the group was eager to fill their stomachs. However, that didn't stop any of them from giving Laurent, Percival, and Solomon peculiar looks.

Their host ate in a consuming silence that Nicholas couldn't stomach. The dining hall had a darkness to it that couldn't be explained. The candlelight burned true, and the doors hung open, practically inviting any to dare an exit, and yet, it was suffocating and entirely untrue. A shimmering web of silk flickering beautifully in the sun while the spider hid under in the shadows.

"What are you up to?" Nicholas finally asked over a half full plate. He didn't partake in the fae food, if only to ensure William didn't mistake any. Laurent had it placed together, after all, no doubt hoping one of them made a mistake.

Laurent leaned back. "Am I not allowed to have guests?"

"You're not fond of human guests less they become a new addition to your toys." He spoke of the attendants lining the hall, ten of them in total. Each was the same; white eyed, bloodied and bruised. There were plenty more wandering the halls and countless crushed under Hill Castle or used as fertilizer for the gardens.

"You once weren't, either, yet here you are, traveling with them," Laurent replied.

"Traveling with them or working with them?" Solomon called from the end of the table. "We should ask what you are up to."

"Father already knows and you don't deserve an answer," he snarled. He never had a family dinner before and decided he was relieved not to because they were horrendous.

Beneath the table, William sat a hand on his thigh. The touch soothed him, but nothing truly comforted him. Not when Laurent sat so close to William, not when he could wave his hand and snap William's neck.

"We appreciate being given this food and rest, Lord Darkmoon," Henry proclaimed. He took to eating his food more comfortably than the others, though Nicholas noted how small his bites were. He practiced caution in his own way. "May I ask how long you want us to stay? We have quite a lot of work to do."

"So I have been told." Laurent took a slow drink. "But I have not been told why this work is so important. Disappearing mortals should be of no concern. Why, there are a few here that others would claim disappeared, though they came to Faerie of their own volition."

"We do not speak of mortals wandering to Faerie in search of riches," said Nicholas.

Laurent's long finger traced the rim of his wineglass. "Then what do you speak of? I suggest you tell me soon if you are in such a rush as you so claim."

"Shadowed disciples," William said. He sat tall and brave, meeting Laurent's eyes without a care. Nicholas both loved and hated him for it. "Shadowed disciples have been snatching mortals from Terra and bringing them to Faerie. We are in search of them."

He took the opening to say, "Let us leave and I will take care of them, as I have been doing until now."

Laurent drank slowly, without a care. He couldn't understand why. Laurent wanted the shadowed disciples gone as much as everyone else, if not more. Fearworn's destruction by Nicholas' hand brought power to the Darkmoon name, even trust. Mortals traveled to Faerie once more. Many would wind up like the attendants, broken and abused by bored fae, then killed once their masters saw no reason to keep them around. The cycle would repeat, and Laurent loved that cycle as much as the next fae.

Mortals were foolish enough to believe the fae that destroyed Fearworn would be more trustworthy. That's what Laurent wanted, more deals to make, lives to ruin. So why have them sitting here? Why...

"This is a distraction," Nicholas whispered. "You don't want us to look into the disappearances."

"If I didn't want you investigating, I could have killed you upon your arrival." Laurent popped a grape into his mouth.

"You would have tried and you would have pissed me off."

Laurent chortled. "You are always angered. That is nothing new."

"Then you should have no issue letting us leave to investigate, though I cannot understand why. Why the distraction?" He stood. The chair shrieked, and the room bore down on him.

"I do take issue with your departure. You did not seek my permission to bring these humans to my lands, and I am shocked by you, Arden."

Arden had his gaping maw open to inhale a roll of meat.

Growling, Nicholas took William's hand. "We weren't on your lands. Even if we were, they do not need your permission. Any are welcome in Darkmoon, so long as they respect it. Come. We are leaving."

William couldn't stand. None could. The table warped. Roots wrapped around their ankles, up their legs, and the chairs shifted behind them. A strangled breath left William's throat when the roots snaked around his torso, then slithered about his neck. The same happened to the others. Fire caught at Charmaine's fingertips. The roots tightened around her wrists until she cursed and relinquished the flames. Nicholas tore at the roots, constricting William. The thorns pierced his flesh. The cent of copper filled his nostrils and fear rang through his heart.

"Release them," he ordered, tearing faster, shredding the roots into splinters that pricked his hands, William's hands. He imagined the room shattering around them, Laurent bloody and dead on the floor.

"Nicholas," William warned. His words choked off from the grip around his neck. Seeing the constriction there, watching it grow tighter and hearing William's breath stutter, forced his heart into his throat.

"I will release them if you assure me they will remain here or return to Terra," Laurent replied. "I am Hill Castle's lord, and as much as it is your home, it must obey me, and I want them here." Laurent stood. His hand fell on Nicholas' shoulder, applying no pressure, and yet, he flinched. "You and Evera have a duty to fulfill, so you will cease this nonsense or come to regret it."

"You're a bastard. You are cold and heartless," William spat between clenched teeth. "But most of all, you fear your son and what he is capable of, so you try to control him, but he is stronger than you will ever be." William turned his attention to Nicholas, speaking low and firm. "He has no control over you. He wants what you have, but this power is yours entirely and he knows, as we all do, that you are better than him in every way."

The roots wrapped around William's mouth. Nicholas spun on Laurent, his nails pointed at the bastard's throat. But then he was yanked under into the stony soil that blackened his vision. He couldn't breathe, clawing at a crushing darkness that made him into a terrified child begging to be set free.

William shouldn't have spoken back to Laurent. Nicholas didn't understand why he would. They were trapped in Hill Castle, captured by Laurent, who could kill them all without care. William had been right. He was cold and heartless and...

Nicholas tore through his lip, tasting blood. He understood he had more power than Laurent in the literal sense, but he had never felt stronger than his father. He shrank in Laurent's presence, never once perceived himself as better, but William believed so. He believed that enough to risk all their lives, to say it to Nicholas' face. If he didn't get out of there, if he didn't stop his father, all of them would die. He would lose William forever.

That fear had him reaching out. Desperation took hold. He tore through the soil, splitting it apart with a crash. Light shone above. He catapulted into the room, where the roots covered his companions entirely. He lunged at Laurent. Hill Castle shifted, the floor trying to swallow him. He wasn't the child he once was. His power awakened in ways he couldn't fathom, that made his mind hazy, but he knew enough; William believed him better, and he would be.

A haze of violet miasma seeped from his form, power taking physical form. It warped around him like armor and crawled across the floor. Laurent wasn't shocked when Nicholas swung at him. His father fought elegantly, too. He moved like water, creating a path through the land, for nothing could withstand its current. Every swing of Nicholas' fist, every burst of his power, was blocked or dodged, though he witnessed a single bead of sweat fall down Laurent's cheek.

William would die before he defeated his father, so rather than going for Laurent, he dropped. His hands sank into the soil, willing it to obey. Much like The Lost Woods, the earth ignored his commands, battling against his will. Laurent had control of Darkmoon and it didn't want to bow to another, but Nicholas forced it with a wild burst of energy.

William breached the soil first, heaving a great breath that sent him into a coughing fit. Charmaine, Henry, Arden, and Evera followed, the latter of whom didn't hesitate to summon blinding light in her palm. Evera's anger burst free in an arch of light, slashing out at Solomon, who dared to try to creep up on them. Nicholas had entirely forgotten about his brothers, so fixated on saving William from their father. Arden tackled Percival, the both of them cackling at the thought of bloodshed.

With a swipe of his hand, Laurent morphed Hill Castle into a maze. William disappeared behind walls of thorns. Evera fell with his brothers into shadow. Charmaine and Henry were gone, their shouts of surprise cut off. The ground rumbled beneath his feet as the walls grew taller, thinner, and the castle he called home became a place of horrors.

Fierce thorns scrambled to rip through his skin. Screaming faces pressed against the skin of the roots like souls reaching out for him. Laurent's voice, cruel enough to cut, hissed through the halls, "Do you genuinely believe you can defeat me, Nicholas? What do you know of power?"

He dashed through the halls, focusing on Laurent's voice. He couldn't sense him anywhere. Hill Castle had become an entity of such force that all he felt was a thrum, like the beat of a great heart.

"You didn't earn your power," Laurent said, and the maze reacted, lashing out with unforgiving wrath.

Fire caught along the roots, summoned by his will. He internally apologized to Hill Castle, hoping that this wouldn't end with the castle as nothing more than a broken mess.

"You're nothing," said Laurent, calmer now, so certain that Nicholas dared to believe him. "You're another Fearworn doomed to craze and death. Nothing you do will ever change your fate."

"Shut up! Shut up! Shut up!" His fear bled from him in waves that withered the walls. They rotted, oozing black across the floor, revealing halls upon halls that reconstructed themselves. Laurent buried him again, differently but still a burial, reminding him what his father was capable of and that he saw Nicholas as nothing. Worthless. Another pawn to control...

"He has no control over you." William sounded so sure. He wanted to be that certain, too. *"He wants what you have, but this power is yours entirely and he knows, as we all do, that you are better than him in every way."*

Nicholas understood that. Laurent was no different from the others. They looked at him in fear or greed. Laurent saw a tool and he would use that tool, bend it to his will like he did all things. He let it happen for years out of his own fear, but William was right. Laurent wanted what he had and, no matter what, he wouldn't be that tool anymore.

He took a breath, standing there motionless, hands listless at his side and eyes closed. Nicholas always let his anger speak for him, spilling from his fingertips like a raging storm. That time, he needed to control the storm as Laurent controlled everything around them. He wouldn't beat his father in a raging fit. He had to be as calculated and careful as him, so he focused on that energy within, letting the sensation of unrivaled power ripple through his veins.

Around him, the walls closed in, sensing his stillness as an opening to attack. Thorns pierced his skin, closing in more and more until he tasted the soil. All the while, he listened to the thrum of Hill Castle's heart, the point of its energy; Laurent. He felt his father moving through the maze, and could somehow see his energy passing below.

He fell through the floor like water. The roots opened for him without hesitation, all controlled by his unbending will. Then his eyes opened as he crashed into Laurent. It was the first he ever seen fear in his father's eyes. Laurent couldn't fathom him being there, one hand caught in Laurent's antlers and the other upon his throat. The miasma pouring from him created a shield that Hill Castle couldn't break through even as he snapped that antler from Laurent's scalp to drive into his chest.

Blood splattered against Nicholas' cheeks, his father's blood. Laurent gawked, his breath coming in through a choked breath. The antler had certainly pierced a lung, and his body struggled to heal with the bone lodged in his chest. Nicholas held it there, pressed his full weight against Laurent as he brought his fist down over and over until he wasn't sure whose blood coated his knuckles. Laurent tore helplessly at Nicholas' arms. His claws ripped through skin. Nicholas felt the blood, but nothing could stop him from hitting Laurent.

A hand fell on his wrist. Nicholas growled until he met emerald eyes. William eased onto his knees, his face cut and clothes torn. Behind him, the maze opened up, withered into a poor excuse of a room. Charmaine and Evera stood together, close enough that their hands brushed, and Henry had his hands up as if he were once speaking. Arden wasn't with them.

"Wait," Henry said, approaching hesitantly.

Nicholas hadn't heard them or realized that Hill Castle relented, or rather, Laurent couldn't force it any further. He laid beneath Nicholas, bloodied and wheezing. He had pressed the antler so deeply that it lodged in the dirt behind his father.

"Why should I wait?" Nicholas whispered, pressing harder and savoring the weakened whimper Laurent released. He was unrecognizable, beaten to a pulp and eyes swollen.

"We need to question him," William replied, keeping a firm hold on Nicholas.

"About what?" he snarled.

"It is peculiar that he didn't want us involved. I believe it is because a fae lord has something to play in all this." Henry eased closer, gazing down at Laurent's limp form. "The disappearances are shadow disciple work, but if Laurent knew we were here, then surely a lord would know if shadowed disciples are on theirs. Someone knows, and that someone is another lord."

"Or the shadowed disciples have their claws dug into a fae lord, forcing them to do their will, and that would look even worse. We can deal with this trouble for you, Laurent," William said with a smug smile.

The meager cuts along Laurent's face healed and his eyes opened as the swelling lessened. "Why would I need you?"

William glared at Laurent. "A lord making moves on another doesn't look good. If anyone learns that the shadowed disciples are working in fae lands, that would spell trouble with Terra, but if you deal with this yourself, it won't go unnoticed."

The corner of Laurent's lip twitched toward a frown. "You wouldn't help without requesting compensation."

"No, we wouldn't. Once we defeat these shadowed disciples for you, quietly, then you will release Nicholas from his deal. He doesn't have to sire children with Evera."

Laurent laughed. Nicholas had never heard a sound so bitter. Hill Castle wavered beneath the sound, as if its lord's laughter empowered it, or frightened it.

"You believe too highly in yourself." He groaned when Nicholas twisted the bone in his chest.

"Damn the deal, let's kill him now," he said, ready to stab that antler through his father's heart.

The ground shook. In Nicholas' distraction, Laurent fell into the soil. He snarled and tore up the dirt until Laurent's voice carried around them. "I suppose there isn't much of a loss in this for me. If you fail, you die, and if you succeed, the disciples are dead. Then all I have to do is wait for Nicholas to make a mistake. He always does. Consider this deal accepted, however, this deal was made between two. Alvina may still call upon you, and know that there will be no help from Darkmoon. You do this on your own."

The ground fell out from under them. Nicholas plummeted into darkness. He panicked for all of a moment before he was propelled into sunlight. He fell among the grass, groaning and looking upon a clear blue sky. More grunts followed. Nicholas sat up. All of them had been spat out of Hill Castle like a nasty spoon full of medicine. The structure reformed, a castle once more, albeit it weeping like flowers after the first frost.

William laid beside him, rubbing the bruise around his neck.

"Gah!" Arden flew above them, spat out last. He rolled safely to his feet, two stakes made of bark in either hand. Percival's blood stained them, though he doubted Arden did much more than irritate him.

"Well," William wheezed. "We better head off to Bloodbane."

"I don't like this one bit." Evera shambled to her feet and shook her head. "I get the feeling he's going to sabotage us."

"Unlikely. He wants this dealt with otherwise, he'd have tried to kill all of you," he said.

Arden dropped his daggers and dusted off his pants that didn't remove any of the blood. "Did you forget he strangled us with roots?"

"That's nothing to him."

Charmaine shivered. "I hate Faerie."

"We'll try not to be here too long." William got onto his feet and scowled at the rip in his jacket. The rip tore through his shirt too, revealing a slim line of silver. "The sooner we end this, the better."

"What happens afterward?" Nicholas reached for William's hand, letting the tips of their fingers brush, then grasped William's wrist. The pulse beneath raced against his fingertips, making his own mirror the beat. "After they are dealt with and I'm free from Evera?"

"Is now really the time for that conversation?" William squeezed his hand, then let go to head toward the others, leaving Nicholas pouting on the ground.

He told himself to be happy. William thought of getting him out of the deal. When they succeeded, and he would make sure they did, he would be free. Free to be with William always.

25

WILLIAM

WILLIAM HADN'T WANTED TO see Laurent again. He didn't want to think of waking in the hospital to discover his arm taken, replaced by what didn't belong to him, by what he hadn't asked for. His fingers flexed. The arm was as much a part of him as anything else. He wished he would come to terms with it, that he would cease mourning the loss of his limb and the loss of his choice.

You're lucky, he told himself, and tasted the same bile as always.

He wiped the sweat from his brow. Behind them, Hill Castle disappeared, leaving Laurent and his troubles. For the time being. Nicholas had shown what he was capable of, what Laurent feared and wanted to control. William hadn't meant to stand up to the bastard, but he couldn't sit there and watch Nicholas be toyed with. Laurent treated him terribly, and William hated him all the more for it. He got what he deserved and would, hopefully, understand the consequences should he bother them again.

Next time, he wouldn't stop Nicholas from killing the bastard. That time, they needed to question him, to ensure Nicholas' deal was broken, and though Laurent said Darkmoon wouldn't help, he didn't doubt that the lord would get involved if Fearworn were not only alive but also ready to start trouble for all of Faerie. Laurent was useful as much as he was awful.

Ahead, Evera led the way. She had a tension to her, an irritation that she rarely showed. Charmaine wandered at her back, having become much better thanks to their distance and rest. Arden sang in a foreign tongue, the language of fae, he guessed. His voice had a high lilt, nothing like they expected, ethereal and haunting in the most beautiful way. Henry traveled at the center, his favorite notebook clutched between his fingers. From time to time, he peered over his shoulder. William pretended not to notice.

"Avoiding your brother won't solve anything," Nicholas said. The wounds upon his knuckles healed. Still, William took his hand to inspect.

"There is nothing to solve," he argued, checking Nicholas for any abnormalities. Of course, he found nothing.

"You remain upset that he fought those red caps."

He crossed his arms. "Now isn't a good time to talk."

"Now is the best time, seeing as we may not survive this endeavor."

William gave him a curious glance. "What were you talking to him about in the hallway before?"

Nicholas hesitated, which meant he was trying to wiggle his way out of telling the truth.

"Did it have to do with me?" he asked.

"He's worried and asked for my advice on how to speak with you." Nicholas scoffed. "Don't make such a face of disbelief."

"Not so much disbelief as surprise," he countered while watching Henry's back. "I didn't think he was so worried that he'd ask for anyone's advice."

"Well, since you know now, you shouldn't avoid it any longer."

Nicholas walked ahead, settling a hand on Henry's arm that told him to linger. While Nicholas walked beside Arden, Henry lagged, as did

William until they walked side by side, far enough away from the others to feel safe but isolated enough to talk.

"We can't jump into danger like that," William said. "You should have talked with the rest of us first before agreeing to the red caps' demands. There could have been a trick involved."

"Does this rule apply to you as well?" Henry challenged. "Earlier, you stood up to Laurent, who could have easily killed us if Nicholas didn't blow a fuse."

His jaw ached from grinding his teeth. "That's different."

"Because it was your life on the line, not mine?"

He didn't answer.

"Need I point out that my life isn't worth more than yours again?"

His fingers bruised his arms from how fiercely he held them.

"What aren't you telling us? There is a truth you have yet to share that burdens you so greatly that you dare to believe your life is lesser than all others. I don't understand and I won't unless you tell me," he said.

"I killed people, Henry."

"You killed monsters."

"Yes, they were the most monstrous of men. I told myself they deserved it and I still believe that. The military didn't teach strength, it taught submission and violence. There were those who dealt pain, and those who fell to it. Cruelty was looked upon as necessary to ensure the masses remained sturdy, but it wasn't sturdiness they created, either. It was broken minds and shattered wills and loathing. Men fought and killed and raped and they were applauded for it," he spat, feeling as if the words soiled his tongue.

"I learned quickly that there were those who would never see justice, so I gave out the one justice I could. But I know how our parents would react, how you and our brothers will react knowing that I've stooped so low as to not only condone such violence but support it unequivocally.

The hatred I have toward myself isn't guilt. I do not regret a damn thing I did to them, but I regret who I have become."

Henry stepped ahead, blocking his brother's path. He caught William's hands, easing them from his arms where his nails had pierced flesh.

"You do not need to explain yourself to me," he said, comforting as the morning sun.

"Don't you want to know what I did? To know what kind of brother you now have?"

"I know exactly what kind of brother I have," he said sternly. "William, what you went through will stay with you all your life. I don't say that to be cruel. I am saying that you survived something you never should have had to deal with, and that leaves a scar. I hope those scars heal as well as they can, but some won't, and I certainly don't expect them to. Our family doesn't, either. That doesn't mean we don't love you, that we dislike anything about who you have grown into being."

"But you have thought about it, haven't you? Who I could have been?" he asked.

"Don't we all?" Henry countered. "We've all imagined other paths we could have taken. I imagine who you may have been if the king hadn't taken you. I curse him for putting you through that, but I don't curse you for what you went through and you shouldn't curse yourself, either."

"I've been trying."

"I know. Sometimes trying is all we can do. That isn't anything to beat yourself up about."

"But what if all I do is try, and nothing gets better?"

"What do you consider better?" Henry asked.

"I don't know."

"If you don't mind me saying, you are doing better. William, when you came home, you wouldn't let any of us leave the house without every detail of what we were doing. You hardly paid attention to us when we spoke because you were too busy looking for the next fight. You carried at least two blades and a gun and you hid some around the house."

William tensed. He hid them so Alice couldn't find or reach them, but the truth remained that he hid weapons in a home where a child could stumble across them because he was too scared of what might happen if he didn't.

"Now, you're running a clinic helping people struggling like you. How is that not an accomplishment for you to be proud of?" Henry asked.

"Because I do so for myself—"

"Who fucking cares?" Henry spat, his hold tight on William's hands. "You're going out. You're doing what you can, whatever that may be. You're helping people who otherwise wouldn't have got it. You have the right to be proud of what you are doing."

Then Henry settled his hand on William's shoulder, the right one. He tried to escape, but Henry held firm. He looked William in the eye when he said, "I know you hate this."

"When I should be grateful?" he interjected.

"No," Henry replied so simply, and yet, the word reverberated louder than anything he had heard. "Nothing you went through should have happened. Do you understand? Fearworn took something from you that is entirely yours, only to wake up and discover something had replaced a part of you that you couldn't even mourn. Yes, it's fortunate you can still do everything you once did, but you are allowed to be angry."

Henry caught him by the back of the head, bringing their foreheads together. There was anger in his eyes, pain and hurt, none of it directed at William. Directed at the world, maybe, and William felt, for the first time, that it would be okay to scream and cry and break down like a child as Henry said, "Be upset. Hurt. Mourn. Curse, if you must, but never tell yourself that these feelings are unjust because they aren't and know there is no time limit on sorrow. Should you mourn your arm until the day you die, so be it. No one has the right to tell you otherwise, not even yourself. Do you understand?"

Henry pulled him into a hug before the first tear fell. William clung to his brother, feeling foolish for not talking to him sooner, and knowing he couldn't have even if he tried. Henry was right. He had scars. Some days would be better than others. He had already learned that. But it was nice to hear Henry say it, to know he wasn't overreacting. And since they were on the topic of sensitive subjects.

"Henry, you should know," he swallowed hard, looking at Nicholas over Henry's shoulder. "Nicholas and I..."

"I know," Henry whispered.

"Do you think our parents suspect...?"

"Doubtful." Henry released him, smiling. "Neither of you have been very subtle while we've been here, but I suspected it long before that."

"Since when?"

He chuckled. "Since the night I met him. I might have been drinking, but I remembered how much he asked about you."

"Fae are curious by nature," he muttered, as if that changed anything.

"They're rarely interested in personal childhood stories. They want information to use, but Nicholas wanted to know about you. That said enough." Henry kept walking. "Although, leave it to you to find the most troublesome man imaginable. Here, I thought we'd have to worry about Richard."

"To be fair, we'll always have to worry about him. Eleanor could always come to her senses."

The two of them laughed, and it felt like old times. All the trying William did had amounted to something, and that felt good.

26

NICHOLAS

THE LAST TIME NICHOLAS visited Bloodbane had been after Alvina saved him. He sat in her castle halls waiting for Laurent, then heard from his father's mouth that he would be betrothed to the pouting daughter at Alvina's side. He hadn't wanted to visit Bloodbane since. It was a reminder of how powerless he was. That his father used him as a tool. But even after over a decade passed, he knew Bloodbane had not looked like this.

Leaves crunched beneath their boots. Sapped of their color, they laid as gray husks of what once was. The trees, too, lost color until they hardly held their ash shapes. Trunks rotted from within, decaying so branches hung, broken from their heart or shattered on the forest floor. The trees of Bloodbane were silent and its fields little more than old, cracking dirt beneath their feet.

Evera knelt. She pinched the debris between her fingers, forehead creased. Nicholas wouldn't dare say aloud that she carried a pain about her the moment they grew close to Bloodbane. All the fae felt it long before they saw it, this sense of emptiness, as if a force had hollowed Bloodbane out from the roots. This was her home, as Darkmoon was his.

If he saw this happen to Darkmoon, if he witnessed Hill Castle crumble, he would hurt, too.

"The red caps weren't exaggerating," Evera whispered. "Something is horribly wrong."

"It wasn't like this when either of you were here last?" Nicholas asked.

Arden pinched a leaf between his fingers. The leaf disintegrated into a fine powder. "There was rot, in some areas, but nothing like this."

Evera tore her nails through the soil. "Last time I was here, there wasn't even rot. We should seek my brother first. He'll have an idea of what trouble she has gotten into."

"Or he'll tell her we're here. He's loyal to Alvina," Nicholas countered.

Laurent and Alvina had their similarities, but more differences. Alvina had better relationships with her children, purely based on the few instances he met her or heard her children speak of her. Evera had a sore spot toward Alvina, for obvious reasons, but he never heard of Alvina mistreating Amos. He obeyed her orders with little question and spoke highly of her, albeit truthfully. He, along with everyone else, knew Alvina veered toward erratic.

"He will be as worried about this as the rest of us. If this has happened to Bloodbane, it could spread." Evera waved her fingers. "This way and keep close."

Together, they descended the rolling hills of Bloodbane, once green and now gray. Evera ran her hands over trees she must have known since childhood. Her pained expression became apparent, so much so that Charmaine offered comfort by a brief touch to Evera's arm. The fae jumped, perturbed by the attention. Then her shoulders slumped.

"I am sure Bloodbane had been exquisite," Charmaine remarked, clearly unsure of what to say.

"It was, and it will be again," Evera said assuredly. "We will fix it."

"We? I thought you didn't like teamwork."

"I will accept it if it means seeing my home as it should be." Evera gave Charmaine a slow once over that had the girl crossing her arms as if she could shield herself. "I suppose the company with me isn't as bad as it could be."

"Would it kill you to compliment us?"

"It may. I'm not risking discovering that truth."

The girls shared a muted glance, then giggled.

"Suspicious," William whispered.

Arden hugged his torso. "The lot of you are suffering from some form of illness. You best not give it to me."

"Whatever do you mean?" asked Nicholas.

"Mortals." Arden made a disgusted face, then put at least ten steps between himself and the group.

Evera guided them through Bloodbane to Sorrows Well. Every fae lord commanded their domain from somewhere. Alvina did so from what most would perceive as an ordinary well. Perched between two slanted burr trees tilted toward one another in a dance, the well sat inauspiciously, stacked ten stones high. Evera stepped onto the ledge, leading to a hole wide enough for a body, but too deep to see.

"What are you doing?" Henry asked. Then Evera fell into the shadows, and Arden jumped in afterward.

Charmaine lurched toward the well, peering within, then looking at Nicholas for answers.

"Go on," he said. "This is the entrance."

"We're expected to jump in?" she asked.

"Yes, you'll be fine."

Henry hefted his pack and stepped onto the ledge. William couldn't get his disagreement out before Henry shouted, "Look out below," and jumped.

"This is mad," Charmaine muttered while shakingly standing on the edge. She took a breath and followed.

He grabbed William's hand and eased him onto the ledge. "I'll be right behind you."

"Why can't fae live in a normal house?" William asked.

"That is so boring."

"But at least it's pleasant."

He chuckled, then William let go of his hand and jumped. He followed immediately, falling through the darkness, then slowing to a stop. In a blink, the shadows faded and ethereal blue light illuminated the narrow dirt hallways. The facade was smoothed into obsidian darkness. Stones embedded in the ceiling covered them in the blue light. William stumbled and caught himself on the nearby wall.

"What a... lovely home," he said. In front of him, the rest of their group waited.

"It is." Evera nodded behind her. "Amos is nearby."

The halls of Sorrows Well were long and winding, changing at random intervals. Much like Hill Castle, the halls changed of their own accord, coming and going, opening to the sky or digging to the harsh rocks below. Creeks ran along the ceiling, clear water so one could see the fish swimming above, and yet nothing dripped upon them.

The hall led into a deep library, six floors below. The glowing stones circled into a spiral and threaded themselves between the carved shelves full of scrolls and books. Evera descended the wooden staircase to a circular room where Amos sat at a table digging through scrolls. He was so fixated on them he didn't notice Evera until she called. Amos stood tall, realizing that he wasn't alone.

"You've brought unwelcome guests," Amos hissed with his attention landing on Nicholas.

Evera glowered. "They may not be so unwelcome. What's wrong with Bloodbane?"

"This is not a conversation to have in front of them."

"We're here because something is wrong in Terra, too," Henry said, earning a worried glance from William. His brother forced a smile. "Now is the best time to be honest with each other. Something is very wrong, and it's affecting all of us."

Amos was likely about to say something smart when William interjected, "There are shadowed disciples kidnapping mortals and bringing them to Faerie. I know of seven, but there are certainly more."

Evera tapped a claw against the scrolls. "You're looking for answers, too. Whatever is happening must be stopped, or we may lose Bloodbane for good. This has something to do with Mother, doesn't it?"

Arden knocked a set of scrolls out of place. They clattered loudly across the floor, earning Amos' murderous attention. Arden kicked those scrolls aside nonchalantly and kept digging, as if he cared about anything in the library. However, his actions put anger on Amos' typically stoic face.

"She has been acting odd," Amos admitted without looking away from Arden. "More paranoid than usual, double checking her alliances like she expects a great evil to befall us, or rather one worse than what we're seeing."

Amos stepped away to snatch Arden by the wrist. Arden heeded the warning and retreated, letting Amos travel between the shelves. The group followed, witnessing the destruction before Amos settled his hand on the wall. A great scar ripped through the wall. A scent like death fell from the wound, making the ground soft so Amos' shoes sunk in the mud.

"I cannot imagine what she is up to, but it's getting worse by the day, and she won't speak to me about it. If what you're saying is true," Amos looked at William, "Then perhaps our mother is to blame. You've visited at the perfect time. She's bedridden."

"Bedridden?" Evera repeated. "Whatever for?"

"She wouldn't tell, but she's weak enough to be in bed the last three nights. I suggest you speak with her before that changes."

Evera snagged Nicholas' arm in a fierce grip. "This is it. My mother is up to no good, and she is weakened. All of Bloodbane is. We solve this for her in exchange for ending our deal, then the two are taken care of."

"Alvina is obsessed with shades. She'll say no," he countered.

"Not if Bloodbane is at stake. Look at this place." She nodded toward the withered wall. "You know as well as I that any lord can be abandoned by their land if they do not protect it. Clearly, my mother isn't, and if she loses her lordship, she will weaken. She doesn't want that."

They had got out of Laurent's deal. It wasn't utterly hopeless to imagine escaping Alvina's clutches.

"Alright. Let's see her." He gestured for Evera to lead the way.

"The mortals should remain here," Evera said. "We don't want my mother to sense we're desperate or play tricks on them."

"She must already know they're here," he argued.

"Not if she's weakened."

"I am not comfortable leaving them alone."

"Amos and Arden will be with them." Evera didn't sound very convince nor did he feel convinced.

"That's worse."

Evera huffed. "They can handle themselves, can't you?"

Henry took to pursuing the library, uncaring of the plans. Charmaine sat at the table, her hands clasped in her lap. William leaned beside her, his expression grim, but he nodded. "Evera's right. We'll wait here."

Nicholas frowned. "If anything happens—"

"I'll call out." William waved his hand. "Go on."

Evera took Nicholas to a lower level, through weaving hallways reeking of damp soil and old moss. The halls became tight, claustrophobic. Being underground hadn't bothered him until now, when he felt the walls brushing against his arms. His breathing became unsteady, panicked, and he stopped. Evera continued on, practically crawling now to get through, grumbling angrily under her breath about Alvina. Nicholas couldn't follow. It was too confined, too much, too dark, reminding him of capture.

"What are you doing?" Evera barked. "We're almost there, and this is a good sign."

He didn't reply. His vision blurred, and he scuttled backward, wanting to run into William's arms.

"Bloodbane is angry to bury her this deep, leaving her halls a mess." Evera ripped a vine out of the way, resulting in dirt falling into her face. She spat it out, then spun, realizing he was not behind her. "Come on."

"You... should go on your own," he said. "I will wait here."

"We need to go together. She will feel cornered."

He already felt cornered, suffocated, trapped. He couldn't breathe. Sweat pooled on the back of his neck. He tasted fear on his lips, blood in his mouth. He sucked on his teeth and pressed his palms to the soil, as if to push it aside.

"Nicholas." Evera caught his wrist, felt the rapid pulse beneath. "You're frightened."

He didn't answer.

"Of seeing her?" Evera pursed her lips, then shook her head. "No, of this." She peered about the hall, how enclosed it was, how the lights dwindled as if Sorrow Well wanted to bury Alvina alive. Or all of them.

"Fear is foolish," he said with clenched teeth, but no more. He couldn't think, so he retreated, trying to rip himself from Evera's grasp.

"Fear is necessary," Evera corrected sternly, sounding more like her mother, which would be unsettling if she didn't add, "Fear prevents fools from acting upon foolish ideas. We'd all die young if we didn't fear."

"Some fear is unnecessary."

"But understandable." Her palm settled on the ceiling. She breathed deep, and the earth rumbled.

Hill Castle had a mind of its own, although it seemed to attune itself to the Darkmoon family. Most of them, while not lords of the land, could convince Hill Castle to play nice, to do what they wanted. None of them could command it though, just as Evera couldn't command Sorrow Well, but she tried. Her expression strained, eyes shut in concentration, then she huffed and became red in the face. The hall expanded, breathing in new life and light, warping around them to form a hall three times the size. He took a breath, his skin clammy from sweat.

"Sorrow Well is upset with all of us," Evera explained while waving her fingers as if the dirt had burned her. "But I assured it that we're working to make amends, so I suggest we keep moving. We wouldn't want to make things worse."

He thought he had made things worse. Evera witnessed his fear, saw clear as day what frightened him most. She should have used it against him, moved to hurt him, smiled knowing she became privy to information that should have been a secret. Instead, she continued on without mention of it.

"You have nothing to say?" he asked, perturbed that she hadn't. It was more frightening.

"About?" she replied.

"What happened just now."

Evera spun on her heel. "We do not have time to dawdle."

"We can walk and talk at the same time. I must know what you plan to do."

"Plan?" She crossed her arms. "Elaborate."

"You know that I am," he didn't want to say it, but he forced it out, "scared of enclosed spaces. If you plan to use that against me, I want you to know you will regret it."

Evera gawked, then blinked, then slapped him over the head. He yelped, confused, then ready for a fight that never came.

"I dislike you," she said. "I dislike you because of what you remind me of, that damned deal, but I do not hate you and I have no interest in your fears. Now, may we continue?"

"We may," he muttered, shocked and confused. He always thought Evera hated him. They couldn't stand being in the same room for most of their years, but she was right. He didn't know Evera well enough to say he hated her. He hated being around her for the same reason, a reminder. They were close to changing that, and so, that hatred for her dwindled.

After another sharp hallway, they came upon a warped door, damp and the doorknob bloodied. Evera entered, leading them to a large, albeit upturned, sitting area. Chairs and a table had been flipped, forgotten in a mess. The ceiling sunk in, roots slithered out and water dripped, soaking the moss crawling across the floor. An open archway led to a bed carved into the wall, more like a bird's nest than anything else. Pillows and blankets overwhelmed the space, but did not hide Alvina's pale and sweaty complexion.

The fae lord bundled in blood stained wrappings leaned against the soil. She had Amos' white hair, pale as snow and cropped short. Her ashen gray skin had a sickly pallor to it, beading with sweat. A pair of eyes, black from side to side, peered at them from the darkness, little more than a glint in the light. Then she smiled, her teeth bloodied.

"Nicholas, what a surprise to see you," she said. "Have you come to fulfill our bargain?"

"No," he replied simply. Evera should do the talking. She knew Alvina best.

"You look unwell, Mother." Evera sat on the edge of the bed. "As does Bloodbane."

The walls groaned as if to agree or to lecture. Based on the state of her room, Sorrow Well didn't appreciate what was happening and expected Alvina to fix it.

Alvina sighed. "I need rest, then I will tend to Bloodbane soil."

More groaning, this time louder, angrier. Alvina pinched her eyes closed, then settled a hand against the wall. Water oozed over her fingertips, dirtying them.

"By the sounds of it, you do not have time to rest. Bloodbane is angry, and you wouldn't want to lose your lordship, would you?" Evera grinned. "Who do you think Bloodbane will choose in your stead? Amos? Me?"

Alvina snorted. "I have been lord of Bloodbane before the oldest tree took root. It would not abandon me for something so trivial."

But Sorrow Well shifted once more, its anger growing hot, making the ceiling sag and Nicholas' feet sank. He retreated from the bed, fearful Sorrow Well would swallow Alvina whole, and them with her.

"This isn't trivial. You've caused trouble, more than even you can handle. What is it?" Evera asked.

Alvina hissed when the walls shrank, threatening to enclose her. Sorrow Well was giving her a chance. Let Evera help or be lost. But the fae lord was proud. Her hesitation lasted long, agonizing moments where Nicholas retreated as the walls closed further around Alvina. Evera left the bed, watching it shrink until the walls pressed around Alvina.

"Fearworn!" she finally bellowed and Sorrow Well relented. The bedchamber cleaned itself, tables and chairs sitting upright, the ceiling flat and secure. The only mess left was Alvina, shaking in bed, holding the blanket over her abdomen where spots of red emerged along the fabric. "Fearworn," she repeated, licking her lips.

"He's dead. I killed him," he said.

"Yes, and no," Alvina replied. "I found his corpse, what remained of it. I wanted to study him, see if I could learn more about shades. However, after bringing him to Faerie, something went amiss. He latched onto us somehow. He started healing."

She hesitated, and Evera laughed. Her words were sharp and accusatory. "And you let him, didn't you? You didn't bother to stop him?"

"I did not expect this to happen," Alvina countered. "It was fascinating watching a body grow from a few fingers, but then I realized Bloodbane was dying. I attacked the corpse. However, things did not go according to plan. He wasn't awake, still isn't, but his body protected itself, and the shadowed disciples appeared, over a dozen of them." She pointed accusingly at Nicholas. "Which you were meant to be rid of!"

"Do not blame him for your own misguidance," Evera interrupted, surprising him. One might say she had stood up for him. "You did this and now we shall fix it, under a condition, of course."

Alvina barked out a laugh. "And why should I make a deal with you?"

"Because Bloodbane will leave you to rot if you don't, and you know you can't handle this, not in your state, and not alone." Evera stood proudly, her hands on her hips. "Release Nicholas and me from our bargain. We will not be forced to have children together. In exchange, we will defeat Fearworn for you and not share your stupidity with anyone outside our group."

"Again," he said. Battles hadn't bothered him once. They did after falling for William, knowing he would be at Nicholas' back, willing to throw his life away to protect him. He couldn't let that happen. He wouldn't lose William.

Alvina gnawed at her bottom lip. She didn't want to make a deal, especially not this one. Her obsession with shades brought this upon them. Had she left Fearworn to rot, this wouldn't have happened.

"Fine," she snapped. "Defeat Fearworn and I'll absolve you of your deal with Nicholas."

"Good." Evera smiled, then nodded at him. "Get the others. They should hear everything she says."

Alvina scowled. "Others?"

27

WILLIAM

NICHOLAS LED THE GROUP to Alvina's room, where Evera waited, more smug than ever. Alvina did not share her daughter's mirth. The injured fae sat in her nest, curled beneath bloodied blankets. She snarled at their entrance, her hatred palpable, but didn't dare to rise. Even William could surmise she was too weak to protect herself.

"You believe you can defeat Fearworn with these mortals?" Alvina laughed.

The mention of that bastard's name brought about a cold sweat. William swallowed hard. His hands shook.

"Tell us everything that happened," Evera demanded.

Alvina spoke of finding Fearworn's corpse, bringing it to Faerie, and how he healed himself by draining the life force of the land itself. That was what caused Bloodbane to wither. William shared what happened in Terra: the missing patients and shadowed disciples capturing them. Alvina listened like he spoke gospel, so enraptured by the information that she made him uncomfortable. Nicholas hadn't said enough about Alvina's hunger for knowledge. No doubt she could repeat his every word, cataloguing it into her mind to find whenever she pleased.

"There were ten shadowed disciples who attacked me," Alvina explained after he finished. "But I can't rule out there being more. They were prepared, so they either knew this would happen or had prepared for Fearworn's return. They're still in Bloodbane. I can feel them, but I don't know why."

"What about the mortals? Do you know why shadowed disciples are bringing them here?" Henry asked from where he scribbled in his notebook.

Alvina gave him an approving look. Apparently, she didn't dislike a mortal who took information as seriously as she did. "My best guess would be for Fearworn. His body healed by latching onto Faerie, but he never woke up. I always believed he used life force to open scars. This might be similar, using life to bring back life."

"So my patients may be alive," said William, uncertain if he was hoping they were. The shadowed disciples had them. They needed them alive, but potentially not unharmed. He brought supplies to help should they find any living, but he may not have enough and, as he learned in the war, breathing didn't mean living. They could practically be walking corpses doomed to death, regardless of their rescue.

"Well, we at least know Fearworn isn't up and about, otherwise things would be much worse," Henry said.

"My biggest concern is that he will remain no matter what is done to him," Alvina added. "He cheated death already. There is nothing to say he won't cheat it again, especially here."

"What if we take his remains to Terra? The magic there is weaker," Evera suggested.

"We'll figure that out once we find him and the shadowed disciples. Where are they most likely to be?" Nicholas asked.

"Likely where I left them at Sky Lake."

"A good place for you to hide," Evera grumbled. "There are cave systems there to hide in and the lake itself is far from prying eyes. Did you learn anything from your experiments?"

"Nothing I can say for certain. My findings are in the library." Alvina waved a hand, clearly giving up on keeping any secrets. "Amos knows where to find them."

"Should we have someone here to watch her?" he whispered to Nicholas.

"No, she isn't going anywhere. Sorrows Well is the only reason she's alive right now," Nicholas replied.

Together, the group traversed to the library where Amos remained. He didn't want Arden there most of all, based on how he watched the fae like a hawk circling a rabbit. Evera instructed her brother to share Alvina's research. He wasn't as reluctant as William expected. Amos tugged leather-bound notebooks from the shelves to lie across the table, though that was the extent of his help. He departed without a word, which William was grateful for. Amos had an unsettling air about him.

Henry took over the duty of reading Alvina's notes. As a researcher, he deciphered them best and pieced together a picture of what to expect, though based on his grim expression, no one would like the answers.

"Alvina is right to be concerned about Fearworn's abilities to regenerate." Henry tapped his fingers, lips set into a grim line. "She found pieces of him, a finger and toe, hair and teeth. I don't know what you did, Nicholas, but there wasn't much left of him."

Nicholas beamed proudly.

"But if he can regenerate from that, then we have to ask ourselves how we'll be rid of him. As Evera mentioned, we could bring him to Terra, perhaps incinerate all that is left of him, because if his shadowed disciples get even a piece of him, I bet he could be brought back."

Evera sat on the edge of the table, one leg crossed and the other dangling. "Then the plan is simple. We slaughter the shadowed disciples and drag him to Terra."

"Except his body protected itself. Alvina said as much," William brought up. "We need to sever the connection between him and Faerie."

"And I certainly do not know how to do that." Henry flipped a few pages. "Neither does Alvina."

"We're also making a lot of guesswork. Alvina thinks he may use mortal life force to open a portal to another realm, but why? Does he expect that to help with his regeneration?" William grumbled.

Nicholas set his hands on the table and leaned forward to speak sternly, "We don't need to know why if we snatch the patients and kill the disciples. Fearworn will be left undefended and without whatever he needs, then we can take some time to research how to sever him from Faerie entirely."

"My mother would work with us to sever him, seeing as what his life has led to. We have to make sure we get his corpse afterward, otherwise she may try something else moronic." Evera hopped off the table. "I vote we go with Nicholas' plan."

"I don't like you agreeing with me," Nicholas muttered. She ignored him.

"We don't have a better option, nor the time to think of one. I wish we did, but the more time we take, the more likely he is to make his move and we have to attack while he's weakest," Charmaine agreed. "Let's rest tonight and leave at first light."

"That could be in days. The sun rises when it wants." Arden poked his head out of the shelves where Amos took to following him. He probably would have kicked Arden out entirely if Nicholas wasn't there.

Charmaine rubbed the back of her neck. "Okay, we leave in six hours? That should give us time for a brief rest."

Henry took to putting the notes away. Arden followed Charmaine and Evera out of the room, the latter of which shouted, "Don't go anywhere alone."

"Then wait for me!" Henry fumbled after them, offering William a smile before he could argue otherwise. With the library safe from Arden's prying, Amos wandered into the shadows.

Nicholas took William's hand. "Shall we be off, then? We should get some sleep."

"We can try to," he replied.

"Oh?" He ran his lips over William's neck. "Do you have something else in mind?"

"I sometimes wonder how your mind can be so dirty when we're in a place like this."

Nicholas shrugged. "We got off in a worse location."

He chuckled and playfully nudged Nicholas' side with his elbow. "Don't remind me of those woods. It gives me the shivers."

Smiling, they walked hand in hand, so blissfully normal that he expected things to turn south. He imagined the walls caving in or Amos coming up behind them to rip out his throat. No such thing happened, and they made it to an empty room without losing any limbs.

The door shut. They were alone. In six hours, they would head out to face Fearworn for the last time, one way or the other. Even if they survived, it would be another nightmare that would stay with him until the end of his days. He couldn't deny that he liked Nicholas' idea, that he'd like to take time to enjoy one another.

"Come here," he said, taking Nicholas by the waist.

The fae fell into him. Nicholas smiled against his mouth. They kissed like it was their first, like they were back in that cold waste of the Deadlands, so overcome by the other they couldn't resist temptation.

He draped his arms over William's shoulders. "You aren't teasing me, are you?"

He propelled them toward the wall, trapping Nicholas between his body. Nicholas' pupils dilated, becoming so black they were obsidian mirrors reflecting his own wanting.

"That depends. What do you want?" He marked Nicholas' neck, savoring the taste of him and the flutter of his heart against the tip of his tongue.

"I want us to be scandalously intimate."

He chuckled against Nicholas' nape. His teeth grazed over the goose feathered skin. Nicholas moaned when he brought their hips together. He slipped a thigh between Nicholas' legs to rub against him. Nicholas caught his fingers in William's hair. He rubbed harder against William's thigh.

"I want you to make a mess of me, my wicked. I want you to crave me as I do you."

"Do you truly believe I don't?" He yanked at Nicholas' clothes. He needed to feel Nicholas. The first brush of his fingers beneath Nicholas' shirt had them moaning. It was maddening to have gone so long without each other, and now to be so desperate for touch, to make up for all the time lost.

"I want you. I missed you," he said with his hands tracing every knot in Nicholas' spine.

"I missed you, too. I thought of you," Nicholas gasped when William's hands found his chest. Nicholas lurched against him, trying to pull them closer. "I thought of you with my hand around my cock. I couldn't get off without thinking about you."

His teeth tore into Nicholas' shoulder as he brought his hand between Nicholas' legs. He felt him, hot and hard and wanting. Nicholas' hips rubbed furiously, uncertain if they wanted his thigh or his hand.

"Did you think about me?" Nicholas panted while tearing at his clothes.

The fabric fell over his shoulders. How relieved he was not to hesitate, not to care as he looked into Nicholas' eyes at the same moment the fae's hand fell on his silver shoulder. In that moment, the appendage wasn't cursed at all, merely another part of him to burn beneath his lover's touch.

Nicholas settled his hands on William's neck, running a thumb over his bottom lip. He took that thumb between his lips to run his tongue over the pad.

"I did," he replied and brought them chest to chest. Feeling Nicholas against him without barrier brought him to a high he so missed. He kissed Nicholas with reckless abandon. "You were always there, in my dreams, around every corner, haunting me. I dreamt about fucking you, about you fucking me. You drive me mad in every conceivable way."

Nicholas caught his thigh to set aside, allowing the fae to drop to his knees. "Then let me drive you mad here. I will make up for every moment you were without me, and I without you."

Slim fingers relieved him of his trousers, leaving him bare for Nicholas' unyielding attention. He cursed when Nicholas grabbed his cock. The shade worked slowly, never breaking eye contact. His breath stuttered, hips trembled, then thrust against Nicholas' touch.

Nicholas kissed his thighs, his words released in a heated breath. "I want you so badly. I want to be reminded what it's like to be yours."

One hand pressed against the wall, preventing him from falling when Nicholas' mouth spread over his cock. The other hand caught in Nicholas' hair, losing themselves in dark curls as he lost himself in Nicholas' mouth. The fae let his hips thrust urgently. Nicholas' hands held his ass, pressing deeper. Nicholas could ruin him completely by using nothing more than his delectable mouth. Those lips, that tongue, they were weapons that could unravel him, and he would be all the happier for it.

When Nicholas retreated, he shuddered. Nicholas didn't leave him entirely. He spread William's pre-cum with his palm. Licking his lips, Nicholas said, "How I've missed your taste, but I so desperately want you to fuck me."

"Then take off your clothes and get on the bed." He watched, transfixed, as Nicholas rid himself of his attire.

Nicholas was more beautiful than ever, more than he could ever want, such eerie perfection that his heart sang a painful longing. The lustful fae caught him in a kiss, then guided them to the bed, where he fell and spread his legs. He held tight to his thighs, giving William an amazing view.

"Such an incredible ass," he said and took his turn on his knees. He marked Nicholas' shaking thighs, moving further and further between his legs.

Holding Nicholas' waist, William licked at his backside. His hips squirmed, pressing hard against William's fervent mouth. He enjoyed teasing Nicholas, pressing his tongue against him, listening to his drawn out whines and pleasured cries. Feeling Nicholas' heart racing against the tip of his tongue made his aching jaw worth it.

He departed only to lavish Nicholas with admiration. "I love the sounds you make." He kissed around Nicholas' cock, burying his nose in the dark curls along his hips. "Tell me you want me."

"I want you," Nicholas repeated over and over after he took to sucking him off. He didn't know why he needed to hear that, why it made his chest burst with fire. Not from the sex, but something more, something deeper that made him want more.

"Again," he said, desperately kissing every part of Nicholas.

"I want you, William. I want my cock in your mouth. I want you inside of me. I want you to ruin me."

The fae released his thighs to dig through the bedside table. William focused on the hot cock in his mouth, bringing his lover to higher ecstasy.

Nicholas caught his hand, pouring oil over his fingers. He wasn't sure how that got in the room, nor did he care.

"Spread yourself for me, trouble," he ordered, wanting that gorgeous view again.

Nicholas did as he was told, moaning when William rewarded him by slipping his tongue past Nicholas' relaxing muscle. There, he stayed, relishing in the sweet whines Nicholas made, the way his ass trembled as William kneaded him. He departed with a lewd pop before slipping a finger in. His palm smacked Nicholas hard enough to make his ass shake, then another joined and another. He curled and twisted his fingers, making Nicholas jerk and moan.

"Are you about to cum?" he ran his tongue up Nicholas' arousal, tasting him.

"Yes, I'm so close, William, don't stop."

"Mm, not yet. There's more to do."

Smirking, his fingers fell away. Nicholas' body lurched toward him before falling, flushed and panting against the mattress. He could have got off just looking at the fae, but there was so much time to make up for. How he could want Nicholas more than ever, he didn't understand. He doubted he ever would understand this ravenous desire tearing through him like roots in the forest.

"William," Nicholas whispered, his tone breathless and eyes a strange hue, as if someone mixed two colors on a canvas and neither wished to give up dominance.

"Keep telling me what you want. I'll give you anything." He leaned over Nicholas, bringing their hips together. They released a shared moan, hips thrusting, feeling their cocks rub against their stomachs.

"Kiss me," Nicholas demanded. William caught his moaning lips. He ran his tongue along the roof of the fae's mouth. "Use your cock to make me cum," he panted.

He guided Nicholas onto his stomach, where he let Nicholas catch his breath. He kissed gently along his back, letting his cock glide between Nicholas' cheeks. The fae pressed his hips back to meet him, grinding, then William spread him. He pressed against Nicholas' entrance, enticing a low groan. That groan became a whimper of William's name when he buried himself to the hilt. Nicholas caught his silver hand to bring to his lips. He took a finger into his mouth, sucking and licking, making William think of how his cock felt in his mouth. He pulled out and brought his hips down hard. Nicholas moaned, and that was all he could handle.

He fucked Nicholas hard, savoring the heat suffocating his cock. Nothing compared to the feeling of Nicholas' body beneath his, withering from their shared pleasure. He caught Nicholas' wrist behind his back, holding tight. The fae moaned into the pillows, body mercilessly rocked by William's ruthless penetrations.

"Harder. Please, my wicked, fuck me harder." Nicholas whimpered when William brought his hand down on his ass.

William had the abrupt urge to devour him. He leaned down to bite Nicholas' shoulder. When he looked up, he fell into the lust of Nicholas' eyes. The fae's lips parted in a low cry that grew louder with every feverish thrust of his hips and the slapping of his hand against Nicholas' backside.

William couldn't get enough of him, his voice, his taste, his body. He couldn't stop biting Nicholas' shoulders, couldn't cease the mad thrusting of his hips, couldn't stop himself from yanking on Nicholas' hair until his neck craned and body shook. His voice crescendoed, beautiful and intoxicating.

"Wait," Nicholas gasped, and he somehow had the mind to stop. "I want to watch you fuck me."

Kissing the back of his neck, he departed from Nicholas' glorious heat. Nicholas rolled onto his back to lean against the headboard. With

Nicholas' ankles in his hands, spreading him far, William didn't wait to continue their fucking.

"You look incredible getting fucked," William moaned. Nicholas' beauty was unrivaled, unfair enough to drive one wild.

"You're welcome to fuck me as often as you like." Nicholas grabbed his arousal, pumping himself in time with Williams' thrusts. He was utterly transfixed by the sight of William's cock entering him. "Mm, I'm nearly there. Fuck, I missed you."

"I missed you too. I missed being inside you. You feel fucking amazing."

Nicholas gasped when he pulled out and slammed back in. His body rocked against the headboard, nothing but a shivering mess for his hips to abuse. Then he clenched around William's cock, hand not stopping as cum spilled over his fingertips.

"Don't pull out," he moaned. "Cum inside of me."

If William had any resolve left, it snapped in the face of Nicholas' pleas. The unrivaled bliss between them, Nicholas' warmth suffocating him, his scent and the taste of his sweat. William's orgasm rocked him, sending his hips into a short frenzy that had Nicholas crying out his name. They fell to the bed, heaving for breath, stinking of sex and clinging to each other, kissing, holding like they were starved of attention all their lives.

Nicholas' eyes were the brightest fuchsia they had ever been. He wanted to drown in them, for them to drown together. At least there, with the world far away, there would be nothing to break them apart, nothing to worry over.

But after Nicholas fell asleep, William slipped out of bed. He had questions, and he needed answers.

He made plenty of foolish decisions in his life. Traversing the halls of Sorrows Well to visit Alvina alone may have been the worst.

The elder fae slept in her nest, awakened by the brush of his feet on the floor. She sat defensively until she realized who visited. A human wasn't a threat, even in her ruined state. Cackling, Alvina planted her back against the earthen wall. Her eyes inspected him, an ant beneath a child's magnifying glass. She could burn him for entertainment.

"You've come to visit me alone. Are you brave or foolish?" she asked.

Foolish, though he wouldn't give her the satisfaction of answering truthfully.

"Can he be saved?" he asked instead.

Nicholas shared how Alvina was always curious about shades, so much so that she unintentionally brought Fearworn back to life. If anyone had answers, if anyone had any conceivable path to take, it would be her. Unfortunately.

Alvina had no sweetness to her smile, only pure cruelty. "No shade has."

"But that doesn't mean none ever will."

Alvina leaned forward like a predator prepared to strike. Her eyes caught the fading blue light, reflected like flames. "Laurent warned me about you, Nicholas' obsession, a mortal medic. What did you do to get him caught in your web?"

He kept a fair distance from her. His gun had iron bullets, if he couldn't run, though he doubted that would do much to her. "After studying Fearworn, what do you genuinely believe? Is Nicholas doomed to follow in his footsteps?"

Alvina clasped her hands in her lap. "I believe you both are doomed, he to obsess over you, and you to lose yourself to that obsession."

He didn't want to hear that, and he had been a fool to seek Alvina out. She wouldn't comfort him, wouldn't promise that the path they walked was the right one and, if she had answers, she wouldn't have shared. He was too desperate to find any answer, anything that would tell him, with surety, that he and Nicholas could last forever without leading to their mutual destruction. Or the destruction of the other people he so loved.

Still, he tried because that's what desperation did, bring us all to utter ruin. "If I were to stay with him, would it make him worse or could we live together?"

"Of course you could until you made the wrong move. Think of Fearworn, boy," she spat. "He loved to create, but he didn't treat those creations very well, did he? Tore them apart, sent them to war, and threatened to destroy us all. Nicholas would keep you close, at first, then never let you see another, perhaps trap you in a deep, dark hole where only he may find you. In the end, you will both lose everything."

"So it doesn't matter if there are moments when he is more like himself?" He gauged her reactions, knowing she would give away as little as she could, but there was something about her, a curiosity that couldn't be sated and he had tempted her.

"What moments do you speak of?"

"When we're together, sometimes his eyes return to what they once were. If what he wants is my love and I give that to him, could there be a chance at relative normalcy?"

Alvina's warped fingers tugged at one another. "There has never been a shade obsessed over love. They have always wanted something else, but I cannot imagine it will end well for either of you, regardless." She cocked her head, making her eyes shine in the dark. "Not what you wanted to hear, dearie?"

He didn't entertain her with a response. He turned away.

"You must make a choice one day. Will you choose your doom, little one?" She laughed, and the earth laughed with her.

He left her in the dark to meander the halls, worrying of what was to come, and hating himself. If Nicholas couldn't be saved, then he would continue to love William. If he could be saved, what if he didn't love

William anymore? It was a sick thought that had him leaning his weight against the wall, trying not to vomit.

Am I a bad person for wanting Nicholas' love to last forever? he thought. He feared losing Nicholas again. He feared losing his love.

But Nicholas proved himself a threat. Would he give up his family to spare them from Nicholas' wrath? Or would he be forced to give up Nicholas to be with his family?

Love came in many forms, and to give one up for another would be painful, lonely, and ultimately, the wrong choice. One needed both to truly live, but one way or the other, he feared having to live without both.

28

CHARMAINE

THEY LEFT SORROW'S WELL behind them. Charmaine had been relieved to learn they wouldn't leave the way they came. She didn't want
to think of how they'd climb out of the well. Evera took them to a back
entrance, where they ascended stone steps into a wide cave that opened
into the dying forest. Over the decayed trees, a mountain sat isolated in
the sky.

Evera pointed at the mountain. "That is where we are headed. It
should be about a day's walk. The land is weakened, but not safe. Watch
where you are going. Call out anything strange."

In Faerie, strange could mean a great deal of things. She found most of
their surroundings strange, but Evera wandered ahead and she followed.
She would not get lost in a place such as this. Bloodbane withered under
Alvina's foolish rule. The trees oozed rot rather than sap. Their limbs
broke free, scattered about the land reeking of death. Bugs infested the
fallen leaves and creatures that had unfortunately eaten the rot, leaving
them as carcasses scattered through the woods.

She shifted between watching her feet and Evera's back. She had a
tension about her that worried Charmaine. Since they came to Bloodbane, Evera gnawed her lip raw. She considered pointing that out, then

thought better of it. Evera didn't need and likely didn't want Charmaine worrying over her, though the fact remained that she did. She wasn't sure when it happened, but her eyes strayed to Evera, admiring her beauty, wanting to talk to her, wondering what she was thinking and what would happen when this was over.

Evera caught her attention. "You look as if you have something to say. Spit it out."

Charmaine hummed. Behind her, Henry and Arden flipped through a notebook. Arden became a walking fae encyclopedia for the mage, informing him which parts of his notes were wrong or right. At the back, William and Nicholas walked hand in hand. Her chest warmed at the sight.

"Well," Evera encouraged.

"I was wondering about Bloodbane," she said, shuffling closer to Evera's side. "You mentioned you want to rule over it, so seeing it like this must pain you."

Evera didn't hide her irritation. She looked upon the tree with unbridled rage, directed entirely at her mother. "Bloodbane could be rid of her for what she has done. I would be happy at the prospect, but Bloodbane shouldn't have to suffer like this."

She ran a hand along the bark of a tree they passed, flinching as if it brought her pain.

"Once we kill that bastard, I will challenge her to rule. Sorrows Well will be angry after such a transgression. She will remain weakened. When I win, nothing like this will ever happen again," she spoke more to the forest than Charmaine and a warm breeze passed as if to reply.

"What will happen afterward? If you're a lord of these lands, then what?"

"I take care of it and throw as many revels as I want," she replied proudly. "I expect you to attend one. There will be no trouble for you."

Her cheeks warmed at the thought. "I doubt your people would want me there."

"I would want you there. That's all that matters."

Her heart skipped.

"And I expect a dress. You must show me your skills. Surely you can work with materials from Faerie. You will be paid handsomely," Evera explained.

"With real money? Not golden nuggets that turn into dirt?"

Pouting, Evera replied, "My plan has been foiled."

Her smile grew so large it almost hurt. Then Evera's expression went dark.

There hadn't been a ring of mushrooms until there was, then Charmaine stood alone. She and the forest where the trunks stood two bodies thick and spaced apart enough for one to force their way through. The world changed in a blink and her companions vanished. Their names caught on her lips, for she did not know if calling for them would lead to help or horror.

The trees formed a perfect circle around her, and in the grass, mushrooms. Perfectly normal mushrooms with their puffy brown tops and pale white stalks. If she weren't in Faerie, she would have plucked them for dinner. Even her stomach growled at the thought of a good stew, fooled by the earthy smell, but her mind knew better. She had passed through a fairy ring.

Treacherous, nasty things, she saw them during the war. They weren't used often as fae had to bury dried mushrooms a day before. Within their circle, there was pain and destruction. Debraks were torn to shreds passing through or ratwings disappeared entirely. She never asked what happened, obviously wasn't interested in speaking to fae about their tortuous charms, but she regretted that now.

How could she escape and what did this ring hold?

Then came a popping sound like pressure released from a wine bottle and Evera stood in front of her, scowling.

"Did I not say to watch your step?" Evera circled her to inspect the forest and, surprisingly, her. Evera tugged at her hand and pushed her head from side to side, eventually deeming her fit and safe. Her chest warmed at the notion and she swiftly stifled the sensation.

"Did you not listen to your own advice?" she replied. "Now you are here with me."

"Because you won't escape without me. You are welcome in advance." Evera held up a hand. She peered through the trees at their backs.

Charmaine saw nothing, heard nothing, not even a summer breeze. The tree tops allowed no light. Shadows engulfed the rays, daring to pass the circle. Nothing moved within, nothing that her sight could track. Evera moved like a beast. She swept around the mushroom rings, keeping herself in the light, but in those shadows, she watched whatever was within.

"What's out there?" Charmaine felt the call for fire, the frantic thoughts whispering to prepare for an assault. She returned to the battlefield, windswept and frightened. Fire could warm them, keep them safe, or set their world ablaze. Surrounded by perfect kindling, she could burn both of them to ash.

"Our captor," Evera replied. "One doesn't set a trap if they don't want to play."

"I wouldn't call this playing."

"Because you are dull."

A twig snapped. She swerved. Evera didn't. A distraction, then, one that she fell for and perhaps would have met her demise without Evera's keen senses.

"How do we escape?" she asked.

"Iron," Evera grumbled. "Your dagger or a gun will suffice."

William ensured they had iron on them. Fae were weakest to the metal. She didn't have a gun like William did. She had her fire, or rather, she was supposed to. She gripped the dagger once tethered to her waist.

"You must be the one to touch the fae who has trapped us here. As you must guess, I am not fond of iron either. Once you do, the ring will break and we will be free." Evera faced a slit between the trees, her body loose and under her perfect control. "Prepare yourself."

A limb speared from the trees. Evera pushed her out of the way. The limb had one too many fingers, each slender and clawed sharper than blades. She couldn't make out more. The limb retracted and gurgled laughter surrounded them.

"A hag." Evera spat. "Vile creatures, ugly things, too."

And murderous, it seemed, as the world went silent. Then two clawed hands pierced the shadows. She ducked. The arms were long and stretched. The skin had a green tint, slightly transparent to reveal the thin bones and veins within. Warts and boils coated the arms.

Evera jumped. The white light from the siren attack appeared in her outstretched palms. Whips of light lashed out. One relieved the hag of one of her arms. The remaining limbs retracted swiftly.

"I think you are doing fine without my iron," said Charmaine. They stood back to back, peering into the forest where the hag circled.

"That did nothing to her. Based on this ring, she's strong enough to regrow that, and her other nine," Evera explained.

"Ten arms." Which meant ten could appear at any moment. "All I must do is touch her with the dagger? I don't have to land a killing blow?"

"No, the iron will ruin the concentration—" Ten arms lept from the trees.

She aimed, but they were too quick. The arms were like strings, swirling and curling. She swung one way, and they yanked the other. Claws snaked around her ankles. A hand caught Evera by the throat. Then they were dragged. Charmaine cursed as another arm held her wrist hard enough to bruise. She left the circle behind, yanked through the thin trees into a black night. Evera disappeared, her laughter becoming one with the hags. She couldn't imagine how one didn't feel fear when death looked them in the eye.

The hands pinned her to the ground, rougher now, real. They had weight to them, the skin no longer transparent as the trees groaned and two yellow lights appeared. Those lights became brighter, bigger, then they sat upon a head three times too big for such a skeletal body. The hag had a crooked hawkish nose, her lips dark green and full of pustules. Her eyes bulged, yellow as a cat's and teeth were pointed and red. Arms flailed from her side and her back, stretching into eternal shadows.

"Fire!" Evera's voice echoed. If she had more to say, the hag's laughter covered it. She sounded like one who hadn't known water, only thirst. When she moved, the trees creaked. A clawed hand reached for Charmaine's throat.

She couldn't use the dagger, not with the hag on the verge of snapping her wrist. All she had was fire, though here, surrounded by perfect kindling, she may send more than the hag up in smoke. But the hag was close, now standing over her with a wicked leer. Her teeth gnashed, sounding like the crunching of bones.

"Fuck." She released the dagger and sought the strings.

She practiced the night before they left, incapable of doing more than letting the fire dance along her fingertips. Fire had once been a part of her, the way she survived and thrived in a world built to consume her. But since the war, fire only brought nightmares and panic. She couldn't light a candle or a match without having the urge to vomit.

Over the hag's laughter and gnawing teeth, Evera's voice broke through, "Charmaine!"

Fire came to life in her palms. The hag shrieked. The flames licked her fingers, burning flesh. In the darkness, the fire blossomed. She commanded it further and further, up the trees that burst into searing red.

Arms flailed, crashing through branches toward her. She summoned the flames to her palms, hissing from the heat. She had forgotten what it felt like, how to protect herself from it. Her fingers would be burned, but so would the hag.

A fireball hit the hag's chest, sending her back. She staggered into the darkness, crying out. The fire spread, hissing and crackling.

"Evera!" she called. She had the dagger clutched in her bleeding hand.

Crashing sounds nearby sent Charmaine running. Her flames followed, growing higher and higher. Their light brought Evera into focus. She battled against three hands, swiping at her. Five hands laid broken around her, having been torn apart.

"Finally here to join the battle?" the fae laughed. "I knew calling for you would work. You're a softie."

"I thought you were hurt," she growled and lunged at the hands with her blade. The hag retreated into the shadows once more.

"I know. That was the point."

"It's manipulative."

"A fae being manipulative?" Evera hopped from one foot to the other, feigning excitement. "Who would have expected such a thing?!"

The hag came out from the trees, already healed. Ten hands shoved the girls forward. They hit the trees, and the hag didn't relent. Another shove, another yank, each one desperate. Then Evera leapt onto a hand, using her body to trap it against the forest floor. The hag moved in, fangs bared. Charmaine scrambled forward, hoping to get there before the hag did. Her blade pierced the hag's palm just as her teeth ran across Evera's back.

It happened in a blink. They were in that darkened forest, then they weren't. Nicholas, William, Henry, and Arden stood near the circle. The ring of mushrooms curled and burned. The hag became small, half her size, frail and screaming. She held her injured hand that burned from the blade, still impaled through the skin. Her angered eyes fell on

Charmaine, but she reached for Evera, still on the ground. Charmaine summoned her fire, roaring in her fingers. She cast them out, setting the hag ablaze. Evera scrambled out of the way as the hag hit the soil. She ripped the blade from the hag's palm, then plunged it into her temple. The hag dropped dead.

Arden whistled. "Impressive!"

William hurried to her side, where he held her arm. "Are you alright?" he gave Evera a brief glance too.

"Yes, yes, we're fine," Charmaine replied.

"More than fine," said Arden with a swift kick to the burning hag. "I am regretting not joining you. Seems like the two of you had some fun."

"It wasn't the best fight I ever had." Evera stood and stretched, nonchalant, like they hadn't been knocking on death's door.

William rolled his eyes. "What kind of fairy ring was that? The ones I've seen led to death, but that took you somewhere."

"Fairy rings grow stronger the longer they stand and the more they are fed," Nicholas explained. "None of the ones you witnessed were older than a night, so they did what little they could."

"Little," she mocked. Those rings tore beasts asunder.

"This one here," Nicholas kicked the dead mushrooms, their stalks withered and their master crisp at the center. "Has been up for a century, at least, and has led plenty of fae to their demise. How unfortunate for its master that mortals, with their nasty iron, came by today. Now come along, we've wasted enough time here."

Nicholas wandered off. Arden followed by singing one of his folk songs. She hated admitting how nice his voice was. Henry took to the mushrooms, where he picked a few to put in a glass jar. Tightening the lid, he put the jar in his pack that had grown twice as heavy since their arrival and followed the fae.

"Are you really alright?" asked William.

"Yes. I'm not hurt," she said.

After a brief inspection, deeming her well, William took after the others, leaving her and Evera alone. The woman gave a half smile, intending to follow the others, when Charmaine stepped forward.

"Evera, I would," she bit her cheek. Copper fell on her tongue.

Evera smirked. "Were you about to thank me?"

"I appreciated your help," she corrected while running a hand over her head. The short hair tickled her palm. "Had you not followed, which you were under no obligation to do, I would have been unlikely to survive."

"Unlikely?" Evera laughed. "You mean certainly."

"You could have died too." Her heart stuttered at the thought.

"Now that would have been unlikely."

"Nevertheless, there was a possibility, so..."

"So?" Evera urged, taking a step forward, too close. If she leaned in, their lips might...

"Why did you help?" Charmaine swallowed hard and looked away, overcome by Evera's unwavering attention. "Here, and with the sirens, and all of this. Surely you are not tagging along and risking your life out of boredom."

She didn't know what answer she sought, if any. She hadn't expected Evera to be so helpful, especially after hearing about her from Nicholas. Of course, the two had a rough history, but fae were troublesome and Evera, well, she was a little of both.

"Why indeed?" Evera reached out, let her fingers ghost over Charmaine's chin to brush a short curl by her ear, then she walked away.

29

NICHOLAS

SKY LAKE WAS NOT a lake in the sky, as the name might entail. Evera stood in front of what she claimed was an entrance to the mountain. Nicholas saw a hole in the wall, tall and thin enough for a person to squeeze through. The mountain envied the sky, unfurling to greet it alone at the center of a wheat field. The tip blended in with the clouds. Grass and soil crept along the rocky crevices, making once barren rocks green with life.

"There is another opening on the opposite side, but my mother's notes said the shadowed disciples use that entrance. They were unaware of this path last she checked, so I suggest we surprise them." Evera leaned against the rock face, prepared to go in first.

He heaved a breath through his nostrils that didn't aid in relieving the tightness in his chest. William laid a hand on his back, the gesture as reassuring as it could be, all things considered.

"Then let us first decide on somewhat of a plan," said Henry. He faced the group, hands clasped at his waist. "We do not know if the patients are in there. We are assuming they are, so William and Evera should make the patients their priority."

"I am not getting between the shade and his pet," Evera quipped, earning a sharp elbow to the side from the shade in question.

Henry raised a hand to silence Nicholas so he could explain, "Nicholas is our best defense against Fearworn should he have awakened by now and he can do the most damage to the shadowed disciples. However, one fae should be by my brother's side in case any of the disciples escape our clutches. Our best bet to stop them is with those who fought against them, such as Arden, Nicholas, and Charmaine."

"But you haven't," William countered. "You do not know what they are like, Henry. They're vicious."

"And I will stick close to Arden because of that. If we are overpowered, we flee. It is better to fight another day than die now."

There would be no chance to flee. The others understood that based on their solemn frowns, but all agreed, if only to lessen the worry festering within.

"Alright, let's go." Evera ducked in first, followed by Charmaine and Arden.

William took his hand. "Keep hold of me." Then William entered with him and finally Henry.

Darkness enveloped him. The walls encapsulated him like a bug caught in a web. He held William fiercely, thinking of how close they were, listening to William's breaths and the shuffling of feet. His breath quickened faster and faster, but there, in the back of his mind, he recalled the fight with Laurent, how he won. If Laurent ever buried him again, he could break free. He could...

"There," said William, holding both his hands now. The medic smiled in the dim firelight cast from Charmaine's fingertips. "We're out."

"Out," he repeated. Over his shoulder, Henry squeezed through the path. His pack had more trouble getting through than him. They were safe. They weren't buried, not yet.

The path led into a chamber taller than it was wide. Water dripped down the rocky facade. Charmaine's flames flickered from the drops dampening their shoulders.

"This way. My mother chose a brilliant place to bring the bastard. One would have to seek this place out, which my mother would know of, and could easily defend from unwanted visitors. The shadowed disciples had no reason to move after she left, or perhaps, Fearworn can't be moved," said Evera at the head of the group. The path opened further, although Nicholas never relinquished the hold on William's hand. He needed someone to keep him steady.

"If he is tethered to Faerie, it may be this exact location," Henry agreed. "If we could get close to him, it could be as simple as moving him from the source he's feeding from at this moment. We won't let him put down more roots."

"I doubt it will be that simple," Nicholas grumbled. Fearworn had been a thorn in all their sides for decades. He should have known the bastard would cause trouble from beyond the grave.

If the others agreed, they didn't verbally say so. They continued through the dimly lit hall. Evera took them through the secret path that swerved and fell. At one point, they slid down the rocks, and moments later, there was sunlight. Evera raised a hand, signaling for them to be stealthy. She fell to the floor, crawling toward a ledge.

The sunlight came from a circular opening in the mountain. Grass and trees once soaked in the light, but now they laid rotten around the lake below. Evera hissed in a breath, annoyed, likely at the sight of the water. Nicholas needn't know that, once, the water had been serene and pure. What they gazed upon was decay, an inky sludge-like substance that laid perfectly still, absorbing the sun like a consuming void.

They weren't alone. Shadowed disciples circled the lake. They had made camp among the ruined trees. The bones and carcasses of rodents scattered around a smothered fire pit. Beside the camp were haphazard cages, but they were more than enough to hold mortals. Fourteen more than William predicted. Nicholas kissed his knuckles when he felt them shake. The patients were alive, but unwell, laying about the cages in their own feces, some with their ribs threatening to rip through skin.

Henry pointed to the black lake where a single mass floated; Fearworn. What became of him, at least. The fae was more corpse than anything, made up of thin gray skin. His once long hair had deteriorated, little more than stray strands peeking through a scabbed scalp. His eyes were open, black as can be, and looking skyward, yet perceived nothing. As dead as he appeared, he remained on the cusp of life. Nicholas felt it, a heartbeat thrumming beneath his fingers, quiet as a bird. He wouldn't have noticed had they not been so silent and still.

Three shadowed disciples swept over to the cages. They yanked on the door and dragged out the patients. Those with enough strength shrieked and kicked. The disciples snapped their wrists. William moved. Nicholas caught the back of his shirt.

"Whatever they are planning, they are doing it now," said Henry. "I fear we don't have time to conjure a better plan."

Certainly not for the disciples dragged the mortals around the lake. Three had been caught in the disciples' hands, standing at predetermined locations.

There would be no plans. There could be no hesitation. He wanted Fearworn gone for good this time. He wanted a life with William afterward without these troubles.

"There's a path leading down. We'll come out at the south side of the lake," Evera explained.

"Too slow," he said before he leapt.

Evera cursed at him, but the disciples were working their magic. By the time they crawled their way down, their ritual would be well on the way, if not completed. The shadowed disciples chanted, their voices ringing as one. The dark sound made the mountain shake. The patients struggled in their clawed grasps, too weak to fight.

He summoned a storm-like wind that ripped trees from their roots and sent the shadowed disciples to their knees. The patients stood in place, locked in a trance, their eyes forced skyward. Strings of coalesced silver spun from their chests to connect near the far edge of the lake. Their skin sagged as they whined and gurgled, incapable of screaming.

He swept a hand across the lake, sending a burst of air that knocked one patient free. Their string shuddered, blinking, then disappeared as they laid, coughing and kicking. He landed beside them, using one hand to grab their shirt. He threw them back to avoid the disciple lunging at them.

"It's too late," the disciple cackled. "You won't stop this. We have more than enough."

Nicholas had always known power. She followed him since birth, a shadow clinging to his back, ever watchful. In the last two years, she had taken on a new form, one he hadn't quite gotten to know. Every moment of every day, he worried what would become of him if he let her in. If he listened to that gnawing need forever grappling for control, what would be the consequence? Even against Laurent, Nicholas knew he had more sleeping within him, a strength that couldn't be explained, and that strength screamed to break forth.

The disciples would give their lives to finish the ritual that would summon their beloved master to his former self. Nicholas hadn't truly beaten him, and he worried he wouldn't, for Fearworn had been living with power for far longer. If he didn't end it all right then and there, he imagined there wouldn't be much of a future left, considering Fearworn or The One Who Waits would devour them all. So, he stopped trying. He let go of those walls he fruitlessly built all his life, and let power burst free.

The disciple called upon spears of ice protecting himself in a wild dance. A wave of Nicholas' hand shattered each of them. He used the ice as his own, hundreds of broken pieces to lash out. The disciple dodged haphazardly, creating a thin sheet of ice to launch. Nicholas shattered what would have sliced him in half. He sent the pieces down in a crash, piercing the disciples' heart. With a gurgled whine, the disciple dropped lifelessly to the earth.

Charmaine's fire raged near the cages where the remaining humans were kept. William cared for them, looking over his shoulder once to catch Nicholas' eyes. He was fearful and determined. Nicholas didn't want to let him down and, perhaps, deep, deep down, he wanted to be more than the monstrous shade others made him out to be.

He attacked the closest disciple that had her claws dug into one of the unfortunate patients used in the ritual. She kept chanting even as he snapped her neck. When she dropped, the strings connected to the mortal's chest didn't dissipate. They flickered momentarily, but the disciples continued their chanting, including those battling against Henry, Evera, and Arden.

He took the mortal by the waist and tugged. The strings flickered in and out. The skin along his chest pulled, threatening to rip him apart, but one last struggle from Nicholas had the strings snapping. The man dropped into his arms. Across the lake, a portal came into being, little more than a thin white cut in the world. They truly were opening a portal, and he wondered if this led to the plane of monsters or somewhere worse.

Two disciples nearby released their captives. Their ritual had left the mortals utterly defenseless, stuck, becoming the fuel for a portal. The disciples stood together, calling upon the mountain to summon a rockslide. The boulders tumbled toward William and his patients. A wall of roots erupting from the soil cut him off. Snarling, he tore those roots to shreds, the power within him so turbulent he had no trouble sending the pieces flying at the disciples and calling upon the avalanche. The rocks hovered midair, leaving William and his patients shocked beneath its shadow. Nicholas sent those rocks flying at the disciples.

The disciples summoned roots to create a shield. Smirking, he pressed the rocks all around them, forcing the pieces to compress more and more around the shield until the disciples within shrieked. With a sickening crunch, he crushed them.

The lake rippled. The water washed over the edge in growing waves, then a force sent him to the ground. He recognized that power, Fearworn's, the same he had used against them in the forest during the war. Through the chaos, the disciples shrieked higher and higher. The ritual—it was ending, he felt it, as if the world itself cried at what was being done. He rose against it, pressing and pressing, the power converging at the point of his back to ram into the phantom force. Then it all shattered, and he leapt to find the portal sparked to life, brilliant in its blinding white hue. The mortals screamed, their pain so palpable he felt it, like someone tore him limb from limb. Blood seeped from their orifices and their skin shriveled as if their insides had gone to mush.

Seven disciples remained. He leapt for three on the farther side of the lake, leaving the remaining four to his companions. The beasts scattered, and he commanded the soil to dissolve into quicksand. The disciples sank, their claws ripping through the murk. Two escaped while the last couldn't overcome his commands and sank to their demise.

One mortal dropped, heaving for breath along the lake shore. Without so many of the disciples' chanting, the strings connecting to the portal withered. Evera and Arden killed two more disciples, leading to another mortal dropping. Nicholas surged after the disciples nearest him, taking their lightning as if it was his own. He morphed the power into a beast rising above his head to snap its jaws, then sent it hurtling forward. The disciple became little more than a smoldering corpse.

The remaining disciple met Nicholas in battle with a whip of fire. He dodged the crackling whip that sent the grass up in flames. Those flames licked his fingertips, becoming an extended part of his form. He raised them higher into a wave that cast the cave in orange light. The disciple surged backwards, unable to escape the destruction. The fire scorched through him, his shriek dying out with the flames that left plumes of smoke rising high.

The last of the mortals dropped, the strings dissipating entirely. Most of them weren't moving. Their milky white eyes were blank, and bodies were little more than gray husks. The portal flickered in and out of existence. He felt its energy waning, little more than a line of sparks that would soon snuff out. They won, in a manner. Lives were spared, some were lost, and deep in the lake, Fearworn slept. Nicholas dared not touch the water. Fearworn would defend himself and, before that, they should get the surviving mortals far from the shoreline.

He lugged one of the breathing mortals onto his back to trek around the lake. Evera brought another, both of them laying the mortals near the surviving five huddled by the cliff side. None spoke, the fear palpable in their eyes, so overtaken by what they went through that they were speechless. He preferred that. He wasn't in the mood to be answering questions.

William took to checking every body, even if all knew it was pointless. Nicholas followed, always a step behind, watching as he settled his fingers against each throat. They came to save his patients, and he had to face the reality that more were lost than spared. Nicholas wasn't bothered by that. He cared about William, the way his eyes darkened and took on that same hue from the war when he tried so hard to close himself off. Then that darkness shivered after he took an elderly woman with a soft face into his arms. There, he sobbed and closed her eyes.

Nicholas stood nearby, uncertain of what to do. He wanted to take William into his arms, ask why he cared so much. They survived, and that was what mattered. They had more work to do, to finish Fearworn off before he could do worse.

"William, there are those left who need you," Henry said in a calming voice he envied. He didn't have brothers to guide or protect him, though he was glad William did, that maybe he could let someone else take the lead from time to time because he wouldn't always be what William needed. Being okay with the thought shocked him.

"For what it's worth, saving some is better than none, isn't it?" Arden muttered. A poor attempt at help, which Evera whispered, but William nodded.

"I appreciate the help you've all given. I..." William paled. He dropped the woman, barely made it onto his feet when Nicholas felt them; claws piercing his waist. "Nicholas!"

Fearworn's decaying teeth remained strong. They tore into his shoulder and then there was pain, a shrieking agony as his body went cold. Fearworn yanked him toward the lake. William reached for his hand, the most he could do as he felt life leave his body. The last he saw was William's terrified expression before he and Fearworn plunged into shadows.

30

WILLIAM

THE LAKE SWALLOWED THEM, and William followed. Fearworn had taken so much; his joy, his sense of comfort, friends, and patients, but he would not take Nicholas.

He risked opening his eyes. A useless endeavor because the black lake held no light. The sun did not dare to enter here. But he called to the Sight, willing the strings around Nicholas' heart to appear. If he was close enough, he would see those convoluted strings and know which direction to swim.

There, a dim light fell lower and lower. He swam to no avail. The light disappeared entirely. Fearworn dragged Nicholas too far down and his lungs screamed. He couldn't make it. Kicking his feet, he breached the surface, gasping for breath.

"William!" Charmaine splashed over, having jumped into the lake, too. His heart swelled in appreciation, then plummeted, for he couldn't withhold a feeling other than pure panic for long.

"He's gone. He's at the bottom of the lake, I know it," he hacked.

He would lose Nicholas forever. He couldn't breathe. His legs and arms went numb. The cavern darkened, shrinking, becoming as dark as the lake. He needed to save Nicholas.

Charmaine grabbed him by the waist to stop him from falling under. He couldn't swim, couldn't breathe, couldn't save anyone. She said something. He couldn't make out the words over his mind shrieking. Then there was Arden, his voice somehow piercing William's panic.

"The bottom? I can get that bastard out of there!" Arden shoved his hands into the mushy shore side. "I suggest you get out of the water."

Charmaine dragged him to the edge where he fell into the muck. The mud cooled his overheated skin. His voice came out hoarse. "What are you going to do?"

Arden snickered. "I am going to make a mess of things."

The ground grumbled. Debris fell from the ceiling. Henry stayed with the patients, using wind to smack any debris aside. He and Charmaine huddled together, keeping each other steady as the shaking got worse and worse. William's panic weakened him. His head pounded and knees trembled.

The water bubbled, rippled, then waves splashed over the edge. Great stalks of vines and roots breached the surface. They wiggled and moved like living things. Soon, the water spread and rose until his ankles sank.

"There!" Charmaine pointed at Fearworn and Nicholas caught between a pair of wiggling roots.

Fearworn had his teeth buried in Nicholas' shoulder and nails pierced his abdomen. Nicholas laid there, motionless, skin an off gray with violet tendrils whipping wildly beneath. His eyes flickered between violet and fuchsia. That violet poured into Fearworn. His once skeletal frame took on muscles, the skin more pale white than gray. He was draining Nicholas, reaping his energy like a leech.

The energy he lost returned in an angry flash. Pure adrenaline propelled him toward the lake. He whipped out his pistol and fired. The bullet pierced Fearworn's shoulder. He didn't flinch. Fearworn's head was too close to Nicholas to chance a headshot. And with the way his eyes swayed, he didn't trust himself not to mess.

He crawled over the roots, moving in more and more, aiming his gun at Fearworn's abdomen. Another bullet ripped through him, but he didn't move. Not until the portal brightened. The strings once connecting to his patients spun toward Fearworn. The shade surged for the portal. The light brightened from the portal, strengthening.

William slipped across the roots, struggling to maintain a hold. They slithered with a mind of their own, lashing out at Fearworn. Corpse-like or not, the bastard was agile enough to weave through the growths.

William cursed his limbs for shaking, for not carrying him further, faster. If he lost Nicholas, he would never forgive himself.

Evera tackled Fearworn. The three of them dropped into the roots. Nicholas fell limply between the crevices. Evera's blades sank into Fearworn's back. Shrieking, he knocked her aside so forcefully she flew across the lake.

William fired the last of his shots. The iron seared Fearworn's flesh that pushed each bullet out. The shade searched frankly for his prey. William scurried for Nicholas, knowing he was too far to get there before Fearworn. The bastard had his claws digging into Nicholas in an instant.

Groaning, Nicholas' eyes fluttered open. The vibrant hue dulled to gray. His skin took on a sickly pallor. He worked up the energy to elbow Fearworn. Fearworn's fangs pierced Nicholas' neck. He jerked this way and that before falling limp once more.

William reloaded his gun, hating that he couldn't do more. What was he in the face of magic, unlike anything he had ever seen and anything he could ever do? Even Nicholas couldn't do anything, the life force being ripped out of him by a rabid shade whose eyes grew fiercer in their greed.

However, that shade hadn't shown his true abilities. William never forgot the terror when Fearworn chased them in the woods to retrieve his book. His power was unimaginable, and that power hadn't shown itself.

Was he too weak to use it? William wondered.

The portal tore through reality, creating a vortex that nearly threw him from the roots. The once white light became a gruesome green. Sparks flickered along the edges, catching fire to the grass, then the roots themselves. Fearworn's need to escape grew more frantic. He didn't dodge Charmaine's flames that hit his back over and over. He was frantic in his escape because whatever would bring him back for good was beyond that portal, and he needed Nicholas.

Fearworn would take him away, like he had taken a piece of William already. That time, the monster threatened to take a piece of his heart that no fae magic or earthly medicine could mend. The pain he felt over the years believing Nicholas used him would be nothing compared to his loss. They had so much to do, a life to live together, as turbulent as it may be. He would take that over nothing at all.

"You can't have him," William said through clenched teeth. "You can't have him!"

He leapt over the writhing vines, so focused on Fearworn that the rest of the world blurred. He didn't care about anything but reaching Nicholas before Fearworn took him forever. Gun raised, he fired and fired until he had to reload. Bullets proved useless. He needed to be closer.

Suddenly, a wire of light wrapped around his torso. The heat of it singed his shirt and forced a hiss from his tense jaw, then he was flung forward. Evera's whip sent him hurtling toward Fearworn. Evera's whip disappeared, and he rolled across the roots, then fell upon the shoreline. Fearworn stood in front of the portal, a violet miasma seeping from Nicholas' form. The miasma curled around Fearworn, slithering into his eyes and making the portal pulse.

Fearworn leapt into the portal. With a desperate lurch, William caught Nicholas' hand, cold and limp. The portal hissed and cracked. It was closing. Fearworn's desperation showed in the whites of his eyes. Fearworn gripped Nicholas' waist. His fangs released, gushing blood.

"It's fruitless," Fearworn growled, his words grave and old like worn paper. "Kill me here and I will revive. Let me leave and I may never return to these lands again."

William knew better than to believe him. Fearworn had to end here without his powers. There had to be a way, something, anything, to save Nicholas by ensuring Fearworn would never return. He couldn't threaten them and their realms ever again.

The portal bristled with violent light. Behind Fearworn, colors bled together. William's hand barely passed the threshold, feeling that peculiar sensation he had when crossing into Faerie, and that gave him an answer.

Keeping hold of Nicholas' hand, he grabbed his revolver with the other. Fearworn cackled as if to frighten him, but William was confident the shade couldn't use his powers. Not without draining Nicholas entirely, which he wouldn't let happen.

Fearworn reached for William's gun. Flames scorched his fingertips. The shade shrieked in pain. Charmaine stood at the sidelines, her hands blazing. She hurtled balls of fire against Fearworn's side, carefully avoiding hitting her companions. Then there was Arden, his hand on a rotten tree. The branches elongated to swipe at Fearworn. Snarling, he smacked them aside, all the while maintaining a hold on Nicholas' waist.

William put the revolver to Fearworn's temple and fired until his gun clicked on empty. Fearworn's mouth sagged, eyes rolled, and grip loosened. The bullets that lodged in his skull made the skin burn black. William pulled Nicholas with all his might, bringing the fae into his chest. Nicholas sagged against him, groaning, one hand hardly capable of twisting into the torn fabric of his shirt.

He held Nicholas and dropped his gun to retrieve the iron blade, the final blow that he plunged into Fearworn's chest. The shade screamed, an animalistic, dying sound. Black blood, thick as molasses, spilled from his orifices. William kept one arm around Nicholas and shot his other hand around Fearworn's throat. The silver squeezed so tightly Fearworn choked, and he pushed.

"What are you doing? Don't send him through the portal!" Evera shouted.

"Trust me," he said.

With a shove, Fearworn passed the threshold. The bullet holes in his skull sizzled, trying to close and failing. The iron blade in his chest became molten red as if plunged into a forge. Fearworn growled when he tried removing the dagger to no avail, then clawed at William's arm. He didn't relent even as silver streams fell and the pain tore through his nerves.

"Release me," Fearworn snarled, his fear palpable, and William knew he had made the right decision.

The portal shrank. Fearworn tried to look behind him. William held tighter, forcing a choked breath from Fearworn.

"Release me," he tried again, his hands incapable of getting a grip. The iron seeped through his skull, visibly moving beneath his skin. The portal shrank to show only his head, the edges crackling with energy.

"Your arm," Fearworn wheezed. "You will lose it."

"I'm okay with that." William watched the portal shrink. Fearworn's claws pierced his arm. The pain had his teeth grinding. He wouldn't relent, watching Fearworn disappear. His eyes showed in the dark, brilliant violet, wonderfully terrified. Then they were gone.

The portal shut. Nicholas fell from his grasp. The pain sent him to his knees, shrieking as the little remnants of silver bled from his arm, leaving a scarred stub. He wept so hard he couldn't breathe, but he didn't regret his decision for a moment.

What he hated was that he never felt he could mourn the loss of a piece of himself because he believed he should be grateful. He saw himself as lucky, no matter what anyone said. But now he wept at the knowledge that he chose the loss that time and that he could choose what to do next.

31

NICHOLAS

EXHAUSTED DIDN'T COVER HOW Nicholas felt laying dirtied by the black lake, his breaths unsteady and limbs cold. The sky showed such a brilliant blue that stung his eyes. Then a shadow blocked out the rays. William leaned over him, face bloodied and silver arm gone. His sleeve hung in shredded tatters.

"Nicholas." William's hand held painfully to his neck. "Nicholas, talk to me."

His mouth tasted of dirt, stale and chalky. He smacked his lips together, seeing as that was all he could move. Fearworn drained the energy from him. If he could sleep for a year, that wouldn't be enough to regain his function. That force forever within him, once stronger than a blaze, flickered like dying embers. He had never ached so terribly, never felt so empty and cold.

"Help me sit him up," William said.

Two hands fell on his shoulders. With a shove, he sat, and the jolt had him wiggling his toes and fingers. That earned relieved breaths from the group. Charmaine knelt on his other side, one hand on his back to steady him. Evera and Arden observed from a distance. Henry sat behind William. They monitored him with a sense of care so foreign he questioned if his mind was deceiving him.

"Look at his eyes," Henry declared. The group gawked, William most of all, somewhat hopeful, somewhat fearful. He caught Nicholas by the chin to force their eyes to meet.

"Is..." he coughed, his throat bitterly dry.

"Water," William demanded.

Henry retrieved a canteen from his pack. He tried taking it, but his hand fell limp. William tipped his head back and poured the water over his parched lips. He gulped down more and more until William retreated.

"Is something wrong with my eyes?" he finally croaked.

"I don't know about wrong." Henry shifted through the pack. He chuckled when retrieving the crystal he used to follow them at the start of their adventure.

"Look." Henry presented the crystal, angling it until he caught a reflection of himself. His eyes were brilliant fuchsia, save around the iris where violet leached into the hue.

"Fearworn was draining you of your powers, what made you a shade, somehow," Evera half said, half asked.

"Then his powers are gone?" asked Arden.

"No." He was weak, but knew he wouldn't be forever. Those dying embers were still embers, struggling to light themselves, growing. He sensed it, like another heartbeat picking up pace. "It's still there, just... quieter."

"Forever or for a short time," Evera muttered.

William fell against his chest, his arm wrapped tightly around the shade's torso. He returned the gesture, savoring the sensation of them being together. He didn't want to upset William but couldn't deny how good it felt to know he worried, that he clung to Nicholas with a lovely vice grip.

"You're safe. Fearworn's gone. We saved who we could. That's what matters," William said, but there was a strangled hope in his voice.

"Are you..." His throat ached when he swallowed. He held William's neck, scrutinizing the shreds falling over his scarred shoulder. Where the silver once bled into his skin were dark lines, like thick veins. "Does it hurt?"

"It's sore and... stranger, but bearable," he answered and didn't sound that dejected at all. Quite the opposite, in fact.

Arden clapped and kicked at the ground. "While the lovebirds chat, I suggest we find any blood from Fearworn and burn it, or something. I don't want anything from him to remain. He may crawl his way out of whatever the portal led to."

Evera and Arden wandered off, bickering over what should be done. Charmaine surprised Nicholas by kissing his cheek. "I'm glad you're safe."

He pondered, briefly, if the warm feeling he had was why William and so many other mortals sought friendships. If so, the feeling was rather nice, and he wasn't entirely opposed to seeking friendships in the future. Then Henry patted his leg, smiling with all his teeth. "You did good, Nicholas."

Henry went to the patients, who huddled together beneath a tree. He gave them food from his pack that they inhaled and thanked him profusely for. They looked worse for wear, but they were alive and he had full confidence that William would see to their health.

"Is it really over?" William whispered.

"I don't know. I don't remember what you did," he answered.

William took his hand. He peered at the spot the others circled, searching for any of Fearworn's remains. Where the portal had been, the grass withered, leaving a pale darkness. Blood stained the ground too, no doubt a little of all of theirs.

"He opened a portal, Nicholas. Call me mad, but I don't think it led to Faerie or Terra. It felt colder, distant, and I remembered what you said." William gave him a stern look. "Don't stray from the path, so I ensured Fearworn didn't have enough time to walk it at all."

"Let us agree that if the bastard dares to defy death again, we let another deal with him," he said.

"Yes, let's." William laughed. "But what shall we do instead?"

"I want to dance at a ball where all can see. I want us to share a meal under the stars. I want us to build a home. I want all my experiences, new and old, to be with you."

William's head fell on his shoulder. He breathed deep like he tasted air for the first time. "You are the greediest and most troublesome man I have ever met."

"Is that a yes?"

"It isn't a no." He kissed Nicholas' shoulder. "I love the sound of that."

"Even if I change again?" he dared to ask, fearful of an answer when he shouldn't have been because William gave a kiss so full of love that his heart couldn't bring itself to rest.

William settled their foreheads together. His eyes were always intoxicating, tempting Nicholas the moment they met and held him captive ever since. "Whatever the future may hold, we will face it together. You *are* troublesome, but you are my trouble."

They shared an elated smile. Then Nicholas held him close and watched their companions burn whatever may have remained of Fearworn, if anything. He dared to believe there wasn't, that they had gotten rid of the bastard for good that time and they could go on living their lives.

Our lives, he thought with such burning hope, his eyes watered. He always imagined his life to be short and meaningless or drawn out and dreadful. He never believed he would be missed should he die or change entirely. There would be no family to mourn his loss, no friends to laugh about him as they told tales, nothing at all. But as he cuddled with William, listened to Henry ask Arden a thousand questions, and watched Evera smirk over Charmaine's nervous responses, he realized that his life had changed entirely.

There would be a family to mourn his loss, friends to laugh about him as they told tales, and a love that made him want to fight to be there. He was not the dog on his father's leash, destined to be nothing more. He had friends and a family; he dared to think.

"What are you smiling about?" William nudged him, his smile sweet as ever.

"Nothing troublesome," he answered. "Quite the opposite, in fact. I've realized something extraordinary." He smiled and his eyes felt watery, though he refused to let that water fall.

"We need to discuss how to tell my family about us."

"What is there to discuss? I can kiss you in front of them." And he did so there, planting a kiss on William's smiling lips. "That is more than enough."

"Absolutely not. They need to get to know you." William smiled like he was delighted by the notion, regardless.

"I love you. Is that not all they need to know?"

William huffed. "Of course not. You'll be part of the family now."

Family, he came to love that word.

"They need to learn about you, as I have learned. You've won over Henry already, so he will be of some help, but you need to get closer to everyone, especially my mother. She will worry." William cast his gaze aside where he gnawed on his bottom lip.

Nicholas kissed him to make him stop and because he wanted to. "I will win her over with my many charms."

William had the audacity to roll his eyes. "What charms do you speak of?"

"Do not dare to ask when you know the answers."

William trudged into dangerous territory by kissing his neck.

"You are tempting me to take you here on the dirty floor," he said against William's smiling mouth.

"We've done that before and I've discovered I much prefer a bed, although," William took his bottom lip between his teeth and released. "I'm not opposed to using my mouth."

Nicholas would have undressed him then and there if William hadn't stood and offered his hand. However, the playful look to his eyes promised Nicholas that once they had the opportunity, they'd have time for themselves.

With William's help, he eased himself onto shaking legs. Fearworn took more than expected, resulting in him using William as a personal crutch.

"I don't know about the rest of you, but I would like to get out of here," Arden declared.

"I would feel safer if we put distance between us and this lake," said Henry.

Everyone looked worse for wear. Though the fae would heal quickly, the mortals direly needed rest, even those who had William's aid.

"There should be an abandoned hag's lair nearby that we can rest in," Evera claimed.

"Good enough for me. Lead the way." Arden gestured toward the exit.

A handful of mortals couldn't walk. Arden used his vines to create a cart that he and Evera pulled. Complaining the entire time, of course, more so Arden than Evera. Nicholas couldn't walk a straight line without William. Henry and Charmaine took the rear, keeping their eyes opened for trouble.

They made it to the abandoned lair in less than two hours. By then, the sun began its descent. Dusk light broke through the trees where Evera tore roots from a hatch leading underground. The earth above formed a series of mounds that wouldn't warn of a lair beneath.

Abandoned or not, the lair had a foul smell and far too many bones dangled from the ceiling to let the mortals rest entirely at ease. Charmaine made a fire. The wounded patients huddled around the warmth where William carefully inspected each of them. His energy drained further after each patient, though his smile never faltered. The patients thanked him profusely, a younger boy crying hysterically against William's chest after the reality of what happened hit them.

Relief washed over Nicholas because he didn't mind. He didn't care if the boy hugged William. In fact, he smiled along with William as he helped each patient until a little color returned to their once dull eyes.

He was of sound mind enough to remember how he would have panicked before. Seeing William so happy toward someone else would have put him on edge. Instead, he rested in the corner, perfectly content knowing William, while he couldn't save everyone, did what he set out to do. He would rest easy and maybe have fewer nightmares.

As if he sensed Nicholas' attention, William looked at him and smiled. His heart swelled, full of love that could only ever belong to William. Two beautifully scarred souls no other could dance with.

"He's not so bad." Evera fell into the chair beside him. "That mortal of yours."

"Did you hit your head today?" he teased.

"Plenty, but that doesn't change what I said." Her attention strayed toward Charmaine.

"Your mortal is quite nice too, don't you think?"

"She's not my mortal." She smirked, not devious but confident and a little hopeful. "Not yet. Suppose I jumped on her tonight. What do you think she'd do?"

"If she knows what's good for her, she'd run." He yelped when Evera pinched his thigh, hard enough to pierce the skin. Then she left to speak to Charmaine by the fire, uttering nonsense that Charmaine fell for based on her nervous smile.

Poor girl, Evera is going to devour her by the night's end, he thought around a laugh.

A moment later, William finished checking on the patients. They crowded around the fire curled up in whatever fabric Henry and Arden scrounged up, which wasn't much, and certainly wouldn't have any remaining for the rest of them. Normally, he would complain, but he was quite tired and William called for his attention.

The medic dropped into the chair beside him, wincing slightly. He rolled his right shoulder as if he forgot the arm was missing. "I'm glad the two of you are getting along."

"Who?" he asked.

William yawned. His eyes drooped. "You and Evera. You're acting like siblings."

"I wouldn't know what that was like."

"I do, and the two of you are acting like it." William glanced toward a door hanging off its hinges. "There are a few rooms here. You should rest in one."

He leaned against William's side, taking in a breath of his scent. "Why don't *we* rest in one?"

"I need to make sure everyone is taken care of." William stood only to lean over and whisper, "But I will join you later."

His heart leapt to a desperate song. "For more than resting?"

William knocked his head aside with his knuckles. But that wasn't a no.

While the others slept, William came to Nicholas' makeshift bed in an old room at the back of the hut. A string of candles lined an alcove in the wall that gave the room a low orange glow. He mended the broken door using roots to create more privacy. William didn't hide his smirk when shutting the door behind him.

"Expecting something, are you?" William whispered.

"I am." He presented a hand from where he knelt among the glade he fabricated. There were no beds to seek comfort from, so he made what he could.

William accepted, and he shuddered as always, as he hoped he always would. Then he was caught between William's legs, descending on his mouth that caught him in a whirlwind. William was the eye of his storm, a comfort among any gloom. There they laid kissing, tracing the shape of one another with fingers and gaze before he couldn't handle it. He craved William with a hunger that knew no bounds.

Their touching grew more fervent, tearing at each other's clothes until William caught the end of his shirt, preventing Nicholas from removing the ruined garment. William glimpsed the bandage wrapped around the end of his right shoulder.

"Are you nervous?" He laid his weight on William, smiling at the content sigh his lover released.

"More than I thought I would be." William kissed his temple and ran his fingers through the fae's hair. "Does it... bother you?"

"No. I never understood why that arm bothered you. When I saw it, I remembered what you were willing to give to save me, and what I did to save you. I was, and still am, grateful, however," he lifted his chin to admire William, "I do understand that you made a decision that is entirely your own and that made you happy, so it makes me happy, too."

William's lips trembled, his eyes foggy. Nicholas kissed him, breathing in his relieved cry.

"Keep going," William said against his mouth. The hand in his hair angled him for a deeper kiss, full of yearning. His hand found William's and guided it above their heads. Chest to chest, he felt William's heart racing in tune with his own.

"No touching." He caught William's earlobe between his teeth. "I want you to just enjoy this tonight."

He traced William's neck with his tongue. His eager hands rid William of his clothes entirely. William did the same, kissing and yanking at his clothes until they were bare against each other. He squeezed William's thighs, pressing their bodies skin to skin. How he wanted to meld, to stitch their parts together piece by piece so they would never part. He could live there, fused to William, captured between his thighs. William grabbed his arm, calling for him as their hips met. He caught that pale wrist to pin above William's head a second time.

"What did I say about touching? I want this to be about you. I want you to be undone by me," he growled.

His fingers pressed against the soil, calling forth mossy vines to wrap around William's wrist. The medic shivered as the vines tethered him, spreading his thighs, giving their master all the space to conduct his work. William flushed from head to toe.

"I don't know if I can," William bit his lip, slightly dejected. "With what happened, the healing, and traveling tomorrow... I don't mean to ruin the mood."

"You aren't. We can do so much just like this." His hands fell on William's chest, savoring how his lover leaned into the affection. "I'll make you cum." He fell forward to take William's nipple between his teeth. "And when we return, when your body is ready and wanting, I will fuck you from sunrise to sunset. Besides, we wouldn't want to be too loud tonight. If any other were to hear you, I can't imagine what I might do."

William withered beneath his feverish attention. He touched every part of his wicked. He kissed and sucked until William panted for breath.

"Touch me," William pleaded. The desperation in his voice had Nicholas chuckling against the skin between his teeth.

"I am touching you." His finger circled William's hole. William squirmed, trying to press his hips against Nicholas' hand to no avail.

"My ass. Use your tongue."

He couldn't deprive William of anything when he sounded like that. His full body blush brought out the enchanting green of his eyes, made Nicholas hunger like a starving beast. He fell to his chest where the vines curled, forcing William's thighs up higher. Then he got everything he wanted.

William called his name beautifully as his tongue thrust between his cheeks. He took care of William's arousal with his hand, pumping him while his tongue worked. William struggled to control his voice. Vines curled over his mouth, muffling his cries that still had Nicholas' cock throbbing.

Nicholas smirked against his ass, spreading and playing with his backside. He would love nothing more than to bring William to ecstasy like that, but he didn't want to stop. Not yet. He retreated to kiss those beautiful cheeks, chuckling when William the vines fell away, allowing William to beg, "Don't stop. Nicholas, let me cum."

"So soon?"

He kissed along William's shaft, smirking at the shivers he invoked. His hands roamed up William's delectable body to play with his nipples while he took William's balls into his mouth. He departed, letting William catch his breath, and reached for his own cock. His arousal throbbed painfully between his legs, wanting attention that he gave. William watched Nicholas touch himself, licking his lips.

"I want to take my time with you," he said, releasing himself before he moved in to capture William in a kiss, one after the other.

"We have all the time in the world now," said William between their lips. He took Nicholas' bottom lip between his teeth, biting down hard, then soothing the wound with his tongue. "You can have me whenever you want, if you behave."

"How can you expect me to behave when you're so tempting?" He traced William's lips, shivering when he sucked on those fingers. "What spell have you cast over me, I wonder? Because I cannot fathom how I could crave one as much as I crave you."

"Why would I tell you? I wouldn't want to risk you ever breaking it." William smiled into their kiss.

"I would never dare."

He descended to lavish William with the pleasure he so deserved. There he stayed, spreading William's cheeks, feeling that erratic pulse racing against his tongue. He switched between sucking William off and fucking him with his tongue. William responded beautifully, a trembling and ravished mess all for Nicholas to worship.

A few more thrusts of his tongue and turns of his wrist had William jerking, eyes pinched shut as Nicholas pleasured him until his body laid spent. The vines released their captive, letting his body relax.

"You are stunning after you cum." He kissed William slowly, letting the medic taste himself. Then pressed Williams' legs together. "Can I use your thighs?"

William nodded, and he buried himself between that warmth. They shared a moan where William squirmed and the brush of his skin, slick with sweat, on Nicholas' arousal had him seeing stars. His hand fell on William's neck, a thumb brushing over swollen lips that took that thumb between his teeth.

He groaned, watching himself take William. The medic ran his tongue around his finger. He thought of all the times William had his cock in his mouth, how that tongue felt inside of him and slammed his hips hard enough to make William jolt.

When they were fully rested and home, he would have William begging for more. But this was enough for the moment, coming undone between William's legs, lost to the lust of his eyes, then the feeling of his chest. Nicholas' hand descended to feel the goosebumps on his lover's skin, every shudder and gasped breath. His palm fell on William's sternum to sense the racing of his heart perfectly in tune with his own. He was close, so close he couldn't stand it.

William smirked, his voice deep and teasing. "You look like you want something. Tell me."

"I want to cum in your mouth."

William opened his devilish lips. Nicholas crawled over him. With a hand in William's hair, he brought that mouth upon his cock. It was pure bliss. He thrust into William's mouth, feeling his moans, the heat and wet of him utterly suffocating. His orgasm rippled through him, leaving his hips rolling against William's tongue. He didn't release William until he was spent, both of them heaving and satisfied.

He fell over to wrap an arm around William's waist. The medic laid there, eyes shut in a peaceful ecstasy, exactly how Nicholas wanted. He wished they could stay fused for all eternity, lost entirely to the other.

"Let me know when you're up for more," he said, grinning when William peeked one eye open.

"Are you that eager to fuck me?"

"At this stage, I think we could call it making love."

William pretended to gag, then rolled over to curl against his chest. His arms fell around Nicholas' waist. He sighed with a contentment Nicholas hadn't heard since they found each other again. A smile spread so large his cheeks ached.

"Don't play the romantic. It doesn't suit you," William teased.

"Says the man who loves a romantic."

"In books." William drew circles in the small of his back. "I love you the way you are, as wicked as I am."

"Love was never a word I thought I would hear from anyone," he whispered, especially not William, even if that was all he could ever want.

"Then I will say it every day." William's eyes became devious. "If you behave."

He groaned playfully. "I've done more than behave this evening, wouldn't you agree?"

"I'll be the judge of that."

William opened his mouth, no words leaving his lips. He pulled away, leaving Nicholas cold and despaired. William got up to wipe himself off with his ruined shirt and tugged something out of his trousers. The item was small enough to hide in his hand. He returned to Nicholas' awaiting arms, where he meant to be forever. William's full body blush darkened as he held that hand against his chest.

Then William took his hand, bringing it from his waist to settle between them. Something dropped, shadowed under William's arm. He caught Nicholas' ring finger, holding it up and Nicholas held it there, letting William slip a ring on that finger. He stared, perplexed, at the roots tangled into a knotted ring. He remembered giving William his, taunting him with a mortal custom that hadn't meant anything at the time. But now, the ring hugging his finger meant everything in the world.

"It won't last forever or hide you from trouble, but that's as good as I can make." Blushing, William kissed Nicholas' knuckles as he had done so many times.

He pulled William flush against him, needing to kiss him, to hold him forever. "Is this your way of asking to court me, officially?"

"It's my way of saying I'll never let you go. I fear I was made for you too, trouble."

He liked that even better. They held each other close all night where Nicholas' heart grew so full he feared it would burst from his chest. He knew the feeling wouldn't go away, never again, because he wasn't alone anymore. He had more than he could ever imagine, more than he would ever dare ask for.

Regardless of what the future held, he was happier than ever and somehow; he knew it was only going to get better.

32

Three Years Later

Every weekend, the Vandervult estate came to life.

Through the week, Lord and Lady Vandervult tended to their garden, read their books, and played with their granddaughter. Having retired last year, Lord Vandervult enjoyed his time away from court, having finally quit smoking those awful cigars Matilda so despised and let their eldest take over so the two could enjoy their later years. Lady Vandervult also took up learning a little fencing, and she was far better than any expected, although her sons greatly regretted encouraging her after they learned her reflexes could not be dodged. They learned swiftly not to make crude remarks lest they risk a smack to the back of their heads.

The Vandervults didn't throw many parties, nor were they invited to many. If they were, they would have declined. Their time in the spotlight ended, and they savored the life they had and the family. Especially the family. They were the reason the estate came to life in a spectacular fashion.

"How is supper coming along, darling?" Matilda called to the chef, who toiled over their meal for hours. After all, they were hosting for thirteen and expecting more in the coming months.

"Nearly done, madam," said the chef, with his tongue poking out of the side of his mouth. He drizzled homemade dressing across their salads. Behind him, dinner cooked, lifting a light haze over the kitchen and a plethora of charming smells that would make anyone salivate.

"Good, good. They will be coming soon." Matilda hiked up her skirts, all smiles and cheer, and went for the door.

Marshall waited for the first carriage to arrive. He opened the door for a very pregnant Amara, who waddled through the doorway with a hand on her plump stomach. Behind her, Arthur carried Alice until she wiggled out of his arms.

"Grandma!" Alice fell into Matilda's skirts, hugging her waist tight. "Good evening."

"Good evening, my dear." Matilda picked her up and kissed her cheek just as Richard and Eleanor dragged their twin boys into the foyer.

She couldn't believe the twins were three already. She could have sworn they were born only yesterday, and yet, they were already running through the foyer in search of trouble.

Amara watched the boys, then glared at Arthur. "If we have twins, you're sleeping on the couch for a year, at least."

Arthur audibly swallowed. "I fear I do not have a say in the child or children we have, my dear."

"Unfortunately for you."

"Twins do run on your father's side of the family. I was always shocked I didn't have a pair," said Matilda, taking joy in putting a little fear in her eldest eyes. She considered it payback for the many years her boys caused such a ruckus, although she wouldn't change any of them for the world.

Richard came in for a hug while Eleanor reassured her sister-in-law, "Oh, I was much bigger than you at this point, Amara. I believe it is safe to assume that you are growing one little baby."

"Thank you, Eleanor, for apparently being the only one on my side here," said Arthur, shaking his head.

"Although the babes could be quite small," Eleanor continued, causing Arthur to grumble about the attacks on him. Richard definitely didn't come to his help. He was having too much fun watching the trouble unfold.

Alice followed her parents to the dining room, where Robert waited to pour drinks. He loved to catch up one on one before dinner, seeing as the table became so full, it was difficult to do so otherwise. Not that any of them complained. Matilda so loved when the family came to visit. The manor had such life about it, constant chatter and laughter in a way she feared they wouldn't have again. She had, thankfully, been proven entirely wrong, and by the last reasons she would expect.

Next, Charmaine entered arm in arm with Evera, their dresses matching in color but not style. Evera would show more skin if there weren't children present, and Charmaine preferred bigger skirts for "twirling reasons." Matilda understood. When she came of age to debut, she wanted a dress with the largest skirt, so when she danced, she would feel like a princess. In fact, she gave Charmaine a fair few of her older dresses to study and tear apart. She much rather they be put to use and Charmaine created new garments as well as bring new life to what once was out of style. Her work was magnificent to watch on the days she invited Matilda to the shop.

"Welcome, my girls," said Matilda, her arms open for a hug that both gave. Evera had been hesitant, as were the rest of the Vandervults, all those years ago. It took nearly two years for the fae to be open to any form of endearment from them. With Charmaine, however, Evera was all over her. Well, they were all over each other. Evera so loved kissing Charmaine's neck just below her hairline where she had recently taken to letting her natural hair grow out.

Henry and Arden came next. She wasn't too close to the peculiar fae that came and went as he pleased. However, Henry took a liking to him since Arden became essentially a Faerie tour guide. He enjoyed going on adventures as much as Henry did. Matilda appreciated a fae kept her boy company when he traveled. She asked once if there was anything between them, to which Henry laughed so hard he snorted. Arden, on the other hand, became so offended that he cursed the flowers in their garden to die. Nicholas fixed them the next day. She didn't ask for further elaboration.

"I'm so glad the two of you could make it. I worried you'd be lost in Faerie on one of your adventures," She hugged Henry and shook Arden's hand. She never chanced hugging that one. He was like a stray cat who determined when, where, and how he could be put. It was best to keep a respectful distance.

"We were. The magical society has been very interested in my findings and has agreed to further my funding for another two years," Henry proclaimed proudly. "But I was due a break, and I promised Arden that we would attend more mortal gatherings. He's very interested in our parties."

"People rarely die at your events. I am curious why you throw so many when they sound so dull," said Arden, which would have shocked Matilda years ago. Now, she found the comment rather tame.

"The gossip at our gatherings is of most interest. I am sure you will find yourself completely enthralled once you find the right people to converse with," she said, then patted Henry's shoulder. "And this one knows exactly who to introduce you to."

"They are typically the ones I avoid," Henry said while the two of them wandered to the dining room.

That left Matilda waiting for their last guests, who arrived minutes later after a long journey that risked them not making it to dinner at all. Her heart swelled when William and Nicholas entered, the latter of whom took her into his arms and spun. One day, she expected her bones to creak and crack, so she enjoyed the theatrics while she could.

"Good evening," Nicholas declared, having yet to detach himself from Matilda's person.

She hugged him, finding that he had been the one most open to any form of physical affection. In fact, he craved it more than her sons. After learning about his upbringing from William, she was insistent on attempting to make up for what he hadn't been given.

Nicholas never complained, always more than eager to hug or offer his arm during an afternoon walk. He was sweeter than she thought fae could be, though he had his moments, the same as the others. Those moments meant little to her anymore. Rather, she would be troubled if the fae in her home didn't bring up a tale of dismemberment once or twice upon their visits.

"Good evening. I'm relieved the two of you could make it." She kissed both of Nicholas' cheeks.

William came upon her next. He no longer smelled of the hospital, having finally been convinced to take a vacation. She found herself oddly okay with William traveling in Faerie for three months, then continuing that journey through Terra for another three. They wrote and, at times, she had panicked worrying that he wouldn't come home, but those moments were brief, and nothing compared to what they once were. The journey had been an arduous one for all of them.

"Luckily, our carriage wheel broke not far outside of town. We were able to get there and have the carriage worked on quickly enough," William explained. He kissed her cheeks then looped his arm with Nicholas', the right arm no longer hidden under a glove, even if it was a noticeable off gray.

The first year after William returned to explain how he lost his arm, he refused to have anything done with it. She and Robert offered to call a doctor to have a prosthetic made, but he always said he wasn't ready. He needed time to mourn, as he didn't have initially. They respected his decision, including the next one, after Nicholas secured a prosthetic for him in Faerie.

"I want to make the choice myself," he said when she asked what made this route so different from what initially happened. There were things she could never understand because she hadn't gone through what William did, but she always wanted to respect his choices, and it had been the right one.

William didn't hide his arm or pretend not to be bothered when someone made a crude remark. He healed a part of himself that he feared would never change. That brought a sense of joy to him that had been previously lost.

"Will you be journeying anywhere else?" She walked toward the dining room with them in tow.

"I've been away from the clinic long enough. I can't believe I am starting to miss the scent of disinfectant," William answered.

"I'm not, nor do I miss the way your patients are so needy of you." Nicholas' eyes took on a faint violet hue that came and went. The color forever stayed around his irises, year by year, growing ever so slightly.

William kissed his cheek. "You will be there with me, so long as you behave yourself."

The hue faded with William's reassurance. The fae smiled a little crooked.

Matilda thought of Nicholas' condition like a cold. Some days he had it, and most days he didn't. When the symptoms showed themselves, they were often thwarted by attention, not even solely William's. While William proved the most effective against an outburst or frustration, Matilda could take Nicholas' hand and ease him into comfort. It had simply become something everyone acknowledged and worked with, as they would anything else.

The three entered the dining room together, where everyone took their seats. Staff scurried around the table, filling it with delights. William searched the perimeter. Once, that would have upset Matilda. Over the years, she learned there were wounds that would never fully heal, but that didn't mean that all was unwell. All lived with their wounds and they could live as happily as any other. Her boys were happy, sat at the table surrounded by family.

Matilda sat at her husband's side. Arthur kissed Amara's cheek. Alice giggled in William's lap as Nicholas made the silverware dance. Henry scribbled in his notebook until Arden threw it out the open window. Evera nearly spit out her drink in laughter. Charmaine squeezed her hand, mildly embarrassed, while telling the twins that they'd grow old and wrinkly in a year if they didn't eat their vegetables. Richard and Eleanor thanked her profusely with their grateful eyes, and Robert stood.

"A toast," he said, smiling in a way he hadn't for so many years. "To family."

"To family," the table cheered.

Matilda smiled over the rim of her glass and made a mental note to buy a bigger table. Their lives changed, as they were always destined to, but they were home and they were happy. That was all anyone could ever want.

About the Author

Twoony is a queer geek writing young adult and adult stories ranging from the always enjoyable teen rom-com to fantasy romances. They posted their first story online at the age of twelve and have been addicted to sharing ever since. Although Twoony graduated from California University of PA with a bachelor's in graphics & multimedia, their true passion has always been writing. After creating original novels and comics on sites like Tapas and Wattpad, amounting over 105k subscribers and 7m+ reads, they have managed to live their dream. They are a full-time writer with three needy cats and not enough bookshelves. If you're interested in their work, please consider subscribing to their newsletter or following their social media to learn more.

@twoonyauthor

ALSO BY TWOONY

Printed in Dunstable, United Kingdom